STORIES TO EXCITE YOU

By
Ken Divine
&
Anna Forrest

Genesis Press Inc.

Indigo Love Stories
An imprint Genesis Press Publishing

Genesis Press, Inc.
P.O. Box 101
Columbus, MS 39703

All rights reserved. Except for use in any review, the reproduction or utilization of this work in whole or in part in any form by any electronic, mechanical, or other means, not known or hereafter invented, including xerography, photocopying and recording, or in any information storage or retrieval system, is forbidden without written permission of the publisher, Genesis Press, Inc. For information write Genesis Press, Inc., P.O. Box 101, Columbus, MS 39703

All characters in this book have no existence outside the imagination of the author and have no relation whatsoever to anyone bearing the same name or names. They are not even distantly inspired by any individual known or unknown to the author and all incidents are pure invention

Copyright© 2003 by Anna Forrest & Ken Divine

ISBN: 1-58571-103-9
Manufactured in the United States of America

First Edition

Visit us at www.genesis-press.com
or call at 1-888-Indigo-1

STORIES TO EXCITE YOU

Dedication

Talent comes from God and it is he who makes all things possible, no matter what form it comes in. Thanks for always watching over me, and keeping me on a straight path.

In memory of those that I hold close to my heart, I dedicate this book to:

Daja Lucky
Sunrise July 03, 1984 - Sunset June 24, 1987

Irene Price
Sunrise September 11, 1927 - Sunset April 24, 1995

Anna Dennis Howard
Sunrise January 08, 1964 - Sunset December 05, 1999

Tess Williams
Sunrise December 24, 1967 - Sunset February. 6, 2003

All of you brought so much to my life at the time you were here, and will remain forever in my heart until I see you again. Thanks for looking out for me up there...I miss you.

FOREWORD
by Ken Divine

"Kiss Goodbye" was the first erotic story I ever wrote. I posted it on my page on the Internet as a message to the woman I was seeing at the time. She didn't respond to it, but dozens of other people did. I got fifteen to twenty notes a day for a week. Most of the people were asking me when would I be posting a new story. Well, seeing how they enjoyed it so much, I decided to write more stories and see if I would get more positive feedback. I did. I had already written a play and I was working on a novel, but I decided to put them on the back burner and start writing erotic stories to publish. But just like the first story I wrote had significance, I wanted the others to have some, too. I thought about all my past relationships and all that I've learned from them and started typing.

My theme for *Stories to Excite You* came from thinking about a nosey ex-girlfriend of mine who spent a lot of time looking out the window, trying to find out what everybody in our building and on our block was doing. She always looked at other couples and asked, "Do you think they're having good sex? You think they're as freaky as we are?" I learned later that she was not the only person who thought about those things. I asked a few of my friends if they wondered those things about their neighbors and most of them willingly admitted they did.

One day, I walked past an apartment building in Harlem, just across from Central Park, and like my ex-girlfriend, thought what it would be like to spy on the residents and see how they handle romance, love and relationships. Instead of spying, I based my stories around fictional residents of that building, but using my own history as the foundation.

There are twenty stories that you will certainly be able to relate to. There is a character that will remind you of yourself, someone close to you, or perhaps someone you may want to know. There is an event that will take you back to something that has happened in your own life, or maybe wish that it had.

Stories To Excite You
By
Ken Divine

Search Engine for Love

This is so boring. No one's talking in these chat rooms. Why do I even bother with this Internet nonsense? Everybody on here is about playing games and finding a booty call. I'm just gonna check my e-mail and shut down for the night.

GMO-67: Hello. How are you?

Oh, brother. Who is this sending me an instant message? Probably just another guy wanting to have cyber sex, or something stupid like that.
SwtGrl: fine. Have we met?

GMO-67: no. I was in the chat room and saw you were not engaged in convo so I thought I'd offer some
SwtGrl: ur right. I was just about to sign off for the night
GMO-67: o are u busy?
SwtGrl: no just bored

I feel you there, sistah. There's nothing happening in these chat rooms anymore. You are my last hope before I sign off.
GMO-67: Well perhaps we could keep each other's interest for a while

SwtGrl: perhaps
GMO-67: I saw ur profile. i c u live in Brooklyn. I live uptown
SwtGrl: Uptown where?

GMO-67: Harlem
SwtGrl: O I C

Ho-hum. I'm still bored.

Damn, she looks good. Thirty-two years old, nice smooth, caramel complexion, big, brown eyes, nice full lips, and the locks compliment her face nicely.
GMO-67: I was just checkin out ur page. u r very attractive.

Oh-oh, here it comes. Next he'll be asking me to tell him what I'm wearing right now.
SwtGrl: thank you

GMO-67: ur welcome. So, what do u do when ur not online getting bored out of ur mind?
SwtGrl: not much. I'm usually real busy w/work or w/my son

Son? Hope he's not real young. That would mean baby daddy drama.
GMO-67: How old is your son?

SwtGrl: he just turned ten a few days ago

Ten ain't so bad, I guess.
GMO-67: Happy belated birthday to him. How did he enjoy it?

SwtGrl: He's still celebrating. My sister took him with her kids to Disney World for the wknd.
GMO-67: Wow, that was real nice of her
SwtGrl: Yeah. She spoils him as much as she does her own
GMO-67: Well, it gives you some time to urself
SwtGrl: That's true. You have any kids?
GMO-67: 1 daughter-17

Seventeen? How old is this guy? Let me look at his page. Hmm, he's not bad. Nice bronze complexion, nice eyes and a goatee. I love a man with a nice goatee. That's so sexy to me. It says he's thirty-five. That means he had a kid at eighteen.
SwtGrl: u started young

GMO-67: how'd u know?
SwtGrl: I saw your age on your page

GMO-67: o of course :-B
SwtGrl: LOL
GMO-67: Hey, I got u to laugh. That's a start

Don't get your hopes up so fast, brotha. I'm laughing at you, not with you.
SwtGrl: Yeah, it's a start

Good, she's loosening up.
GMO-67: it's Saturday nite and it's still early. What were u gonna do with ur evening once you got offline?

Do? I was about to make it a Blockbuster night.
SwtGrl: I have a ton of work to catch up on.

GMO-67: I hear ya. I figured I'd check out a movie
SwtGrl: By yourself?

Not unless you care to join me.
GMO-67: I always go by myself. I'm a movie buff and when I want to see something I don't wait

Sounds like you have no friends.
SwtGrl: I never go anywhere alone. It's kind of depressing I think

You're probably out on a different date every weekend.
GMO-67: No, it's not depressing at all. I have just as much fun by myself

I bet you have a whole lot of fun by yourself. Your right hand is probably the best friend you have.
SwtGrl: I hear ya. I prefer company, tho

GMO-67: don't get me wrong, company is always better, but I just don't have any 2nite

Riiiight!
SwtGrl: Well, enjoy ur movie

GMO-67: Well, since u think it's so much better to have company, why don't you be mine for the evening.

Is this fool crazy? I don't know him.
SwtGrl: No thanx. I'll have to pass

GMO-67: C'mon, no strings attached. Just a friendly nite at the movies
SwtGrl: We don't even know each other
GMO-67: This would be a good way to get to know each other

Yeah, this is a good way for you to try to get some and bounce.
SwtGrl: I don't think so. Maybe another time. Like I said, I have a ton of work.

GMO-67: Work? On Saturday nite? What kinda living is that?
SwtGrl: It has to get done.

She's just scared. She's probably heard all kinds of horror stories about Internet dating.
GMO-67: Have u been on a blind date from the net b4?

SwtGrl: I've been on a couple.

Oh, she's not an Internet dating virgin.
GMO-67: They didn't go too well I guess

SwtGrl: One of them was okay but the guy just wasn't my type. The other one was a disaster. The guy lied about everything. He didn't look anything like his picture, he was much shorter than he said and he was broke.

Bad experiences. I knew it had to be something.
GMO-67: Well, that's really me on my page. 100% Like I said b4, no strings attached. I'm just looking for company for the movies 2nite. Ur the one who said it's better to go with someone

Yeah, but I wasn't talking about me.
SwtGrl: It is, and maybe we will go out one day, but it's too soon right now

She's just trying to be difficult. I guess women are supposed to play hard to get.
GMO-67: R U sure I can't change ur mind? We can meet at the theater, see the movie, grab something to eat, and go our separate ways. It's just a way to get more acquainted. If there are no romantic sparks, I'll at least have someone else to add to my Christmas card list

SwtGrl: LOL
GMO-67: I got you to smile again :-)

He's trying real hard. Maybe I should go. What do I have to lose?
SwtGrl: I'm not dressed to go out and I really don't feel like pulling anything out. I have on jeans and a t-shirt
GMO-67: u don't have to get all dressed up. I have on sneakers, sweatpants and a t-shirt. I think it's better to go on a first date dressed down anyway. I only want to dress up for someone I know I like
SwtGrl: I can understand that
GMO-67: so does that mean u'll come?
SwtGrl: I'm thinking about it
GMO-67: Why don't you call me? 212-555-1234 My name is Gerald

Hmm, either this brother is a nut, or real desperate for a date. I can handle the latter.
SwtGrl: Okay, give me about 10 minutes. My name is Michelle

GMO-67: OK, Michelle. I'll be waiting
I wonder if she'll call?

Let me look at his page again. He is a good-looking brother and he didn't say anything out of line. I don't know why I'm doing this. I'm in rare form tonight. What the hell? I'm game.
SwtGrl: Okay, talk to u in 10 minutes

YAHOO! MESSENGER: SwtGrl has logged out.
YAHOO! MESSENGER: GMO-67 has logged out.

Oh, God. Here I go, again. Why do I waste time doing stuff like this? I swore after my last Internet fiasco that I wouldn't do this anymore. Aw, what the hell? He's right, I have nothing to lose. I get to see a movie, grab a bite, and come back home without breaking a dollar. Yes, this does have its advantages. But what if he's an asshole? Spending four or five hours with a man who only talks about himself, his exes or sex is just plain torture. And God, if he's like the last guy I went out with, I'll go crazy. That guy was just plain stupid. I tried to ignore all the so-called "typos" he made when we were chatting and corresponding emails, but then he took me to a restaurant and told the waitress he wanted to order an entry. The man didn't say entrée, he said, "ENTRY!"

I wonder if she's really going to call? I think she will. Hmm, but what if she's loud and obnoxious? What if she's snobby and stuck up? What if she has a bad attitude? What if she smokes? Damn, I forgot to ask her if she smokes. With my luck, she'll be a damn chimney. Okay, let me take it easy. She might be real cool. She has two minutes left to call. If she's punctual, I'll know she's not scared or second-guessing. If she's early, I'll know she's excited or curious. If she's late, she's pondering. If she doesn't call at all, she's a fuckin' liar...

— Ring —

That's her. She's early.

— Ring —

"Hello."

Here we go. "Hello. May I speak with Gerald, please?"

"Hi. This is Gerald."

He has a sexy voice. "Hi, Gerald. This is Michelle."

"I'm glad you called, Michelle."

"Did you think I wouldn't?"

"Well, it's hard to tell. You really don't know what people are thinking when you talk to them online."

"Yeah, that's true."

"So, are you ready?"

"I don't know. Like I said, I'm not really dressed for a date."

"I told you, I think it's better this way. Let your hair down and be yourself. Determine whether or not you like me enough to want to fix up for."

"Are you just saying that because you don't want to get fixed up for me, or is that how you really feel?"

"That's how I really feel. You know, usually when people meet at work, on the street, or in a supermarket, they aren't dressed their best and all made up. They meet, establish that they want to go out, and then they dress up. When you meet someone online, you don't get the full effect of their physical being or the opportunity to look them in the eye. So, the way I see it, every first Internet date is more like a meeting. It should be toned down to a very casual blind date since we are meeting for the first time."

"Then perhaps instead of going to the movies, we should meet in the supermarket."

"Ha, ha, ha. That's cute." *She has a sense of humor. That's good.* "Well, I just stocked up a couple of days ago, but if you need to go, I'll be happy to go with you."

"You'd give up your movie night to go to the supermarket with me?"

"Hey, it's not about the movie. It's about the company."

Okay, I'm feelin' him a little bit. So far, he doesn't sound like his brain is there just to give his head some weight. "Okay, since you put it that way, I won't put you through the agony of having to shop with me – this time. We can go to the movies."

"Well, thank you for sparing me."

"You're welcome. What theater are we meeting at?"
"I'd like to go to Times Square. Can you meet me there?"
"Yeah, that's no problem."
"Okay, then meet me at seven-thirty at the AMC Theatre on Forty-Second Street and Eighth Avenue."
"Seven-thirty? That's fine. What are we going to see?"
"You like science-fiction?"
"I like comedy."
"Oh, that's cool, too. There are some comedies that just came out that I'd like to see."
"Good. Well, I'll be wearing jeans and a yellow t-shirt with 'Sexy' written on the front."
"Okay. I have on blue Nike sweatpants and a white t-shirt that says, 'Above The Rim' across the chest."
"Okay, I'll see you at seven-thirty."
"Okay."

7:24 PM EST – The AMC Theater

"Excuse me, are you Gerald?"
"Yes. Michelle?"
"Yes."
Hey, she is sexy. Umph, nice lips. "Well, the show starts at eight o'clock. The only comedy showing is The Crazy Man. Is that alright?"
"Oh, yeah. I heard that was good."
"Let's go in and get the tickets, shall we?"
He's not bad. He's taller than I expected, and he's wearing the hell out of that goatee. "Sure, let's go."

TICKETS FOR THE EIGHT O'CLOCK, EIGHT-THIRTY AND NINE O'CLOCK SHOWS FOR THE CRAZY MAN ARE ALL SOLD OUT. THE NEXT AVAILABLE SHOW IS AT NINE-THIRTY.

"Did you hear that announcement, Michelle?"
"Yeah, that gives us two hours to kill."
"Would you like to see something else instead?"
"I don't mind. It's your movie night. Whatever you choose is fine."
"How about if I chose to skip the movies. I've been wanting to do some DVD shopping. Then we can just grab something to eat and get acquainted."
"Sounds like a plan. Let's do it."

7:40 PM EST – HMV STORE

He held my hand. What made him think I'd want him to? Maybe he did it because Times Square is so crowded and he didn't want us to get separated. Yeah, that's it. He let go as soon as we got into the store. I don't want to think he's trying to move too fast. He's just being a gentleman. He did open doors for me and walk on the outside of the sidewalk. His hands are big and strong, yet soft. I doubt if he does any kind of manual labor. Um, he has a nice wide back. I like a man with broad shoulders and a strong back.

She seems okay so far. She's not standoffish. Damn, she's sexy as hell. I'd say about 36-29-39. Stacked like a brick house. She purrs when she talks and she has an arousing sashay. Yeah, she's a dime.

9:13 PM EST – ESPN ZONE RESTAURANT

So far he's doing well. He's interesting, funny, and he didn't say entry. "So, Gerald, I take it you've been on a few Internet dates before, yourself?"

"A few. This is the sixth."

"Sixth? You mean to tell me you've been on five other dates and they've all been busts?"

"Well, I think it's me. I'm picky and hard to satisfy."

I bet if I were all over you, you'd be hard and satisfied. "Really?"

"Yeah, really. There was nothing terribly wrong with any of them except for the fact that I wasn't connecting with them in one way or another. We either had very little in common, weren't physically attracted to each other, or something. There was usually something."

"And of those five, there were no second dates?"

"Oh, yes. I went out at least two times with all but one of them."

"What was the longest you dated any of them?"

"I saw one woman regularly for about four months. We both knew we wouldn't make it in a committed relationship together, so we just shared an open, adult relationship instead."

"It was purely physical, huh?"

"Yep."

"Yet, you keep trying. Why?"

"Because I love meeting people and I am an optimist."

"Those are good traits."

10:55 PM EST – J & B Cocktail Lounge

"Would you like another drink, Michelle?"

"No, thank you. Two drinks are enough. I tend to lose my head when I drink. It's too soon for you to see that side of me."

"I know. This is not the place to be dancing on the table."

"Ha, ha, ha. Table dancing. I got your little repartee. You're not too far off base, though. When I drink, I do get freaky."

"Bartender!"

"Stop it, silly. Like I said, it's too soon for you to see that side of me."

Too soon? I hope that means she wants me to see that side of her, eventually. "Sounds as though you can get pretty wild."

"I don't know about wild, but I will say that I am uninhibited."

"Admirable. That's something else that you and I have in common."

"Is that so?"

"Yes, it is."

"You come across to me as being a bit reserve, Gerald. Those characteristics usually carry over into what you do in the bedroom."

"Oh no, my dear. I believe quite the contrary. I think it's the quiet, reserve types who are the biggest freaks in bed. I, for one, am totally uninhibited, very creative and extremely spontaneous. But anyone can tell you that about themselves. Action speaks louder than words."

Okay, let me chill out. I don't want to give him any false hopes despite the fact that my panties are drenched. "Well, Gerald, where do we go from here?" *Shit! That might not have been the right thing to say.*

I don't know, your place or mine? Nah, chill. I'll be cool. I like her. "Excuse me?"

Whew. He let me off the hook. "Are we going to try to catch a late show, or are we calling it a night."

She's having a good time. That's a good sign. "I didn't know you were still interested in seeing a movie. If I had, I would've bought tickets then for now. They're probably all sold out, again."

"Yeah, you're probably right. It's just as well. I have to hike it all the way back to Brooklyn tonight and I don't want to be on the subway too late, anyway."

"Oh, don't worry, I'll put you in a cab."

11:15 PM EST – Port Authority Bus Terminal's Taxi Station

"Well, here's my cab."

"I had a great time tonight, Michelle. Thank you for coming out to keep me company."

"The pleasure was all mine." *Okay, here it comes. Mmm, his lips feel so good on mine. Oh, my goodness. I may have to stop and pick up some batteries. I may be working my vibrator over-*

time tonight. "I'll call you tomorrow afternoon after I get in from church."

"Okay, I'll be waiting." *I got a good feeling about this one. She's a lady - respectable and smart. I see good things happening.* "Goodnight, Michelle."

"Goodnight, Gerald."

THE FOLLOWING MONDAY - 7:39PM EST

Oh, good. I'm glad he's online.
SwtGrl: Hey, Gerald. How r u?

GMO-67: Hi, Michelle. I'm fine. How r u?
SwtGrl: I'm doing okay. Thank you again for a wonderful date.
GMO-67: Ur thanking me? I should be thanking you.
SwtGrl: LOL Okay, ur welcome.
GMO-67: I'm glad u said that, because I'm looking forward to our second date.
SwtGrl: To tell you the truth, so am I.
GMO-67: That's good, because a colleague of mine gave me 2 tix to see The O'Jays and Stephanie Mills at the Beacon Theatre Saturday night. I was going to call you later today to ask if u were free to go.

Oh, my God. He's going to score major points for this one.
SwtGrl: I'd love to go. I just have to get a babysitter.

GMO-67: Oh, how is ur son?
SwtGrl: He's fine. A handful as always. How's ur daughter?
GMO-67: Shoot, you know teenagers. She's all bent out of shape right now because I told her she couldn't get her navel pierced.

Oh-oh. I hope he doesn't have anything against piercings or tattoos. I didn't tell him about mine.
SwtGrl: Wow. Does she have any other piercings or tattoos?

GMO-67: No.
SwtGrl: None that you know of, eh?
GMO-67: Hmmm Don't have me ACCIDENTALLY walk in on that child with a magnifying glass while she's in the shower.
SwtGrl: LOL You better not. Well, do you have something against piercings and tattoos? Is that why you don't want her to have it?
GMO-67: No, not at all. She can do whatever she wants to herself once she's legally an

adult and paying her own bills.

SwtGrl: Oh, I hear that. So, where is your daughter this wknd?

GMO-67: Her mother's on vacation and they went to New Orleans for the week to visit family.

SwtGrl: O I C Well, what time is the concert?

GMO-67: 8:00 I figured I could pick u up around 6.

SwtGrl: No u don't have to come all the way to Bklyn just to go back uptown. I can meet u like I did the last time.

GMO-67: Are u sure? I don't mind u know

SwtGrl: No, don't be silly. We can meet in front of the theater at around 7.

GMO-67: OK, if u say so. But if u change ur mind let me know.

SwtGrl: Don't worry, Gerald, it'll be fine. I'll call you later in the week to confirm.

GMO-67: OK, I'll talk to u then.

SwtGrl: Okay, take care.

I guess he likes me enough to get dressed up for, which means I have to fix up for him, too. Well, this gives me an excuse to buy that dress I saw in Macy's. Mmm, I'm gonna make him mine for damn sure.

Okay, now if she can make it past phase two, I think she'd definitely qualify as a keeper. I'm not going to jump the gun just yet, but I have a good feeling.

Saturday - 4:43PM EST

— RING —
— RING —
"Hello."
"Hi, Gerald. This is Michelle."
"Hey, Michelle. You sound like you're outside."
"I am. I'm calling from my cell phone. I went to Macy's to get something to wear tonight. It's crowded as hell down here, but I'm on my way home, now. I may be running a little late, though."
Here we go. "Oh, really? How late?"
"The way I see it, I'll make it home around six o'clock, shower, get dressed and be out of the house by seven. That means I'll arrive at the theater right around eight o'clock."
She'll never make it. Is this her way of backing out of the date? "That's cutting it real close."
"I know. I'm sorry. I had no idea I'd be up here this long. I was out here since eleven-thirty this morning."
"What? You've been shopping for five hours?"

Damn, he makes it sound so bad. "Yes."
Maybe I can make this work. That is if she's not playing games. "Where are you?"
"I'm on Thirty-Fourth Street."
"Do you have anything else to do at home besides get dressed?"
"No. My son is at my sister's already. I just have to shower, get dressed and be on my way."
"So, why don't you just come here and get dressed? You're much, much closer to me than you are home. You can do whatever you have to do here and we won't have to worry about being late."
What? Come to your house? "I don't know about that, Gerald..."
"C'mon. You can catch a cab and be at my house in fifteen-twenty minutes tops. This way we can get ready and have some time to spare."
"Well...I guess..."
"Good. Take my address and jump in a cab."
Shoot, he did it again. And I'm giving in again. Oh, what the hell...

5:20 PM EST

Wow, this is a very nice building. It's right in front of Central Park, too. It must've cost a pretty penny to get up in here. Gerald must be really doing all right for himself. Here it is, 3B. Well, here goes.
DING-DONG
"Yes?"
"It's Michelle."
"Hey, sweetie. Come in. Wow, don't you look sexy. You're working those cut-offs." *Down, boy!*
"Thank you. I'm sorry I took so long. I had to go back into Macy's to get some toiletries."
"Oh, I should've guessed."
"Hey, you know how that goes. Nice big apartment. Wow, I could do a lot with this place."
"Yeah, I'm sure. I'm not big on decorating, too much."
I see. "I see."
"Is it that bad?"
"Naw. It's the typical bachelor's pad. I can tell no woman has stayed here for any period of time."
"You're right about that. Actually, you are the first guest I've had over since I moved here."
"You gotta be kidding me."

"Nope. No one else has been here except my daughter."

"You really are a loner, huh?"

"I told you. Anyway, the bathroom is right down the hall on your right. When you're done in there, you can go into the bedroom directly across the hall and get dressed."

"Where will you be?"

"I'm going to shower while you dress and get dressed after you're done."

"Sounds like a plan."

"There are towels in the closet next to the bathroom. Here, I'll put your bags in the bedroom for you."

"Thank you."

5:30 PM EST

Oh, shoot. I left my bath gel in one of those bags Gerald took into the bedroom. Let me wrap a towel around myself and run in there...on second thought, I think I have a better idea. Man, if we don't end up together, I'm just a slut. "Gerald! Could you come here a minute, please?"

"What is it? Is everything okay?"

"I forgot my bath gel in one of my bags. I've already taken off my clothes and I don't want to come out in just a towel."

"Geez, you really are shy."

"Yeah, I'm sorry. The gel is in the little green bag."

"Don't be sorry. You don't have to be shy in here. Just make yourself at home. Here you are."

"Thank you."

Damn, she is seriously fine. I just wanna gobble her up. "You don't need any help in there, do you?"

You read my mind...finally. "No, I don't need any help. I've been bathing myself for a long time now."

Yeah, I've missed a lot. "Okay. I was just trying to be helpful."

Damn, he's sexy. "Wait. Come back."

Please, don't let this be for lotion. "What's wrong?"

"I said I didn't need any help. I didn't say I didn't want any."

Michelle had been peeking out of the bathroom. When Gerald walked back toward her, she opened the door all the way and unwrapped the towel from around herself. Gerald gazed at her smooth, caramel skin and her swollen, brown nipples that pointed out from her well-formed breasts with a tattoo of Pegasus on the left one. His eyes moved down across her stomach, which was slightly padded, but it didn't take anything away from her. Her hips were wide and shapely, and there was another Pegasus tattoo on the outside of her right thigh. Her vagina was shaved clean and a small silver ring hung from her clitoris. She had muscular, athletic legs. Gerald always loved a great pair of legs and was overly impressed with Michelle's.

Gerald entered the bathroom. The shower was running and it was beginning to get steamy in there. Michelle stepped forward and lifted his t-shirt over his head revealing his broad, muscular chest. It was a little hairy for her taste, but not too much. She stepped closer and kissed him passionately. She slammed the door shut and pushed him back against it. Their tongues wrestled with each other as Michelle tugged at Gerald's sweatpants. The string finally gave and she pulled his sweatpants down to his ankles, and then pulled them off with his socks together.

Gerald stood against the door in just his briefs looking down at Michelle undressing him. She started planting a series of kisses up his legs as she reached up and pulled his briefs down. Gerald's erection stood straight out and hovered above Michelle's head as she removed his underwear and tossed them to the side along with the rest of his clothing. She stood up slowly, running her hands along the backsides of his hairy legs, then took his hand and led him into the shower. The hot water beat down on their bodies as they kissed and caressed each other. She put both hands on his shoulders and pushed him down to his knees, giving him a close-up of her womanhood. She placed her right leg up on the side of the tub and offered herself to him. He opened his mouth wide, moved his head forward and began to indulge himself with her. His tongue played with her ring, and then waltzed within her erogenous zone as the moans of her euphoria played the symphony.

Michelle's body began to shake as she felt the tension of her first orgasm. She placed her hands on Gerald's face and motioned him to stand up. He stood to his feet and she threw her arms around him and they kissed lovingly. She could feel his anticipation wedged between their bodies and his hands tightly holding onto her buttocks. She reached down behind him and turned off the water.

"Let's get in the bed," she whispered. Then she took his hand and led him out of the bathroom, and across the hall into the bedroom; both of them still soaking wet and leaving a trail of water behind.

Michelle pushed Gerald back onto the bed. She reached down into her purse, pulled out a condom, opened the package, and put it into her mouth. She climbed onto the bed, took his penis into her hands and lowered her mouth down over it. Gerald became more excited and his organ began to throb as Michelle rolled the condom on with her mouth. She wanted him inside of her and the feeling of emptiness within her womb had become unbearable. She climbed up and mounted him, lowering herself down slowly, feeling every inch of him go up into her. She placed both hands on his chest and moved her hips back and forth. She closed her eyes and began humming a tune, continuously gyrating her hips and dancing to her own melody. Gerald reached up and cupped her breasts in his hands, fondling and kneading them. Michelle's hums became moans and she began bouncing up and down, swinging her head from side to side until she felt another explosion come from within.

Michelle's movements became slower and steadier as her orgasm began to subside. Gerald was still massaging her breasts and thrusting his hips upward, sending his full length up into her. Before she knew it, Michelle felt the tension building up inside of her a third time. Gerald got a good hold of her hips as his strokes became more intense. Soon, they were both screaming as they grinded each other until they reached a simultaneous climax.

6:55 PM EST

"Wow, Michelle. All eyes are going to be on you tonight. That dress is off the chain. You might have to walk in front of me so I can look at those legs all night."

"Stoppit, silly. He-he. You look really nice, too. You fix up really well."

"Thank you. So, are you ready?"

"Yes, let's go."

"Let's see, I have the tickets. Okay, we're outta here. This is going to be great, Michelle. I promise."

"Yes, I'm sure it will."

Jackie

Life was moving kind of slow for me five years ago, before I started my own business. I was out of work and my girlfriend of seventeen months yielded to her own selfishness and abandoned me. Before I knew what hit me, I didn't have anything - no girlfriend, no job, nothing. Eight months had passed and I was still unemployed and unloved.

I didn't have my own computer at the time, so I spent most of my days at the library surfing the Net for work. While online, I also set up a few personal profiles on several dating sites. A woman named Jackie answered one of my ads and we started to correspond regularly. One Friday night, I checked my email at my friend Glen's house and discovered that Jackie had left her telephone number. Glen and I got all excited because she said in her email that she was entertaining a couple of her girlfriends that night. We thought this would be an opportunity for us both to get in on some action. We called and tried to get them to meet with us, but Jackie insisted that she wasn't prepared to meet right away. She did, however, agree to meet the following evening. Glen wasn't able to make it because he had made other plans, so I went alone.

Jackie turned out to be very nice, smart, and had a great personality. The night we met, however, I didn't really want to give her a chance because she was overweight. When I first noticed her and her friend, Pam, standing at the ATM, I prayed they were not the women I was supposed to meet on the corner that night, but I knew in the back of my mind that they were. They didn't notice me at first, and I just stood there hoping that the women I was waiting for would come walking from another direction.

I stood on the corner of One Hundred and Tenth Street and Broadway with my back to the bank and waited. My personal profile had a photograph, so Jackie knew what I looked like. I never even asked her for a description of herself. When I spoke to her on the telephone, her voice sounded so sexy and seductive, my mind told me she'd look like Toni Braxton.

"Keith?" I heard a voice call out. I turned around and saw the women from the ATM walking toward me. I started to pray that Pam was the one I came to meet. She was about five-two and thin with a sandy complexion. The woman that stepped forward was five-nine, light brown-skinned, wore thick glasses, and fat. "No way," I thought to myself, but I didn't let it show up on my face or come out in my voice. I was as nice as I could be and greeted her pleasantly with a smile. I thought I might've been able to dump Jackie and get with her friend, but I found out that Pam, who was visiting from Memphis and leaving the next day, had some New York booty already waiting for her.

So we were off to Pam's friend James' new brownstone for his housewarming party. It was a very beautiful house and James hadn't done much to it yet. We were all awed. I didn't say much of anything when we first arrived, but I loosened up a few Heinekens later. It turned out to be a nice little social gathering. There were five other guys there besides James and myself, and five other women besides Jackie and Pam. Jackie and Pam were the only African-American women. There were two Hispanics, an East Indian, an Asian, and a Caucasian. All of the men were African-American professionals, a corporate lawyer, an entertainment lawyer, a stockbroker, an investment banker, and a computer program designer. I doubt if any of them were older than me, and I was thirty-three at the time. I wasn't jealous or intimidated because I didn't have a job, but I knew I had to do something with my life right away. I had been planning to start my own business and decided right then and there to move forward with that idea and make it work.

Anyway, the night went well. The whole group left James' and went to a small social club on Eighty-Fifth Street for drinks. Jackie and I only stayed at the dance club for about an hour. She got into a cab and I got on the subway convinced I'd never see her again. Even though I had fun with Jackie that night, I couldn't picture myself being with a woman her size. She had to be, at the very least, three hundred pounds. I couldn't help it. If something turns you off, it just does. It was hard for me to look past how big she was despite all the other positive things she had to offer. She was funny, witty, intelligent, and very much down to earth, but all I could think about was her exterior.

After that night, Jackie and I spoke on the phone a few times. I didn't call her the next day like I said I would because I never planned on seeing her again, but I thought that would be inconsiderate. I wasn't a total jerk. I called her about three days later at her job, and she called me back later that night. The conversation got steamy and I found out that Jackie was a freak. All she wanted to talk about was sex, so we spent most of the night having phone sex.

"I wanted to kiss you so bad when we were on the dance floor," she said in her usual sultry voice. "You looked so fine in your linen outfit. I had to restrain myself because I just wanted to eat you alive."

I wondered if she meant that literally as I chuckled to myself. "Is that a fact?" was all I could think to say.

"Yes, it is. You were looking and smelling real nice."

"Well, thank you. You were looking rather nice yourself."

"I know you wanted to kiss me, too. Am I right?"

"Of course," I lied, rolling my eyes up in my head. "Would you have let me?"

"Absolutely. I was hoping that you would. I love to kiss. I love to use my lips."

"Hmm, is that a fact?"

"Oh, yes. My lips are one of my three best assets, don't you think?"

"Indeed. You do have a very nice set of lips." I was being sincere at this point. I did notice that Jackie had nice, full lips that looked very soft and juicy. I remembered staring at her lips when we were at James' house and wondering how well would she be able to slob my knob.

"You know what my other two best assets are?"

"What are they? I asked as I got off my couch and laid down on the carpet in front of the coffee table.

"My other two best assets are my other two sets of lips."

"Is that a fact? I don't know why I didn't know you'd say that."

"I don't know. Maybe you underestimate me."

"Perhaps I did."

"Well, don't. I can offer a lot. When I am into a man, I make sure that he reaps all the benefits of me. I have no trouble keeping my man satisfied."

"Is that a fact?"

"Yes, that's a fact. Is that all you ever say?"

"No; I'm just a little surprised to hear you talking this way. You don't come across..."

"I told you, baby, don't underestimate me."

I was into playing the game at this point. I knew she wanted to get into some arousing, in-depth, sexual conversation, and I wanted to see exactly how far she'd go. "So, what would you do to keep me satisfied?"

"Well, I take real pride in my ability to give a really great blow job. I love doing it. I've mastered a technique that I know will drive you out of your mind."

"Oh, that's good, because I really love to get a good blow job."

"I'm sure you do, but I don't give good blow jobs. I give great ones. As a matter of fact, they're outstanding."

"What do you do?" I asked as I reached into my boxers, pulled out my erect penis and began to stroke it slowly.

"Mmmm, wouldn't you like to know?"

"Yes, I would."

"I'd rather show you."

"C'mon, don't do me like that."

"Oh, trust me, you won't do anything except enjoy whatever it is I do to you. And *that's* a fact."

"I'm sure it is."

"What are you doing right now? You're breathing is kind of heavy. You have your dick in your hand, don't you?"

"Yes," I confessed, and began stroking faster.

"Good. I'm playing with myself, too. I have two fingers buried deep in my pussy and I'm using my thumb to rub my clit. Oh! Oh! I think I'm about to cum."

So was I. I stroked myself harder and faster until I ejaculated, and a wad of semen shot up into the air and landed on my stomach. More of it oozed out as I continued stroking and squeezing my cock until there was no more. I could hear Jackie on the other end giggling.

"Now, doesn't that feel better?" she asked in that soothing, deep voice of hers.

"Oh, yes," I muttered.

"Good. That should hold you over until we get together again. By the way, when are we getting together again?"

I held the telephone to my ear with my shoulder so that I could remove my boxers and use them to wipe the cum from all over myself. "We can get together this weekend if you want."

"Yes, that would be great. We can meet up and catch a movie or something. I love to go to the movies."

"I do, too. The movies it is. We can go this Friday."

"Call me at work and I'll tell you where to come to pick me up."

"Okay. I'll talk to you then."

"Okay. Goodnight, Keith."

"Goodnight, Jackie."

I picked Jackie up from her job on Wall Street at seven o'clock the next Friday evening and we took the subway up to a theater on Fifty-Ninth Street. In the theater, we sat in the back and she snuggled close to me. I tried hard to put her size out of my mind because I knew she was horny and so was I. She got really hot and squirmy and started rubbing my thigh and in between my legs. I slipped my hand under her shirt and bra and kneaded her huge nipples. Her breasts were gigantic. I'd never seen anything like them before. I could've used one of her bra cups for a hat. We continued to kiss and feel each other up throughout the entire show. After the movie ended, we took a walk to Central Park. I wanted to go to her apartment instead, but she claimed she didn't want to move too fast. Go figure.

We found the darkest and most deserted spot in the park that wasn't too far from an exit. Jackie just moved to New York from Tennessee six months ago and heard many Central Park horror stories. We kissed and fondled each other for about twenty-five minutes, and then Jackie changed her mind and decided that we should go to her apartment after all. We got on the C-train and went uptown to her apartment on the other end of the park where we talked and listened to music for a while. At about one a.m., we agreed that I should stay overnight.

Jackie went into the bathroom and started running water in the bathtub. She came back into the living room, took my hand and escorted me back into the bathroom where she removed each article of my clothing very patiently. The bathtub filled with hot, bubbly water and Jackie instructed me to get in. She got on her knees beside the tub, lathered up a large sponge and began giving me the best bath I've ever had in my life. We didn't talk the whole time. Jackie had an Al Green CD playing, and we were both humming and singing along.

I got out the tub and Jackie let the water out and began to dry me off. Then, she wrapped me in the towel, led me into her bedroom and instructed me to lie across her king-sized bed. I laid on my back and Jackie removed the towel and took it with her back into the bathroom. I heard the shower come on as I lay there nude, enjoying Al Green, and I began to drift off into a slumber. I was awakened by Jackie's hand massaging my scrotum and her lips gliding along the shaft of my semi-erect dick. My eyes fluttered open and all I could see was naked brown flesh positioned over my mid-section, and the top of Jackie's head slowly moving up and down. I closed my eyes again and imagined that it was my ex there with me instead. Jackie's lips felt really soft, and my excitement grew causing me to become fully erect. Her lips were locked tightly around my shaft and her tongue glided up and rolled down. Then she pressed her lips around the head and flicked her tongue into the opening at the top. She continued to massage my balls with one hand and stroke the length of my dick with the other. She opened her mouth again, taking all of me in, and let it follow her hand up and down on my dick. She was turning her hand and flipping her tongue as her head bounced up and down faster. My legs started shaking and I felt like I was ready to explode, but I couldn't. Jackie had a rhythm of going up and down fast, then around and around slowly, while keeping a firm grip on my balls and massaging them. Finally, I felt myself release. Jackie aimed my dick at her enormous breasts and I doused them with milky-white cum. She certainly backed up the story she told me on the phone about her being the queen of fellatio. I stayed with her the rest of the week.

A few weeks later, I went back to Harlem to spend the week with Jackie again. The bottom line is that I was feeling very, very lonely because I had nothing or no one. It didn't justify me using this poor woman, knowing that I was in no way attracted to her. I did like her, but I couldn't get past how big she was. I guess that made me a small person. I'm sure if it were not for the loneliness and the horniness, I wouldn't have even been able to keep an erection around her. I let those feelings influence my better judgment even more because I had unprotected sex with her. I let the wrong head do my thinking for me. Before then, I would've sworn that I was too mature to let something like that happen. I have to admit, however, that having sex with Jackie was really nice. She felt really good and she was right about her other assets. I got caught up with her because she was so active and always had multiple orgasms. She loved to do it doggy-style, which was fine with me, because my dick is only six inches and I had trouble staying inside of her any other way. She couldn't keep her legs up missionary-style, and I certainly couldn't hold them up. I just felt so ashamed of myself because she was such a nice person.

After seeing Jackie every weekend for about three months, her personality overwhelmed me and I started getting real feelings for her. I didn't care about her size anymore because she was so loving, caring and endearing. I began thinking that I may be in love. I decided that I'd put aside my immature, superficial feelings because I wanted to get serious with her and I couldn't wait to let her know. I showed up at her apartment with flowers and wine so I could create the ideal setting to reveal my feelings to her. After I knocked on the door several times, Jackie answered with an attitude.

"Who is it?" she snapped. I had never heard her use that tone of voice before.

"It's me, Keith," I responded.

"Keith?" She sounded surprised as she opened the door dressed in a sexy black night-gown.

"Wassup, baby?" I said as I started to walk in. Jackie put her hand on my chest and stopped me.

"Wait a minute," she said. "It's not like you to come over without calling. What if I wasn't here?"

"But you are here. Is there a problem?"

"Well, Keith, I'm entertaining right now."

I couldn't believe what she was telling me. I found myself getting angry. "You mean you got a dude in there?"

Jackie covered her mouth and started chuckling. "Aw, c'mon now. I know you're not getting bent out of shape behind this, are you? It's not like we were going to get serious or anything. That's not what we were doing. We're just kickin' it, right?"

It's a good thing I'm good at hiding my thoughts. I gave her a "C'mon please" look and said, "C'mon, please. We're fine just like this. I'm not even trying to start trippin' with no relationship talk. I was just in the mood for some freaky deaky, but I wanted to get a little romance on, too."

"That's real sweet, baby," Jackie said, taking the wine and flowers out of my hands, "but like I said, I'm already entertaining. Next time call."

She kissed me on the cheek and closed the door. I was mortified. I stood there for a few minutes feeling like a complete ass. After about five or ten minutes, I finally got up the strength to turn around and go home.

Sow Her Oats, Plant His Seed

Diane sat at her desk sorting her upcoming cases. The beautiful accident and workers compensation lawyer was usually very busy, but she worked very hard to organize enough to make some free time for herself. Enough free time to spend some quality time with the man she'd been chatting online with for the past month. She was finally able to meet her new friend the day before, and was looking forward to spending an evening with him again after work. Diane smiled widely when his instant message flashed up on her screen.

MrKlean: Good morning, Diane. How's my favorite lady doing this morning?
XOXO: Hey what's up, Mark? I'm fine & u?
MrKlean: Better now that I'm online w/u. Thanx for having lunch w/me yesterday. I had a good time, and u are fine as hell
XOXO: well thank u. I had a good time, too, and ur quite a specimen urself
MrKlean: whatcha doin? Working hard or hardly working?
XOXO: today I'm not working so hard. It's kinda lite
MrKlean: That's good because I don't want u 2 b 2 tired for our date 2nite
XOXO: o no I'm looking forward to it
MrKlean: that's good. me 2
XOXO: so what r u doin? working hard or hardly working?
MrKlean: I'm takin it easy. I wanna be right for 2nite. LOL
XOXO: lol why? What do u have in mind?
MrKlean: I figured we could have dinner at that Mexican place in Chelsea, then go to the Paramount for some drinks and shake our booties a little
XOXO: lol I like that. Since we're going dancing, I think I'll wear that little black dress I just bought
MrKlean: yeah u do that. :D
XOXO: if I do what am I gonna get out of it? :">
MrKlean: maybe I'll have a special treat for u at the end of the night if ur a good girl
XOXO: maybe the night won't end if ur a good boy

MrKlean: promises promises

XOXO: lol I guess u'll have to wait and see

MrKlean: why don't u give me some incentives?

XOXO: u mentioned dinner, drinks and dancing. Well, if dinner is good, when we go back to ur place I'll be sure to feed u. As for drinks, what I'll feed u will quench ur thirst as well. And as for shakin our booties, well, use ur imagination

MrKlean: damn baby, there's smoke coming outta my modem

XOXO: LMAO it's not as hot as it can get

MrKlean: All right now u talk a good game. Just don't let ur mouth write a check that ur ass can't cash

XOXO: u must not've taken a good look at my ass yesterday

MrKlean: oh yes I did

XOXO: then u should know that I always have funds available

MrKlean: <— is clearing the smoke

XOXO: LOL

MrKlean: LOL

Diane's direct line rings. She looks down to see her fiancé's cell phone number on her caller ID.

XOXO: I gotta take this call. BRB

MrKlean: ok np

"Hey, Hector. What's up, baby?"

"Hey, sweetheart. I'm just checking in. What's going on?"

"I have a lot of work here. It looks like I'm really going to be swamped today. I'll probably be working very late."

"Damn, Diane. We were supposed to hang out with the gang tonight."

"I'm sorry, baby. This has to get done, though."

"Well, what time do you think that you'll be finished?"

"Around nine or nine-thirty."

"Shit, it doesn't make any sense for you to have to work so late on a Friday night."

"I know. I'm sorry."

"So, why don't you just meet us after you get off?"

"I'll be too tired. My sister is going to pick me up, and I'm going spend the night at her house so I won't have to take the subway all the way back home. She's going to drive me home in the morning."

"Forget it, then. I'll just come pick you up after work and we'll stay home together."

"No, you go ahead and hang out. Don't let me stop you from having a good time. I'll be fine at my sister's house."

"You sure?"

"Yes. Go out and have a good time. Tell Jerome and Neicy I said, hello. Watch Jay's ass. Don't let him drink too much and cause a scene. And tell Katina to keep her crusty lips off of you. Don't bring your ass home with her slobber all over you. I'll kick both your asses."

"Okay, okay, Diane. Well, call me later so I'll know you're okay."

"You see, Hector, that's why I'm marrying you. You're always looking out for me."

"I have to, because I love you."

"I love you, too."

"Alright, Diane. I'll talk to you later."

"Okay."

Diane hung up the phone and let out a loud sigh. She was proud of how well she played Hector and how easy it was to make him believe her. She knew that was only the first step, though. The next phase of her plan would surely be far more difficult.

After organizing her thoughts, Diane returned to her chat session.

XOXO: u still there

MrKlean: yes wb

XOXO: sorry about that. These damn clients ask the same stupid questions over and over

MrKlean: LOL be patient with them. They don't mean to be a pain in the ass

XOXO: I know, but they are

MrKlean: Well u handle ur business and call me b4 u leave

XOXO: I will. I get off at 3:00

MrKlean: ok I'll talk to u around that time

XOXO: ok

MrKlean: take care

XOXO: u 2

"Alright, it's time to put my plan into phase two," Diane thought aloud. She let out a deep breath and hit the speed dial on her telephone.

RING - RING

"Hello?"

"Trisha."

"Hey Diane, what's up?"

"I need you to look out for me tonight."

"Look out for you how?"

"Hector wants me to go out with him and the gang, but I'm not feelin' them tonight. I told Hector that I'd be working late and I'd stay with you."

"And I take it that's not what you'll really be doing?"

"No; I'm going out, but I'm hanging out somewhere else."

"Uh huh. Somewhere else with whom?"

"With a friend, Trisha."

"What kind of friend, Diane? A male friend or a female friend?"

"A male friend."

"Oh, hell no!"

"What?"

"I'm not getting in the middle of this."

"C'mon, Trisha…"

"No. No. No."

"Why not?"

"No. Find someone else to be your flunky. I ain't down."

"Hold up, sis. When did you acquire this liking of Hector? Weren't you the one who said that I'd have to be crazy to marry that man?"

"Yeah, I said that. I still don't like him, but I don't want to get in the middle of you steppin' out on him. You do that on your own."

"Oh, shit. Let me find out that you've developed some sense of morality in the last three days."

"In the last three days? I'll have you know, little sister, that I have never, ever stepped out on anyone I've been with in my life. I cannot condone that type of thing, nor will I be a part of it."

"Damn, Trisha. I would've done it for you."

"You're not hearing me. I wouldn't ask you to do anything like that for me."

"Look, I just want to go out, have dinner, maybe dancing, and have a good time without Hector tonight. I'm not going to sleep with this man. I just want a change of pace."

"Then just be honest with Hector and tell him that."

"I can't believe this. Just the other day you were giving me every reason why Hector is so bad for me, and telling me how much of a mistake I'd be making if I married him. Now, all of a sudden, you got this holy attitude. I don't get it, Trisha."

"It's very simple. All I see is you being Hector's trophy, a showpiece for him to show off to his friends. You're a twenty-seven-year-old lawyer. You're intelligent, successful and beautiful with so much going for you. Meanwhile, his two-bit, underachieving, fat ass dropped out of medical school. What's he doing now? Managing a damn music store."

"So what, Trisha. It's a respectable job. It's not like he's out on the corner selling drugs."

"No, but he is hanging on the corner drinking forties with his pants hanging off his ass. I just think that's a bit much for a thirty-year-old man. Particularly one who still refers to himself as the 'Puerto Rican Prince.' But despite all that, I still believe in honesty. If you're going to go out with another man, you should ask Hector for some space so you can get this urge to be with other men out of your system. You know, the mere fact that you're even considering stepping out on your fiancé just reassures me that you're making a mistake by marrying him. Still, I think it's wrong for you to go out behind his back."

"I don't know what the fuck to think, Trisha. All you've done is confuse me. I do know that I find Mark very interesting, to say the least. He's smart, motivated, and damn, fine as hell. I love Hector, but I like Mark, too."

"Mark, eh? Who is this Mark character? Where'd you meet him?"

"We met online."

"Online? The Internet, Diane?"

"Yes, the Internet. There's nothing wrong with that."

"What do you know about this Mark character?"

"He's a 29-year-old investment banker that lives out on the suburbs."

"He can tell you anything online, Diane."

"Give me more credit than that, Trisha. I have called his job and he's called here. We had lunch together yesterday. I just want to get to know him better. I just want to have a little fun with a man without a bunch of other people for a change. It's something different, not something permanent. If I do what you said and asked Hector for space, it may change everything between us, and I certainly don't want that. All I'm asking is that you look out for me this one time so that I can release. Let me get this out of my system. I promise you that it's nothing more than that. Please?"

"What makes you think Hector won't call or come looking for you?"

"Girl, please. Hector is not even coming to your house. He doesn't like you either, you know. He says you're stuck up and you talk down to him like you think you're better than he is. Personally, I don't know what would ever give him that idea."

"Very funny. This is the first and last time, Diane. I mean that from the bottom of my heart."

"Thank you, Trish. I owe you big."

"Oh, you have no idea."

"Take care. I'll talk to you later."

"Okay, bye."

Diane hung up the telephone, sat back in her chair and spun around in it. "Yes!" she shouted. "It's going to be a good night."

Diane and Mark arrived at his house around two a.m. Diane was staggering a bit from the shots of tequila she downed at the club. She was not much of a drinker, but she was trying to show out. Mark held Diane's arm and escorted her inside. She was immediately awed upon entering. She walked to the middle of the living room and slowly turned in a full three-sixty.

"My goodness, Mark," she said. "You have a very, very nice place."

"Thank you. I'm glad you like it," Mark said, proudly.

"Oh, I love it. Who is your designer?"

"Uh...designer? Nah, I did it all myself. No designer."
"Really?" Diane asked, surprised and impressed at the same time.
"Really."
"Shit. Well, you have impeccable taste."
"Thank you, very much."
"You are full of surprises tonight."
"What do you mean?"
"I had no idea you could dance Hip Hop so well."
"Why didn't you think I would be able to?"
"Well, can I be honest?"
"Absolutely."
"You seemed a little tight to me at first."
"Tight?" Mark echoed, raising a brow at the notion.
"Stuffy."
"Stuffy?"
"Well, yeah. No offense, but you just seem more like the black tie, ballroom type rather than the get down and boogie type. You're so clean-cut and proper. I was really surprised when you said we'd be going to the Paramount. I expected to spend most of the night at a table drinking and socializing. I thought that maybe we'd get on the dance floor for a couple of songs and you'd do a two-step to Nelly."
"Ha haha ha haha. Well, I am so happy to have disappointed you."
"Oh no, my brotha. I am not disappointed one bit."
"Well, you are quite a dancer yourself. I love the way you move. You're energetic, and sexy as hell. I tried to be cool, but you were making it hard for me."
"Well, I was trying to make it hard for *me*."
"Ha haha. I think you succeeded."
"You have a great laugh."

Mark walked over and stood in front of Diane. She closed her eyes and waited for him to take her. He gathered her into his arms and kissed her passionately. Their tongues rolled and wrestled while their hands probed each other's bodies. He slowly unzipped her dress and let his fingers dance up and down her back, sending surges of excitement up her spine. Diane removed Mark's blazer and let it fall to the floor. She unbuttoned his shirt and began to plant gentle kisses all over his broad, muscular chest.

Mark pulled the straps of Diane's dress over her shoulders and let it fall to her feet, exposing her perfect round and firm 36Cs with large light-brown nipples and her flat stomach. Her thin waist and round hips made up her perfect hourglass figure. Marks eyes feasted on the sight of Diane's silky, golden-brown skin tone as she stood there in her black thong. Her dress gathered at her feet, hiding her black leather pumps as her long, shapely legs extended upward. Mark was convinced that Diane was a perfect ten as he gazed into her brown eyes that slanted slightly. Diane's mother was part African American, part Japanese, and her father was part African American, part Cherokee Indian, which explained her slanted eyes and her long straight hair. People often mistook her for being Latin of some sort.

Mark removed his shirt, revealing his six-pack abs and large muscular arms. It was obvious that he worked out regularly. His smooth, bronze complexion made Diane gasp. He had a thin goatee, deep set alluring eyes and a short, wavy haircut. He picked Diane up, carried her into his bedroom and laid her down on his large Roman-style bed. He stood over her for a moment gazing at her beauty. "She could've very easily been a model," he thought to himself. "She's absolutely perfect." He removed his pants and stood there for a moment longer in just his black silk boxers. Diane smiled devilishly at the sight of his bulge barely being restrained.

Mark kneeled on the bed and slowly rolled Diane over on her stomach. He reached on the nightstand for some massage oil, removed her shoes and began rubbing the oil on her feet. Diane jumped and squirmed slightly. She had sensitive feet that were easily tickled, but Mark's foot massage didn't bother her too much. He knew how to touch her.

Mark poured more oil into his hands and started up Diane's legs, taking his time on each one. Diane let out soft moans of pleasure from the touch of Mark's strong and firm, yet soft hands. He got more oil to coat her round, firm posterior. His hands caressed and kneaded her buttocks and she could only close her eyes and smile. No man had ever made her feel this good.

Mark continued to massage Diane's back before turning her over again. He started his procedure over, working from her feet, up her legs, to her stomach and breasts. After Diane's body was completely oiled, Mark removed her thong. Her bikini wax exposed her vagina that looked like a blooming rose, and her clitoris poked out like a tiny pearl. Mark kneeled on the side of the bed and ran his fingers up and down Diane's wet vagina, softly stroking the inner and outer folds. Her back arched and she spread her legs wide as he inserted one finger, and then another into her.

Diane tugged at Mark's boxers until she pulled them down enough for his ten-inch erection to spring free. She grabbed his butt with one hand and the head of his penis with the other. She lifted his dick upward and ran her tongue up and down the under-shaft. Mark's fingers were fucking Diane harder and faster and he used his other hand to hold on to the headboard. Diane took as much of his dick into her mouth as she could and sucked greedily. Mark felt the tension building up in his loins and began stroking Diane's love hole faster.

"Ohhh, I'm cumming!" he bellowed, and began spurting semen into the back of her throat.

Diane drank and swallowed as quickly as she could, trying not to waste any of Mark's delicious protein shake. It was truly good to her. "He must eat really well all the time," she thought. As hard as she tried, she could not keep some of it from escaping to the sides of her mouth and chin. She used the head of Mark's dick to smear it all over her lips, and then licked it off with her tongue.

Mark turned Diane over on her stomach again and spread her legs wide apart. He reached over on the nightstand for a condom, opened the package and rolled the prophylactic onto his still erect penis. Diane moved her ass around in a circular motion with anticipation. Mark pulled her up on her knees and pressed the head of his cock against her vaginal opening. Slowly, he entered her inch by inch. Diane threw her head back and let out a loud moan. It was her turn to hold on the headboard now, and she did so with both hands as Mark thrust in and out of her with long, slow strokes at first, then faster, harder and deeper. His balls slapped against her clitoris as he pounded into her, causing her to climax in waves. Diane's juices soaked Mark's balls and pubic hair and dripped down the insides of her thighs. She didn't stop cumming the whole time he was inside of her. Finally, he felt the tension in his loins once again. He grabbed her hips on both sides and shot another load.

Diane and Mark collapsed on the bed together panting heavily. Mark looked over at the clock that read three thirty-four. "Sweetheart, that was fantastic," he whispered into her ear.

"Um hm," she panted.

"Don't go to sleep, baby. I have to take you home."

Diane lifted her head and looked at Mark with a puzzled expression. "Take me home? Oh, I just assumed..."

"I'm sorry. I just don't think that it would be a good idea for you to stay over."

"Oh, of course. I'll get my things." Diane jumped up from the bed and quickly put on her thong.

"Look, I'm sorry if I gave you the wrong impression."

"Don't worry about it," she said as she slipped on her shoes and hurried out of the room to get her dress. By the time Mark put on his boxers, pulled his house shoes from under the bed and slipped them on, Diane was gone.

Ten days had passed and Diane hadn't heard from Mark, and she refused to call him. She felt that he should have called her with an explanation a long time ago. However, she could not resist the urge to send an instant message when she finally saw him online.

XOXO: good day, sir.
MrKlean: hi Diane
XOXO: I haven't seen u online in a while
MrKlean: I've been really busy
XOXO: O I C
XOXO: I thought you'd call me
XOXO: maybe send an e-mail or something
MrKlean: oh sorry, but I've been really wrapped up

XOXO: I understand. I know how it can get
XOXO: :-)
XOXO: u still there?
XOXO: Mark?
MrKlean: yes I'm here
XOXO: can I ask u a question?
MrKlean: of course
XOXO: why couldn't I stay at ur house that night? Why was it so important for me to leave?
XOXO: are u married?
XOXO: do u have a girlfriend?
XOXO: Mark? Are u there?
MrKlean: sorry dear. I'm still very busy so if I take a while to respond please forgive me
XOXO: o ok
XOXO: I'll be here waiting for u to respond
MrKlean: I might've explained it to u that night if u would've hung around long enough. u left kinda abruptly
XOXO: I was very upset at the moment
MrKlean: I understand, and I apologize
XOXO: yeah ok
MrKlean: What are u doing after work? Are u busy?
XOXO: I was just going home. Why?
MrKlean: I want to come pick you up if you can get away for a couple of hours
XOXO: I don't know
MrKlean: I can pick you up around 5:15. I promise you'll be home by 8:00
XOXO: where r we going?
MrKlean: now there's no need to discuss that unless u can go
XOXO: well, I'm free, but I still don't know
MrKlean: What's there to know? Didn't you enjoy being with me last week?
XOXO: yes, up until it was time to go home >:(
MrKlean: then you must let me make it up 2 u the best I can for a couple of hours tonight
XOXO: I need to know why things had to go down like that
MrKlean: we'll talk about it when I pick you up. 5:15 be ready. I gotta go. I'll see you then :x
XOXO: wait a minute. I didn't say yes
XOXO: Mark?
XOXO: Mark?

XOXO: r u there?
XOXO: Mark?

"Shit. Fuck him, then," Diane muttered. "I'm not going. If he wants to see me he'd better... Hmph. Oh God, what am I doing?"

5:33 P.M.

Mark led Diane down Eighty-Sixth Street and started to smile as he looked her over.

"Damn, baby, I almost forgot how fine you are."

"Really? I was hoping I'd leave a lasting impression. I guess it's out of sight, out of mind as far as you're concerned."

"Why are you so bitter? I'm just trying to say that you are even more beautiful than I remember."

"I guess you wouldn't have had to say that if this wasn't the first time I saw you, or spoke to you in ten days."

"Well, I missed being with you. That's why I invited you to come with me today."

Mark noticed the "don't walk" light starting to flash and grabbed Diane's hand.

"Oh-oh, come on," he said, pulling her across Columbus Avenue. They got to the other side just as the light changed.

Diane began to get impatient. "Where are we going, Mark?"

"For a little walk in the park."

"A walk in the park?"

"Yeah, come on."

"Are you married? Is that it? Is that why I had to leave; because your wife was coming home?"

"No, *I'm* not married."

"What was it then, a girlfriend?"

"No."

"Boyfriend?"

"Ha haha. Now, you're trippin'."

"What then? Please, tell me something."

Mark stopped, faced Diane and looked her over. "I don't understand why you're so bent out of shape about that. I thought that you and I were just out to have a good time. I thought this was a no-strings-attached deal. Am I wrong? Isn't this just a game being played by two consenting adults looking for some wild action?"

"What the fuck gave you that idea?" Diane asked, acting as if she was appalled.

Mark grinned at Diane's futile attempt, gathered her in his arms and kissed her passionately. Diane tried to resist at first, but as much as her mind told her, "no," her body said, "yes." Mark had guided her to a spot right near the reservoir in Central Park. It was usually very deserted over there. The area looked like a miniature forest. It was a warm and slightly breezy day, ideal weather for any type of outdoor activity. But Diane realized that she may be playing too close to home.

"Mark, I live on the other side of this park," Diane said, once again pulling away, "right on Central Park North."

"So," Mark said, pulling her back close to him. "What, are you afraid that someone you know may see us?"

"No. Well, yes. What I mean is, um, I'm just saying..."

"Don't worry," Mark told her. "It'll be fine. Just trust me."

Mark took Diane by the hand and led her deeper into the midst of the trees where he thought joggers running along the reservoir and other park strollers would not be able to notice them. Diane attempted to resist again, but her protests fell on deaf ears. Not that she tried that hard, anyway. She knew what Mark's intentions were, and the thought of having sex outdoors, and possibly being an exhibitionist in the process, excited her. She had never done anything even close to this before. She read erotic novels and fantasized about doing all the things the characters in those stories were doing, but never did anything so exciting. She never brought up any ideas to any of her six past lovers fearing that they would think that she was too freaky or worse.

Mark led Diane about thirty yards through trees and bushes, stepping over rocks and branches. Finally, they came upon a large tree and he swirled her around. He pushed her back against the tree and started planting kisses all over her neck as he eased the strap of her pocketbook off her shoulder and let it fall to the ground. He continued his series of kisses as he removed the blazer to her work suit, which fell right over her purse. He used his tongue to unbutton her blouse and began kissing the top of her breasts before running his tongue up and down her cleavage.

Diane was moaning loudly as she began to open Mark's belt and zipper. She unbuttoned his trousers as she felt his hands moving up her thighs, lifting her skirt. She felt his finger poking the crotch of her pantyhose until he popped a hole in them and ripped them open from back to front. Just as fast as he made the opening, he spun her around again, pressing her breasts into the tree. Diane threw her arms around the tree and hugged it tightly. She felt Mark rip her pantyhose open wider and tear away her panties completely. The evening breeze rushed up between her legs, sending chills throughout her entire body.

Mark pushed himself against Diane using his leg to spread hers wider apart. She felt the head of his erect penis stabbing at her inner thigh. He rubbed and caressed her round, plump, firm ass, enjoying the feel of her silky, smooth skin. He spread her ass cheeks apart enough for his dick to slide into her waiting, wet pussy. Diane closed her eyes real tight as she felt Mark push in hard. He fucked her with long and hard strokes, making loud slapping sounds against her backside. Diane whimpered "uh, uh, uh" with each of his hard thrusts into her. Her breasts were pressed hard against the tree trunk as she held on for dear life. Finally, Mark let out a long groan and Diane cried out as they reached their orgasms together.

They took their time and cleaned themselves up as best they could before coming out of the midst of trees. It was obvious that they had been spotted because there was a couple sitting on a bench about fifty feet away with big, wide smiles on their faces. The couple watched them as they made their way up the little hill and back to the path at the edge of the reservoir and the man gave them a thumbs up. Mark returned the gesture and Diane blew the couple a kiss. Diane had never felt so lively before. Mark gave her an unfamiliar feel of satisfaction. She didn't think about Hector one time while she was with him.

"Mark, please don't wait so long for us to be together again. I'd die if I didn't see you, or talk to you everyday."

"Diane, listen. Just as I said before, I just wanted to play this little game for a while, that's all. It seems you want more than that and we both know that can't happen. I'm not looking for a relationship right now. I just got out of a three-year relationship with someone and I just want to take it easy."

"I'm not looking for a relationship either, Mark. I just want to keep this game going and play it more often."

"That's what you say now, but the more time we spend together, the more we are prone to start having feelings for each other. Geez, if we start out spending the night together, soon we'll be leaving clothing and hinting about moving in."

"What? Hold on a minute..."

"No, it's true and you know it."

"Mark, you got me all wrong..."

"Do I? I don't think so. And I'll be damned if I be the cause of breaking up someone's happy home. Aren't you married, or about to get married?"

Diane became wide-eyed and her words trembled as she spoke. "What makes you think that I'm about to get married?"

"That big, pretty ring you're wearing. You forgot to take it off today just as you did the day we had lunch together. It's cool, though. It's part of the game, right?"

"Mark, let me explain this to you."

"C'mon, Babe. There's no need to explain anything. We both got what we wanted. Let's leave it at that. It's best if we don't go on any further with this. You've sowed your oats, now go ahead and live your life and be happy. I'll find that special someone one day, too."

Mark hailed a cab after he and Diane exited the park. "Thanks for a wonderful time," he said, then kissed her on the cheek, got into the cab and waved to her as the driver pulled off.

Diane never saw Mark again, and neither of them tried to contact the other. Two months later, Diane found out she was pregnant and got Hector to move their wedding date up. She didn't want her baby to be born before they were married.

Hector was so happy to be a father. It changed a few things about him, including Trisha's opinion of him. He wasn't hanging on the corner drinking forties with the boys anymore. He didn't want to go out with the gang every weekend anymore. Hector's life now revolved around his loving wife, Diane, and his pride and joy - his son, Mark.

Birthday Celebration

Rashida got home from work disappointed that her twenty-sixth birthday was nowhere near what she'd expected. So far, the day sucked. It was a Monday that was gloomy from rain that never came. It was just cloudy and misty all day long. She thought, at the very least, that her co-workers would surprise her with some cake and ice cream, but that didn't happen. She thought her family would have called and said that they were coming over, but that didn't happen either. She was alone and bored.

Rashida decided to change clothes and surf the Net for a while. When she logged on, she saw she had received an email from Duane, the guy she'd been chatting with for over two years. Although they never met, she and Duane both talked about how well each of them felt they knew the other because they chatted so frequently and told each other everything. She opened the email to find that Duane had sent her an electronic birthday card. It read:

HAPPY BIRTHDAY. I HOPE YOUR DAY IS GOING WELL AND YOU ARE HAVING A GREAT TIME. I REMEMBERED YOU SAID YOU DIDN'T HAVE ANY PLANS, SO OF COURSE I CAME UP WITH ONE. I'M SENDING YOU ON A BIRTHDAY SCAVENGER HUNT. HERE'S WHAT YOU DO: FIRST, YOU MUST GO TO THE MALL. ENTER ON THE SOUTH SIDE AND GO DOWN THE HALL, ALL THE WAY TO THE PAYPHONE RIGHT PAST THE STORE WITH THE BALL. PICK UP YOUR FIRST GIFT, AND THEN YOUR NAME DO CALL.

Rashida read the e-card ten times before she said to herself, "What the hell. It's not like I have anything else to do. Besides, if he went through all this trouble to get me a gift, I should at least go see what it is."

She got into her car and took the fifteen-minute drive to the mall. She followed Duane's instructions and came upon a store called Zelda's. In the window were two mannequins in bathing suits leaning up against an oversized beach ball. One of the mannequins had a sign hanging around its neck with "Rashida" written on it. Smiling, she hurried into the store and inquired to find that Duane had bought her both bathing suits.

Rashida got her first present and was walking out the store when she remembered something about making a call. She exited the store and looked to her right where she saw three payphones against the wall. She walked over to them and looked around for another clue, but didn't see anything. She read her printout of the card again, and then it hit her. "Oh," she said, thinking she should've caught on sooner. "It says, 'your name do call.'" She dialed the seven letters of her name and got a voicemail.

"HELLO, RASHIDA. I HOPE YOU LIKE YOUR BATHING SUITS. I REMEMBERED YOU SAID YOU LIKED THE BEACH AND WAS PLANNING ON GOING A LOT THIS SUMMER. I JUST WANTED TO DO MY PART TO MAKE SURE YOU ARE THE FLYEST WOMAN ON IT. FIGURE OUT THIS RIDDLE FOR THE NEXT PART OF THE HUNT: YOUR NEXT GIFT IS KIND OF BAD; BUT LIKE THAT RED BIKINI, IT'LL MAKE MY EYES GLAD. I WANT TO TAKE OUR RELATIONSHIP UP - TO THE NEXT LEVEL AND RING YOUR BELL. SHHH! DON'T TELL! DON'T TELL!"

The message ended and another recording came on:
PRESS ONE TO SAVE, TWO TO DELETE, THREE TO REWIND, AND FOUR TO MOVE ON TO THE NEXT MESSAGE.

Rashida played the message back two more times before she solved the riddle. She took the escalator up to the second level and walked around to the other side of the mall. She remembered the vendor who sold custom-made, hand painted bells – right in front of Victoria's Secrets. She made double-time getting to the store and blushed when she saw what Duane picked out for her. "He doesn't even know me like that," she said to herself. "Shit, they're too nice, and damn sure too sexy not to accept, though."

The clerk wrapped her unmentionables and Rashida headed out the store. She didn't see any more clues and figured the scavenger hunt was over. As she walked back to the escalator, a woman walked up behind her carrying a box.

"Miss, you dropped this," the woman said.

"That's not mine."

The woman turned the box over and showed her the writing on it. "Well, isn't this your name on it?"

Rashida smiled and took the box. She went back to her car and found an envelope on her windshield. She opened it and saw that it was a dinner reservation for two along with another card. The card said:

I'VE BEEN DYING TO MEET YOU AND I'VE PUT IT OFF LONG ENOUGH. IF YOU WOULD ALLOW ME THE PLEASURE OF YOUR COMPANY FOR A NICE DINNER, I WOULD GREATLY APPRECIATE IT. ALL YOU HAVE TO DO IS DON YOUR LAST TWO BIRTHDAY GIFTS AND MEET ME AT THE RESTAURANT IN NINETY MINUTES.

Rashida hurried right home. She still didn't know what was in the box and couldn't wait to see. As soon as she got to her apartment, she opened it up and raved to herself over the little black dress that was enclosed.

Rashida arrived at the restaurant and was shown to her table by the hostess. She ordered a glass of white wine and waited for Duane to arrive. Five minutes later, he came in from the back of the restaurant carrying a birthday cake, followed by six waiters and waitresses singing Stevie Wonder's rendition of Happy Birthday. Then, they all broke out into a chant of Fifty Cent's "It's Your Birthday." Rashida laughed until she cried. It was the most hilarious, and the most romantic thing anyone had ever done for her.

Duane was taller and broader than he appeared on his profile picture. Rashida figured his picture must not have been recent because his locks were much longer, as well. He wore an attractive black suit that complimented her dress, with a uniquely designed, gold-colored necktie. He sat the cake on the table and took Rashida's hand. "Happy Twenty-Sixth Birthday, sweetheart," he said. "You look ravishing; absolutely breathtaking."

"Thank you," Rashida said, blushing.

"Make a wish and blow out the candles."

Rashida closed her eyes tightly and blew away the flames with one big huff and smiled from ear to ear as all of the patrons clapped and cheered. Duane instructed one of the waiters to take the cake away until after dinner and sat down. The two of them talked and got acquainted, but they were mostly joking around and laughing out loud. They were having so much fun they had to shush each other on a few occasions. They shared a piece of cake and had the rest put into a box before leaving the restaurant.

Rashida handed the valet her ticket and noticed that Duane did not. "Where's your car?" she asked.

"Oh, I don't drive. I'm a true New Yorker. I live in a Harlem condo, and I take the subway everywhere. I got here and had a cab drive me around New Rochelle all day."

"Well, can I drop you off somewhere?"

"The bus station would be nice."

"What time does your bus leave?"

"Oh, I don't know."

Rashida grinned and shook her head. "You are a piece of work."

"Yep. That's what they tell me."

They arrived at the bus station at ten o'clock that evening, just as the rain began to fall, and discovered that Duane's bus wasn't due until eleven-thirty.

"Well, what do we do in the meantime?" Rashida asked.

"We can park somewhere and kill the rest of that cake," Duane suggested.

"Deal," she agreed. "I know the perfect place, too." She drove a few blocks to the local supermarket and parked. It had been closed for about an hour so they had the whole parking lot to themselves. They ate the cake with their fingers as they laughed, joked and acted silly. It was raining steadily now, which set an intimate mood. Duane watched Rashida lick frosting from her fingers and took her hand.

"Let me help you with that," he said, and proceeded to insert her index finger into his mouth. He then licked each of her fingers individually until all of the frosting was gone. Rashida looked at her hand, looked at Duane, looked at her hand again, and then grabbed a big chunk of the cake with both hands.

"You're not finished," she purred. Then she took both hands and smeared cake all over Duane's face. He laughed and took the rest of the cake and smushed it all over her face and neck, as well. There was cake and frosting everywhere.

"Look, you got cake on my brand new dress," Rashida complained.

"Oh, let me help you with that," Duane said as he wrapped his arms around her and kissed her passionately. He worked one hand around her back and slowly lowered her zipper. Rashida responded by snatching his jacket off his shoulders and loosening his tie. Duane slid the straps of her dress over her shoulders as she unbuttoned his shirt. Then, he pulled her dress off over her head, revealing the lacey, black lingerie ensemble he purchased for her. Her Balconette bra revealed her pierced, erect nipples, which Duane wasted no time sucking on. He slid his hand between her legs and stroked her clitoris through her crotchless panties.

"Wait a minute," Rashida said as she pushed Duane away. He sat back in his seat with a puzzled look on his face. "Take off your clothes and follow me," she ordered, and stepped out the car into the rain. Duane watched as Rashida walked around to the front of the car and lay on the hood. She had on nothing but her lingerie and her pumps as the warm rain poured down upon her. He quickly removed every stitch of clothing and hurried out to join her. He stooped down in front of her and spread her legs apart. Rashida closed her eyes and let the rain beat down on her face as Duane flicked his tongue on her clit and ran it down into her pussy. She propped her legs up on his shoulders and let him feast on her womanhood. Her body started shaking from her first wave of climax.

Duane stood and pulled Rashida up to him. Once again, they embraced and kissed passionately, and she licked the remaining frosting mixed with her love juices from his face. He then gently pulled Rashida off the hood, to her feet, and they traded places. She squatted down in front of him and stroked his thick, elongated manhood in both hands before taking it into her mouth. She gripped its base tightly with one hand and massaged his scrotum with the other as she sucked the shaft of his dick up and down rhythmically. Her hair was soaked and laying down on her face, but she refused to move her hands from his dick and balls and sucked with more intensity. Finally, he exploded, depositing his thick, hot semen all over her face and neck.

Rashida stood up and removed her lingerie. The only things she was wearing besides her jewelry was her pumps and a smile. Duane didn't even have on shoes so he had her beat.

"Lay down across the hood this way," Rashida instructed, to which Duane happily obliged. He waited as she walked around to the passenger side, opened the door, threw her lingerie inside, and took a condom from the glove compartment. She opened the package and threw the wrapper back into the car. Then, she climbed up on the hood and rolled the condom onto his throbbing dick.

Rashida then climbed up on top of Duane and mounted him. His thickness stretched her open and her body responded as she immediately came a second time. Her muscles pulled and milked his dick as she rose and fell repeatedly. Duane grabbed her hips and guided himself in and out of her while matching her rhythm. He moved his hands up and cupped her firm breasts as she once again took over the pace. Rashida threw her head back to welcome the rain again, and came a third time. Her body trembled as she collapsed on top of her lover.

Duane quickly flipped Rashida over on her back and held her legs up with his arms as he thrust into her with long, hard strokes. Suddenly, he moaned aloud and his body tensed. He withdrew his dick and removed the condom, allowing streams of his jism to spurt out all over her breasts and stomach. They both lied there and let the rain rinse their bodies of all the sweat, semen and cake they had all over them.

"This was the best birthday ever," Rashida said. She and Duane agreed to get together every weekend. They told each other that if they'd known things were going to be like this, they wouldn't have waited two and a half years to meet.

Beautiful Music

I lay back on the bed enjoying the delightful melody as Jennifer serenades me. I close my eyes so I can take in the harmonious tunes of her love song.

I'd been playing the saxophone since I was ten. Now, I have my own band and my first CD hits the stores in three weeks. I love to make music. Jennifer wanted to make her own kind of beautiful music especially for me. She asked me to teach her how to play.

I met Jennifer a year ago at Smith's on the East Side. She sat alone, staring at me on the stage, never turning her attention away. As I played each song of each set, I felt her big, brown, alluring eyes locked in on me, sizing me up, analyzing my every feature - undressing me. I admired her full lips as she pouted them out at me. I thought she was trying to discreetly blow kisses at me.

I'd seen her once before. She was there when my band played at the Blue Note the previous month. I remember her sitting at the bar. Some guy was jumping over hurdles trying to pick her up. His back was to the stage and she was looking past him, directly at me. I don't think she heard a word he was saying. I made contact with her eyes, which were as big as pools and I wanted to dive in. Still, more than those big beautiful eyes, I was drawn to her perfect mouth and full lips. I was anxious to finish my set and go say hello to her, but before I could, three other women came and rescued her from the guy at the bar and the four of them left the club.

When she walked into Smith's a month later, she was alone. She wore a short red dress that was cut low in the front. It showed off her long, slender, well-shaped legs and put the cleavage of her well-endowed breasts on display. She was the most beautiful woman in the place. She sashayed through the lounge and sat at a table right in front of me. She crossed her legs giving me a view of her silky, copper-toned thigh as she raised her hand to hail a waiter. She ordered her drink without turning her attention away from me for a moment. She gazed into my eyes and I became mesmerized. In my mind, I stood on the stage alone, playing for only her, and she was the only person in the audience. It was time for the last number of my band's final set. She had already made the first move by presenting herself to me. It was my move now.

"I dedicate this last number to the beautiful lady right here in the red dress," I said, doing my Barry White impersonation. The audience applauded and cheered, and it became apparent that she and I were not alone at all. Everyone had observed the flirting that was going on between she and I. Jennifer tilted her head slightly and smiled as she waited for me to serenade her. I turned to cue the band and all the guys had that "you lucky dog" grin on their faces. I think that was the first time I blushed since I was fifteen.

I played the lead to our rendition of Regina Belle's song, "Baby Come To Me." I watched Jennifer cross and uncross her legs repeatedly. She squirmed and swayed in her chair, shifting her legs from side to side. She occasionally fanned herself with one hand and ran her fingers down the front of her neck with the other. I played my heart out for her, and it was getting her more and more excited.

The song ended and the audience gave us a standing ovation. Jennifer didn't clap. She just sat there with her head tilted, stroking her neck, and still smiling. Finally, she stood up and walked to the stage. I stepped down to meet her.

"Thanks for the song," she said. Her exotic voice was soft and deep. Her words danced over her tongue and past her luscious, full lips. "I love the way you play."

"Thank you very much," I said as I took her hand in mine and kissed the back of it gently.

"I would love to learn to play, but I just want to play for you. Will you teach me how to play for you?"

Jennifer and I are now celebrating our first anniversary together. In just one year, she has learned how to blow masterfully. Her lips were made for playing. She studied my instrument and all its parts until she knew every detail of it. The first time she put her lips on it, I knew she'd be a natural. When she plays, I lay back and relax. Her melodies are so soothing. Her songs begin with tantalizing intros, which lead to comforting verses and invigorating choruses. Then, she takes me to the bridge, changing the flow so she can close out with powerful and exciting riffs. Every song she plays causes something inside me to churn, boil and eventually explode. She plays and I get weak. I submit to her. I worship her. I yearn for more.

Right now, I feel her playing her rendition of Anita Baker's song, "Sweet Love." As she comes to the chorus I sing along:
SWEET LOVE, HEAR ME CALLING OUT YOUR NAME
I FEEL NO SHAME, I'M IN LOVE
SWEET LOVE, DON'T YOU EVER GO AWAY
IT'LL ALWAYS BE THIS WAY

I start to get a tingling sensation as I get that feeling of something churning within me.

The bridge comes:
> THERE'S NO STRONGER LOVE IN THIS WORLD
> OH BABY, NO
> YOU'RE MY MAN, I'M YOUR GIRL
> I'LL NEVER GO
> WAIT AND SEE; CAN'T BE WRONG
> DON'T YOU KNOW THIS IS WHERE YOU BELONG

I open my eyes momentarily because I want to see her work my instrument. Her lips are closed tightly around it. One hand is holding the instrument securely as she uses the other to stroke it up and down.

> OH SWEET STREAMS, HOW LOVELY, BABY
> STAY RIGHT HERE; NEVER FEAR I WILL BE
> ALL THAT YOU NEED
> NEVER LEAVE 'CAUSE, BABY I BELIEVE IN THIS LOVE

Now that churning feeling begins to boil. I can feel my muscles tense and I get more involved with the song. She moves me, and I feel the need to sing out loud as she continues to play:

> SWEET LOVE, HEAR ME CALLING OUT YOUR NAME
> I FEEL NO SHAME I'M IN LOVE
> SWEET LOVE, DON'T YOU EVER GO AWAY
> IT'LL ALWAYS BE THIS WAY

Oh, I can't follow the riffs. They're too intense. From here, I just enjoy the ride she's taking me on. I'm overwhelmed. I explode with excitement, gratification and satisfaction.

She takes the instrument from her mouth and licks her lips. "You really like that song, huh Mike?"

"Baby, I enjoy every song you play. They all make me feel the same way."

"I'm glad. I love making you happy. I always wanted to learn to play for someone special, but I never found that someone before I met you. When I first saw you on that stage, I knew you were the one I wanted to teach me to play. I wanted to play the best music you've ever heard, but only for you. I love you."

"It is the best. The best that has ever been played for me. I'm honored and privileged to be your chosen one. We make beautiful music together. I love you, too."

We kiss passionately. I love to feel her soft, sweet lips pressed against my own. I turn her over on her back and we make sweet love into the wee hours of the night.

Afterwards, I pick up my saxophone, walk over to the window and begin to play. Jennifer curls up on the bed in a fetal position, pulls the covers over herself and drifts off to sleep as I play her favorite lullaby. When she wakes up, I'll have a special song prepared for her. I love the way she blows my horn. But she has an instrument that I love to play, as well.

Richard

Harold is the sweetest man I've met in a long time. He's smart, caring, respectful, understanding, and he'll give me whatever I ask for. I know I should appreciate all that, but there's more, much more that I need. I need spontaneity, excitement, confidence and stamina in a lover. Oh yes, lots of stamina. Harold doesn't always provide me with all of that, but his best friend, Richard, fulfills my desires.

Harold introduced me to Richard three weeks after we started dating. He never mentioned anything about his closest friend before, and I thought that was a bit strange because most men mention their best bud during the first or second date. I wanted to know the company my man was keeping, and since he never said much about him, I figured I'd ask. I didn't know it would happen, nor did I expect it to, but as soon as I laid eyes on Richard I knew I wanted, needed and had to have him. Ladies, he was everything a woman could dream of.

Richard has a smooth baldhead, a long, dark chocolate, beautifully sculpted body; he always stands tall and at attention, and his natural musk aroma is an aphrodisiac. Damn right I fell for him right away. I couldn't wait for the opportunity to get my hands on him and devour him. I wanted to kiss him on the top of his head and run my tongue down the length of his entire body. Harold knew right away that I liked Richard a lot, but I don't think he had any idea how much.

Harold and Richard spent their whole lives together, and as inseparable as they were, they were very, very different. Harold was not a go-getter. In fact, I pursued him. I saw this tall, dark, handsome man with deep-set eyes, a strong jaw, a short tapered cut, and a killer goatee. I was ready to chase him down, and chase him down was exactly what I had to do. Damn, I never had to go so far out of my way to get a man's attention before. I did some investigating first, so I knew that he wasn't married, had no girlfriend, and no kids. He was a single, educated, gainfully employed, twenty-six-year-old black man and he was going to be mine.

I expected to play hard to get for a while, but Harold flipped the script. I saw Harold in the park everyday after work. I'd be out walking Mimi, my West Highland White Terrier, and I'd see him sitting on a bench or in the grass pecking away on his laptop, totally engulfed in his work with his round specks sitting on the edge of his nose, looking nerdy as a muthafucka. I usually wore biker shorts or sweats to go walking in, but I wanted to get Harold's attention and entice him, so I started wearing my sexiest little mini-skirt or my tight little boy-shorts so he could see my long, slender, shapely legs. I would wear a halter-top or low-cut tank top to give him an eyeful of my perfect thirty-six Ds, my flat stomach, and my silky-smooth, butter pecan complexion. The first couple of days, I'd strut pass him and wait until he lifted his head so I could lower my shades and let him see my big, almond-shaped, hazel eyes beckoning him on. He'd just smile and go right back to pecking. Finally, after being ignored for four days, I decided to go ahead and make the first move.

I sat beside Harold on the bench and extended the leash so Mimi could play in the grass. I introduced myself, we chatted for about an hour, exchanged numbers, and two weeks of phone courting later, we went out on our first date. I admired the fact that Harold and I were able to indulge in insightful, intellectual conversation. Most men I date just want to talk about their exes, my exes, sex, and try to flatter me and shower me with gifts thinking that'll get them some. But it's not about what they want; it's about what I want. When I want my back dug out, I pick the date, time, place, and terms of which any digging will get done. With Harold, however, it was like it didn't matter to him when or if we ever got intimate.

Ah, but when I finally met Richard, he was eager to get a taste of my peach. That's what I was used to, and dammit, that's what I liked. That's how I'm able to control the situation when it comes to men. I like to see how well they can pace themselves even though they're dying to just get a whiff. Harold was too well paced. But when I finally met Richard, he was right on point.

I never understood how Harold and Richard were so close, yet so different. How come they weren't on the same page when it came to pleasing me? Harold *thinks* he's pleasing me all the time, and Richard *wants* to please me all the time. When Harold makes love to me, it's routine. When I take sex from Richard, it's the only time I get a real thrill. It wasn't until recently I understood that because I love Harold and really wanted to be with him, I'd have to bring out in him what Richard brings out in me. Even though it requires so much more than sex, even if it's great sex, to get a commitment from me, "great sex" is still very important. I decided that the time had come for me to be honest with Harold and tell him why I've been so attracted to Richard, but he confronted me first.

I got off of the elevator, coming in from getting my hair done, and saw Harold waiting for me in front of my apartment door. "Darlene, I have a problem with you," he said with a saddened look of discomfort on his face. "I've been working very hard to make things right between us. I want to marry you someday, but I can't do that because I feel that you only want one thing from me. All that I'm working for to prepare a life for us gets overlooked because all you want to do is be with Richard." My attempt to respond was stifled by Harold's finger pressed against my lips. "Please, don't try to deny it. I know how fascinated you are with Richard, and how much you lust for him. You're a smart girl, Darlene. I thought you'd appreciate more than just a good roll in the sack."

"Harold, I love you. Regardless of what you think, I appreciate you and everything you're doing for me and for us. You need to understand, though, that the way you hold me, kiss me, and make love to me is just as important as anything else. I like the way you make love to me most of the time, but baby, sometimes I just need to get fucked. I need you coming at me from all directions. I need your dick every way I can have it and I need you to give it to me like that. I'm tired of taking it and just doing whatever I want with it. Give me that dick hard and mercilessly."

"Ooh, Darlene. Please, I asked you not to say that word. It sounds crude. I told you, if you insist on calling my penis something, call it Richard so no one else will know what you're referring to."

"Dammit, Harold, no one else is here. Dick. Dick. Dick. Dick. To hell with Richard! I want your dick because your dick, excuse me, Richard, is always ready to go. I don't see how that thing can be attached to you. We make love, you cum, and Richard is still standing and ready, even when the rest of your body is comatose. That's just some amazing shit to me. I'm tired of sucking Richard off and riding it until I'm satisfied and all you do is lay there. I want some damn reciprocation from you. Fuck me with your dick, dammit!"

Yes, yes, yes. That was the first time I truly felt I got *everything* I wanted from Harold. He pulled me into the stairwell and started kissing me as he reached under my mini-skirt and pulled my thong to the side. He ripped open my blouse, reached behind me and unfastened my bra. After frantically unbuckling his belt and unzipping his pants at the same time, he lifted me up and began sucking on my breasts. I wrapped my legs around his waist and he drove all ten inches of Richard's body into me. We began kissing again as Harold moved his arms under my thighs, spreading my legs wider apart. He clutched my ass with both hands and pinned me against the door while thrusting into me with hard, rapid strokes. I wrapped my arms tightly around his neck and enjoyed the ride of my life.

Suddenly, without warning, Harold turned around and put me down. He stepped back and pulled his pants down to his knees. I looked down at Richard pointing at me, calling me, inviting me. I dropped to my knees and started stroking his shaft as I pressed my lips against his head and slowly took him into my mouth. My tongue danced and rolled while my lips slid back and forth. I closed my eyes and enjoyed the mixed flavors of Richard's chocolate and my own peach until I felt streams of thick cream fill my mouth and flow down my throat, and I savored that delectable taste as well. I stood to my feet again and looked at Richard; still vibrant and glistening from the bath I just gave him.

"Turn around and bend over," Harold ordered, and I happily obliged. I lifted my skirt and gave my man a full view of my firm, round backside. I leaned over the rail and looked down the staircase leading up to my floor. Harold grabbed my hips and pushed Richard's full length into my wet pussy, again. I let out a yelp of delight that echoed down to the lobby. It's a miracle that no one came in or went out the whole time. I don't know, maybe some of the neighbors were looking out of their peepholes. It didn't matter and I didn't care. I just wanted Harold to give me more of Richard, which is exactly what he did.

My huge breasts bounced over the rail as Harold drove Richard into me again and again. I became dizzy with delight, and my juices flowed like a dam was broken inside of me. Harold had a handful of my hair, pulling my head back as he pounded me violently. My new 'do was wrecked, but it was a small price to pay. Harold came again, soaking my ass, my skirt and the back of my blouse. I turned around, grabbed a hold of Richard and led them both into my apartment. We weren't even close to being finished.

Most men call their penis by its nickname, Dick, which is short for Richard. Well, I guess my man's "dick," being as good as it is, deserves the formality.

Kiss Goodbye

Nikki didn't come home last night. I expected as much. We had a great morning together yesterday before she cursed me out and stormed out the house. She gets in her shitty moods ever so often, but something was different about her this time.

"Damn, what did I do this time?" I thought as I downed my ninth beer. I pondered and searched within myself, and though I knew what the problem was already, I thought back to yesterday morning just before we got up to go to work. I turned over to face Nikki as she was waking up.

"Hey, baby. Good morning," she said in that sexy, deep voice she has when she first wakes up.

"Good morning, sweetie," I responded, and started kissing her forehead as she cuddled closer to me and rested her head on my chest.

"The sun sure is bright this morning."

"Yeah, it's supposed to be really nice today."

"Mmm, can we stay home, then?"

"Why? What are we gonna do at home all day?"

I knew what her response would be. She loved to tease me, talk dirty to me, and the way I'd get when she told me of all the things she wanted to do to me. "Let me show you," she said as she rolled over on top of me. I always say action speaks louder than words, and she was definitely about action that morning.

Nikki rubbed her hands all over my chest and shoulders as she gazed lovingly into my eyes. I looked up at her beautiful round face and let my eyes fall down to her small, perky breasts. I always liked the fact that she was in the I.B.T.C. Her breasts fit perfectly in my palms. Anything more would've been too much for me. I reached up to grab them, but she stopped me by pinning my hands to my sides.

"I'm doing this," she demanded. "You just be patient and follow my lead. Don't do anything until I tell you it's okay."

A broad smile came over my face. I knew she was going to be bad and it was going to be good. Nikki threw the covers off us, exposing our naked bodies to the morning sunlight. Then, she leaned forward and started whispering into my ears, nibbling at them and sticking her tongue in between words.

"Why do you think everything has to be the way you want it?"

"What do you..." I started to respond, but Nikki put her hand over my mouth.

"You see. Shut the fuck up. I told you not to do anything unless I told you to. That meant talking, too."

She never stopped nibbling on my ear as she gave me my orders in a husky, seductive tone that enhanced her faint Spanish accent. I was down to play the game. I liked being the submissive one once in a while.

"Shit," she continued as she resumed rubbing her hand over my chest, "is it so damn hard for you to do what I say? Be a good boy and good things will come to you."

Nikki ran her tongue down from my ear to my neck and onto my chest. She nibbled and sucked on each nipple as she let her hands glide down from my chest to the sides of my thighs. Then, she reached around, grabbed my butt and squeezed it hard while biting down on my nipples at the same time. It sent a surge through me and caused my penis to jump up and stab her in the stomach.

"What the fuck?" she said. "Don't you have any self-control? What's wrong with you?" Her voice was never harsh. She was teasing me for sure. "You want me to put it in my mouth, don't you?"

"Hell, yeah!" I blurted out.

"Why?" she asked as she moved her head down over my stomach and nibbled on my navel. "What have you done for me lately?"

"I do whatever you want me to."

"No the fuck you don't. But you will today if it's the last thing you do." She continued running her tongue down past my pubic area and held her mouth open, hovering over the head of my penis. I could feel her breath on the tip and my dick started jerking back and forth. She looked up at me with a devilish smile, and then stood up on the bed. She walked over me and stood directly over my head. "Why do I always have to start this? If I don't you won't, will you?"

"Won't what?" I asked, looking straight up into her vaginal opening.

Nikki plopped down to her knees, letting her sweet pussy land directly on my mouth. I opened my mouth wide and stuck my tongue into her inviting hole. She reached back and cupped my balls, kneading them as she moved her hips back and forth on my face. It felt like she was doing a belly dance. Her juices started flowing into my mouth and all over my face as I massaged her clit with my tongue. She was grinding her groin into my face, suffocating me as her body bucked and jerked with each orgasm. I reached my hands up to fondle her breasts, but she slapped them away again as she jumped up off me.

"What the fuck are you, dumb or stupid?" she snapped. "What the fuck did I tell you? Keep your fuckin' hands down." She flipped over into a sixty-nine position and grabbed my dick in both hands. "Don't touch me with your hands, your tongue, or anything else," she ordered.

Nikki cupped my balls again with one hand and tilted my stiff dick to the side with the other. She locked her full lips around the shaft and moved up and down while flicking her tongue. Then she stuck her tongue out and licked its length down to my balls, bathing each one. She let her tongue run the length back up to the head, tightened her lips and pressed against it. It felt like a virgin cunt was descending down onto me. I became frenzied, so she placed one hand up on my chest as if to tell me to calm down. She sucked my dick long and slow, pacing us both very well.

After what seemed like eternity, Nikki got up from on top of me and rolled over on her back. I waited anxiously for her next order. Finally, it came. "C'mon," she cooed.

I rolled over on top of her, aiming my dick at her waiting pussy.

"What?" I asked like a teenager who had just seen a vagina for the first time.

"Do what you do," she said, using her hands to present herself to me.

I lowered my mouth down to hers and let our tongues dance about. Finally, I was able to lovingly squeeze, knead and caress her beautiful breasts as I pressed my pelvis into hers. As I entered her, I felt the familiar feeling of warm honey that made me vow to her that she would be the last woman I ever made love to for the rest of my life; she'd be my wife.

We ignored the annoying sound of the alarm clock as we fucked like wild animals. It was her. She was so loud and wild. She wrapped her legs around me and thrust upward, meeting my strokes until we both came.

"Get the fuck off me," Nikki panted as she pushed me away. I rolled over on my back and stared up at the ceiling. I had to focus on something blank because the room was spinning. Nikki got up and went into the bathroom. "I'm so fuckin' tired, Jay," she said. "I need to do something different because this shit ain't for me."

I didn't get it at first. Now I know for sure that she was talking about us. Everything she said while we were making love was a message to me. I didn't realize it then, but she was saying all the things to me that I said to her whenever we had disagreements. "You never listen to me. Why can't you do what I tell you?" Damn. It didn't sound like that when I was saying it. I certainly didn't mean it like that. I guess it's all about how you go about doing things. Nikki, honey, no matter how long it'll take; I aim to keep my vow.

Cheater

Katina giggled and squirmed as Russell ran his tongue along the area behind her knees. "Stop it," she said, "you know that's my ticklish spot."

Russell grinned and continued running his tongue up the back of her raised leg to her foot. He opened his mouth to take in her heel and sucked on it. He then ran his tongue past her arch to her toes and took each one into his mouth individually, sucking on them with poise and patience, allowing her to bask in the delight of her favorite form of pampering. Katina closed her eyes and let her mind wander off into a fantasy of the two of them lying on the beach of Saint Croix, and him giving her the same treatment.

After Russell repeated his procedure on Katina's other foot, he moved down between her legs and inhaled the sweet aroma of her heated pussy. He closed his eyes and rubbed his nose gently back and forth against her clit while planting soft, gentle kisses on the folds of her outer lips. Katina raised her arms above her head and stretched with anticipation as Russell ran his hands up and down her thighs. He cupped her plump, supple ass in both of his hands and lifted her inches from the bed, feeding himself like he was drinking soup from a bowl. He let his tongue maneuver its way past the outer and inner folds and wiggle into the depths of her tunnel of love. As he continued to tongue kiss her wanting cunt, she caressed her own lovely breasts and tweaked her hardened nipples.

Russell proceeded to suck on Katina's exposed clitoris, locking his lips on it tightly, and letting his tongue flicker on it. Katina continued squeezing on one of her breast with one hand and placed the other on top of Russell's head to make sure he didn't stop before she wanted him to. With him holding her up off the bed by her ass and her pressing his head down into her crotch, the intensity of his oral assault increased ten fold causing her to cry out. "OH, YES! I'M CUMMING, RUSS! OH, LIKE THAT! YESSS!" Russell rubbed his lips and tongue up and down Katina's pulsating cunt as she doused his face with her delicious nectar.

Russell let Katina down gently on the bed and freed his head from her hold. He planted gentle kisses up past her shaved pubic area, along her stomach, and darted his tongue into her navel. He then continued up to her breasts and fondled them as he sucked, bit and licked her swollen nipples, taking his time on each one just as he did her toes. Katina ran her hands over Russell's muscular arms and back as he continued to feast on her melon-sized mounds, and at the same time ran her feet along the backsides of his well-toned thighs.

Russell continued kissing and licking past Katina's neck and to her lips, allowing her to taste her own juices, which she loved. He then reached down under her thighs and held her legs up and opened wide as he let the enormous head on his ten inch dick pry her vaginal opening apart. Katina threw her arms around his neck and held on tight, waiting for him to push deeper into her. Her vaginal walls expanded and welcomed his massive organ like it had so many times before. Her eyes rolled back into her head and she gasped for air as he drove his dick up into her to the hilt. She let her arms drop down and dug her fingernails into his shoulder blades as he started his rhythm of thrusting in, circular grinds, and slowly out again, repeatedly. She raised her legs and wrapped them around his hips as his balls smacked hard against her ass with each thrust, and laid heavily against it as he grinded into her. Her body trembled as she released her next orgasm.

"Tonight's the night, baby," Russell whispered into Katina's ear. She sighed loudly, letting out a deep breath as she prepared to keep her promise. Russell slowly withdrew his rigid, elongated dick from her pussy and helped her turn over. He mounted a bunch of pillows under her stomach as she propped up on her knees. He lowered his head and kissed all over her beautiful, firm posterior before spreading her cheeks apart and stabbing his tongue into her puckered anus. Katina closed her eyes again and let her mind escape once more to the white sand beaches of the beautiful Virgin Islands, imagining Russell was doing this to her there. She felt him remove his tongue and prepared her anus for its next intruder.

The warmth of the oily lubricant being squirted onto her, running down from her asshole to her clit, made Katina's heart begin to race with anticipation. Then, as she felt the tip of Russell's dick press against her anal opening, she gasped for air a second time and clutched her pillow. Very, very slowly, and with extreme caution and patience, Russell pressed his dick into her asshole. Katina's teeth gritted and she bit her bottom lip until it squirted blood as she could feel every vein of Russell's dick moving up into her. Russell wanted to make sure she'd maintain a level of pleasure that would balance the pain so he moved his hand down in front of her and slid his fingers up into her pussy. As Russell's dick made its way into Katina's asshole, he finger-fucked her slow while massaging her clit with his thumb, which he knew she adored.

After a while, Katina's body submitted and Russell was moving in and out of her with steady strokes. He still had his finger thrusting in and out of her pussy simultaneously, and Katina felt an unimaginable and immeasurable pleasure that she never thought was possible.

Their bodies rocked and the bed squeaked loudly as they moaned and the perspiration poured off them. Katina came harder, and more times than she ever had before in her life. The euphoric ecstasy she endured made her dizzy as she felt Russell plunge into her hard, and his warm, thick semen filled her bowels.

Russell had long gone home and Katina lay still in the same spot, her head throbbing, until she drifted off into a comatose-like slumber.

Mitch came home and walked into their bedroom where he found his fiancé lying face-down, nude and barely covered. They were due to be married in six weeks and had been living together for the past ten months. He walked around to the other side of the bed observing the scene carefully. He noticed the open bottle of KY-Jelly and the smell of sex lingered. Mitch knew that Katina had been unfaithful in the past, but he thought that all the counseling and them relocating from Chicago to New York City had made a difference. He knew at that moment that he was wrong. "Damn, Katina," he said, his eyes flooded and his heart racing. He packed his suitcase and left.

Everything is Perfect Now

I was in the Virgin Megastore in Times Square browsing around when I saw her down in the lower level looking at culinary videos. She was absolutely beautiful. Her long, slim body stood six feet tall. She had a short, stylish haircut and a smooth, peanut butter-colored complexion.

"Excuse me, Miss," I said in my deepest, sexiest voice.

She turned around slowly and looked me over as if she was sizing me up. "Yes," she responded as if she wasn't in the mood to be bothered.

"I was wondering if you could help me out," I said with a big smile on my face. "I can't find any of the sales people, and I was looking for the sports videos."

"Oh. Well, I don't know where any sports videos are. Maybe if you go to the cashier, they'll be able to help you." She spoke as if she was trying to get rid of me, and immediately turned away and continued to look at the videotapes. If anyone were watching, they would swear that I had just been shunned.

"Excuse me, again," I said. Her response was a deep breath through her nose as she turned her head toward me, cutting her eyes at the same time. "I don't mean to be a bother you, but I'm from out of town. I've been here since early this morning, and alone the whole time. I came to visit a friend, but he had a family emergency and had to leave town. Now I'm on a seven day vacation with nothing much to do."

"And?"

"And I was wondering if you were alone, and if you would mind having dinner with a total stranger?"

"I don't think so," she snapped as she turned away from me.

"We can go where ever you want," I persisted, "and I promise that the only thing I'll bite is my dinner." That remark got her to chuckle.

"I'm sorry, but I don't just go off with strange men," she said while walking away.

"What's so strange about me? Is it so strange that I think you're beautiful enough to buy you dinner at your favorite restaurant just for your company?" She stopped and looked back at me. I opened my arms invitingly. "C'mon, at very the least, you can show me around Times Square for a little while. Would that be so bad?"

"And what do I get out of this?" she asked.

"I told you, a nice dinner if you want it. All I want is a little company. No strings attached. I promise."

"I don't know. You could be a psycho rapist killer or something."

"Yeah, but so could you." That got her to laugh out loud this time. I held my hand out to her as I introduced myself. "My name is Carl."

"Natasha," she smirked as she placed her hand in mine and gave me a friendly shake.

"Well, Natasha, how about you show me where the hot spots around here are?"

"Hot spots?" she asked, giving an uppity glare. "I'll show you some of the places I like to go, but they're not fast paced and loud."

"That's cool. I'm open to whatever."

"Okay, let me make a call first." She took her cell phone from her bag, went into the bathroom and returned about five minutes later. "Okay, let's go."

Natasha became my tour guide through Times Square for about an hour before she exposed me to the New York City subway system. We took a train uptown to a nice little jazz club where we ate, drank and talked for hours. I told her that I was visiting from Los Angeles and it was my first time coming to the East Coast.

"I just moved here from Los Angeles eleven months ago," she said. "I have family there."

"Wow, what a coincidence," I said. "I don't know anyone in New York City except my friend, Shawn. We were best friends since eighth grade. He moved here after he got out of the army and got married."

"Is his wife from here?"

"She was," I said. "She left him; got a new job and moved away. I miss Denise. She was a great girl."

"I'm sorry to hear that," Natasha consoled.

"Yeah, he took it pretty hard. He's still pretty depressed so I came here to spend some time with him. As soon as I got here, though, he had to go to Phoenix to be with his sister because she was diagnosed with breast cancer."

"Oh man," she said. "Your friend is having it hard right now. You were a good friend to come all this way to be with him."

"That's what friends are for, right?"

"It sure is," she agreed. "So, where are you staying?"

"I'm staying at a hotel on Fifty-First Street. Where do you live?"

"I live a few blocks from here. Across the street from Central Park."

"Ha! No wonder you wanted to come to this area."

"Yeah, I wanted to be close to home just in case you turned out to be a jerk and I didn't want to be bothered with you anymore. I wouldn't have far to go after I dumped you."

"Well, I guess I'm doing okay since we've been together for almost five hours and I haven't been dumped, yet."

"Yeah, you're doing okay," she said with a smile. "I'm having fun. I hadn't had a good time out like this in a while."

"Good. I'm glad you're enjoying yourself as much as I am."

"I had a great time tonight, Carl. Unfortunately, time does fly when you're having fun."

"Yeah, it's almost three o'clock," I said looking at my watch. "I guess you have to get up early?"

"No, not really. I just don't want to over do it."

"I understand. Well, at least let me walk you to your door."

Natasha hesitated for a moment, then smiled and agreed. We left the club and walked four blocks to her apartment building. She held onto my arm and walked closed to me. Before now, she stayed a safe distance away. In Times Square, she walked about three feet over with her arms folded. On the subway, although we sat next to each other, she sort of turned herself away from me as if to give the impression that we weren't really together. Now, after spending a few hours together, she had finally loosened up and became receptive of me. I was proud of myself for making the decision to approach this woman, and being persistent with her without being too pushy. At first, I thought she was going to be a snob the whole time we were together, but she wasn't. Besides being F-I-N-E, she was smart, funny, caring, and very interesting.

"Can I call you tomorrow?" I asked as we stood in the doorway of her building, both of us gazing into each other's eyes, waiting for the moment to give each other the infamous kiss goodnight. "I can't wait to see you again."

"I don't want this night to end, either," she said. "Please, call me tomorrow afternoon. I'll take you to do some more sight seeing."

Then it happened. At first it was a soft, gentle peck. Then it became long and passionate as we embraced tightly. Ten minutes later, we were in her bed. I devoured her entire body, sucking, licking and kissing every part of her. I buried my face between her legs and inhaled the sweet fragrance of her heated vagina. She put both of her hands on my head and pinned it to her as she grinded her pelvis into my face. Her head flung from side to side as I flicked my tongue on her clit and let it slither in and out of her hole. Her juices flowed into my mouth and all over my face. I freed myself from her grip and placed her legs up on my shoulders. She grabbed and pulled the sheets as I entered her ever so slowly. I held her legs on my shoulders as I pushed deeper into her.

"Ooh! I'm cumming!" she shouted. She grabbed my legs, and I could feel her fingernails digging into my flesh behind my thighs.

Still grinding myself into her, I tried to open her legs wider, but she immediately wrapped them tightly around my waist. She now had both hands on my back and all ten fingernails dug into my shoulder blades. She pushed her pelvis up hard to meet my down strokes and our flesh smacked loudly. Sweat rolled down my face, neck and chest, and a stream of blood began rolling down my back. Natasha was also covered in sweat as she clung to me with all her might.

We made love over and over until dawn. I couldn't get enough of kissing her, caressing her and the wonderful feeling of being inside of her. She was the best I ever had. No one else I've ever been with came close.

It was a little after noon when I woke up. I stared up into the ceiling thinking about the wonderful night I just had. Natasha's head was rested on my chest and she awoke shortly after. She looked up at me smiling. "Good morning, sweetheart," she said. Her voice was husky from just waking up, and a little scratchy from all the screaming she was doing the night before.

"Good morning, my dear," I said as I kissed her gently on the forehead.

"What time is it?"

"It's ten after twelve."

"After twelve? Oh man, I have to get up."

"You have something to do?"

"I have to call my husband and tell him I'm coming home."

My eyes widened and I jumped up. "Your husband?" I shouted. "Home?"

"Yeah," Natasha said as she got out of the bed and put on her robe. "He still lives in Los Angeles. My job moved me here to set up a new office. Everything is up and running now, so I'm going back to L.A. next week."

"What? You're kidding?"

"Nope. I told you I had family in California."

"Yeah, but I didn't know you were talking about a husband."

"Yep, a husband and a seven-year-old daughter. I can't wait to get back there to them."

"You're serious, aren't you? You're really moving back to L.A."

"As soon I finish packing."

"That's great!" I yelled, and jumped out of the bed. I grabbed my wife and pulled her close. "Why didn't you tell me, Denise?"

"Damn, Shawn," Denise said. "You stepped out of character. We agreed to keep role-playing for three days. I knew I shouldn't have said anything until the last day. You ruined it."

"I don't care. You're coming home?"

"Yes," she said, and threw her arms around me. "Things went well and we got finished ahead of schedule."

"But you're supposed to be here for another seven months."

"Well, I'm coming home; back to my own office, back to my baby girl and back to you."

"Oh, Denise. This trip has turned out to be much better than I dreamed. You're coming home to be with our daughter and me. Everything is perfect now."

Me and the Girl Next Door

I tossed and turned on my futon, trying to find a comfortable sleeping position because my back was hurting so badly. I was in a car accident two years ago, which caused my herniated disk. Now, my back gets sore and I occasionally get muscle spasms all over. I'd had enough tossing and turning. Although it was one-thirty in the morning, it was time for some drugs. I got up and threw on a sweater, jeans and a coat, and headed out the door en route to the all night mini-mart for some Doan's Pills. I opened the door and saw Penny, my good friends and neighbors' daughter, standing by the window in a long, pink bathrobe and big, fluffy, pink slippers. As I came out my apartment, she turned around.

"Hey, Penny. What are you doing in the hallway this time of night?" I asked like a concerned neighbor and good friend should.

"Hey, Mister Moore," she replied. "Nothing. Just standing here. I couldn't sleep."

The top of her robe hung open revealing her large left breast. I could see her half dollar-sized, brown areola through her sheer, pink camisole. I tried not to change my expression and pretend I didn't notice. I made eye contact with her and locked in. "Do you know what time it is?"

"Yes. I'm going back in soon. I just want to stand here awhile."

"Where are your folks?"

"They're in there," she said, nodding her head toward her apartment door. "They just got home a half-hour ago. I don't know where they went, but they sure came in happy and to' up."

"Oh, I see. Well, don't stay out here too long. It's cold and you'll get sick."

"I won't," she said, finally noticing how exposed she was. She closed the front of her robe and drew her belt tightly. "Hey, where are you off to?" she inquired as I started off down the hallway.

"My back is killing me. I'm going to the store for some pills."

"You're driving all the way to the mini-mart at this hour, as cold as it is?"

I held the elevator door open and looked back at her. "I have to. I can't sleep."

"We have some Doan's pills in our medicine cabinet. I'll get you some if you want."

"No, you don't have to bother."

"It's no bother at all. I'm just going right inside."

"Well, okay. That would be great," I said, relieved.

"Okay, I'll get them."

I let the elevator door close and headed back up the hallway. "Thank you, Penny. You're a lifesaver."

"No problem. I'll be right back."

"Well, I'm going back inside. I have to go to the bathroom now."

"Okay, I'll knock on your door."

"I'll leave the door open just in case I'm not out yet. Just let yourself in."

"Okay, Mister Moore."

Penny was always a nice girl. She was always smiling and always had a good attitude. Her parents moved to this building twelve years ago. I watched her grow up from a little, overweight, snot-nosed tomboy into the beautiful young woman she is today. She's attending the local university, and her folks are saving money by making her commute rather than live on campus.

Penny went into her apartment and I went back into mine. I went into the bathroom to handle my business, and then I took my clothing off and put my pajama pants back on. I plopped down on the futon on my stomach and waited for Penny with the pills. She was taking a long time. I started thinking that maybe she didn't have any more or couldn't find them. I hoped not. That would've been unbearable. About five minutes later, I heard a light tapping at the door. Then, I saw the door open and Penny peeking inside.

"Come in, Penny," I called out to her. She came in and closed the door quietly behind her. "I'm sorry, it's kind of dark in here. The light switch is on the wall on your right."

Penny flicked the light switch on, and I looked up to see her standing there, still in her bathrobe, holding the pills in one hand and a small jar in the other. "I figured you could use a rubdown, too," she said.

I sat up slowly on the futon. "No, you don't have to do that."

"It's okay, trust me. I can't sleep anyway, so I may as well help you. No sense in both of us being up all night."

As bad as I wanted to object, I couldn't. The thought of a massage sounded real good. "What the hell," I thought. This is Penny. She's not a little girl anymore. She's a very intelligent, focused, respectable, twenty-two-year-old college senior. "Well...thank you," I agreed.

"Just take off your t-shirt and lay back down," she instructed. Then she went into the kitchen and got a glass of water for me to drink. I took two pills and lay back down on my stomach. Penny climbed on the futon and straddled me, sitting over my back thighs, and began to rub the ointment all over my back. She had soft hands and rubbed my back with firm strokes.

Penny and I had never been this physically close to each other before. She smelled really nice. I inhaled her sweet aroma as she massaged and caressed my back all over. I closed my eyes and let my mind wander off into limbo. I could feel the muscles loosening up with every stroke of her hands, but the disk in my lower back was still throbbing.

"Could you rub lower down?" I managed to mumble through my moans of pleasure.

She brought her hands down lower and started rubbing. "Is this good?"

"A little lower. Right here." I pulled my pajama pants down giving her the plumber's scenery, and pointed to the spot above my tailbone. She massaged me there, sending me back into limbo, totally relaxed.

After giving me a thorough massage for about twenty minutes, she finally got tired.

"Is that better, now?" she asked in a whisper.

"Oh, yes. Thank you," I moaned. I was so relaxed I couldn't move.

Penny got up from the bed, wiped her hands with a towel, and started toward the door. "Okay, Mister Moore, I'm leaving."

I turned my head to see her standing with her back to the door and her hand on the doorknob. She looked as if she was waiting for me to say something else. I found enough strength to speak one last time. "Thanks again, Penny. I'll see you around." With that I dozed off.

I got up around eleven that morning and went out to do my regular Saturday routine. I had brunch at IHOP, and then I went to visit my father and let him beat me at chess. From there, I did some grocery shopping and made my way back home. As I drove up to the apartment complex, I saw Penny coming up the street. I parked my car and waited for her, holding two bags of groceries in my arms. She saw me and smiled. She looked so cute in her red snorkel, blue jeans and red Timberlands. I always thought Penny was a very beautiful young lady. The boys her age on the block teased her growing up because she was overweight. They stopped teasing when she started kicking their behinds. They all wanted to be her "friend" by the time she turned seventeen or eighteen. Although she was still chunky, she wore it well. Now, I'd say Penny's probably about a size sixteen. She has big watermelon shaped breasts, wide hips and booty for days. Her red sweater-cap covered her burgundy-dyed flip feather cut. She has a very light-golden complexion, and her cheeks had turned as red as her hat and coat in the twenty degree weather.

"Hey, Mister Moore," she said as she approached me. "How is your back feeling?"

"It doesn't hurt as bad as it did last night, at least not right now."

"Oh, well let me help you with your bags. I wouldn't want you to strain yourself."

"It's no problem. I can manage."

Penny huffed and gave me scolding stare. "Why do you do that? Is it a macho man thing?"

"Do what?" I asked, puzzled.

Penny took one of the bags from my arms and headed into the building. "Why do you say, 'no' when you really mean yes? How come when I offer to help you, you feel you have to decline like you're sparing me somehow?"

"That's not it at all," I said as I followed in behind her. "I just try not to burden anyone else with my troubles, that's all."

"But if I offer to help, and you need help, say yes. You're not burdening me if I'm offering."

For a split second, I thought that Penny viewed me as a broken down, lonely old man who could use all the help he could get. Not that I'm so old; I'm forty-five. But I've never been married, and I don't have any children. To a twenty-two-year-old, that could easily classify me as an ancient artifact. Then I realized whom I was dealing with. Penny knows me better than that, and I should know her better, too. Her concern had to be genuine.

"I guess you're right, Penny."

"I know I am," she assured me as she held the elevator door open. I hesitated and started to insist that she go in before me, but I looked into her eyes and knew I'd lose that fight, too. All I could do was grin as I walked in past her. Penny walked in behind me and pressed four. I watched her standing there holding the bag of groceries in her arm, looking beautiful and self-assured. "She's a proud, independent woman," I thought to myself.

We reached our floor, and Penny held the elevator door open again and waited for me to exit.

"You know, I'm supposed to be holding doors for you," I said. Penny just smiled and batted her eyes. I let out a surrendering sigh and walked out past her. I don't know why I hadn't learned my lesson.

I reached my apartment and turned to Penny to take the bag from her. "Thank you, dear."

She shook her head and smiled at me again. "You have to get your key out and open the door first."

I started to tell her that I could manage, but I caught myself. I took my keys out of my pocket and opened the door. Penny stepped up close to me and gently placed the bag in my free arm. Her being so close allowed me to get a whiff of her sweet fragrance again. I began to float.

"Here you are, Mister Moore. I didn't mean to sound pushy, but you're a nice man and you don't bother anybody. I just figured that I could be nice to you sometimes."

"Well, I appreciate that very much, Penny. That's very, very sweet of you."

"You're welcome. And if there's ever anything I can help you with, you just ask."

"I appreciate that, too. But the only thing I'd ever need is good back massage and..."

"Cool," she interrupted, "I'll see you later tonight."

"Oh no, Penny. I was going to say, you've done that already and I'm grateful."

"I'll do it again. I don't mind. It can only help." I didn't expect her to be so eager, but she was wide-eyed and grinning from ear to ear. "So do we have a date?"

"Okay," I agreed.

"Good. I'll see you around eleven, eleven-thirty."

Penny walked past me and went into her apartment without looking back. I stepped inside my place and began putting the groceries away. My thoughts were all over the place. I found myself really attracted to this girl. The same girl whose parents and I went to high school and college with. Shoot, I helped her parents get their apartment. As a matter of fact, I even changed Penny's diapers a few times. I prayed to God for help. I had to get a hold of myself. The best thing to do would be to call her and tell her not to come over. No. There was no way I could do that. What if Milton or Regina answered the telephone? How could I explain asking for their daughter?

I went into the bathroom and stared at myself in the mirror. I tried to figure out what it is about me that made this girl attracted to me. I'm an average looking man, nothing to write home to Mom about. The last woman I dated told me that all the gray hairs I have peeking through my mustache and beard makes me look distinguished. She said that my salt and pepper hair, although there are only a few grays scattered about, complimented my mahogany complexion. Shoot, who am I trying to fool? That gold-digger would've said anything as long as I kept clothes on her back and money in her pockets. I would've thought a forty-one-year-old woman would be beyond that. I was terribly wrong.

I figured I was a fool for thinking Penny was really attracted to me. She never said that she was. She was probably just being nice to her parents' friend next door because she thinks I'm nice. That girl is beautiful, and stacked enough to have any man she chooses. Look at me; I'm five-ten, a hundred and ninety pounds with a bad back. There's nothing extraordinary about me at all. I had to be kidding myself. Oddly, that brought on a sense of relief. It would be better if this were all innocent. Still, I felt I was doing something wrong.

It was around eleven forty-five P.M. when Penny knocked on my door. I opened the door and saw her standing there dressed in a flannel nightshirt, holding a jar of Icy Hot. I was wearing my gym shorts and a t-shirt. My first thought was to tell her never mind and send her home. Of course that didn't happen. I invited her in, took off my t-shirt, and proceeded to the futon and lay on my stomach. Penny climbed on and straddled me, just as she did before, and began to rub my back. I immediately felt relaxed and at complete ease. I inhaled her scent, which was even stronger than before. I figured she must have just gotten out of the shower. She gave off pheromones that drew me to her like worker bees to the queen.

I lay still and allowed her to work her magic for about ten minutes. Her hands did wonders on my back, but like the previous night, she neglected the area that bothered me the most, my lower back.

"I need you to massage down here again," I said, pointing to my tailbone area. She pulled my shorts down a bit and began to rub the area. She wasn't rubbing low enough so I pulled my shorts down some more.

"Why don't you just take your shorts off?" she asked.

That rendered me speechless. All I could do was stutter. "Uh...er...eh...huh?"

"Don't worry, I've seen naked men before. Just take them off and let me do this right."

Before I could respond or react, Penny was pulling my shorts off for me. She pulled them all the way down and tossed them to the floor. I was totally nude. She positioned herself beside me on the futon so that she could massage down my back. She was kneeling closer to my shoulders now. "Does this feel better?" she asked.

"Oh, yes," I grunted. Her aroma filled my nostrils even more and began to intoxicate me. I was getting more excited and I had an erection, but she couldn't see it because I was still lying on my stomach. I reached between her legs with my left arm, hugged her left leg and pulled myself closer to her. I rubbed my face against her leg and inhaled her scent. I had to have her and the time had come.

I began kissing up and down her thigh as I moved my hand up under her nightshirt and slowly rubbed her big, round butt through her silky panties. Penny grabbed her nightshirt, pulled it off over her head, and her huge breasts bounced as she freed them.

"Come. Lay down," I said as I sat up on my knees. Penny laid on her back in front of me and spread her legs open wide. I laid down on top of her and pressed my lips gently against hers. She closed her eyes and parted her succulent, full lips, and I kissed her deeper. She ran her hands up and down my back, continuing to massage it as we kissed lovingly. I moved my body down over hers, kissing and nibbling at every part of her anatomy. I ran my tongue past her neck and down between her gigantic breasts. I gently bit and chewed on her large nipples, then lowered my head and rubbed my face in her crotch. I inhaled deeply as I rubbed my mouth all over her moist panties. Penny became impatient. She reached down, pulled her panties off and tossed them to the side.

"Eat it," she moaned in a whisper. "Please. Eat it for me."

I lowered my head again and pressed my mouth against her thick, furry pubic patch. I sucked on her large clitoris as she held the back of my head with both hands. She lifted her legs up off the bed and pressed down against my head harder. It felt like she was trying to push my whole head up into herself. I continued sucking hard at her clitoris and poking my tongue into her vaginal opening. I moved my mouth down and traced the opening of her anus with my tongue before sticking it into that opening as well. My penis became as hard as a roll of quarters embedded in cement. Penny was moaning and gyrating her hips as I moved my tongue up and down from her huge clit to her pouting rectum.

"Oooh, Mister Moore, I need you inside of me. I need you inside of me now."

I wanted to be inside her as much as she wanted me to, but I had one concern. "Wait. I have no protection."

"Don't worry. I've been on the pill for two years. I've only had two other partners, one long term and the other I used protection with."

That was all I needed to hear. I moved up between her legs, and she whined with delight as I penetrated her. She held her legs open with her arms, pulling her knees all the way back to her shoulders. She was extremely flexible. Our bodies rocked together with every stroke. The harder I thrust down into her, the more she cried out in pleasure. Finally, I felt myself getting closer to climaxing.

"Oh, yes! I'm cumming!" Penny moaned. Hearing her say that made me reach my own climax faster. Both of our bodies tightened as we came in unison. I collapsed on top of her as she let her legs down and hugged me tightly. We kissed passionately until we were both heated again. Penny rolled me on my back, lowered herself down on me and rode me long and slow. Her vagina muscles gripped and pulled on my penis, milking it each time she rose and came back down.

"Oh, Penny. Oh, Penny. Oh, Penny," I chanted repeatedly.

"Yes, Edward," she replied each time. I saw her eyes squint and felt her body tremble, and I knew she was reaching another orgasm. She wailed as she released a second time, then a third, and then a fourth. Finally, I felt myself about to reach my boiling point and I ejaculated again.

After about fifteen minutes of holding each other, Penny got up and rolled me over on my stomach. She got the jar of Icy Hot and started massaging my back again. I fell asleep minutes later, feeling better than I had in twenty years.

Penny and I are in love. Today is our wedding day. I proposed to her the same day she graduated from college. Milton and Regina finally gave us their blessings, but it took them months to get used to us being together. I am happier now than I've ever been before. Life couldn't be better.

The Way She Makes Me Feel

Oh, goodness. I love the way she makes me feel. "Please, Mama, do that again. Oh, yes. Like that. Like that. Yessss!" Oh, I feel dizzy. The room keeps spinning. I'm cumming again. Oh, this is the fifth time. No, no, no. How can I endure? "Ahhh! Ooooh! Ummmm! Wait, wait, wait, baby. You gotta gimme a minute. Hold on." Oh, please hold on, sweetheart. My heart can't take this. I thought I was ready for this, but now I think I'm in over my head. I should've hooked up with someone my own speed. I like this young girl because she's lively, ambitious, and she keeps it real, but perhaps that's all more than I need right now. However, I do like that for a twenty-one-year-old, she is mature beyond her years. Although I am fourteen years older, she is able to relate to me on my level. She's not about all the childish games and antics that girls her age usually play. The one thing I don't like about her, however, is that right now she's being hardheaded. I asked her to stop, but she keeps going, and going, and...ahhh...going. Doesn't her damn tongue ever get tired? Ah, shoot! Here I cum again.

"Where the hell do you get all this energy, baby? Ooooh!" Look at her. She's in another world. I don't think she's heard a word I said. Oh, but she's so damn cute. I just adore those big, brown, glossy eyes, her beautiful mahogany complexion, those wonderful box braids, her perfectly upright, melon-like breasts, thin waist, flat stomach, well-rounded hips, and her big, round, heart-shaped ass. Whew! Men are always gawking at my big, plump ass and my sexy walk, but she's more stacked than I am. Yes, this girl's a dime.

We met at my cousin Angela's birthday party this past April. She was Angela's younger brother Melvin's date. Melvin, who is a D.J. for a Hip-Hop artist, was home for three days from their summer tour and picked this girl up at a club the night before. She looked just like a groupie video ho, wearing what looked like a handkerchief barely covering her breasts, and a tiny piece of material around her hips that she tried to disguise as a skirt. The darn thing barely covered her behind. I thought it was a shame because she had such a beautiful face and smile, and such a nice body that she could've worn a sweatsuit and no make-up and still would've been the finest girl in the club.

"Everybody, this is Robin," Melvin proudly announced with a broad smile on his face.

His short, dumpy, crispy ass was so ecstatic to have a girl like that on his arm he didn't know what to do with himself.

"Hi, Robin," I said as I extended my hand to her. "I'm June, Melvin's cousin. Pleased to meet you."

"I'm pleased to meet you, too," she said as she took my hand in hers. When we touched, a strange feeling came over me. Robin had a firm grip on my hand and gazed into my eyes. She had a bigger smile than Melvin's, showing off all of her pearly whites. It was obvious right at that moment that this girl was attracted to me. I had always been curious about sleeping with another woman, and I was pretty content with it just being a fantasy, but the way this girl touched me and looked at me brought out desires in me that gave me goose bumps.

"Well, I'll be talking to you," I said as I let go of her hand and tried to get a hold of myself.

"Okay. Make sure you do that before the night is over."

I just smiled politely and walked over to the bar. I definitely needed a drink. I sat at the bar and watched Robin chat with family and friends before Melvin lured her off into the men's bathroom. I started getting excited thinking about what they were doing in there. I imagined being in the stall with her instead of Melvin. Just as I was about to visualize the parts of her body she actually left for the imagination, Angela interrupted me.

"Girl, this is my birthday party. Why ain't you up shakin' yo' ass wit' one o' these fine ass men up in here?"

"Because I ain't as drunk as you are yet. A couple more of these Long Island Ice Teas and they'll look good to me, too. I'll dance then."

"Girl, you sound like a damn fool," Angela said as she grabbed my hand and pulled me off of the barstool. "C'mon out here and let's cut a muthafuckin' rug."

Once on the dance floor, I started feeling the music and got into the mood. Two men came over and cut in on Angela and I dancing with each other and we really started to get loose. I must've been dancing with this one guy for a about a half-hour, and we were grinding and getting real freaky. I was humping on him from behind when Robin came up behind me and started humping on me. I felt her breasts pressed against my back as she wrapped her arms around my partner and I and joined our rhythm. Robin ran her hands down along my thighs, then back to my butt and squeezed. My panties got soaked immediately.

"Excuse me," I said, breaking free of my two dance partners. "I have to go to the bathroom."

I hurried to the ladies' room to put some water on my face. I was shaking and breathing heavily and that was bugging me out. I knew it was this girl that was making me feel this way, and as much as that excited me, it also bothered me. The last time I felt this way was when I was met my ex-husband in college. Humph, his sorry ass couldn't leave other women alone, so I had to leave him alone. But why was Robin making me feel this way? A woman? No, no, no. I knew I wasn't gay, nor will I ever be. I couldn't imagine myself being in love with a woman no matter how much fucked up shit men do. Oh, but my nose was open and I didn't even know this girl.

I pulled myself together and dried my face, fixed my makeup, straightened up my clothes, and started to head out of the bathroom when Robin walked in.

"Hey, Ma," she said in her gleefully, high-pitched voice. "This party's fun. I'm glad Melvin made me come."

What a choice of words. I started to tell her how she'd made me cum, but I bit my tongue. "Oh, he had to make you come?"

"Not make me, but you know what I mean. I wanted to go somewhere else, but he said this was a big deal for his sister turning thirty-five and all, so I told him we could come for a little while. I had no idea older people could party so hard."

"Older people? What do you mean, 'older people?'"

"You know, people in their thirties and forties. I think you, me and Melvin might be the only people here under twenty-five. I know me and you are definitely the finest - especially you, Ma. You really got it goin' on. The blouse is hot, and you're wearing the hell outta those leather pants. Those boots are off the hook, too. Where'd you get them from?"

It was confirmed. I was being macked. "Uh, they were a gift. I have to thank you for the compliment, but the fact is that I am not under twenty-five. Actually, I'm thirty-five."

"No way."

"It's true."

"I hope I look as good as you when I get your age."

"Well, just how old are you?"

"I'm twenty-one."

"Oh, you're still a baby."

"Hardly. I graduated college last year, I'm gainfully employed, and I have my own apartment. No babies I know got their shit together like that."

"I hear ya, girl," I said, giving her a high five.

"I still love to party, though," she said, moving closer to me. "Shit, I work hard so I can make the type of money that'll allow me to play hard."

"What kind of work do you do?" I asked as I turned away from her and looked into the mirror, pretending I was still fixing my makeup.

"I work for an advertising company doing illustrations and graphic design. I also do video editing sometimes."

"Wow. I would've never thought that."

"I know. You thought I was a chicken head, didn't you? You saw me come in here dressed like this with your celebrity cousin and just knew I was a starfucker, right?"

"No...Robin...I...uh..."

"It's cool, Ma. We can keep it real. I'm still an around the way girl from the projects. That ain't never gonna change. You know what they say, 'you can take the girl outta the 'hood, but you can't take the 'hood outta the girl.'"

"I guess that's true to some extent. So, uh, you and Melvin are hitting it off real well, huh?"

"Melvin? Yeah, I guess. He's cool. Smart."

"Yes, he is. I wish he'd gone to college. It's a shame he's not doing more with his brain."

"Maybe he will. Don't give up hope. Besides, he made a success out of the life he chose. Be happy for him."

"Yes, you're right. Are the two of you..."

Before I could finish my sentence, Robin stepped to me again and placed her hand gently on my face. "Shhh. I don't want to discuss Melvin. I want to know more about you. You're so beautiful and nice. I would really like it if we got closer and became friends."

My body tensed and I swallowed hard. "So would I," I confessed.

"Would you, really?"

"Yes, I really would."

Robin smiled at me and her eyes sparkled as she moved her face closer to mine. Our lips touched gently, just as the bathroom door flew open. We quickly stepped away from one another as Angela staggered in.

"Ooh-wee," she whined.

"Excuse me, I gotta go." Angela crashed into the door of the first stall, made her way inside and locked the door behind her. A few seconds later, we heard her sigh in relief as her urine flow splashed against the toilet water. I don't think she even knew it was Robin and I in the bathroom. She probably just saw two silhouettes. I was embarrassed for her.

I looked at Robin standing there grinning and admired her beauty. She walked over to me again and stuck her card into my bosom. Then she placed her hands on my shoulders.

"We'll have to finish this another time, I guess," she whispered to me. Before I could respond, she pressed her lips against mine, and I responded in kind. She then turned around and walked out without looking back.

Now, here we are in my bed, three months, two hundred and seventy phone calls, ten dates, and a countless number of drinks later. Robin is openly bisexual, but I found out that she had been with more women than men. Although I always told myself that if I did ever get with a woman it would be with someone who was also doing it for the first time, it turned out to be better that I got involved with someone already experienced. She knew how to pace things and waited until I was ready. She made me feel comfortable and at ease.

Robin and I hooked up earlier this evening at my favorite bar. We had about three drinks each and danced and mingled with some of my friends that I met there every Friday night. It was the first time she and I hung out like this. Usually, we'd have lunch or dinner or do some shopping. We took time to get to know each other and established a very good friendship. We both knew, however, that tonight would be different. We both knew that it was time we consummated our "relationship."

Robin and I left the bar around three in the morning and took a cab back to my apartment. We had a couple more drinks and chatted for about an hour. We were sitting very close, and Robin had her arm draped behind me, across the top of the sofa, and was playing in my hair.

"June, I'm tired of sitting here," she whispered into my ear as she licked the lobe.

"I guess we should go to bed then, huh?" I couldn't believe I was so forward. It might've been the drinks talking, but my body was yearning for this girl. I wanted her and it was time for me to have her.

Robin smiled, stood up and began to undress. "I'd like to take a shower first, if you don't mind."

"Not at all. The bathroom is on your right past the bedroom. The towels are in the closet right outside."

After we both showered, I gave Robin one of my nightshirts and we got into bed together. I surprised myself again by not being apprehensive at all when Robin took my face in her hands and gave me a long, passionate kiss. It felt so natural. She removed our nightshirts, climbed on top of me and caressed my breasts as she ground her crotch into mine. I broke our kiss so that I could suck on her erect nipples. Robin rolled me over on my stomach and spread my ass cheeks wide apart. I spread my legs open wide as she let her tongue journey into my love canal. I came three times in that position, and then she turned me over on my back and started lapping away at my clit.

Oh, yes, it feels so natural. It feels so damn good. No man has ever gone down on me and made me feel this good. "Ohhh, yes! Oooh, baby! Oh, do it like that! I'm cumming again! Ohhhhhhh!" Damn, that's seven times. "Oh, I love you, Robin. I love the way you make me feel."

Have Faith in Rome

Faith sat at the table and swayed to the music as she sipped on her drink. She wasn't happy with her girlfriends' choice of club this night, but she had to admit that the DJ was doing his thing. The problem with the club was that the patrons were too young for her taste. At thirty-five-years old, Faith was looking to be approached by an older, more sophisticated type of man. Everyone in this place looked and dressed like hip-hop junkies.

"Damn," she said to herself, "I paid my twenty dollars to get into this shit shack and I can't wait to leave. I'm gonna get Tracey and Rita for this. They owe me big."

On cue, Tracey and Rita came off the dance floor and rejoined Faith at the table. "Girl, are you gonna sit here all night like a bump on a log?" Rita asked.

"I don't feel like dancing," Faith whined.

"Don't feel like dancing?" said Tracey. "The way you're always shakin' your big ass? That's a surprise. What's the matter, are you sick or something?"

"Yeah," Faith snapped. "I'm sick of being in this club full of teenyboppers."

"Teenyboppers? Girl, you're crazy. There aren't any teenyboppers in here. I don't see nothing but grown men."

"That's right," Rita agreed. "I mean, I admit they're a little younger than we expected, but there aren't any teenyboppers. The men in here are rollin' long and strong."

"Oh, my goodness," Faith said as she rolled her eyes at her two best friends. "Y'all must be drunk and the alcohol is affecting your eyesight as well as your brains."

"Hm? What did you say?" Tracey asked, too busy looking for men out on the dance floor to listen to Faith complain. "Ooh, girl I just found the man I'm leaving with tonight." She got up from the table and started to walk away.

"What?!" Faith shouted as she grabbed a hold of Tracey's arm. "I know you don't mean that, do you?"

Tracey snatched her arm away and proceeded out to the dance floor. "You damn right I do."

"Rita, would you say something to her, please?" Faith pleaded.

"Ooooh, you go, girl!" Rita cheered. "I'll be out there right after I finish my drink."

"Rita? What's wrong with the two of you?"

"Shoot, girl, what's wrong with *you*? Get with the program and stop being a fuddy-duddy."

"I can't believe this."

"I can't believe you. I never knew you were so uptight and shit, Faith. Why don't you loosen up and have some fun?"

"I don't like it here, Rita. I mean, the music is cool and it's a nice place, but I'm not feeling this crowd."

"Okay. Well, if you decide to leave, call me tomorrow." Rita turned up her glass and downed the remains of her drink. "Now, if you'll excuse me, I think I've just zeroed in on my target, too." She got up from the table and began to walk off, then stopped and turned around. "Faith, if you do decide to stay, think of this as being in Rome. You know what they say: when in Rome..."

Faith sucked her teeth and turned her head. She sat back in her seat and tried to enjoy the music as she contemplated whether she should just leave or wait around to see if Tracey and Rita meant what they said. Just then, she heard a soothing baritone behind her.

"Excuse me," the voice said. "I'd really appreciate it if you'd join me for a dance."

Faith was tempted to turn around, but instead, she just waved her hand at the person standing behind her. "No, thanks. I'm sure you can find plenty of women over there who'd love to dance with you."

"This is true," the voice replied, "but I asked you. There must be a good reason for that, don't you think?"

That response prompted Faith to look over her shoulder to see whom she was dealing with. She looked up and down at the chocolate covered, broad man with a thin-shaved mustache, dressed in a black suede suit with a matching derby, and a gray silk mock-neck. He wore a confident smile as he moved around the table and sat beside her. Faith rolled her eyes up in her head and let out a disturbed sigh. "And what reason could that possibly be?" she sneered.

"Well, for one, you are by far the most attractive woman in the club. Second, you seem mature and sophisticated. Third, I have a feeling that you dance very well."

"Oh, is that a fact?"

"Well, you being the most attractive woman here is definitely a fact. As far as you being mature, sophisticated and a good dancer goes, well, that's what I came to find out. I figured we'd dance, talk, get acquainted, and see where things go from there."

Faith snickered and took another sip of her drink. "That's what you figured, eh? Well, I'm sorry to have to disappoint you, uh..."

"Oh, I'm sorry. My name is Rome."

"Rome?"

"Yes; short for Jerome. I just like Rome better."

Faith laughed to herself as she thought about the last thing Rita said. She and Rome sat and talked for about an hour before he finally convinced her to accompany him on the dance floor. She found out that Rome was ten years younger than she, which she wouldn't have usually cared for, but she found him to be very intellectual and that turned her on.

On the dance floor, Faith and Rome were in sync. They bodies moved together and they complimented each other's rhythm. Rome really liked Faith's thick frame, wide hips and large breasts. He admired her ravishing smile and lovely, honey-toned complexion against her cream-colored, spaghetti-strapped party dress as she danced with one hand in the air and the other on her hip. He moved close and put his hand on her waist, and stared into her big, brown, bedroom eyes. Faith responded by moving closer and rotating her hips to the music. She noticed how Rome moved back a step and knew that meant he was getting excited.

"Humph, this young boy wouldn't be able to handle me," she thought to herself.

Faith didn't see Tracey or Rita anymore that night. She figured they both must've cashed in on their respective prizes.

"Well, they can go ahead and be as loose as they want," she told herself. "They'll be calling me complaining about how much their little one night stands with their little boy toys wasn't even worth it."

It was four-thirty a.m. when Rome pulled up in front of Faith's apartment building. She looked over at him and smiled. "Thanks for a wonderful evening, Rome. I didn't think that I'd have a good time tonight, but because of you, I did."

"I had a great time, too. You are a very special lady, Faith."

"Thank you," she blushed. She looked over at Rome again, thinking that he was quite attractive. She stared at him looking straight ahead figuring he was tentative about asking her for a goodnight kiss. She was right. Rome didn't want to move too fast. He respected Faith and didn't want her to think that he was only after one thing. He knew that she was apprehensive to start and didn't want to ruin his chances of seeing her again. Faith, on the other hand, wanted that kiss and waited a few seconds before deciding it probably wasn't going to happen. She was disappointed because she'd become extremely attracted to Rome. He was different; he was a gentleman. He also seemed shy about making a move and that turned her on more. She thought back to how he backed away from her on the dance floor when he started to get an erection and chuckled under her breath.

"Goodnight, Rome," Faith said as she opened the car door and started to get out.

"Wait..." he called out to her.

She looked back at him figuring he finally got up the nerve to make his move. "Yes?"

"Uh, I think I should walk you to your door."

"Well, how chivalrous of you," she said with a grin.

Rome parked his car and escorted Faith up to her apartment on the eleventh floor. He waited as she unlocked her door and turned to face him. An awkward silence filled the air before they simultaneously stepped toward one another and kissed tenderly.

"Well, goodnight," Faith said as she started backing up into her apartment.

"Goodnight, Faith," Rome replied, and very slowly began to backpedal down the hallway. He blew her a kiss when she peeked her head out of the door.

"Um, I'm sorry, Rome. I could've at least offered you a drink or something."

"No, thank you," he said, holding up his car keys. "I have to drive, remember?"

Faith stepped back out into the hallway and removed the straps of her dress off of her shoulders. "Well, if you want, you can wait until morning to drive."

Rome marched back over to Faith and took her into his arms. They engaged in a passionate kiss that led to them disrobing each other, leaving a trail of clothing from the front door to the bedroom. Rome laid on top of Faith, kissing all over her face, ears and neck. She closed her eyes and tilted her head back while running her hands up and down his back and across his wide buttocks. Rome moved down and planted kisses all over her chest and ran his tongue down between her breasts. He used his hands to press her breasts together and flicked his tongue on her nipples. Then, he moved down more and licked her navel, causing her to giggle and push his head down further. He ran his tongue over her pubic patch and let it rest against her clitoris. Faith let out a tiny squeal and opened her legs wide. Rome pressed his lips down hard on her love button and sucked on it masterfully.

Faith's toes curled when Rome opened his mouth and probed inside her moist vagina with his tongue. He reached underneath her, grabbed her butt and held it up as he greedily ate her pussy like he was devouring a watermelon.

As Faith cried out in ecstasy, Rome just pressed his lips harder against her pussy and continued until he felt her trembling body start to relax as her wave of climax passed. He let her down on the bed gently and sat up on his knees.

Faith noticed Rome's thick, hard penis sticking straight out at her and nodded her head to the left at the night table. Rome looked over and saw the box of condoms and quickly rolled one on. Faith propped some pillows under her butt, opened her legs wider and held them up high. Rome bent down and lapped her waiting pussy some more before entering her. He drove into her again and again while pushing her knees back to her shoulders.

"OHHHHHH!" Faith bellowed as she came a second time. The expression on her face was flushed as she closed her eyes tightly and clawed and pulled the sheets off the mattress.

Rome withdrew his penis and turned Faith over on her stomach. She positioned the pillows under herself so that only her hips were raised off the bed. He mounted her big round butt and drove his throbbing erection back into her love ravine hard from behind. He pumped into her furiously, causing her to have to hold on to the headboard for support.

"Yes! Yes!" Faith repeated as Rome rammed into her. Her juices were now flowing continuously and tears streamed down her face from the overwhelming pleasure.

"OHHH! I'm cumming!" Rome moaned.

"Wait!" Faith yelled as she reached back and pushed him away from her. She quickly spun around and snatched the condom off his pulsating dick. Then, she held onto his butt with one hand, his dick with the other and took it into her mouth. She sucked and stroked with one rhythm while holding him in place.

Faith felt the first squirt hit the roof of her mouth and took it out to receive the rest of his Rome's juice all over her face and neck. Then, she put it back into her mouth and sucked on it slowly until she felt it submit and go limp.

Faith invited Rome to stay over for the weekend, which he gladly accepted. That was four years ago. He's still there.

The Official Scores

"Aw, c'mon!" Derek exclaimed. "What kind of call was that?! Geez, you are the worst! I mean, the absolute worst!"

Brenda tried to ignore Derek's rants as she ran up the court with her whistle locked in her lips. She cut her eyes at the coach from across the court and smiled slightly. He was skating on thin ice, and although she didn't really want to, she decided that if she heard one more outburst from him, she'd administer the first half of his ejection process.

Derek coaches an academics through athletics basketball program for girls thirteen to eighteen years old, and he did a lot to help his players become above average student-athletes. Brenda had just become a certified girls basketball official a year earlier and got a lot of work in most of New York City's summer leagues. Usually, before games, Derek greeted Brenda cheerfully with a smile. But once the game started, she became his least favorite person. As of late, it seemed to him that she was officiating all of his games. He was right, and it was Brenda's doing. She worked as many of his games as she could get, and made sure to do what she could to draw his attention. It wasn't her intention, however, to make him angry with her over calls. That was a bonus – extra attention.

Before this game, Derek saw Brenda come out the locker room with her partner and he sighed in disappointment.

"Oh, God," he said to Monica, his assistant coach. "We got this ref again. Damn, why is it she gets every game we play in this tournament? She's horrible."

"Why don't you ask the tournament director not to assign her to our games?" Monica suggested.

"That's a good idea," Derek agreed. "I'm going to make sure I do that right after this game."

"You think it may be personal?"

"Personal?" Derek pondered that possibility for a brief moment. "No, why would it be? She's always real nice and stuff when she's not officiating. I just don't think she's a good ref, that's all."

"I don't know, Derek. I think it is personal."

"Why? Why wouldn't she like me? What have I ever done to her?"

"Actually, I think the contrary. I think she *does* like you. I think she wants you."

"That's what you think?" Derek asked, displaying a puzzled frown. "That's ridiculous."

"Okay, if you say so. But women know these things about other women. Believe what I tell you. She wants to get with you."

"Well, she *is* a cutie. No doubt about that. But, nah..."

Unconsciously, Monica's observation weighed on Derek's mind. He was especially hard on Brenda this game. Every time she made a call he didn't like, he'd yell at her. Finally, Brenda's partner, Beatrice, gave Derek a warning.

"Okay Coach, that's enough," Beatrice said, walking over to him. "This is your warning. Now, have a seat and tone it down."

Derek rolled his eyes and took his seat. Beatrice ran back out onto the court to take the ball from Brenda so she could resume play. As Brenda handed her the ball, she quietly blasted her partner.

"You didn't have to do that," she scolded. "I can handle myself out here."

"He was getting out of line..."

"I said I can handle myself," Brenda snapped, cutting Beatrice off, "and I can handle him, too."

Just then, Beatrice caught on to what was happening. She shook her head at Brenda and proceeded to resume play without making another comment.

"YEAH! Let's go!" Derek cheered as one of his players stole the ball from the other team and dashed down the court. Brenda immediately gave chase, running hard to get into position to make a call if necessary. Derek's player leapt for a lay-up and the chasing defender jumped to block her shot. Their bodies bumped in the air as the ball hit off the backboard and swished through the hoop. Derek looked over at Brenda, waiting for her to make a call, but her whistle never sounded.

"For cryin' out loud!" he yelled as he jumped up out his seat. "Call the foul! What are you out there for?!"

Now, Brenda had no choice. Derek had been warned and there was nothing left to do. She blew her whistle and used her hands to form the letter T. "I have a technical foul on the red-team coach," she told the bookkeeper as she walked toward the scorer's table. She looked over and saw Derek walking toward her with his arms spread open. Brenda imagined he was inviting her into them and had to refrain from running over and jumping on him. Although his face was balled up with anger, Brenda looked into his brown, bedroom eyes and admired his dark-chocolate complexion, neatly-tapered cut, light-shaded goatee, broad chest and...

"A tech?! For what?!" Derek yelled, interrupting Brenda's fantasy.

"Unsportsman-like conduct," she responded, immediately switching back into professional mode. "Now, go back and have a seat. One more tech and you're going to be ejected from the game." Before Derek could say or do anything else, Brenda quickly turned her attention to the opposing coach and asked her to select a player to shoot the technical foul free throws. As Beatrice went to administer the ball to the shooter, Brenda strutted to take her position on the other side of the court. She knew her black official's pants were fitted enough to show off her wide hips and big, plump butt, and she wanted Derek to get an eyeful.

"Look at her switching her big ass across the court," Monica whispered in Derek's ear. "Who do *you* think that's for?"

Derek didn't respond, but he was beginning to realize that Monica was right. He looked across the court at Brenda and caught her looking at him. Their eyes locked, and at that moment, everything Monica said was confirmed. Although Derek had noticed Brenda enough before to recognize how beautiful she was, his mind was too consumed with basketball to recognize her attraction to him. But that wasn't the case anymore.

After the opposing player swished the two free throws, Derek looked over at the scoreboard and saw his team was still up by two points. Unfortunately, the technical foul also gave the ball back to the other team and they were able to score right away, tying the game. Derek regained his composure and focused on coaching his team. Brenda smiled to herself, proud that she had taken control of the situation and was able to tame Derek. She felt good about that because she was used to him being able to intimidate most refs and getting his way. Now, all she needed to do was get him to have his way with her, control the situation between her legs, and tame the desires burning within her.

The game ended, and Derek had a fifty-five to forty-nine victory. He led his team over to the opposing team's bench to shake hands, and then he walked over to Brenda and Beatrice.

"Good job," he said as shook Beatrice's hand.

Brenda took a breath and prepared for him to address her. He extended his hand to her and displayed that familiar wide smile, showing off his pearly whites.

"Thanks, ref. Good job."

Brenda returned a smile and took his hand in hers. She felt his strong, firm grip and wondered how it would feel to be totally wrapped in his arms. She imagined him holding her tight and her body totally submitting to him.

"Thank you. Take care," she cooed.

Their eyes locked again, just before Derek turned away and walked off. Brenda admired his butt through his blue nylon sweatpants and pouted a kiss at him before she went into the locker room to change.

Monica had to hurry and leave to go meet her husband, so Derek waited around for his players to finish getting changed. Before they came out their locker room, Brenda came out the official's locker room carrying her black gym bag. Derek's jaw dropped and he became mesmerized. He had never seen Brenda in street clothes before. She wore a flowery, light-blue, low-cut mini sundress that showed off her muscular legs and the cleavage of her well-endowed breasts. Her plum lipstick drew attention to her luscious, full lips and complimented her smooth, walnut-colored complexion. She let her shoulder-length hair with gold and brown streaks hang loose, and she wore round designer frames that made her look very studious, yet extremely sexy.

"Goodnight, Coach," she said, waving at him as she headed for the gymnasium's exit.

"Goodnight. I'm sure I'll see you around, soon. You always seem to get my games."

Brenda stopped and turned toward him.

"Yeah. Funny, eh?" Her smile was inviting as she held her gym bag across her shoulder, her head tilted slightly and her body curved in an S form.

Derek wasn't sure of what to do right then. Although he thought he was reading her correctly, he needed to be absolutely sure.

"Yeah, it is kinda strange," he said jokingly. "You wouldn't be following me, would you?"

Brenda bit her bottom lip seductively and turned to walk away again, her body language suggesting that she would like him to follow her. Now, Derek was definitely sure he was reading her right. But as bad as he wanted to follow her, he knew he couldn't because he was still waiting for his team and had to drive some of his players home.

"Wait a second," he called out to her. She stopped and turned to face him again. "Are you free later? I'd like to hook up with you, perhaps take you to dinner or something."

Brenda displayed a broad smile and eagerly accepted Derek's invitation.

"Sure, I'd like that." They exchanged telephone numbers just before the team came out the locker room and she quickly exited the gym.

Derek hurried his players home and rushed to his apartment to get ready for his date. He got into the shower and replayed over and over in his mind how good Brenda looked. What a fool he'd been for not noticing her. His preoccupation with coaching was the same reason his last girlfriend left him.

"Maybe it won't bother Brenda as much being that she's into the game, too," Derek thought aloud.

"This woman may be exactly who I need to be with right now. I hope she is. I don't want to jump the gun, though. I mean; it's only our first date. We may not even hit it off at all. No, think positive. She definitely likes me. I just have to make sure I don't do anything to screw this up."

Brenda took out a similar styled pink sundress and hung it up outside her closet. She spread her white bra and thong ensemble across the bed and waited for Derek to call. She sat naked on the side of her bed as she sipped on her glass of Chardonnay before deciding to walk over to the balcony door and look out from her twentieth floor view of Central Park. She could see the entire park and some of the bright lights of Times Square a distance away. She loved the scenery, and smiled to herself as she thought about Derek.

"I hope he doesn't stand me up. That would be so terrible. I'd never speak to him again. Oh, who am I fooling? Of course I'd speak to him again. I'd make sure he wouldn't want to stand me up anymore. I'd see to it that he'd be begging to get with me."

At that moment, the telephone rang. Brenda walked back to her bed, sat down and picked up the receiver on the third ring. "Hello," she answered in a smooth, sultry voice.

"Hello? Brenda?"

"Yes."

"This is Derek"

"Yes, hello."

"Hi. Uh, well, are you ready? Are you still up for this?"

"Absolutely. I'm looking forward to it."

"Good. So am I."

"So, do you want to meet or…"

"Oh. Yeah. What's your address? I'll come pick you up."

"I live in the building in front of Cathedral Circle, right on the corner of Central Park North and a Hundred and Tenth Street."

"Oh, I know that building. I don't live too far away. That's cool. I'll be there in fifteen minutes."

"That's fine. I'll be waiting out front."

Derek drove up in his red Dodge Caravan. Brenda watched him park and walk toward the building. He had changed into a stylish, beige, two-piece linen outfit, and she was pleasantly surprised at how well he cleaned up. She opened the front door and stepped outside to greet him.

"There you are," he said as he approached her, looking her over again. She actually looked more beautiful to him than she did three hours earlier. They embraced, and Derek inhaled the fragrance of White Diamond as they gave each other a simultaneous cheek kiss. "Let's go. I know this nice little Italian restaurant down in Greenwich Village that I'm sure you'll love. Uh, you do like Italian, don't you?"

"I love Italian food," she smiled enthusiastically. "It's my favorite."

"Good. You're really going to enjoy yourself, then." Derek took Brenda's hand and escorted her to his minivan. He opened the door and started tossing scorebooks, clipboards and stats sheets from the front passenger seat into the back. Brenda looked inside and noticed a mess of tournament shirts, basketballs and other junk all over. "Sorry about the mess," he said. "I've been meaning to get my team to clean this out."

"That's alright. In fact, let's just take my car. I love to drive, anyway."

"Are you sure?"

Brenda looked at the mess again and reassured him.

"Oh, I am definitely sure," she said with a grin. "Just leave your car here; it'll be fine. This is a good spot."

She led him to the building's parking lot and got into her silver BMW X-Five. They arrived at the restaurant and got a table near the back wall. The place was dimly lit by candlelight, one at each table. They indulged in idle chitchat about themselves and basketball as they got acquainted.

"I picked up some weight since college," Brenda said. "I used to be a toothpick."

"Well, I don't know about then, but you look great now."

"Humph, flattery will get you everywhere," she teased.

Derek grinned at the statement. "Where did you play college ball?"

"I played at the University of Kentucky from Eighty-Five to Eighty-Nine," Brenda said. "I was the starting point guard in my junior and senior years."

"Really? That's cool. I didn't really start following women's basketball until around Ninety-One, so I missed you by a couple of years."

"Oh, I see. Did you play in college?"

"I played at Howard University from Eighty-Four to Eighty-Eight. I played point, too."

"So, how'd you get into coaching women's basketball?"

"My best friend's sister and her friends were always playing and they said they wanted to get into some tournaments, but they needed a coach. I was coaching a boys' team at the time and my friend asked if I could do both. Being the basketball lover that I am, I graciously accepted. Now, I've given up the boys and only coach girls."

As Derek told his story, he noticed how Brenda was gazing attentively into his eyes with an endearing look on her face. She leaned forward, resting her elbows on the table, and her soft breasts pressed down against her arms. Derek looked down into her cleavage and felt the saliva trying to escape from his mouth. He swallowed hard to keep from drooling and quickly grabbed his water glass and gulped without stopping.

"Thirsty, huh?" Brenda asked, teasingly.

"Yeah. For some reason I just felt dehydrated."

"Well, it is a bit hot in here. Perhaps that's what's making you so thirsty?"

"Oh, I'm sure that's what it is," he confirmed.

Brenda tilted her head and batted her eyes. "I know how you feel. I'm feeling very thirsty, too."

Derek grinned coyly and picked up Brenda's water glass. "Wha...um...well, have a drink."

"No, thank you," she smiled, devilishly. "That's not what I'm thirsty for."

Derek put Brenda's glass to his mouth and drank with the same intensity. Brenda put her hand to her mouth and chuckled at his discomfort.

After dinner, Brenda drove back uptown to Riverside Park. She and Derek walked hand-in-hand through the park and Brenda closed her eyes every time a gust of wind blew.

"Oh, I just love the summer time," she said. "The wind feels so good. I just want to take off all my clothes and lie down in the night air."

"Yeah, I feel the same way," Derek agreed.

"I hate wearing clothes, anyway. If I could, I'd just walk around naked all the time."

"Do you walk around your house in the nude?"

"Of course. I sleep in the nude, too."

"But, you make sure all your curtains and blinds are drawn, right?"

"No way. I don't care if anyone sees me. I have nothing to hide as long as I'm in the privacy of my own home."

"I hear that," Derek said as he led Brenda to a bench. "Let's sit here awhile."

They sat on a bench looking out over the Westside Highway into the Hudson River enjoying the pleasant, eighty-degree night breeze. Derek put his arm around Brenda's shoulders and hugged her lovingly. She opened the top button of his shirt and let her fingers gently tickle his chest.

"So, I've been meaning to ask you something," Brenda said.

"What's that?"

"Why do you get so emotional when you coach? Are you like that all the time? Do you react with such emotion to every situation that you're displeased with?"

"Actually, no. In fact, I'm usually very laid back. I'm not usually so aggressive. It's just that when the game is going on, my adrenaline gets going and I get crazy. That's because I'm such a competitor. That's the way I used to play. I hated to lose, and did whatever I could to win."

"Oh, I see."

"You asked because it seems like I ride you, right?"

"Oh no," Brenda thought to herself, "I'm going to be the one riding you."

"If so, I don't mean anything by it," Derek apologized. "I never carry it off the court, either."

"Oh, I know. I don't take it personally. If I did, we wouldn't be here right now."

"I guess that's true."

"It is true. I'll tell you something else, too. I asked to be assigned to your games."

"Really?"

"Well, I didn't come right out and say give me all of Derek Pierce's games. I just requested the dates and times I knew you were coaching. I did it because I wanted to see you and I wanted you to notice me."

"Why didn't you just say something to me if you were interested? Why do women have such a hard time making the first move?"

"Oh, so you like when women make the first move, huh?"

"Absolutely."

Brenda climbed up on Derek's lap and they began to kiss passionately. She squirmed and wiggled, causing his excitement to build. Derek began rubbing Brenda's thigh, and gradually worked his hand up under her dress and between her legs. She let one leg down off his lap, opening herself up to him. Derek stroked and caressed Brenda's clitoris through her wet thong. Then he pulled her thong to the side and inserted a finger past the folds of her moist vagina.

Brenda had both arms thrown around Derek's neck, kissing him violently. As their tongues entwined, he worked his other hand up her back and unfastened her bra. Brenda moved her hands down to unbutton Derek's shirt just as he began to rip away her thong. The material finally gave away and he tossed her torn underwear to the ground. Brenda stood up and pulled her dress over her head and tossed it over the back of the bench. Then, she removed her bra and threw it to the same place. With the exception of her clog-heeled sandals, she was totally nude. Derek's eyes widened and he looked around to see if anyone was watching. To his right he saw a couple out walking their dog about thirty feet away. To his left were two women smoking marijuana four benches away.

Derek thought that when he tore away Brenda's thong, she'd sit in his lap and let her dress drape down over them. Instead, they were in jeopardy of getting arrested for indecent exposure. "Brenda, there are people out here," he pleaded.

"To hell with those people," she said while reaching down to unfasten his pants. "They don't have anything to do with us."

"But..." Derek's attempt to plead again was stifled by Brenda's lips pressed hard against his. She worked his pants and boxers down past his knees, exposing his massive erection to the night air. Without hesitation, she mounted his lap and lowered herself down onto him.

Brenda moaned loudly as she felt Derek's thickness push into her vaginal walls. Derek quickly put his reservations to the side and began sucking on her nipples. His hands clung to her ass tightly as she pounced up and down on top of him. He managed to stand to his feet, and Brenda wrapped her legs tightly around his waist. Their tongues entwined once more as they ground their pelvises into one another.

Brenda let herself down out of Derek's arms and his penis slipped out of her releasing a wet, slurping sound. She trotted to the bench and climbed up on her knees, holding onto the back of it with both hands. Derek looked at her big, round backside sticking out at him and moved up behind her with his pants down around his ankles. He looked around to see if the people were watching and found that they were. The couple was standing by a tree pointing at them, and the two women had moved a bench closer to get a better view.

"Come on!" Brenda demanded, just as Derek was about to hesitate. "Give it to me!"

Derek looked at the beautiful woman kneeling on the bench in front of him and forgot all about the people watching. He moved closer and entered her. He reached around and grabbed her large dangling breasts as he drove into her with long, hard strokes. Brenda squealed and moaned loudly as Derek thrust in and out of her, causing his balls to slap against her clit. Her orgasms were coming one after the other, and Derek held on to her hips as he felt himself about to release. His whole body began to shake as he withdrew from her and sprayed thick, hot semen all over her back.

The two women, who had now moved yet another bench closer, began to clap and cheer. The woman of the couple by the tree stood in disbelief with her hand over her mouth, and her male companion was laughing at her. Derek pulled up his pants, and Brenda put her dress back on. She left her bra and ripped thong behind, and led Derek back to her car. When Brenda pulled into the garage and parked, she rolled her eyes at Derek and proceeded to open her door.

"What?" Derek asked, defensively.

Brenda closed the door, sat back in her seat and folded her arms. She looked at Derek and huffed. "You owe me a bra and panty set."

Derek jerked his head back and raised a brow. "Brenda I...uh..." he muttered.

"I spend a lot of money on my lingerie, you know. I mean, you could've moved them to the side or taken them off me. You didn't have to rip them off."

Derek was confused at this point. He had no idea that Brenda would react this way. "I'm sorry. I just thought..."

"You know what?" she interrupted. "I don't want to wait for you to buy me a new set. I think you should make it up to me instead. And the only way I can see for you to do that is by coming upstairs and spending the night with me."

A look of relief came over Derek's face and he laughed out loud. "Oh, man. You are something else."

"I mean it," Brenda demanded, trying to refrain from laughing. "That's the only way you can make it up to me."

"Fine," he smiled. "But, if that's my punishment, you may end up without any underwear at all."

The next morning, Derek woke up to the smell of turkey sausage and pancakes. He sat up in the bed, rubbed his eyes into focus and looked over at the clock, which read seven-nineteen. He heard Brenda in the kitchen singing and he smiled to himself. As he was about to get out of her king-sized bed, she walked into the room, totally nude, carrying a tray of food.

"Oh wow, baby. That looks delicious. And the food looks good, too. Goodness, how long have you been up?"

"I got up at a quarter to five," Brenda said as she placed the tray on a small table beside the bed.

"What? We just went to sleep at two-thirty."

"I know," she said as she crawled on the bed and climbed on top of him. "I wanted to clean out your car before I made breakfast and left for my games at West Fourth Street."

"You cleaned out my car?"

"Yeah, I took your keys and went downstairs," she said while planting kisses all over his face. "Everything is in perfect order now. I hope that's not a problem. I wasn't out of line, was I?"

"Oh, no, no, no, not at all. I'm actually very, very grateful. Wow, you are something else."

"It was my pleasure. I think you are a beautiful, wonderful man, and I want to make you happy. Anyway, I see you didn't have a problem sleeping."

"Well, I had a long, wonderful night."

"Oh, yes. Me too. I'm not finished, though."

"What? You want more?"

"Oh yes, baby. I'm a morning person, anyway."

Brenda pulled the sheet off Derek, exposing his naked body to the morning sunlight. She took his semi-erect penis into her hands and began to stroke it. She lowered her head and let her tongue flicker across its tip before suctioning her lips around it. Then she took the head into her mouth and sucked noisily while continuing to stroke with both hands. As Derek's dick began to stiffen, Brenda opened her mouth wide and took it in, feeling it get harder and thicker. She stroked faster and bobbed her head up and down on his manhood, taking as much of it into her mouth as she could.

Derek's legs started shaking and he was making short squealing noises as he felt himself about to erupt. "I'm cumming!" he shouted and gently patted Brenda on the back of the head so that she could move. Instead, she locked her lips around the head and continued to stroke. Derek grunted and moaned loudly as he spewed globs of semen into her mouth. She drank greedily while squeezing his dick, milking it for all she could get.

"Wow, you are loaded," Brenda said. She sat up and wiped cum off the side of her face with her fingers and stuck them into her mouth. "Didn't you give me three loads last night?"

"Oh, I don't know," Derek panted.

"Let's see. You gave me the first load on my back in the park. Then, you gave me another load all over my breasts when we came upstairs. Then, you gave me another load all over my legs in the shower. Mmmm, yeah, I was right. I like that. I like to have lots and lots of it. The more you give me, the more I want. So you're going to have to give me some more later, okay?"

Derek, unable to speak at the moment, grinned and nodded.

"Okay, baby." Brenda climbed off the bed and pulled the sheet back over him. "Sit up so you can eat your breakfast. You need to fuel up."

Derek did as he was told and Brenda sat the tray across his lap. "Aren't you going to eat, too?" he muttered.

"You just gave me my breakfast, baby. All I needed was that protein shake you just fed me. I'm good to go now."

Again, Derek grinned and shook his head. "What time is your game at West Fourth Street?"

"Ten o'clock. I have three games, so I'll be finished by two-thirty or three o'clock. Then I'm going to come home and take a nap. What's on your agenda?"

"My team is playing in Brooklyn at Tillary Park at noon. After that, I'm going to do some diamond shopping."

"Diamond shopping?"

"Yes. I want to buy a ring for you because I want you to marry me."

"Oh, stop playing, silly," Brenda laughed.

"I'm not playing. I mean it."

"Just like that?"

"Why not?" Derek shrugged.

Brenda looked into his eyes and was able to see his sincerity. Her eyes widened, her heart started to beat faster and her nerves started jumping. "You *are* serious, aren't you?"

"You think I'm crazy?"

"No, I..."

"I'm not crazy. Impulsive perhaps, but I'm not crazy. I know what I want, and I know I want you. You're smart, funny, beautiful, successful, and totally sexually uninhibited. I'm thirty-six years old, and I've never been so sure about anything, ever."

Brenda curled up on the bed beside Derek and rested her head on his shoulder. Tears began streaming down her cheeks. "I fell in love with you the moment I laid eyes on you. I was ready to be your wife then. But...but I had no idea that you'd feel this way, too."

"I do. I guess what got me is that I could see and feel all that love from you. Of course it's not going to happen tomorrow, but I want us to be together and work toward that goal for the near future. I know this is right. Will you have me?"

Brenda sobbed and threw her arms around him. "Yes," she said.

Lady Baller

Garrett looked across Frederick Douglass Boulevard and noticed a jeep pull up and park in front of his SUV. His eyes locked in on Tamara's legs as she swung them out onto the sidewalk and followed her six-foot-three frame up as she stood to her feet. "Son, check out the honey," he said, tapping his friend Tariq on the arm. The two of them were standing in front of their building waiting on Bruce, the third member of the trio which was always together.

Tariq looked across the street, gave Tamara a once over, and twisted his lip slightly. "She's a'ight, Son. She ain't all that."

"Ain't all that? Son, I'm talkin' 'bout the tall chick that just got outta the blue Four Runner."

"I know. She's a'ight. I've seen better."

Garrett ignored Tariq's comment. He always had an eye for athletic women and Tamara was just that. As far as he was concerned, she was the most beautiful woman he'd ever seen in his life. He watched her as she withdrew a piece of paper from her wallet and read the writing on it. His eyes followed her long, thick, muscular legs up from her white Nikes to her tiny, denim cutoffs. His eyes moved up her torso to her firm breasts that looked like a pair of grapefruits covered by a white WNBL t-shirt. He admired her full lips, high cheekbones and deep dimples. She wore no makeup, her eyes were hidden by large, round sunglasses, and her medium-length hair was combed straight back into a ponytail. She had a dusty-gold complexion, and a tattoo of a basketball with the number twenty-two on her left arm. She fit the description of the woman of his dreams.

Garrett smiled as Tamara began walking toward the building. She was looking up at it, giving it a nod of approval. She directed her attention to Tariq, who had started walking toward her. "Excuse me, I'm looking for the management office."

Tariq shrugged her off by pointing his thumb over his shoulder at the front entrance. "There's a security guard in there. He'll help you."

"Thank you," Tamara said, politely. As she walked toward the automatic doors, Tariq looked back at her butt. He squinted his eyes with astonishment and mouthed, "oh shit" at how big, round and well-toned it was.

"C'mon, I'll show you where it is," Garrett volunteered. "I live right across the hall from the management office."

"Thank you," Tamara said, smiling.

At that moment, Bruce came walking across the street. "What's up?" he shouted. "Y'all ready to go, or what?"

"We were waitin' on yo' slow ass," Tariq responded just as loud. "Yo, Gee, we out. Let's go, Son."

Garret held up his hands, signaling his friends to wait. "Hold up, Son."

"Yo, Son, let's go," Tariq shouted again.

Garrett ignored him and escorted Tamara into the building.

"Right this way, Miss. The office is by the elevators."

Tamara gave Garrett a polite smile.

"Thanks again," she said as she walked in behind him.

"Just sign the visitors book, Ma. We hold it down in here. No one gets in without seeing security. You'll appreciate that when you move in. You are movin' in, right?"

"Maybe. It depends on how nice the apartment is."

"The apartment is slammin'. It's on the second floor. The lady that lived there just moved out about a week ago, and she had it hooked. It was already nice, but she made it better."

"Why'd she move?"

"She really lives in Cali, but she was here because of her job. She was supposed to be here longer, but she finished early."

"Oh, I see. You two must've been close."

"Yeah, Denise was my girl. We were real cool." Tamara nodded, and then Garrett picked up on her implication. "Not like that, though. Nah, we were just cool, you know what I'm sayin'?"

"Yeah, I hear you. Well, thanks again."

"No problem, Ma. I'm sayin', though. I live right there in One B. You know, if you need anything, or just wanna kick it, holla, a'ight? My name's Gee."

"Gee?"

"Yeah. Gee."

"Okay, Gee. I'm Tamara Bingham."

Garrett shook Tamara's hand and gave her another once over from head to toe. She stood four inches taller than him and outweighed him by ten pounds, which he liked very much.

"Okay, Tamara. I gotta go. You'll like it here. It's peaceful. Nobody's about no bullshit, you know what I'm sayin'? Nice neighborhood. Nice, hard workin' folks. Nobody bothers nobody else, and everybody minds their own business. So, hopefully you'll take the apartment and I'll get to see you again."

"Yes. Hopefully."

Tamara's response brought a broad smile to Garrett's face and his confidence grew.

"Well, can I have your number or something, just in case you're not feelin' this place and do decide to move someplace else? You know, so then I can still kick it with you and we can go out or somethin'."

"I don't know about that. I have a very busy schedule and I travel a lot. I don't think I'll have much time for socializing. Not for quite a while."

"Oh, Ma. Don't treat me like that. There's always time for socializin'. You can't be busy all the time; it's not healthy. You feel me?"

"I know what you're saying, but the fact still remains."

"Look, let me give you my number, and the first chance you get, you give me a call, a'ight?" Garrett took a business card from his pocket, then took out a pen and wrote on the back of it. "Here, Ma. You got my cell, my office, and I wrote my home number on the back. Holla at me."

Tamara took the card and put it into her wallet. "Okay. Well, let me go in here and see about this apartment."

"You do that. Holla, Ma."

Tamara smiled at Garrett and headed into the office. He watched her walk away and could see why Tariq made such an expression a few minutes ago.

"Yo, Gee!" Tariq called out again. "C'mon, Man!"

Garrett went back outside and stared at Tariq and Bruce standing near the curb and shook his head. "You know you niggas ain't right. Why y'all gotta be cock blockin' and shit?"

"Nigga, please," Bruce said. "That chick ain't givin' yo' little scrawny ass no play, you burnt, crispy, black, ashy muthafucka."

"Word, Son," Tariq agreed. "Honey do got a fat ass, but she ain't 'bout to let you sniff none o' that poo-poo."

Garrett smiled and nodded as he joined his doubtful best buds that were laughing at him.

"Fuck y'all," he said matter-of-factly. "Let's bounce."

The three men got into Garrett's Lincoln Navigator and drove off.

Six days later, Garrett woke up to the sound of the alarm clock. He reached over and hit the snooze button before turning over to catch a few more winks. Before he could get back to sleep, however, he heard the soft, soothing blow of a woman's whisper fill his ear.

"No, don't go back to sleep, baby," she said. "You have to wake up so you can give me some before you go to work."

Garrett smiled as he felt her hand reach around in front of him and start to stroke his penis while placing gentle kisses along his back and shoulders. He felt himself getting excited, and his erection started to grow in his lover's hand.

"You sure you want this?" he asked. "You might be too tired to get up and go to work afterwards."

"I don't care," she replied. "I want it. I need it. I have to have it."

"Okay, Diana. You asked for it."

"Give it to me, Daddy."

Garrett rolled over on top of Diana's full-figured body and kissed her deeply. He grabbed as much of her forty-four double D-sized breasts as he could and squeezed them hard. Diana loved to have her breasts manhandled. It drove her crazy. She moved her hands down Garrett's bony back and clutched his tight, little backside as he moved his head down and wallowed his face between her enormous mounds.

"Ohhh, yes!" she moaned. "I like that, Daddy."

Garrett took turns sucking and biting each of Diana's nipples while continuing to squeeze her honey-colored breasts as hard as he could, causing her to writhe beneath him uncontrollably. He then moved himself up so that he could slide his penis between her breasts and squeeze them around it. As he moved his hips back and forth, she opened her mouth to take in its head with each of his forward thrusts.

Diana pushed Garrett back off her and turned over on top of him. She ran her tongue down from his navel, through his bushel of pubic hair, and up the length of his erection. She locked her lips around the head and poked the tip of her tongue into the slit before letting her mouth glide back down. She locked both hands around the base of his rigid cock and slid her lips and tongue up and down until Garrett's life force started cascading down her throat. Diana drank and slurped, swallowing hard and smacking her lips until she got every drop. The alarm clock sounded a second time and Garrett reached over to turn it off.

"I want you inside of me, baby," Diana pleaded.

Garrett moved from under her and sat up on the side of the bed.

"We're both gonna be late if we don't get up. And you gotta take Avery to school first, so you better go get him up and get in the shower so y'all can get your asses up outta here."

"Fine," Diana complied. She got out the bed, put on her bathrobe and headed into the next room to wake up her son. Garrett put on his pajama pants and went to the closet to pull out something to wear for work. Diana came back carrying an armful of clothing. "Avery's taking his shower first," she said.

"I'll take mine afterwards. I'm going to start on breakfast and iron our clothes. Do you have anything you need to be ironed?"

"Nah, I'm straight. You go ahead. I'mma catch the morning news for a minute."

"Okay, baby."

Diana went into the kitchen, and Garrett sat down and turned on the television. Just as the traffic report was about to start, the telephone rang.

"Who the fuck..." he said to himself as he picked up the receiver.

"Hello?"

"Good morning. Is this Mr. Garrett Orr?" Tamara asked in her most professional voice, trying not to laugh, and hoping that Garrett had a sense of humor.

"Yeah. Who's this?"

She was glad he sounded puzzled and a little concerned. It made her little prank more fun. "This is Miss Tamara Bingham. I'm calling to find out about your good neighbor policy."

"Good neighbor policy? Who is this, again?"

Tamara covered her mouth a second to hold in her laughter. "Uh, this is Tamara Bingham calling. I was asking about the good neighbor policy you were informing me of the other day."

"I was telling you about a..." Garrett could only laugh when he caught on to the joke that was being played on him.

"Okay, you got me," he confessed. "Wassup? You get the apartment?"

"Yes, I did. I moved in two days ago. I thought you might've known, and then I remembered you said people in this building mind their own business, so I decided to call. Sorry about calling so early, but I have a long week ahead of me and I wanted to touch bases with you before you left for work."

"Yeah, I'm about to get up outta here in a few."

"I see on your business card that you're into show business."

"Yeah, I'm a talent scout. My agency represents comedians, actors, singers, and models. I see you got jokes; you should stop by my office."

"I'm sorry. I was in a pretty good mood, which isn't often, and I just felt like acting up."

"It's cool. I'm feelin' that."

"Are your buddies from the other day in the same line of work?"

"Nah. Tariq, the first dude I was standing with, is a director at a mental institution. His crazy ass should be one of the patients, though. The other cat, Bruce, does something with computers at a bank."

"Oh, I see. How old are you, Gee?"

"Twenty-six. Why?"

"I was just wondering. You look younger than that."

"Oh, you thought I still had my mama's milk on my breath, huh?"

"Ha-ha. Yeah, sorta."

"How old are you?"

"I'm twenty-seven."

"The age ain't no problem is it?"

"No, it's no problem at all."

"What's your gig, Ma? You say you're so busy and what-not."

"I play basketball for the New York Empire."

"Word? You in the WNBL?"

"You ever watch any games?"

"Nah, but I will now to see you."

"Yeah, I got traded here last season from Cleveland. I'm also going to be an assistant coach at Columbia University, and that's why I moved."

"Word? Where're you from?"

"I'm originally from Saint Louis, but I've lived in Ohio since college. I went to Ohio State, then I got drafted by Cleveland so I just stayed there."

That moment, Diana came back into the bedroom. "I'm finished ironing, and I'm going to take my shower now," she said.

"Hold on a second," Garrett told Tamara before covering the telephone. "A'ight," he said to Diana, "where's Avery?"

"He's getting dressed."

"A'ight, you go ahead, then."

Diana slowly walked out the bedroom and into the bathroom, looking back at Garrett the whole time. He knew she wanted to know whom he was talking to, so he waited until she closed the bathroom door behind her before resuming his conversation with Tamara.

"So, Tamara, how'd you get the gig at Columbia?"

"The former assistant coach at OSU got the head job there last year. When I got traded to New York, she offered me a job."

"A'ight. Well, what's up with us getting together? You got tickets to a game or somethin'? I can roll to your game, then we can hang out and chill for a while, you know?"

"We have a home game tonight, then we leave tomorrow for a three-game road trip to Phoenix, Los Angeles and Minnesota. I'll be back next Thursday."

"I'm sayin', what about tonight's game?"

"Sure, I can get you some tickets. How many do you need?"

"If I can take you to dinner or somethin' afterwards, I'm rollin' solo."

"I really can't be out late because I have to get up early. But okay, I think we might be able to do a little something, even if it's just having you escorting me home. You know, being that we're coming back to the same apartment building and all."

"Yeah, yeah, that'll work, too. How am I gonna get the tickets?"

"I'll leave them at Will Call for you. After the game, meet me by gate twelve. I'm not going to drive. I'll take a cab to the game since I'll be coming back with you, so don't stand me up."

"Oh, never that, Ma."

"Okay, then it's on."

"A'ight. I'll see you tonight."
"Okay. Have a good day, Gee."
"You too, Ma."

Garrett hung up the telephone and went into the bathroom. Diana smiled when he pulled the shower curtain back. "You come to finish what we started in the bed, baby?"

Garrett was tempted, watching Diana standing there all suds up, but he thought about it and declined. "No, I just wanted to tell you, before it slips my mind, that I'm going out tonight so you and Avery should just go on home."

"Okay, baby. Will we see you tomorrow?"

"Oh, no doubt. I'll probably roll up to your crib, though."

"Okay, that's no problem. What time are you coming?"

"I'll be up there sometime between six and seven. Do me a favor and make a sweet potato pie, a'ight?"

"Sure. I can do that."

"Thank you, sweetie."

"I love you, baby."

Garrett felt a chill go through him because he knew Diana meant what she just said. He could hear it in her voice, and he could see it in her eyes. He felt terrible for not feeling the same way. Instead of responding, he leaned forward, gave her a lingering kiss, and then walked out.

That evening, after the game, Garrett was driving Tamara home. She was not in a good mood because of her team's performance, and sat with her arms folded, staring out the side window. Garrett tried to make small talk, but Tamara wasn't receptive at first.

"So tell me, what would it take for y'all to get into the playoffs now?" Garrett asked with sincere interest.

"Hm. Oh. Uh, we have seven more games. We have to win five to insure a spot. This was our third straight loss. It hurt us big-time."

"Y'all a be fine, Ma. Damn, I did think y'all were gonna pull this one out, though. You played a hell of a game, too. You was kickin' homegirl's ass down in the post. How come she's doin' all those commercials? She ain't shit. *You* the shit, Ma. I was screaming your name like a maniac every time you put a move on that chick. I was like, 'Tamara! Tamara!' Yo, I was having a good time. I'm coming to the next one, too. I've never been to a WNBL game before. It was cool."

Tamara was able to let a little smile break through her frustration. The thought of having a man there to support her made her happy. The fact that he got into it and was giving her words of encouragement pleased her even more. She hadn't been romantically involved with a man in two years, and her ex-fiancé was not supportive of her career. That was the reason she sought other alternatives in her life.

When Garrett pulled up in front of their building, Tamara attempted to open the door and get out, but he stopped her.

"Hold up, Ma. Just sit tight for a sec," he instructed, and then jumped out and ran around to open her door.

Tamara looked at him standing there smiling, holding out his hand to help her down. She couldn't help but to smile back as she took his hand and climbed down out of the truck. Garrett closed the door behind her, took her arm in his and escorted her into the building.

"Well, I know you said you want to turn in early," he said as they walked to the elevators, "but I really would like to just sit and kick it for another hour or so. You know, just so we can spend a few moments to get acquainted. We ain't gotta talk about the game, or about basketball at all. I wanna find out your favorite color so I can buy you a dress. I wanna find out your favorite movie so I can go rent the video for us to watch together when you get back. I wanna know what your favorite food is so I can order it, put it in some pots, invite you down and tell you I cooked it."

Garrett's sincerity made Tamara's heart start to race. She looked into his eyes and felt warmth and comfort. He was not like the kind of man that she used to date: six-foot-eight jocks with muscles. He was only five-eleven and weighed about one-sixty. He usually wore baggy jeans and over-sized jerseys with designer's names or team logos all over it, Timberland boots or sneakers with loose laces, and his hair in cornrows. Yet, he was a perfect gentleman who was trying very hard to lift her spirits.

"I can't spare an hour, Gee. I'm going to change, make a cup of coffee and go to bed."

"A'ight then, Ma. I can respect that," Garrett submitted, and moved closer to give her a kiss on the cheek. Tamara put up her hand to stop him.

"Wait," she said. "I could probably spare a half-hour. I would like it if you joined me for a cup of coffee. You do drink coffee, don't you?"

"Not usually, but I'm sure I'll enjoy having a cup with you."

"Come on up then. Just one cup, though."

"No doubt."

Garrett sat on the couch and waited while Tamara made the coffee. She still had most of her things in boxes and her furniture out of place.

"You know, I can help you get things organized in here when you get back if you want," he called out to her.

"Listen to you. Are you always so nice?"

"It's not hard being nice to you, Ma."

"I bet you say that to all the girls."

"Ha! I bet I don't."

"How would you like your coffee? I drink mine light and sweet."

"Oh, that sounds just like you, Ma."

Tamara came into the living room carrying cups in both hands. "Thank you. Well, I made yours light and sweet, too. I figured since you're not a coffee drinker, this way would be best."

"Whatever, Ma. It's all good."

She handed Garrett a cup and placed the other on the coffee table.

"I'll be right back," she said, and hurried into her bedroom. Garrett sipped on his coffee and waited for her. Five minutes later, she returned wearing a pair of tiny boy shorts and a sports bra. Garrett was in the middle of swallowing when he looked up and saw her and nearly choked.

"Hey, are you okay?"

Garrett coughed a bit more and cleared his throat. "Yeah. Yeah, I'm okay."

"Don't you die in here. It won't be hard for me to hide your body in this mess. I'll act like I never saw you."

"Oh, Ma, you'd do me like that?"

"No," Tamara said as she sat close to Garrett on the couch and put her legs up, "you're too nice for that. You, at least, deserved to be found. I'd probably drag you out and leave you in the stairwell."

"Damn, you're cold."

Tamara giggled like a little girl and snuggled closer. Garrett sat back and put his arm around her.

"Can you pass me my cup, please?"

"Oh, yeah. Here you go."

"Thank you. Mmmm, that's good."

"Yeah, it's pretty good," Garrett agreed as he sipped from his own cup. He looked down at Tamara curled up under his arm and noticed that although she was joking and smiling, her eyes seemed to be focusing on something else. He figured her mind was still on the game and knew he needed to say something to bring her around. "Ma, you got some seriously muscular arms. And later for a six-pack, you got a whole damn case. Y'all workouts must be intense. What're you pumpin'?"

"Um...let's see. I bench about two-twenty, and I do about two hundred to three hundred crunches about three or four times a week. We have to work hard and stay in shape. That's part of the job."

"I can tell. The results are all over you. You're definitely holdin' it down."

"When do I get to see what you do? I know working in the entertainment business has got to be fun."

"Yeah, it's the real shit, Ma. You know I'mma take you to some shows and concerts. No doubt."

"Okay. That'll be nice."

"You know, you're in the entertainment business, too?"

"Yeah, I know. Sports." Tamara sat up and placed her cup back on the coffee table. "I don't think we did too much entertaining tonight, though."

"Hey, now don't you start that," Garrett said as he placed his cup on the table, as well. He then used his finger to gently lift Tamara's head by her chin. "I was very entertained."

"I hate losing," she whined. "We may not go to the playoffs."

Garrett stood up, took Tamara by the hand and pulled her up to her feet. He held both of her arms up, took a step back and looked her up and down.

"Look at you, Ma. You're built like a goddess. You got mad skills on the court. You're smart as a whip. You even got jokes and shit. You are definitely a winner."

Tamara threw her arms around Garrett and kissed him with all she had. They began rubbing and feeling all over each other until they fell back onto the couch. She reached up under his shirt and ran her hands up down his narrow chest and back. She felt him lift up her sports bra and begin to knead her nipples. It had been two years since she'd been with a man, and her body was yearning to be pleased that way again. Her mind said, "no," but her body was screaming, "Take me, now!"

Tamara spread her legs as Garrett slipped his hand down the front of her shorts. He ran his fingers threw her soft, curly pubic hairs and gently stroked her clitoris. He let one finger dip in through the folds of her tight vaginal opening and moved it steadily deeper inside. Tamara gasped aloud and her legs seemed to open wider of their own volition. Garrett moved his finger around inside her until she suddenly pushed him away.

"No. We can't."

"Oh, Ma..."

"Please, Gee."

Garrett took a deep breath and got up off the couch. Tamara quickly sat up and pulled her sports bra back down over her breasts.

"You a'ight, Ma?"

"I'm sorry, Gee. I told you that I have to get up early, and I need my rest. Besides...you know..."

"I know. We're movin' kinda fast, right?"

"Yes."

"I know. Don't worry, it's cool."

Tamara leaned forward and put her face in her hands. Garrett sat down and put his arms around her. "I'm so embarrassed," she whined, and started to sob.

"No, Ma. You ain't got nothin' to be embarrassed about. I told you, it's cool. I'm not sweatin' that. It'll happen when it happens."

Tamara sat up, and Garrett wiped her tears with his thumbs. She threw her arms around him, and they embraced and held on to each other tightly. Finally, they released one another and Tamara stood up and extended her hand, which Garrett took and stood up, as well. They embraced again and kissed passionately. Tamara's heartbeats started to pick up its pace. She felt her nipples harden and her vagina start to tingle from the inside out. She broke their kiss and stepped away.

"You'd better get going, Gee."

"A'ight, Ma," Garrett said with an agreeing nod. He watched her lovely, enormous butt bounce with her gluteus folds peeking out from under her shorts as she led him to the door. Her long, well-toned legs took long strides along the way. He shook his head and bit his bottom lip as he admired her thin waist and muscular back, wishing she'd turn around and tell him she'd changed her mind. Instead, he found himself standing outside of her door.

"I'll call you when I get to Phoenix."

"Yeah, do that. I'd like that."

Once again they embraced and kissed, and then their night finally ended.

Tariq and Bruce knocked on Garrett's door around seven-thirty the next evening. Garrett was on the telephone, so he just opened the door and walked away.

"Yo, what's goin' on, Son?" Tariq said in his usual loud, high-pitched voice.

"Sheeesh. Can't you see I'm on the phone?" Garrett snapped before resuming his telephone conversation. "Yeah...Yeah...You know what, make it three dozen...Yeah, a dozen red, a dozen white and a dozen pink...Hook it up real nice, and make sure you get it there by halftime...Yeah...How much is that gonna be now?...Damn, Son!...Nah, it's cool...A'ight, thanks."

"What's up, Gee?" Bruce said while looking through the refrigerator. "You ordering flowers for somebody?"

"Yeah."

"Who?"

"The girl I met the other day."

"What girl?"

"Not that Amazon chick that was tryin' to move in here?" Tariq jumped in.

"Yep, that's the one," Garrett proudly admitted. "She got the apartment, too. It's on now."

"Man, I told you that chick ain't givin' you no ass," Bruce said, laughing as he pulled some beers from the refrigerator.

"Word," Tariq agreed. "She got a nice, fat ass, but she looks like she's into bodybuilding or somethin' like that. She probably dates those huge, cock-strong muthafuckas - or other chicks."

"Word. And Gee is too scrawny to be a bodybuilder, and too ugly to be a chick."

Tariq burst out laughing as he took a beer from Bruce. "You're right about that, Son."

"Nigga, please," Garrett said to Tariq while also taking a beer from Bruce. "I know you ain't talkin' 'bout nobody being ugly and skinny. Look at the cracked-out, no chest, no ass havin' rag dolls you be runnin' around with."

"Whatever, Son. I like little, petite girls. I don't need all that excess T and A. Big asses are just good for lookin' at. I need a chick I can toss around and flip and shit."

"Both of y'all trippin'," Bruce said. "You like tiny pencil-like chicks, and Gee like those big ass, boulder liftin', Zena wannabes. I'm the only sensible one. Look at my wife. Hannah has perfect 36Cs, a nice 25-inch waist and well-rounded 36-inch hips. Her hair comes down to the middle of her back and it's real..."

"Yeah," Tariq interrupted, "but she got buckteeth and a big ass nose, so shut the fuck up."

"Word," Garrett laughed in agreement. "Get her ass a nose job and some braces, and then you can come back and talk that shit."

"Oh, it's like that, huh? I'll tell her that the next time y'all come over and she starts cooking for your punk asses."

Garrett put on a straight face and opened his arms in a pleading gesture. "Why you gotta be like that, Son? Why you gotta take food outta our mouths?"

"You see," Tariq added, "he always gotta take it to the next level. He can't just take a joke. He always gotta be threatenin' niggas."

"Yeah," Bruce said, grinning. "I thought y'alla change your minds."

"Word," Tariq said. "I don't know how we got on everybody else girl, anyway. We were talkin' about that Amazon chick that Gee's tryin' to get wit'."

"Yeah, Gee. What's up with that? You orderin' three dozen roses for this chick and whatnot? What's up?"

"Yo, I'm feelin' this girl, Son," Garrettt began as he led Bruce and Tariq into the living room. "I'm like Jonesin' or whatever. I don't think of no other chick like I do her. She ain't like no other chick."

"So, what's up with Diana?" Tariq asked. "I thought you were tryin' to get serious with her. You're always takin' her and her son places, and they're always staying at your crib and shit. You just gonna drop her?"

"Diana? Oh, damn. I was supposed to go see her tonight, too. I forgot all about her. But that's what I'm sayin', Tamara's got me trippin'. Yo, the moment I saw her I knew she was the one. Bruce, you should know what I'm talkin' 'bout. You said the same thing when you first met Hannah."

"True," Bruce reminisced. "It was like...magic or something. Something just felt right. I knew she'd be mine forever."

Bruce and Tariq sat on the couch as Garrett picked up the remote control and sat in his recliner. "That's what I'm sayin'," Garrett related. "I got serious feelings like that, Son."

Tariq sat forward and rested his elbows on his knees. He twisted his lip and gave Garrett a doubtful look. "You came to this conclusion just by showin' her the way to the management office?"

"No, dumb ass," Garrett snapped. "I mean, yeah. I mean, it started there, but I knew for sure when we were hangin' last night."

"You went out already and didn't tell your boys?"

"Yeah," Bruce said. "What's up with that?"

"It was a last minute thing. I went to see her play, and then we came back and hung out in her crib for a minute."

"See her play? What does she play?"

"She's the starting power forward for the New York Empire."

"Word? She plays pro ball?"

"Yeah. She's got game, too. I'm about to catch her on TV, right now."

"Oh, turn that shit on, Son. I gotta see this."

Tariq put his hand on his chin and stroked his beard as he thought out the scenario. "Let me get this straight," he said. "The chick plays pro ball? Not only that, but she starts, too?"

"Yeah," Garrett confirmed, "and after the season she's gonna coach at Columbia."

"Columbia? Columbia University down Broadway? The Ivy League Columbia?"

"Yeah, why?"

"Man, please. That chick ain't hardly tryin' to mess with you."

"She might," Bruce said. "It sounds like she's just like you, Tariq."

"In what way?"

"You said you like petite women you can toss and flip. Maybe that's why she likes Gee. It wouldn't be hard for her to toss and flip his ass."

Garrett gave Bruce and Tariq the finger as they laughed and gave each other fives. He sat back in the recliner and chugged his beer as he turned to the game. The starting lineups were just being announced.

"They're in Phoenix," Bruce noticed. "You ordered flowers to be delivered in Phoenix?"

"Yeah. I just called FTD in Phoenix. What's wrong with that?"

Bruce gave Garrett a serious nod. It was that moment he knew how serious his best friend of eighteen years was about this woman. He then became a bit worried that Tariq's comments, although said somewhat in jest, may not be too far off base. "Son? I'm sayin', it's cool for you to step to any female any way you like. Do you; you know what I'm sayin'? But...I'm just thinking...maybe you're hittin' her in the head kinda hard, right now. Maybe you're doing a little too much."

Garrett smiled and took another chug of his beer. He thought back to him and Tamara lying on her couch the night before. He remembered how good she smelled and how moist and tight her vagina felt around his finger. "I got this, Son," he said confidently. "I know what you're thinkin', but I got this, a'ight?"

"A'ight," Bruce surrendered.

"There she is," Tariq said, pointing at the television. "Tamara Bingham. She better be good, Son. You know I'mma talk about her ass if she ain't."

By the time half-time came, Tariq had fallen asleep. Garrett was glad because Tamara wasn't playing very well and her team was down by nine points. Tariq's mouth would've been running a mile a minute, and he didn't feel like hearing anything negative. Garrett and Bruce both loved their friend, but they knew he didn't know when to shut up and he often said the wrong thing.

Bruce stood up and stretched. "Ohhh! I gotta go to the bathroom."

"Shhh. Don't wake that muthafucka up," Garrett said. "Let him sit right there, snorin' and droolin'."

Bruce nodded in agreement and walked out. Garrett got up and went into the kitchen for another beer. As soon as he reached the refrigerator, he heard Tariq's annoying, high-pitched voice project through the apartment.

"Yo, where did everybody go? I'm starvin'. Whose turn is it to buy the food?"

"It's your turn," Garrett shouted back to him. "Don't act like you don't know."

"What're we orderin'?"

"What does it matter?" Bruce said as he came out the bathroom. "We'll order it and you'll pay for it. Now go back to sleep until it gets here."

Garrett didn't hear Tariq respond and figured he must've done what Bruce told him to. He called Jimbo's Restaurant and ordered some cheeseburger specials, and then went back in to watch the rest of the game. The second half started and Tamara caught fire. She was scoring from all over the floor and even hit two three-pointers. Her tenacity fired up her teammates and rallied a comeback. Garrett, Tariq and Bruce ate their cheeseburgers and watched Tamara score twenty-one second-half points, finishing with twenty-seven for the game and leading The Empire to an eight point victory.

"That was a good game," Bruce said. "Your girl was holdin' it down, Son."

"I told you. She was killin' like that last night, too, but her team didn't have her back like they did this game."

"See if you can get us some tickets to her next home game," Tariq requested.

"Ah ha! You knew you were enjoyin' that shit, Son."

"It wasn't like watchin' the Knicks, but it was still good. I'm feelin' it."

"Me too," said Bruce. "If you can get some tickets, let us know. Try to get six so that I can bring my wife and daughter, and just in case Tariq can get a date."

"What? I can get a date, Son. How you sound?"

"Well, hold out on that until I find out if she can get us the tickets," Garrett said. "I know she said she could get some, but I don't know how many. We'll see."

Later that night, after Bruce and Tariq had gone home, Garrett was reading Tamara's profile on the WNBL website when his telephone rang. "Hello?"

"Hi, Gee."

"Hey, what's up, Tamara? I watched your game tonight. Congratulations."

"Thank you. And thank you so much for the roses. I never expected that."

"Oh, cool. I'm glad you liked them."

"I loved them. They came right on time, too. When we went into the locker room at halftime and everyone saw that enormous bouquet, we got all excited. When I found out it was from you, I started crying."

"Tears of joy, I hope."

"Oh, yes. Absolutely. But guess what else?"

"What?"

"Well, I hope you don't mind, but since there were so many roses, I gave one to each of my teammates, the coaching staff and the trainers."

"Really?"

"Yes. I wanted them to feel what I was feeling, so I shared my joy with them. Did you see what happened? Did you see how well we played in the second half? That was because of you, Gee. You helped us win."

"Nah, y'all just did y'all thing, Ma, that's all."

"No, it was you. It was like your flowers were our 'Secret Stuff.'"

"Your what?"

"You saw the movie 'Space Jam', right?"

"Yeah."

"Do you remember when the Looney Tunes were losing, and Bugs Bunny put water in a bottle and told them that it would make them play better?"

"Oh, yeah." Garrett laughed.

"Well, that water was their 'Secret Stuff', and the roses you sent was ours. We all took off a petal and kept it on us in the second half. I put mine in my sports bra, right next to my heart. Believe me when I say it made a difference. Now, we're all going to wear a petal on us for the rest of the season, win or lose."

"Yo, that's cool. I'm, like part of the team now."

"Yeah. Oh baby, I can't wait to see you again. I thought about you the whole time we were on the plane. You've stirred feelings up in me that I never thought I'd have again. My life had changed so much after I broke up with my ex-fiancé. But now, I feel a new hope. Just from spending that short time with you. Oh God, I probably shouldn't be saying all of this. I'm probably just scaring you away."

"No, Ma, not at all. I'm feeling that way, too."

"For real?"

"No doubt. I couldn't stop thinking about you, either. I was telling my boys how you had an unfamiliar effect on me. I like what you do to me, Ma. I'm happier knowing that I have the same effect on you. It makes things easier, you know what I'm sayin'?"

"Well, I'm glad. Listen, baby, I can't talk long, but I'll call you every chance I get."

"Okay. Listen; see about getting some tickets to your next home game. Tariq and Bruce wanna roll and Bruce wants to bring his wife and daughter. Tariq may bring a date, too. You know...if it's possible."

"What's that, six tickets altogether? That shouldn't be a problem."

"Thanks, Ma."

"You're welcome. Well, let me go. I'll talk to you soon. Thanks again for the roses and for making me so happy."

"There's more happiness to follow, Ma."

"Goodnight, Gee."

"Goodnight."

Tamara hung the telephone up and sat on the edge of the bed staring into space. Her mind wandered back to her and Garrett sitting on her couch. She thought about how comfortable she felt with him, and how good it felt to be close to him.

"This guy sure has got you open," a voice spoke from behind. Tamara jumped and yelped from being startled. She turned around to see her roommate standing by the door. "I've never seen you like this before."

"Oh, my God, Ellie," Tamara said, placing her hand over her heart. "You scared me. I didn't even hear you come in."

"You're scaring me," Ellie said as she slowly walked over and joined Tamara on her bed. "What's up? You sound real serious about this guy."

"I am. Why wouldn't I be?"

"I don't know. It's apparent that he's pretty serious about you. No man goes out their way like that just to send a woman flowers unless he's totally whipped. You must've put it on him good, girl."

Tamara rolled her eyes, stood up and began to undress.

"No, we haven't gone there, yet."

"You haven't?" Ellie asked, and leaned slightly to look at Tamara's butt as she bent over to step out her sweat pants. She reached out and stroked her posterior through her silky panties. "Mmm, I sure wouldn't have wasted an opportunity to get with you."

Tamara quickly slapped her hand away turned around. "Stop it, Ellie."

"Oh, just like that, huh? Last week you were all upset because we were both on the rag, but now since you've met this guy, you don't want to be bothered with me anymore. That's how it is, huh? We spent eight months together, and now you just want to toss me away like an old pair of shoes. You never even told me about him, Tamara. How long have you been seeing this guy?"

"Look, I don't have to justify my actions to you. I told you a hundred times that you and I are not a couple. I can never call myself being in a relationship with another woman. You knew that what we had was purely physical."

"What we had? Had, Tamara? You're saying it's over between us? Just like that?"

"Come on, Ellie; don't do that."

"Do what, Tamara? Ask for some consideration? Ask to be kept informed of your intentions? Those sound like reasonable things to me."

"You see, that's your problem. You're not even trying to hear me. I'll say it once again: our relationship was purely physical. We never had, nor will we ever have, a relationship. Not like the kind you want. I can't get down like that."

"Oh, I see..."

"Oh, no you don't. Don't even do that. I am not the bad guy. I've been telling you this all along, Ellie. You heard this speech many times before, so you need to just stop. Besides, you think I don't know about you and Christina? You think I'm blind or stupid? I'm not. I know what's going on."

"You're right, I have been seeing Christina. But I don't feel for her the way I do for you. You don't understand..."

"Oh, but I do. It's just that you're my Christina, and I don't feel for you the way I do for Garrett. I love him. I could never love you."

Tamara wanted to take back her forwardness with Ellie as she watched her green eyes fill with water and her face turn beet red. She sat down beside her and hugged her close.

"I'm sorry. I didn't mean for it to come out like that. You've been really good to me and I appreciate it. What we had together was great. You're a great lover and a great friend, but I'm not gay. I'm not even bisexual after tonight."

Ellie lifted her head, streams of tears rolling down her face, and gazed into Tamara's eyes.

"After tonight?" she asked. "You mean..."

Tamara smiled, leaned forward and kissed Ellie softly on the lips. She wiped her tears and cradled her face in her hands. Once again she leaned forward, but this time Ellie threw her arms around her and they kissed hard. Ellie pulled her t-shirt over her head and unfastened her bra, exposing her firm, round breasts with large brown nipples. Tamara pulled off her own t-shirt and sports bra in one motion and threw them on the floor. Ellie pushed her back on the bed, reached up under her hips and pulled her panties off. Tamara lay across the bed totally nude and watched as Ellie finished undressing. Ellie removed her shorts and panties, revealing that she is a natural redhead. Tamara looked up at Ellie's slender, six-foot frame and opened her arms invitingly. Ellie climbed on the bed between Tamara's legs and spread her knees apart. She lowered her head, locked her lips on Tamara's swollen clitoris and sucked on it like a pacifier. She stopped for a moment to stick her fingers into her mouth, lubricating them, and then inserting them together into Tamara's tight vaginal hole. She then returned to sucking on her clitoris with a vengeance, sending her into a frenzied state.

Ellie continued pumping her fingers in and out of Tamara's pussy, fucking her violently while keeping her lips pressed hard against her clit. Tamara seemed to be trying to get away as she began moving backward from kicking her heels into the bed. Ellie wrapped her free arm around Tamara's thigh and tried to hold her in place as best she could. The more Tamara bucked around on the bed, the more violently Ellie pumped into her.

"I'm cumming, Ellie," Tamara whimpered loudly. "Oh, my goodness, yessss!"

Tamara's body went limp and Ellie crawled up on top of her, planting kisses along her chest, neck and face before kissing her deeply. Their tongues entwined, allowing Tamara to taste her own juices. Their breasts pressed together as Ellie ground her crotch hard into Tamara's. The two women held on to each other tightly and continued to grind until they both came.

Tamara and Ellie pulled a sheet over themselves, laid on their sides and snuggled close. Ellie was lying behind Tamara in a spooning position and hugging her tightly. She could hear Tamara's breathing getting heavier and knew she was falling asleep.

"I'm going to miss you, baby," Ellie whispered.

"Um. You'll be fine, Ellie," Tamara grunted. "You have Christina, now. Make the best of that. You'll be happy together."

Ellie moved closer and held on tighter and they both drifted off to sleep.

The Empire finished their West Coast trip, and returned to New York on a three-game winning streak. Tamara lit up the scoreboards in Los Angeles and Minnesota, scoring thirty-seven and thirty-four points, respectively, and earning WNBL Player of the Week honors. She and Garrett talked everyday, which kept her motivated. She and her teammates also kept their roses and wore their petals in every game.

Tamara arrived home around four-thirty Thursday afternoon anxious to see Garrett. She thought for sure that he'd be waiting for her, but he was nowhere to be found. She called his apartment, his cell and his office and left messages at each number. Four hours later, she still hadn't received a call back so she decided to take a walk to the store for some groceries.

Garrett was sitting outside the building in his SUV with Diana. Her eyes were filled with tears from the hurt, anger and confusion she was feeling. She couldn't understand why Garrett was saying the things he was telling her. She listened to his explanations over and over, but couldn't stop asking...

"Why? It still doesn't make any sense to me, Gee."

"I don't know how else to explain it to you, Diana. What else can I say?"

"I don't know. All I know is that you're telling me you never really loved me because you want to leave me for some other bitch you just met."

"I'm not tellin' you that *because* I met somebody else. I just never felt for you the way you feel for me. I thought that maybe my feelings would grow if we spent more time together, but they didn't."

"Yet, you're telling me that you've acquired those feelings for a woman you've only known for a week?"

"I knew right away, Diana. I don't know how to explain it. I went out with her one time and I was sprung."

Diana cut her eyes at Garrett and her nostrils flared in anger. The tears were rolling down her cheeks steadily and she felt herself start to shake. "You went out with her one time, eh? Humph, I guess I'm just not good enough for you. What is it; I'm too fat? Is my complexion wrong? Is it because of Avery? Your new bitch don't have any kids, right?"

"No, it's not because of Avery. Avery's my little man; you know that. And it's not because of the way you look, either. I've always told you that you're fine. I meant that. You're beautiful on the outside and the inside..."

"So why don't you love me, then? We've been together three months and I've never given you any problems. We haven't had one argument. Now, some other woman comes along and you're dropping me like I'm nothing. I guess you don't love me if you can do this to me. You've already gone out with her, for crying out loud. That's probably where you were last Saturday night when you had me waiting on your two-timing ass. I made a sweet potato pie for you and everything, and you didn't even give me the decency of a call. Her stuff must be really good."

"Come on, Diana. Why are you saying that?"

"Because I want to know. Did you fuck her, too? Have we been sharing your dick? You getting your jollies off by fucking two women?"

"No, it's nothin' like that. I haven't had sex with her, yet..."

"Yet? So you want to?"

"Of course I want to if I'm talkin' 'bout getting with her..."

"Fuck you, Gee!" Diana opened the door and started to get out, but Garrett grabbed her arm. "Let me go, you bastard!" she screamed as she pulled her arm free and continued out the truck.

"Diana, I didn't want it to end like this. Please try..." Garrett's sentence was cut short by the thundering sound of the door being slammed in his face. He watched Diana run down into the subway station in front of the building, and then he noticed Tamara standing in the doorway of the building.

"Aw, damn," he sighed aloud.

Slowly, he got out his truck and walked toward her. He watched her standing there, waiting with her arms folded, and he swallowed hard. As he approached her, he put on a wide smile and tried to act cheerful.

"What's up, Ma? Did you just get home?"

Tamara's facial expression displayed her disappointment and anger. She took a deep breath before responding.

"I guess I never did ask whether you had a girlfriend already, or not. I see now that I should've."

"I'm sorry. I should've been honest and told you that I was seeing someone else."

"Yes, you should've."

"I didn't say anything because I knew I wasn't going to be with her anymore."

"Look, Gee, I don't want to come between you and your girlfriend. I wouldn't be comfortable thinking that I'm the reason for you breaking up with her."

"No, don't think that. That's not true. I would've left her eventually, anyway. I just wasn't feelin' her. She was cool and everything, but for some reason I couldn't get close to her. I found myself having way more fun being with her ten-year-old son than with her. I just stayed with her as long as I did because I thought that maybe my feelings for her would grow, but they didn't. Then, when I met you, I felt so much different. All I knew was that I had to be with you. I felt that you were a Godsend."

"Well, what if I were married?"

"Oh, Ma, I would've bugged. I would've had to handle it, but I wouldn't have wanted to. But things don't happen that way. When two people are meant for each other, nothing can come between that. The universe doesn't allow two good people who were meant to be together to meet, and then have a hindrance like a husband or a wife. No, God wouldn't do me like that."

"Really? God and the universe approves of you dumping one woman for another?"

"I told you, I would've broken up with her even if you and I hadn't met. At least that's what I wanted to do. For whatever reason, you came into my life and it gave me a reason to move on it faster. It still took me a while, but I finally had to let her go. She and I were in each other's way. Just like I know that you and I were meant to be together forever, I know that there's another man out there somewhere who's perfect for her and her son. He's probably on that train, seeing her crying and offering her encouraging words right now. What just happened between me and her was probably exactly what she needed to meet him."

"That's what you really believe, huh?"

"Yeah, Ma. She's a good girl, and bad things don't happen to good people. She may think it's bad now, but good things are waiting for her. You're a good girl, too. I know I'm the good thing that's happening to you. That's what I want to be. That's what I'm going to work to be."

Tamara's expression changed. She started thinking about what Garrett was saying and how much he affected her life in the short time they'd known each other. One gesture on his part gave her life a turn for the better and put her on track toward success and happiness. She couldn't deny that. "What are you saying, Gee?" she asked in a humbled tone.

"I'm saying that I want everything that you and I do, from this moment on, to be about us. I want us to be best friends, lovers and partners. No more secrets, I promise."

Tamara dropped her eyes and thought about what Garrett said. "No more secrets" rung out in her mind and she looked up at him again. Staring into his eyes, she could see the love and sincerity, just as she had before. She already knew that she had fallen in love with him, and he just confirmed that he felt the same way, too. With that being the case, she felt compelled to share her secret with him, as well.

"Okay, Gee," she said after exhaling hard. "No more secrets, right?"

"No more," he confirmed. "There ain't much more to me. That's all I had."

"Well, I have something. I had to let someone go from my life, too."

"You had a man?"

"No. The truth is...well...I sorta had...a woman."

Garrett's eyes widened and his mouth hung open at first, then he gathered himself, took a step back, looked Tamara up and down and started grinning.

"Okay, you got that one. You had me for a minute there. A woman."

"Yes, a woman," Tamara reconfirmed. "I'm not joking, Gee. For the past eight months, I've been sleeping with one of my teammates."

"You're not joking, are you?"

"No, I'm not. It was just for physical pleasure, though. She wanted more, but I told her that I could never see myself being in a real relationship with another woman. I didn't want to give myself to any more men after I broke up with my ex-fiancé. I still got horny, though. So when she propositioned me one day, I accepted. Well, my body accepted because sex was all I wanted from her. It was the first time I'd done something like that."

"And now it's over?"

"Yes, it's over. I swear."

"Fine. We've both laid out all of our cards, now. From here, there's nowhere to go but up. You ready to do this?"

"Yes."

"Let's go then," Garrett said, then took Tamara's hand and led her into the building.

Tamara laid face down on her bed with her arms tucked under her head and her eyes closed. She wore a dreamy smile as she waited for Garrett, who was standing beside the bed observing the beauty of her nakedness. He made a trail with his finger from the nape of her neck, down her spine, and between the cheeks of her buttocks. He moved his finger in deeper, tickling and teasing her anus with the threat of entry. He then moved his hand down further to caress the folds of her moist vagina and massaged her swollen clitoris. Tamara moaned with delight from the feel of his hand, and spread her legs further apart so that he could give her more attention.

Garrett kneeled on the side of the bed and placed both hands on the hills of Tamara's large, round posterior and gently caressed, squeezed and kneaded. He then made a trail with his tongue from her foot, up her leg and to her buttocks where he planted tiny kisses and gentle bites all over it.

Tamara continued to grunt and moan as Garrett feasted on her derriere. She gasped each time he let his tongue swipe across her tiny virgin asshole, and jumped whenever he let his tongue journey inside. Her eyes fluttered as he spread her ass-cheeks wider apart and moved his tongue from one opening to the other. Her moans became louder as she experienced her first orgasm of the night from Garrett's tongue invading her two holes.

Garrett sat up and turned Tamara over on her back. She closed her eyes and rested her arms under her head again as Garrett caressed her breasts and leaned forward to suck her nipples. He took his time to milk each one, licking, sucking and nibbling on them continuously. He eventually worked his way down, kissing and licking her stomach, letting his tongue dance in and out of her navel, making a trail down into her full pubic patch, sucking her clitoris, and then letting his tongue dwell within her love tunnel once again. He French kissed her there until her body quaked and her juices made a stream down his chin.

Tamara cradled Garrett's face with her hands and guided him up to her. They kissed savagely while grinding their groins into one another. She reached down and grabbed his throbbing erection and held onto it tightly. She rolled him over without breaking their kiss and laid on top of him. She sucked and licked her way down his neck to his chest. She sucked each of his nipples while stroking his penis, then moved her lips down across his torso. She took the crown of his penis into her mouth and swirled her tongue around the tip as her full lips locked tightly around it. She opened her mouth wide, let his dick slide over her tongue, relaxed her throat and accepted it into her esophagus. His pubic hair tickled her nose and her bottom lip rested on the top of his scrotum.

Garrett was gritting his teeth as Tamara's head rose and fell, taking his full seven and a half inches into her mouth, releasing all but the head, and leaving the shaft glistening with her saliva. Her fingers were massaging his balls and he found it hard to keep still as she sucked his dick more intensely. She made a ring with her thumb and index finger on her free hand and locked it around the base of his shaft, which prevented him from ejaculating too fast. Garrett's legs trembled and he clutched the sheets. Tamara had to get on top of him and turn around in a sixty-nine position to keep him from moving too much. Garrett made the most of that by repeating his earlier procedure of ravishing her hot, wet pussy and her tight, pouting anus. Finally, he cried out announcing that he couldn't be held at bay any longer.

After Tamara finished drinking Garrett's love potion, she turned around and reached over to take a condom from the nightstand. She opened the package and carefully rolled it onto him. Garrett flipped her over gently and they kissed passionately once more as he guided himself into her. Tamara held on to him tighter as he penetrated her, her vaginal muscles contracting and pulling him in, and she raised her legs to receive all of him. Their bodies moved in unison, rocking, grinding, tossing and turning. Their perspiration soaked the sheets that they eventually pulled from the mattress. Tamara had already had multiple orgasms and Garrett finally reached his second. They clutched each other and held on with all they had as they came together and collapsed from exhaustion.

Garrett rolled over on his back and stared up into the ceiling while trying to catch his breath. Tamara snuggled close to him, rested her head on his chest and pulled the sheets over them.

Over the next three months, because of their schedules, Garrett and Tamara only saw each other six times. The Empire's season ended with them losing a game three, double overtime thriller in the semi-finals. But Tamara earned herself a spot on the U.S. National Team and spent the rest of the summer and early fall competing in the Olympics. Immediately after she helped the United States win the gold medal, she started her job at Columbia University. Meanwhile, Garrett spent most of his time traveling and scouting new talent. He signed three new acts, including a singer whose CD he co-produced.

It was New Year's weekend when Garrett and Tamara finally got an opportunity to spend quality time together and brought in the New Year together on vacation in Las Vegas. When they returned to New York City, Mr. Garrett Orr and Mrs. Tamara Bingham-Orr bought a four-bedroom penthouse in the same building so they could prepare to start working on a family the following winter. Two years later, they had their first of three children and lived happily ever after.

More Than a Crush

I was already hyped up for this game coming in because the team we were playing had guys from the NBA playing with them. It was my first time playing in the Entertainer's Classic at the Rucker, and in my first game I was given the nickname "Helicopter" because of my hang time. Now, in my fourth game, I had to show that I was one of the best and that nobody could hold me. I scored sixteen points in the first half, and the crowd was going crazy over how I hung in the air and maneuvered around guys. But that was nothing compared to what I planned for the second half. I had added motivation to perform because I saw her.

Our coach, Happy, a wannabe streetballer who was really just a scrub, was rambling on about something, but I had long since tuned him out. I just kept staring at this girl sitting up in the stands, hoping she'd eventually look my way so I could make some kind of gesture, give some kind of signal, or something. I saw her standing at the bus stop on my way up to the park, but I didn't stop to talk to her because I didn't want to be late for this game. If I knew she was coming here I would've offered her a ride. She was rooting for the other team, but that was all right. She was fine enough to root for whomever she wanted to. Her wide smile showed off her beautiful, straight, white teeth and made her eyes squint. Her skin looked like smooth, rich chocolate, and her hair hung loose down past her shoulders. Umm-umm, she was fine. I just needed to get her attention through the crowd.

The horn sounded to start the second half and I was walking out onto the court when I decided to look up her way again. That's when it happened; we made eye contact. But before I could wave at her or anything, she quickly turned her head and started screaming for Rack 'em Up. Rack 'em Up? I couldn't believe she was there to see that punk ass albino. His real name is Nigel Armstrong, but they call him "Rack 'em Up" because he can score in bunches. When he gets into a groove, he'll drop thirty or forty points before you know what hit you. But he's a loser. He was a McDonald's All American who ended up going to a junior college because of his grades, and then got kicked out of school for selling weed on campus. He probably could've gone to the league, but all he does now is hang around the way selling weed, smoking blunts and getting drunk. We went to the same high school. I was a freshman and he was a senior, so he got all the play. I wasn't hatin', but I knew I was going to have to bust his ass. He already had twelve or fourteen points I think, and I knew he'd go all out to win this game but I couldn't let that happen. Damn, why do women like those drug-dealing thugs like Nigel anyway? Don't they know that the money they're getting from them is just a temporary fix?

"Yo, Todd," I heard Happy calling me. "Getcha head outcha ass and get into the game!"

I don't know who this chump thought he was talking to like that. He couldn't coach his foot into his shoe and he was trying to tell me what to do. I wasn't going to blow up his spot, though. Not right then.

"Chill, Happy," I yelled back. "I got this!"

The second half started and I went right to work. I wanted Nigel to check me, but he kept switching up with one of the NBA cats. It was just as well, I scored my twenty-two second half points, victimizing whoever stepped up. The thirty-eight points I scored that game was my second highest point total. I scored forty-one in my first game out there, but that was against a wack team.

Nigel's team won the game, ninety-three to ninety. He totaled twenty-two points, and the two NBA cats scored twenty-four points each. I busted all three of their asses thinking I'd have that girl riding my jock, but apparently all I did was piss her off. Every time I scored or made a wicked pass (did I mention that I also had nine assists) she'd boo and hiss, waving her hand at me or giving me the finger. I couldn't win for losing. And when the game ended, she ran out of the stands and into Nigel's arms. I put on my hat and turned the brim to the back as I proceeded to exit the park. Nigel and his girl were walking a few feet in front of me holding hands. She was wearing some short booty huggers that showed off her big ole butt and thick, strong legs that looked so smooth and soft.

My sister's girlfriend, Robin, was walking into the park and I saw her stop and talk to Nigel's girl for a moment. I don't know exactly when my oldest sister, June, turned to the other side, but she'd been seeing Robin for about a year from what I understand. I always stayed with June during the summer when I wasn't playing ball overseas, but last summer I got a part in a movie so I stayed in California. Anyway, an immediate smile came over my face when I saw Robin talking to this chick. I knew that I could get the inside track.

Robin noticed me walking toward her as she and the girl said goodbye to each other. She walked up to me with a puzzled look on her face.

"Todd, where are you going?" she asked.

"I'm going home, I just finished playing."

"What? I came to see you play. I thought your game was at seven o'clock."

"Nah, it was at five."

"Shit, I knew I shouldn't have listened to June. She always gets shit mixed up."

"What made you want to come see me play, anyway?"

"I told you I was going to come one day. I wanted to see if you could back up some of the shit you be talkin'. So, did you win?"

"Nah, we lost by three."

"Oh, sorry to hear that. Did those NBA guys play?"

"Oh, that's why you came. You just wanted to see those cats."

"Well, yeah I wanted to see them," she grinned. "But I really wanted to see you play against them, too."

"Well, you missed it. We lost, but I had thirty-eight. I was the game's high scorer."

"Well, at least you did your thing. I'll catch the next one, I promise."

"No doubt. We play next Friday at seven. Come by the house and I'll bring you with me."

"Bet. You goin' home now? Can I get a ride with you?"

"Yeah, c'mon. I need to ask you something anyway."

I drove downtown and Robin sat quietly beside me waiting to hear what I had to ask her. I knew she thought it had something to do with her and my sister, being that I never said anything to her regarding that situation, but I don't pry into my sister's business. I looked into my own eyes in the rearview mirror and reminisced about the brief eye contact I made with that girl. It was that moment that Robin's patience wore out and she interrupted my daydream.

"What was it you wanted to ask me, Todd?" she asked with a huff.

"It's about that girl you were talking to when you were coming into the park."

"What about her?"

"She's the finest girl I ever seen in my life. Who is she?"

"Oh," Robin said, seemingly relieved. "You know that's her man she was holding hands with, right?"

"Dammit, girl. I didn't ask you about her man. I know Nigel, we played ball in high school together. I want to know who that girl he was holding hands with is."

"Damn, it's like that? You ain't got no kinda respect for your boy, huh?"

"He's not my boy. And if he's really tight with his girl, a little competition won't phase him."

"Oh, that ain't right. You're foul, Todd."

"Whatever. How well do you know her?"

"Her name is Bridgette Wells. It's funny that you said you went to school with her man because she and I went to high school and college together. In high school, we were real tight. We went separate ways in college even though we went to the same school and were in the same sorority. She was living the typical college life, partyin', hangin' out and shit like that. I was a bookworm. I was all about studyin' and getting out with the quickness. I love partyin' and shit too; I did a lot of it before I got to college. But I wanted to get out early, so I put that stuff on hold for a while. Now, I've been outta college a year and a half and I party whenever I feel like it. Bridgette is just now going into her senior year and we started at the same time. She's still cool, though. She's real smart, too."

"She can't be that smart if she's running around with Nigel's punk ass. You know he drives an Escalade and lives right on a Hundred and Twenty-First Street, yet I saw his girl standing on One Sixteenth waiting on the bus. What's up with that?"

"Yeah, I know what you mean. She can definitely do better, but it's her choice and she's gonna have to live with it."

"Well, maybe I can save her before she gets in too deep. How long have they been together?"

"About five months."

"Oh, so they're still relatively new," I grinned enthusiastically. "This shouldn't be too hard."

"You're wrong, Todd. You're supposed to respect other people's space, not invade it. How would you like it if somebody did that to you?"

"I'll cross that bridge when and if I get to it. I'm not going to worry about that right now."

"Okay. Just remember, even if you do get her, what goes around comes around."

"I'm not worried about anyone pulling a woman away from me."

"Yeah okay, all the ladies love you, right? Well, just know that when it comes back it's not always the same way. Think about that."

I did think about it. I thought about it, and I thought about Bridgette everyday that week while I was working out and practicing. I thought about laying her on her stomach and massaging her back while listening to a Smooth Grooves CD. Damn, I never wanted a woman as much as I wanted her. I just couldn't figure out why a girl like that, with all her smarts, would be dumb enough to get with Nigel. I guess people can't help who they fall for.

Friday rolled around and I jumped in my coupe and headed uptown around four-thirty. I wanted to get to the park early enough to see Nigel's team play, hoping that Bridgette would be there, too. I drove up Lenox Avenue and stopped at a light on a Hundred and Sixteenth Street. I happened to look over at the bus stop, and like she just appeared out of nowhere, there was Bridgette eating an ice cream cone. I did a double take because I saw the bus pull away just before the light changed and I could've sworn no one was left standing there. But there she was, licking on her ice cream so unconsciously seductive. I knew I had to take advantage of this opportunity, so I blew my horn and waved at her. She looked into my car with a frown and I saw her mouth, "Who is that?"

I lowered my window and called out to her. "Hey! Your name is Bridgette, right? Are you headed to the Rucker to see Rack?"

"Yeah. Who're you?" she shouted back to me.

"C'mon, I'll give you a ride up there."

"I don't think so. I don't know you."

"My name is Todd Green. They call me Helicopter. I played against your man last Saturday."

"Oh, yeah," she said, showing off that beautiful, broad smile of hers. "That was a good game. You tried, but you should've known you couldn't beat my man's team."

"Yeah, well I can set you straight on that on the way up to the park. Hop in." I knew she really wanted the ride even though she still hesitated because it was ninety-three degrees outside and the sun was beaming right in her face.

"C'mon girl, the light's about to change."

She trotted over in her short, form-fitting jersey dress with the NBA logos all over it, trying not to drop her ice cream cone. As she got into the car, her attempt to keep her ice cream from spilling failed and some of it dripped down onto her leg.

"Damn," she said as she quickly wiped her leg with the napkin she was holding, "I knew that was gonna happen."

I looked down and once again admired her silky-smooth, cocoa-colored legs. I get hard just thinking about them. That was the only time in my life I could remember making a wish and seeing it come true right before my eyes because as soon as she finished wiping her leg, she fumbled the cone and it flipped over in her lap.

"Shit!" she exclaimed.

"Don't panic," I said, "Let me pull over so we can get you cleaned up."

I turned the corner on a Hundred and Nineteenth Street and parked. I reached pass her and opened the glove compartment to take out some napkins and looked down into the cleavage of her full, round breasts that were big and ripe like a pair of honeydew melons. Bridgette threw her cone out the window, took some napkins and began to wipe her legs off again. I took some napkins and started helping her. I knew I was taking a chance, but it paid off because she didn't stop me. She welcomed the help and smiled with appreciation. I decided to take things a step further and see if I'd get similar feedback.

"Damn, look at all of this ice cream wasted. I bet your legs taste real good now."

Bridgette snapped her head back and cut her eyes at me. "What? Man, please. I don't need anything on me to taste good. I'm always sweet."

"Yeah?" I smirked. "I'd give anything for a taste."

I expected Bridgette to either slap me or come back with another snappy comment, but instead she reclined her seat, pulled her dress up and pulled her thong to the side. "Taste what, this right here?"

I wasted no time lowering my head and placing a trail of kisses up her thigh. I let my hands dance across her tender flesh from her ankles to her high calves and across her firm outer thighs. My kisses turned into long licks as I used my tongue to clean up the remaining vanilla ice cream, and then I moved up from her inner thighs to the opening of her juicy vagina. Bridgette twisted her body around and raised her left leg so that I could get to her better. I pressed my mouth hard against her neatly trimmed pussy and entered her with my tongue. I took my time sucking her hot vagina while my tongue rolled around inside her and I fingered her tiny, tight anus. She came continuously in my mouth as she bucked and squirmed in her seat. Bridgette was right, she was naturally sweet and I had a good time eating her dessert.

I forgot that I promised to bring Robin with me to the game, so I went back home to get her. When I got there, she and June were in the room with the door closed. I knew they were in there doin' it because their clothes were on the floor in front of the room's door. It was cool, though. It gave me a chance to wash up and brush my teeth. Still, I made sure to make enough noise to alert them that I was in the apartment, hoping they'd wrap things up if Robin was still coming to the game. I wanted to get back up there as soon as possible. I had to see Bridgette and let her know that her days of being Nigel's girl were numbered. I couldn't let him have her; it wasn't right.

As I was coming out of the bathroom, June came out of her bedroom with a sheet wrapped around her.

"Hey, Todd," she said, and proceeded to gather the clothes off the floor. "It's about time you got here. Robin was waiting for you. We thought you stood her up."

"Nah, I just lost track of time, that's all. So, uh, is she still coming?"

"Oh, yeah, for sure," June replied with a devilish grin.

I picked up on her repartee and just twisted my lip. "Well, I'm ready to go. Tell her to come on."

Robin came out, also wearing a sheet.

"Just chill a minute, dude," she said, taking her clothes from June. "I gotta freshin' up first. I'll just be a few minutes."

She headed into the bathroom and I stepped aside to let her pass. June followed in behind her.

"Whoa, where are you going?" I asked my sister. "I told you I'm in a rush."

"Boy, please," June said, waving her hand at me. "Go sit down somewhere. We'll be out in five or ten minutes."

I started to ask June if she was coming too, but I didn't want to give her any ideas that'll have those five or ten minutes turn into fifteen or twenty. Instead, I said, "Oh, are you joining us?"

"No, I'm going to the supermarket. We need some food in this house."

"Damn, Sis. You used to love to come see me play. Now I can't pay you to come to a game."

"Oh, don't be like that. I've just been busy, that's all. I know you're the man. Get your ass in the league and I'll definitely come to see you then." She winked at me, stepped into the bathroom and closed the door behind her.

Women are hard enough to understand, but bisexual women the most confusing of them all.

Instead of going into my bedroom, I sat on the couch loungin' around thinking about Bridgette until Robin came out of the bathroom.

"Okay, let's go," I said as I jumped up and marched toward the door.

"Damn, why are you in such a hurry?" June asked as she followed out behind Robin.

"I got some business to take care of in the park before the game starts."

Robin rolled her eyes up in her head and turned around to give June a goodbye kiss. "I'll see you later on, Ma."

As Robin and I got out of my car and walked to the park, we saw Nigel and Bridgette standing across the street. He was angry with her about something and had his finger all up in her face. She had a frightened look on her face and was trying to plead her case. I wanted to go over there and pull her away from him, and dare him to utter a word to me or make a gesture like he was going to do something. Robin must've seen the look in my eyes because she grabbed my arm and pulled me toward the park entrance.

"Bring your ass on, Todd," she said. "That ain't none of your business."

I wanted to make it my business. I wanted to go over there, punch Nigel in his face and hold Bridgette close to me so she wouldn't have to be scared anymore. What was he doing outside anyway? The game had already started and he was supposed to be inside playing.

"Come on, I said," Robin demanded, as she pulled on me harder.

When we got inside the park, I saw that Nigel's team was already up by twenty-two points in the second quarter. The bench was in the game having a field day, which explained why Nigel wasn't playing. I still wanted to go back out and see what was going on with Bridgette, but Happy came over and talked Robin and I to death. Just before halftime, I saw Nigel walk into the park with Bridgette in tow. Now she was smiling from ear to ear and he wore the frown. Apparently, she somehow managed to flip the script. I watched as he led her to get his bag, and he pulled out a knot, peeled of a couple of bills from it and handed it to her. She looked in our direction and waved at Robin.

"Hey, girl," she shouted.

"Hey, Bridgette," Robin waved back. "What's up?"

"Nothing, girl. I see you're here a lot. Who're you here to see?"

"I came to see my boy Helicopter play next," Robin said, pointing her thumb at me.

"Oh," Bridgette replied after glancing at me briefly. "Well, I gotta run. I'll catch you later."

"You're not staying for the rest of the game?"
"No. I gotta go get my hair done."
"Okay, take care."
"You too, girl."

I watched Bridgette standing there as she shoved the bills into her Coach bag, her navel ring hanging from her stomach matching the charm on her body bracelet, her long legs descending from her low-cut denim mini-skirt and her nipples trying to force their way out of her tube top. My whole body got hard, my dick, my nipples, my tongue, everything. I'm telling you, I've never been this hung up over a woman before. Especially a woman I didn't even know. Meanwhile, she paid me no mind and quickly turned away making double-time out of the park.

I gave Robin a performance to go back and rave to June about as I totaled thirty-six points, which included eight high flying dunks over and around defenders, and an array of aerial feats that people will be talking about for years to come. My twelve assists and ten rebounds made for my first triple-double of the tournament. I perform best when I am really excited or really upset. I was upset seeing Nigel all up in Bridgette's face the way he was, and also because she left before I could talk to her. I took it out on the opposing team and made Happy very happy with the ninety-eight to seventy-three win.

The following Tuesday I drove out to Kings Plaza Mall in Brooklyn. My boy Curtis manages a Foot Locker there so I get my sneakers and basketball gear on discount. The last person I expected to see there was Bridgette, but there she was standing by the payphones getting ready to make a call. I started to walk over to her when I saw - you guessed it - Nigel. He was walking toward her from the opposite direction with his arms full of bags, so I ducked into a store so he wouldn't see me. I didn't even want to speak to his punk ass. I peeked out to see if they were leaving and which way they'd go and saw Bridgette pointing, sending Nigel in my direction.

"Would you just go?" I heard her say to him. "I'll be there in a minute."
"Who you callin'?" he asked her.
"None of your business. Just go."
"Why you usin' a payphone? Where's your cell phone?"
"The battery died. Now get out of here."
"Who you callin', Bridgette?"
"I'm calling my mother to see if she wants those drapes we saw. Damn. You want to stand here and take minutes on our conversation, or do you want to get my jacket like I asked you?"
"Keep bein' smart and yo' ass won't get shit, bitch."
"Whatever."

Nigel headed right for the store I was in. Since I couldn't avoid the inevitable, I stepped out of the doorway.

"Ohhh, shit!" he said when he saw me. "My man Helicopter. What's goin' on, nigga?"

"What's up, Rack?" I said cordially as we embraced in a shoulder hug. He reeked of alcohol. "I never expected to run into you out here."

"Yeah, my girl just had to have a dress she saw in Macy's. We went to Thirty-Fourth Street and to Fulton Street and neither one of them had it, so we ended up all the way the fuck out here. That's what I get for havin' a high maintenance bitch."

"Well, you know how women are; it's all about the loot."

"Yeah, well her constant need for the loot is gonna get her ass the boot."

He let out a roaring, drunken laugh at his own joke and held out his hand to me. I faked a grin and gave him a pound to humor him.

"Yeah, but that's my heart, though," he admitted. "I love her to death."

He told me he loved her. The words stabbed through me like a spear. There was a humbled expression on his face and sincerity in his eyes. What was I doing? I started to think that Robin was right. No matter how bad Nigel seemed to be treating her, it would be wrong for me to come between them, or as Robin put it, "invade their space." I looked at Nigel standing there exposing his heart to me, then looked past him at Bridgette standing at the payphones. She was so radiant. She stood out like a shining star in a black sky. That's when my cell phone rang. I excused myself and answered.

"Can you get rid of your boy so I can talk to you, please?"

I went into temporary shock. I looked past Nigel again and saw Bridgette gesturing for me to get rid of him.

I swallowed hard and muttered my response.

"Ah, yeah, yeah, I can do that. I've been wanting to talk to you anyway. Hold on." I turned my attention back to Nigel. "Yo, I'll catch up with you later, I need to take this call."

"No problem. I gotta get in here anyway before my girl starts buggin'. I'll see you on the courts."

"Yeah, no doubt."

We gave each other another shoulder hug and Nigel went into the store as I slowly strolled toward the payphones while resuming my phone call.

"Hey, what's up?"

"You. Robin told me that you were trying to get in contact with me."

"Yeah, well, you know..."

"I asked her for your number to call you. I figured it would be safer than you calling me at an inappropriate time. You know what I'm saying?"

"Yeah, I hear you," I said as our eyes locked and I continued to walk toward her.

"So, what's up? Why were you trying to reach me?"

"I think you know the answer to that, especially after what happened last week."

"Oh, so I take it you haven't had your fill. You hungry for more?"

"No doubt," I said as I finally reached her, gazing deeper into her big, brown, almond-shaped eyes. "But I want all of you this time, inside and out."

She smiled teasingly and turned her back to me. "I'm sure you do. But if I let you have more of me you might get hooked. Why should I risk what I have with Nigel just for a good lay?"

"I'm not asking you to risk anything with Nigel," I said, turning my back to hers, "and I'm not just looking to give you a good lay. When I said that I wanted all of you inside and out, I didn't just mean your body. I want your heart, soul and mind, as well. You have no idea what you do to me and how strongly I feel about you. Trust me, it's not my style to step on people's toes, but when it comes to you I don't care who I have to step on to get to you; especially if it's somebody like Nigel. You know he's not the one for you. You're a smart girl, and you're not blind."

"What makes you so different? I mean, if the way you use your tongue is any indication as to what making love to you would be like, I know for sure you have what I've been missing and I definitely want more of it. But still, that doesn't mean that you're the man for me. How do I know that you're the one who can love me the way I need to be loved, and treat me with the kind of respect that I deserve? Nigel is wild, but I can handle him most of the time. Besides, I get everything I need and all that I want from Nigel. I know what I have, but I don't know what I'm going to get."

"And you'll never know if you don't give yourself a chance. You need to escape that glass house he has you living in. You aren't getting all that you need and want from him if you say the intimacy needs work."

"Yeah, it definitely does. That's for sure."

"So, what are you doing? You're settling that's what. And I know he doesn't give you all the respect you deserve because I saw how he was all up in your face at the park last week. Next he'll be whipping your ass, and don't think it won't happen."

"I'm not saying that. I know what you're saying." She let out a heavy sigh. "What are we going to do?"

At that moment I saw Nigel walking back toward us. "Look, why don't you come see me tonight. I'll have Robin call you and give you my address."

Nigel approached her. "You ain't finished yappin' yet?" he shouted. I turned and faced him to let him know he was disturbing my phone call. "My bad, Son," he said, and lowered his tone. "Girl, get off that phone and come on."

Bridgette thought fast and gave me my reply. "Okay, Mommy. I'll get it and come by tonight. Bye."

Nigel got loud again as soon as Bridgette hung up the telephone.

"I ain't stoppin' in no more stores, Bridgette! Fuck that! You buy your mom's curtains on your own time. I got your jacket, so we're gettin' the fuck outta here!"

"Whatever, Nigel," she said, ignoring his antics. "Come on, the store is right there."

Bridgette walked off without looking back and Nigel followed her back into Macy's complaining the whole time. I put my cell phone away and walked away smiling. I hurried home to prepare for my date.

I had to promise to chauffer June around town all day the following Saturday in order to get her to vacate the premises and stay with Robin that night. Bridgette called and said she'd be there at nine o'clock, which gave me enough time to set the mood for us. I put on some Mighty Romancer love songs CDs, lit some candles, ran a hot bath and placed some rose petals all over my bed. No, I wasn't getting ahead of myself. Sex was the one thing Bridgette definitely wanted. She was just missing the romance part of it. My mission was still to get her to be mine forever.

I didn't trip when Bridgette arrived eighteen minutes late. After Seven was singing "Ready or Not" when I opened the door, and I was awed at the sight of her. I didn't think she could get any more beautiful but I should've known. She wore a blue, silk dress with matching sandal pumps, and her hair was up in a French Roll leaving her long, slender neck exposed. Without saying a word I took her into my arms and kissed her with all I had. She threw her arms around me and responded in kind.

"I love you, Bridgette," I blurted out, still holding her close. "I know we hardly know each other, but I know what I feel and how strongly I feel it for you."

"I know," she smiled. "I can tell. That's why I came tonight."

"You're all a real man can ever want, and ever ask for."

"You sure you're not just infatuated?"

"This is real love, baby. This is more than a crush. I need you. I want you to be my wife one day. I want to take you overseas with me if I don't make an NBA team this season. And if I do, I want you there with me wherever I end up. You don't need Nigel and all the bullshit he brings uptown with him. With me you'll be drama free."

Bridgette walked past me to the middle of the living room and turned around. "Okay," she said, "you're right. I know what I have is not even close to being good enough. I want to be with you." She removed the straps from her shoulders and let her dress fall to the floor. She wore no underwear and I drooled at the sight of her beautiful brown body. "Now come give me what I need," she whispered.

SWV sang to the sound of "Rain" and I began undressing myself as I walked over to her. When I stepped out of my pants, she dropped to her knees and ran her fingers along my hard penis. She stroked it gently with one hand while massaging my scrotum with the other. I watched as she parted her lovely, full lips and placed them softly against the crown. Then she closed her eyes, opened her mouth wider, stuck out her pierced tongue and licked it around and around slowly. I reached down and stroked her thin-waxed eyebrows with my thumbs as she kissed and licked the head of my dick some more. Finally, she opened her mouth wider and patiently received my organ into her throat. She continued to stoke it while massaging my balls as she took her time and sucked my dick with expertise. No wonder Nigel said he loved her.

Bridgette's head moved back and forth and she hummed with delight, but all I could do was fight to keep my balance as I threw my head back and closed my eyes. When I finally came, Bridgette closed her mouth tight and let my sperm ooze out all over her lips and drip down her chin and onto her neck. Then she took my dick into her mouth again and sucked a little faster while stroking it a little harder. She never stopped massaging my balls, and within a minute or so I was shooting out another load. This time she drank every drop. I fought to keep my wobbly knees from giving in.

"Okay, I think you're ready now," she said while licking her lips as she stood to her feet.

"Ready for what?" I asked, dumbfounded.

"Ready to please me slow, hard and long," she replied in a seductively husky tone. "We have a long night ahead of us, baby."

I raised a brow as all sorts of naughty thoughts filled my brain. I was going to give her exactly what she was asking for and much, much more. I took her hand and led her into the bathroom. We got into the bathtub together and she sat between my legs and leaned back against me. The contrast of her smooth, dark skin and my light-golden complexion was a perfect match. I rubbed her shoulders and arms while nibbling on her earlobe and kissing her neck. She raised her legs out of the water and rested them on the sides of the tub. She had incredibly beautiful feet with a French pedicure and rings on two of her perfect toes. She ran her long fingernails back and forth along my thighs under the water and laid her head back against me. I moved my hands around to her breasts and cupped them in my palms. Then I took the sponge, lathered it up and gently washed her neck, chest and breasts.

Bridgette was moaning softly as I moved the sponge across her body, and she moved her hands from my thighs to between her own. I squeezed soapy water from the sponge all over her back and chest and her perky, erect, dark nipples pointed straight out. She took two fingers on her right hand and buried them deep inside her vagina while she used two fingers on her left hand to rub her clit. I continued washing her body as she fucked herself violently and cried out with pleasure. My rock-hard dick was aching from being wedged between our bodies instead of up inside her. I was real tempted to enter her at that moment, but I wanted to see her make herself cum. Finally, her body shook and made the water splash all over the place.

"OH! OH! OH!" Bridgette cried. Her eyes rolled back in her head and her toes pointed as she reached her climax. I was smiling from ear to ear and just kept rubbing the sponge all over her until her breathing calmed. Then she laid back and rested against me and I washed our bodies over again.

We got out the tub and I made Bridgette just stand there while I dried us both off with an oversized towel. Then I cocooned her in it and carried her to my bedroom. She just submitted to me and lied limp with her head rested against my chest. We got to the bedroom and the moonlight was shining through the window, setting a romantic atmosphere. I let Bridgette down and unwrapped the towel from around her letting it fall to the floor. Then I picked her up again and went to place her on the bed, but she threw her arms around me and we kissed deeply. We stood there for what seemed like hours with her cradled in my arms, her soft lips pressed against mine and her arms locked tightly around my neck. I finally let her down on the bed and she squirmed and giggled a bit from lying on the rose petals. She playfully rolled over on her stomach, hugged a pillow and kicked her feet up and down. She looked so comfortable, totally at home and completely relaxed.

I climbed up onto the bed and placed my hands on Bridgette's beautiful, round, ample ass and squeezed tightly while I admired the curvature of her back. She slid her legs open wide as I moved on my knees behind her. I spread her cheeks apart and licked my lips at the sight of the lovely folds of her vulva and her pouting anus. I continued to hold her cheek open on one side while I ran my fingers into her moist vaginal opening and my thumb caress the entrance of her rectal cavity. Bridgette raised her hips from the bed to receive my hand, but I needed to taste her again, so I lowered my head and briefly teased her anus with the tip of my tongue. I then moved down, making a trail to her delicious pussy and wiggled my tongue past her tender folds into her sweet hole. I ate her pussy like it was my last meal, occasionally having to raise my head and take in some oxygen.

The time had come. I turned Bridgette over on her back and gently spread her legs apart. I looked down at her and she was looking up at me with an endearing expression. Her eyes were glassy and she let out tiny pants as she eagerly anticipated what was about to happen next. The intro to Michael Jackson's song "Lady in My Life" came on, which was ideal because Mike said everything in that song that I wanted to say to Bridgette. The timing was impeccable.

I entered her as I whispered in her ear, "I dedicate this song to you because the lady in my life is exactly what I want you to be."

As she received me, Bridgette gasped and whispered, "Yes, Todd."

Her velvety warmth pulled me in, engulfed me and held on tight. Our bodies drifted out into an ocean of love and we swam together in timeless currents of pure bliss.

A tapping at my door awakened me the next morning. I rolled over and stretched. "Come in," I grunted.

June opened the door and peeked her head inside. "Don't ask me why," she said, "but I feel like cooking this morning. You want some grits, eggs and salmon cakes?"

"Oh, hell yeah, Sis. That'll definitely work."

"Okay. Hey, what happened in here? Why are your sheets pulled all of the bed? You have a bad dream or something?"

"Nah, Sis." I grinned. "I had a good dream."

June frowned and turned to leave the room.

"That's nasty, Todd. You're twenty-five years old and still having wet dreams. You should be ashamed of yourself."

I laughed out loud as June closed the door when she left the room. So, now you know. All of last night was just a dream, a fantasy played out in my subconscious mind while I slept. I daydream about Bridgette so much that now I'm having real dreams about her. I went to sleep thinking about what would've happened if she really was talking to me on the phone at the mall instead of to her mother. What would've happened if I would've actually saw her at the bus stop again last Friday? I know that if I ever get the chance to really talk to her, I would definitely make my fantasies reality. For now, though, I'll take heed to Robin's advice and respect her relationship with Nigel, even if he is a pothead, drunken asshole. He told me he loves her, that part was real. He'll mess up soon enough, though. When he does, I'll be right there waiting.

Pleasure Apartment

Camille eagerly opened the letter she received from the Dunns, her former landlords. Before she got married and moved into her husband's New York City condominium across from Central Park, she lived in the Dunns' four-story walk-up in South Philadelphia and shared a very unusual landlord-tenant relationship. She had the best setup any single woman could ask for.

Camille thought back to the day she called Missus Dunn upstairs to her apartment. She wanted her to ask Mister Dunn if she could do the maintenance work around the building, and perhaps even clean their apartment for them because she had just been fired from her job. She was already living from paycheck to paycheck and had no extra money saved, so she was willing to do anything to keep a roof over her head. She knew Mister Dunn always did all the work in the building himself when he got home from his day job, and figured she'd be doing him a favor by taking over for him. Missus Dunn had a different idea.

"Well, Camille," Missus Dunn said with a sigh, "I don't know. My husband loves working around the building. He loves his tools, and he loves using his hands."

"Well, maybe I could assist him," Camille pleaded. "We could work together. Please, just until I find another job. I don't want to lose this apartment. I love it here."

"I know you do, and we love having you here. You're our favorite tenant. We talk about you all the time."

Camille was surprised to hear that since she hardly spoke to her landlords. She lived in that apartment for almost two years, but usually only saw them when it was time to pay the rent, and sometimes when they passed in the hallway. "You talk about me all the time?"

"We sure do. Les says you remind him of me thirty years ago when I was about your age. I must say I have to agree. I used to have a figure like yours, and long, pretty hair. Is it yours, or is it sewn in?"

Camille grinned at Missus Dunn's forwardness. "No, it's not sewn. My mother took real good care of my hair when I was growing up, and I make sure I do the same."

"Yeah, my mama did the same thing. You see, Les was right about us. I just hope not in every way."

"What do you mean, Missus Dunn?"

"Sit down, dear." The two women sat down at the kitchen table across from one another. Camille looked at Missus Dunn and wondered if she was going to look like that one day. Missus Dunn was still very beautiful. She grayed very early, but it highlighted her fudge-colored complexion. The years and four sons added pounds to her, but she carried herself very well.

"How old are you, sweetie?" Missus Dunn asked.

"I'm twenty-seven."

"Twenty-seven. Hmm. Why aren't you married?"

"I just haven't found the right man yet, that's all."

"Waiting for a knight in shining armor?"

"Oh, no. I just want to meet someone nice who's not a liar, doesn't have kids all over the place, not into playing games, and just wants to love me for me. Nothing or no one else would matter. No wandering eyes either."

"Well baby, that's all nice, but what are you going to give him in return?"

"Everything. Everything I am and everything I have. For the man that's right for me, there's nothing I wouldn't do."

"It's good you feel that way. I'm not as strong. Les is good - real good to me - but there is just one line that I've never been able to bring myself to cross. You see, I was raised to believe that anything except conventional, missionary-style lovemaking was vile and disgusting. I was always taught that everything else is a sin. I never got over that. I haven't been the best of a bedmate for Les and I know that. I won't let him touch me certain places and I cannot stand to have him slobbering and licking all over me. We've been married thirty-three years and have never had oral sex once."

Camille eyes were about to pop out of her head and she covered her mouth in disbelief. She would've never guessed that Missus Dunn would talk to her about this. She was always so proper and diva-like. "Missus Dunn, I...I...don't know what to say," Camille stuttered as she removed her hand from her mouth and placed it on her chest.

"I think you know what I'm asking, Camille. You're young, beautiful and unattached. You wouldn't have to do anything. In fact, I insist that you don't. All you have to do is lay there and let him perform on you. Nothing else. Les doesn't even know about this yet, but I know my husband and I know I can get him to agree to it. You're in a situation, sweetie. And this is an ideal way to solve both of our problems. In lieu of paying rent, you allow my husband to spend an hour with you twice a week. No penetration and you don't have to reciprocate."

Camille was sweating all over and her heart was racing. She still couldn't believe what she was hearing. The Dunns were such mild-mannered, wholesome, respectable people. She pictured Mister Dunn in her mind. He was short and stocky, but not unattractive. He didn't have nearly as much gray as Missus Dunn, his coffee-toned face was always clean-shaven, and he always spoke very politely. She looked at Missus Dunn sitting across from her with a serious expression on her face. Either this woman was very serious about her proposition or the best actress she'd ever seen. After forty-five minutes of discussing the dos and don'ts and all of the other particulars, Camille tentatively agreed to go through with Missus Dunn's indecent proposal.

Missus Dunn went back to her apartment to propose the idea to her husband and Camille went into her bedroom and sat on her bed. "Oh, God," she thought to herself. "I am such a whore for going through with this." She got up and stood in front of her full-length mirror and looked herself over. She shook her head at herself and decided that she couldn't go through with it. "Oh, forget it," she said aloud. "I can't do it. I *won't* do it. I'll just have to go out and look harder for work. When I leave this house tomorrow, I'm not coming back until I have a job."

Camille crawled into her bed and closed her eyes. Before she knew it, she had drifted off to sleep. After a while, she could feel a hand pinching her nipples and another hand stroking her clit. She fluttered her eyes open to see Mister Dunn lying between her legs with one hand reaching up under her t-shirt. She looked over and saw her shorts and panties thrown to the side of the bed. "How could I have slept through all of that?" she thought to herself. Then, she felt Mister Dunn insert his fingers into her pussy and she lifted her knees to open herself up to him. He continued massaging her nipples with one hand and pumped his fingers in and out of her with the other.

Camille closed her eyes tight. She felt her body begin to quake and her juices start to cascade out of her. She tossed her head from side to side and began shouting, "Oh, yes! Like that! Yes!" until she heard the telephone ringing. She opened her eyes and looked around the room. There was no sign of Mister Dunn. She looked down at herself and saw she had one hand on her breast and the other between her legs with her own fingers buried inside of her cunt. "A dream," she said. "It was just a dream."

Smiling, Camille slowly withdrew her fingers from her love hole. The answering machine picked up and Missus Dunn's voice came from the speaker. "Hello? Camille? Are you there, sweetie?"

Camille picked up the telephone and answered, "Yes. Hello. Missus Dunn?"

"Yes. Did you fall asleep or something?"

"Yes, I did. Sorry."

"Oh, that's okay. I just called to say that everything's a go for tonight on this end. Are you still up to this?"

"Uh...well..." Camille hesitated.

"Look, there's no pressure. You probably didn't have enough time to think about it since you fell asleep. Why don't you just get back to me tomorrow?"

"No!" Camille blurted out unintentionally. "What I mean is...well, sleeping on it actually helped my decision." She inhaled deeply and blew out hard. "Yes. We...uh...we can get together tonight."

"Very good. We'll come upstairs in an hour."

Camille thought Missus Dunn sounded like they just confirmed a business date as she hung up the telephone. Then, she realized that it was exactly that. Mister Dunn is the only one who is supposed to be getting any pleasure out of this. "Fuck that!" she said as she jumped out of the bed. "If I'm going through with this, I'm going to get more out of it than..." Suddenly, her enthusiasm wilted. "No, this is business. I have to approach it that way and make sure it stays that way. Damn, I *am* a whore."

Camille couldn't help but to keep debating with herself back and forth as she showered, douched, perfumed up, put on her makeup and donned her purple teddy. Again, she stood in front of her full-length mirror staring at herself. She was beautiful if she had to say so herself. She finally put the thoughts of her compromising her morals or selling herself short out of her mind and decided that she was getting the best of this deal.

"Wow," she said, smiling into the mirror, "I get to live here rent free and get my pussy eaten twice a week. I've got it made."

At that moment, Camille's doorbell rang. She opened the door and let Mister and Missus Dunn inside. Mister Dunn displayed a broad smile as his eyes danced all over Camille's body. Camille looked over at Missus Dunn who had a blank expression on her face.

"Well, I guess we'd better go into the bedroom," Camille suggested.

"No," Mister Dunn said, grinning from ear to ear. "Let's go into the kitchen."

"The kitchen?" both women asked in unison.

Mister Dunn took both of them by the hand and led them into Camille's kitchen. He pulled a chair out for his wife to sit down and instructed Camille to sit on the edge of the sink. "Hold on to the handles on the cabinet doors," he said as he helped her up. Then he reached behind her and turned on the water. "Now, don't move. This is going to be cold." He took a cup out of one of the cabinets, filled it with water and poured it slowly onto Camille, soaking the front of her teddy and causing her nipples to stand at attention. Camille gasped out loud as she felt her body shiver. Mister Dunn filled the glass again and again and continuously doused Camille until her teddy was completely soaked and sticking to her. Her body trembled as she held on to the cabinet doors tightly.

Mister Dunn put the cup down, turned off the water, squatted down and positioned his face between Camille's legs. He grabbed both of her legs and began running his tongue from her right knee, along her cold, wet inner right thigh, and over her wet purple panties. He started over at her left knee and followed the same routine. Then, he stood up, reached up under her and removed her panties. He squatted down again and began flicking his tongue on her cold, hard clit. He opened his mouth wide, covering her entire vaginal opening, and began sucking loudly on her outer lips. He stuck his tongue into Camille's throbbing cunt, which was rapidly heating up, and she began to whimper. Soon, her whole pubic area was heated. Mister Dunn let his tongue probe deep into her pussy causing her juices to flow into his mouth.

Camille was moaning loudly as she threw her head back and closed her eyes. She felt Mister Dunn furiously sucking on her clit and felt another orgasm building up inside of her.

"OHHHH, YESSSS!" Camille yelled as she came hard from Mister Dunn's tongue darting inside of her and his mouth pressing against her pussy lips again. He didn't stop his oral assault for another thirty minutes. Camille became weak from cumming so many times, and her clit was numb.

Mister Dunn stood to his feet and helped Camille down off the sink. Her knees were weak, and she stumbled to the table and sat on the chair beside Missus Dunn, who still had the same blank expression on her face. She looked over at Mister Dunn, who was smiling and licking his lips.

"You okay?" Missus Dunn asked Camille.

"Uh huh," she mumbled and rested her head down on the table.

Missus Dunn stood up and took her husband by the hand. "Come on, Les," she said. "We have our own business to take care of."

Camille watched as her landlords walked hand-in-hand out of the kitchen and back into the living room. She sat there trying to get her strength back when she realized she didn't hear them leave the apartment. Slowly, she got up from the table and went into the living room. There they were, laying on her couch completely nude, making love. Camille watched them hug tightly and kiss passionately. She watched Mister Dunn's backside rise and fall, then make circular motions on top of his wife. Missus Dunn's legs were spread open wide, one foot on the floor and the other leg resting on the top of the sofa. Her eyes were closed and she had a dreamy look on her face. Camille curled up in the loveseat facing them and watched until they finished.

Camille found a job three weeks later, but still spent Friday nights in the Dunn's apartment and they spent Saturday nights in hers for a year. Each time, Missus Dunn would watch Mister Dunn eat Camille out to his heart's content, then Camille would watch the two of them make love. Sometimes they'd go out for dinner first, or one of them would cook. The games stopped when Camille met a man, fell in love, got married and moved away.

The Dunns wrote in their letter that they finally found a suitable replacement to rent Camille's apartment to.

"It took us five months," the letter said, "but we finally found a girl who is just wonderful. It took a little while to convince her that we were serious, but it was worth it. We're all doing just fine."

Anything For Neicy

"Why, Jerome? Why not?" Neicy kept asking as she followed me from the bedroom to the kitchen.

I opened the refrigerator door and searched aimlessly throughout. "Because I can't get with the whole submissive, no control thing," I told her for what seemed like the millionth time.

"That's some bullshit. I can't believe this. What do you think I'm going to do to you? Do you really think I'd hurt you?"

"No. I'm just paranoid about things like that. I hate being defenseless and unable to use my hands."

"But that's what makes it exciting. I want to have complete control without you eventually taking over the situation."

I grabbed a jar of strawberry preserves from the refrigerator door and walked over to the cabinets. "I can't help it, babe. You're so damn sexy, and you get me so damn hot. I loose control when I'm with you. I can't resist your fine ass even though it has been filling out more these days."

"Fuck you, Jerome," Neicy barked. She knew I was just joking. I love the way she looks. But she had been gaining weight over the past year and it was getting to be more noticeable. Neicy was always in good physical shape because she played volleyball and ran track in high school and college. Even after we got married and had three children, she continued to work out regularly, so her body was still fabulous. Then, one day, she just stopped and her metabolism went to work on her. She is still in no way fat, but she's not a size six anymore either. At thirty-four years old, she stands five-nine with long muscular legs, broad shoulders and a set of beautiful, round breasts. Her hips were widening, though. And there was a little bit of fluff in her mid-section. She always had a nice round butt, but it has filled out to what is better known as ghetto booty.

It doesn't matter to me, though. I love how Neicy has filled out. It was her who complained about getting fat. I always assured her that she was still the finest woman on earth, but I do tease her when she starts nagging me, hoping that she'd get mad and leave me alone. It's not right and I know it, but it usually does work. It didn't work this time. She was adamant about getting her way, and nothing I said or did would suffice until she got it.

"Well, you can fuck me," I said sarcastically as I took the peanut butter down from the cabinet, "but I won't be tied up when you do it."

"I bet if I gave you your fantasy..."

"Ahh, but you won't," I interrupted. "You'd never let me have a *ménage à trois* with you and another woman."

"Why should I? That's just giving you permission to fuck somebody else. I'm not doing that. I'll never, ever give you permission to fuck another woman."

"Just like I'll never, ever give you permission to tie me up."

Neicy let out a long loud sigh as she folded her arms and leaned back against the adjacent counter. I took the bread from the breadbox and started making my sandwiches. I tried to ignore her as she glared at me, looking me over from head to toe. Just as I finished making my second sandwich, she sucked her teeth and headed out the kitchen.

"Talking about me," she said. "You're the one who needs to lay off all that sugar and bread. Black ass Santa Claus."

That wasn't right. She didn't have to say that. So what, I got a gut. I'm thirty-six. Most men my age have at least a little playground for their woman to play on. I've always been husky. I'm two-twenty and solid. Still, she didn't have to go there. Dang. I can dish it out, but I can't take it too well. I don't care. I still ate those damn sandwiches.

A month later, Neicy and I celebrated our eleventh wedding anniversary. Her best friend, Tania, threw us a nice dinner party at our apartment with nine more of our closest friends. I had to admit that it was very nice, despite the fact that Tania put it together. It was about time she did something right. She and I never got along. Our friends called us Martin and Pam after the characters from the show "Martin." It was a good comparison.

To me, Tania was just a stuck up floozy. She thought the sun rose and set on her ass. She ran through men and women like kids run through sneakers. She would fall in love with a guy, which only would last for two or three months, then go back to hating all men. Then she'd go find a girlfriend to be with for two or three months. It was an ongoing routine of hers. She had no problems getting men or women either. I mean, I guess she could be considered attractive if you like short Philippine women with long, wavy hair. Whatever.

Tania outdid herself with the party, though. I think I even caught myself smiling with her at one point during the evening. The catering was splendid, the decorations were amazing, the atmosphere was exotic; it was all - unbelievable. I knew that the next day Tania and

I would be back at each other's throats, but right then she had it going on.

The party ended and I thought I ate and drank myself into oblivion as Neicy helped me climb into bed. I knew I was drunk as hell. Shoot, we all were. Everyone had gone home except Tania who was cleaning up.

"Why is Tania still here?" I asked rudely.

"C'mon, now. Don't start," Neicy said as she tucked me in. "She gave us such a great anniversary gift. Don't mess things up by being nasty."

"You're right. She hooked us up."

"Why didn't you thank her, then?"

"I thanked her when I didn't curse her ass out once tonight."

"You can be such an asshole sometimes, Jerome."

"I love you too, honey."

That was the last thing I remembered before blanking out and wandering off to La-La Land. Neicy calling my name softly in my ear awakened me about an hour later. I could feel her naked body draped all over mine. I opened my eyes, and then I realized that I wasn't naked when I went to sleep. I also realized that Neicy had lost her damn mind, because I was spread eagle on the bed with my hands and feet bound to the bedposts. The room was dimly lit with scented candles, and I could hear soothing jazz instrumentals playing on the stereo. Dammit, Neicy. She just had to have her way. I tried not to get angry. I wanted to keep the mood, but I wanted her to untie me more.

"Baby, stoppit. You know I don't like this. Untie me, please."

"Relax, baby." Her voice was soft and seductive. I always loved the way she talked to me in bed and on the phone. The sound of her voice always gave me an immediate hard-on. "I need you to trust me right now, okay?"

"But I'm uncomfortable with this and you know that."

"You're gonna feel much, much better in a minute if you just relax and trust me."

All of my feelings at this point were scrambled. I was really paranoid about being tied up, but Neicy had me really excited. As she suddenly got up off me, my dick sprung up and pointed straight at the ceiling. Neicy leaned over to the nightstand and picked up a bottle of baby oil. She poured a stream from my right arm all the way down the right side of my body to my foot. Then she started another stream at my left foot, back up to my left arm. She poured some more oil into her hands and began rubbing it all over me. Her hands felt so good as she massaged and caressed my entire body. My tension gradually went away and I became more relaxed.

Neicy finished my rub down, and then she took a silk scarf from the drawer and tied it around my mouth. That uncomfortable feeling started coming back again and I started to pitch a bitch. That's when I saw the silhouette of another woman at the foot of the bed. I focused in on her face as the candlelights flickered and realized that it was Tania standing there, totally nude. I was in absolute shock at this point. My body froze and I couldn't utter a sound as bad as I wanted to scream.

Neicy was sitting on the edge of the bed on my left. She poured more baby oil in her hands and began stroking my dick and balls. Tania walked slowly around the right side of the bed, running her fingers up my leg, over my stomach and all over my chest. My eyes were as wide as saucers as I watched Tania climb onto the bed and straddle my chest. I looked up and saw her perfect round breasts topping off her hourglass figure and four pack stomach. The flickering flames highlighted her golden complexion. Humph, I never said Tania wasn't fine. I just said I don't like her.

I could feel Tania's neatly shaved, wet pussy pressing against my oil-slicked chest as she made slow, circular grinds against it. She reached down and traced the outline of my face with her fingers and teased the outline of my lips through my silk gag. Neicy got behind Tania and straddled me. She rested down on my groin causing my dick to slide up the crack of her lovely, big ass. Then, she leaned forward, grabbed Tania around the waist and pulled her back close.

I watched as Neicy worked her hands up Tania's sides to her firm breasts, and she began to caress and knead her nipples. Tania threw her head back and her long hair draped across my wife's left shoulder. She ran her tongue up the right side of Tania's neck and nibbled on her earlobe. I couldn't believe my eyes. I saw what was happening, but I couldn't believe it.

Tania stood straight up on the bed and my eyes followed her legs up to the opening of her vagina glistening in the candlelight. Her juices mixed with the baby oil she absorbed from my body. I swallowed hard and inhaled as much air as I could threw my nose. Neicy slid her body against mine up under Tania. She positioned her head between Tania's legs and turned over on her back. As Tania squatted down, Neicy opened her mouth wide and stuck out her tongue to receive her best friend's wet pussy. My dick was still rock-hard and being restrained under my wife's back as she sucked on Tania's cunt. I never imagined Neicy would even consider being with another woman, but I was sure excited watching her with one.

Tania began to moan and grind against Neicy's face as she ate her out. The pressure from the weight of the two women didn't bother me at all as they both bucked and squirmed about. Tania began panting heavily as she came in Neicy's mouth. My beautiful wife just pressed her mouth harder against Tania's pussy and let the juices flow all over her face.

Tania stood up again, allowing Neicy to turn over on her stomach and slither her way up my body until she and I were face to face. "Tania tastes real good," Neicy said. "I want you to taste her, too. If I take the gag off, do you promise to be a good boy?"

I nodded my head so fast I almost shook my eyeballs loose. Neicy removed the scarf from my mouth, pressed her lips against mine and attacked my tongue with her own. I tasted Tania's sweet nectar as I kissed my wife deeply and licked all over her face. Tania squatted down and sat on Neicy's back and I braced myself to support their weight. Tania began rubbing Neicy's back and shoulders and playing with her long braids. Neicy began wiggling her hips around until she positioned herself for me to enter her. Tania let up so Neicy could raise her pelvis and lower herself down on me very slowly. Neicy's pussy was soaking wet and as hot as fire. It gripped my dick like a vice and pulsated as she contracted her muscles.

"Baby, I never knew you liked women," I said.

"I don't usually. I'm doing it for you. You see. I'm willing to compromise."

"You like it, though, don't you?"

"Mmmm, yes."

"It's really turning me on, too."

"Remember, you promised to be a good boy," Neicy reminded me.

"I know. I will be."

"Okay. No matter what happens, don't move. Do not, I repeat, do not try to thrust upward or grind me in any way. Is that clear?"

"Yes, baby."

Apparently, that was Tania's cue because she moved down behind Neicy, spread her asscheeks open and began licking and sucking both our genitals with me still inside. Neicy and I began kissing passionately again. I felt Tania's tongue working furiously all over the both of us. After a while, I couldn't feel Tania's tongue anymore, but I could feel her breast rubbing against my inner thighs and Neicy was moaning and squirming. "What is she doing to you, honey?" I asked.

"Ohhhh!" Neicy grunted. "Her tongue...her tongue is...it's in my asshole! Ooooh!"

I looked down Neicy's back and saw Tania's face pressed against her ass, making rapid circular motions, and she was humming with pleasure. Neicy started grinding down harder against me causing me to go deeper into her. Tania continued her assault on Neicy's anus until she cried out, "OHHHH! I'M CUMMING! OHHHH!"

I felt Neicy's juices flow down over my dick and balls and down my ass. Tania sat up on her knees and Neicy began riding me harder shouting, "Come on, daddy! Come on! Come on!" I unloaded what seemed like a gallon of semen into my wife. She pressed down hard against me and let me fill her up. "Oh yes, daddy. Ooh. I know you put baby number four in me just now. Mmmm, I hope it's a girl this time."

I caught my breath and looked up at my lovely wife. She looked so radiant and happy. Yeah, she's pregnant again. I remembered that glow from three times before. She knew she was pregnant immediately those times, too.

"Nah, hopefully we'll have twin boys this time, and I'll have my starting line-up for my basketball team."

"It's a girl. I feel it."

"Whatever. They have the WNBA now, so it's cool."

Tania walked around to the side of the bed and plopped down on the edge. "I guess I'm no longer needed here, so I'll get dressed and head on home," she giggled.

"Yeah, good lookin' out," I said. "Don't crash with your non-drivin' ass."

Neicy slapped me across the forehead. "What did I tell you about being rude?"

"What? Oh, that applies to her, too?"

"I see you want to stay here tied to the bed for the rest of the night. I think Tania and I will go in the kitchen and have some coffee and leave you here to think about ways to be nice."

"Nah, stop playing. Untie me. I was just joking."

"You'll be fine. Don't worry."

"No, I won't. Stop playing, Neicy."

"Oh, and say goodbye to Tania. She has a new job and she's moving to Buffalo the day after tomorrow."

"The day after tomorrow?"

"Yeah," Tania said. "Neicy thought it would be nice to surprise you with that news the same time we surprised you with your anniversary gift."

"Yeah, but it's cold as hell in Western New York. Well, peace and good riddance."

"You see. There you go with the rudeness," Neicy said, shaking her finger at me.

"What did I say?" I asked innocently.

"You do need to just lie here awhile. In fact, you probably should stay that way until morning."

"C'mon, Neicy!"

Neicy ignored me, grabbed Tania's hand and led her toward the bedroom door. "Tania, you don't have to go home tonight. It's late and you have a long ride. I think I'll sleep with you on the sofabed since we won't be seeing each other for God knows how long. Besides, there's no room for me on the bed with him spread out like that."

"Oh, yeah," Tania eagerly agreed. "We can still have a lot more fun with each other, too." She pulled Neicy's face to hers and gave her a long, deep kiss. The two women then trotted out the room as Tania looked back and stuck her middle finger up at me.

"NEICY!" I screamed.

"Quiet, you'll wake the neighbors!" she shouted back at me.

"NEICY! NEICY! I'M SORRY! NEICY!"

She beat me again. What am I going to do with her? She got her way just like she always does. It's cool, though. At least she thought of me, too. She gets on my damn nerves sometimes, but God, I love that woman. I'll do anything for Neicy.

You Send Me Swinging

People bumped and brushed past Tara as she stood close to the door on the crowded C-train on her way to work. She didn't mind. In fact, she hardly noticed. Her mind was still on her weekend. She couldn't believe the things that took place and how much she enjoyed it all. She looked around the subway car at all the people wondering how many of them were into doing what she did and sharing the way she had.

"How many of you are into the swinging lifestyle?" she yelled out, but only in her mind. Although she knew most subway riders in New York City would not have been stunned by her outburst, she still managed to bite her tongue. If she had said it, however, it would not have mattered because being open like that could not have compared to how open she was Saturday night.

Smiling, Tara thought back to how it all started. Bryan, her husband, had been asking her for two months to let him take her to a swingers club, but she didn't want any part of anything like that. She started to regret telling him about her fantasies of being with two men and being with another woman. She never thought that he would condone her acting on it, or that he would want to get in on it, too. To her, it was just a fantasy, not something she expected to actually happen. Bryan was intrigued, though. His fantasy has always been to participate in an orgy.

"C'mon, Tee," he'd say. "This would be the perfect opportunity for us both to fulfill our fantasies and get it out of our systems."

"No way," she would respond. "I don't want to do that. I don't want to see you fuckin' some other bitch."

"Why? It wouldn't be just me. You'd be with other men."

"I don't want to be with no other man. I just want to be with you."

"It's not like we're going to start a relationship with these people. It's just sex, and just for one time. You and I both have had one-night stands before. This ain't that much different. Just like you never saw that one-night stand again, we'll probably never see these people again."

It was a lousy argument and Tara let Bryan know it every time he asked. Then, one day, Bryan sent her an email with a link to a site for couples that wanted to be swingers. Tara read some of the posts people put up on the message board and got into some of the chat sessions. She never knew that swinging was a lifestyle for many people. There were mostly married couples who were uninhibited and believed in "sharing their love and sexuality" with other couples who were looking for the same thing. Many of those people started by fulfilling each other's fantasies, just as Bryan wanted to do with her. Tara did not want her and Bryan's fantasies to turn into a lifestyle the way it had for those people, but she had become curious. The stories people told about their first time adventures, the clubs they had been to and the other couples they had been with turned her on.

Two weeks ago, the club's founders, Ray and Theresa, sent out invitations to the swing party they were giving at the Marriott in Brooklyn. The fact that Tara had been chatting regularly with them and several other couples who were going to attend made her a little more comfortable with the whole idea. She liked the fact that the party was an invitational for club members only. Bryan didn't waste any time to RSVP after Tara mentioned that she thought she might want to go.

"I just wanna make sure we're on the list," he lobbied. "If you decide you do want to go, we'll be able to get in. If you change your mind, it's no big deal."

Butterflies stirred in Tara's stomach as she and Bryan approached the hotel suite. Bryan knocked and a tall, thin, dark-skinned man with long dreadlocks opened the door. "Can I help you?" the man asked in a deep voice.

Bryan introduced himself and Tara using their screen names. "Yes. I'm Krazy Man and this my wife, Wonder Girl."

"Oh, yes. How are you? I'm Ray, also known as Swingman. Come on in."

Bryan and Tara went inside and Ray showed them where they could change and leave their things. Then, he led them back into the front room and they began to mingle. Tara downed four apple martinis and started to loosen up. Bryan stayed close to her to make sure she was doing okay and feeling comfortable. At about midnight, Ray and Theresa gathered everyone together and had them take turns introducing themselves, starting with the three couples that were attending their first swing party. Eleven couples were there altogether, seven of them married.

After introductions, most of the people made their way to one of the two bedrooms. Ray and Theresa came over to Bryan and Tara and sat next to them on the couch.

"Now, you two just relax and have some fun," Theresa said. "We're going to break you in. We've been waiting for you. Girl, it's about time you let your hair down and came out to a party."

"Yeah, I know," Tara smiled shyly. "I'm having fun so far."

"Girl, the fun hasn't even started, yet."

"That's right," Ray agreed. "The real fun is about to start right now."

Ray moved close to Tara and started rubbing her shoulders and arms. Theresa got up, sat her long, thin, mocha body on Bryan's lap and threw her legs across Tara's and Ray's. She took Bryan's hand and placed it inside her red lacey teddy and he began squeezing and caressing her large breasts. Ray was planting tiny kisses on Tara's neck as he removed the straps of her blue teddy over her shoulders and down her arms, revealing her handfuls of thirty-two Bs. He grabbed and squeezed one of Tara's breasts and Theresa reached over and squeezed the other.

Theresa felt Bryan's hard dick pressing against her ass and swung her legs off Tara and Ray. She tapped Bryan's hand so he would let go of her breast and got down on her knees in front of him. She grabbed his silk boxers and pulled them down to his ankles before leaning forward and taking his dick into her mouth. Bryan leaned back and watched Theresa stroke and suck his dick at a slow, steady pace. He looked over and watched Ray nibbling and sucking on Tara's nipples. Ray's hand was between Tara's legs and he had his fingers buried deep inside her wet pussy. Ray's dick was sticking out the front opening of his silk boxers and Tara had a firm grip on it, stroking it hard.

Theresa removed her mouth from Bryan's dick and reached over and removed Ray's hand from between Tara's legs at the same time. She moved on her knees from between Bryan's legs over to between Tara's legs and buried her face in Tara's crotch. Tara moaned loudly as she felt Theresa's mouth press against her pussy lips and her tongue flicking against her clit. Thanks to Theresa, Tara's first fantasy was being fulfilled. Her body trembled with nervousness, but she welcomed the touch of another woman.

Ray sat on the top of the couch and aimed his dick at Tara's lips. Tara stared at his semi-erect member and examined it for a moment. She never saw an uncircumcised penis before. She stuck out her tongue and poked it up under the foreskin a few times. Suddenly, she felt Theresa's tongue slither its way up into her, and as she moaned out loud, Ray's dick plopped into her mouth. She sucked and groaned causing it to become fully erect. She always enjoyed the feel of a penis growing in her mouth.

Bryan grabbed a condom from the dish on the end table and positioned himself on his knees behind Theresa. He rolled the condom on and slowly slid his dick into her wetness. Theresa continued eating Tara out as she enjoyed Bryan fucking her from behind.

Tara's eyes were closed as she continued to slowly suck on Ray's dick. Suddenly, she felt him move away from her. She opened her eyes to see Ray being pulled away by another woman who made him turn around so that she can suck on his smooth eight inches as well. Tara watched for a moment as Irma, the woman she knew online as Diamond Diva, wrapped her thick, full lips around the base of Ray's dick and sucked up and down with the most masterful technique she had ever seen. She thought this woman could easily be a porn star.

At that moment, Tara felt a pair of hands reach under her arms and lift her up off the couch. It was easy for people to move her because she was so petite. At five-one, she was all of a hundred and five pounds. Tara was glad to see that it was Kevin, also known as Black Knight, carrying her from the couch into one of the bedrooms. She saw Kevin's picture on his profile and thought he looked like the actor Leon. Seeing him in person, she thought he was even more handsome. She looked back just before Kevin entered the bedroom to see Bryan still fucking Theresa and Theresa's head buried into the seat of the couch where she was sitting a few seconds ago.

There were two beds in this room. On the first bed, three women were in a triangle with each one eating the other out. One of them was Dawn, Kevin's wife. At the foot of that bed, a man was sitting on the edge with a woman bouncing up and down on his dick while sucking another man off who was standing in front of her.

Kevin placed Tara on the bed next to a man whom she recognized as one of the other first timers. Tara looked between his legs and smiled at his thick eleven inches. A wide smile came over her face as she could foresee that her second fantasy was about to be fulfilled like she never imagined. A newfound confidence came over her.

"Mmm, you gotta pretty dick," she said. "What's your name, again? I'm sorry, I forgot."

"My name is Charles," the man said eagerly.

"Yeah, that's right. Pretty dick Charles. It's so fat and long and straight. You gotta let me suck it, please?"

"Be my guest, pretty lady," Charles encouraged.

"Damn, I got the two fattest dick men in the house," Tara said licking her lips. She leaned over and began sucking and licking on Charles' dick, trying to mimic what she saw Irma doing to Ray. Kevin removed Tara's teddy, propped her up on her knees and squirted some lubricating gel on his ten-inch, condom-covered dick. He moved up behind her and pressed the head of his penis against her vaginal opening. He continued to press, pushing his way into her inch by inch as far as he could go. Tara groaned as she felt Kevin penetrate her, but she refused to remove her mouth away from Charles' dick. Kevin began thrusting slowly in and out of her and Tara felt her pussy stretch to accommodate his massive tool. As Kevin stroked Tara's pussy longer, harder and faster, she sucked Charles' dick more intensely.

"Argh!" Charles cried as he pulled himself out of Tara's mouth and shot streams of jism all over her face and neck. Tara felt her stomach churn and her blood boil as she reached her own climax. She screamed and clutched the bedspreads as her juices flowed out of her, down her legs, and down the legs of Kevin who was still thrusting in and out of her. Suddenly, Kevin slowly withdrew from her. Charles laid down on the bed and rolled a condom on his still erect dick. Kevin picked Tara up by her waist and lowered her down onto Charles who guided himself into her. Kevin then climbed on the bed and positioned himself to enter Tara's ass. Slowly and very carefully, Kevin slid his dick into Tara's rectum. She braced herself as best she could, and although it felt like she was being impaled, she just bit her lip and took it. Charles' dick in her pussy felt really good and made things easier for her.

Any pain Tara felt immediately turned into pleasure as Kevin and Charles both held onto her waist and hips and slowly moved her up and down rhythmically. Kevin's dick slid into her ass as they lifted her up and Charles' dick slid into her pussy as they lowered her down. Tara's eyes rolled back up in her head as the ecstasy overwhelmed her, causing her to cum again and again.

Tara and Bryan didn't speak much during the drive home. They just smiled and gave each other adoring looks ever so often. They got in a little after six-thirty in the morning and made deep, passionate love until they both fell asleep. Tara awoke around three in the afternoon thinking about the party. She loved the way she felt. After all she experienced, Bryan still made her feel special. The sex at the party was really good, but the love she made to the man she loved was much, much better.

Tears streamed down Tara's cheeks as she leaned over and whispered to her sleeping husband, "Thank you for sharing."

Caught in the Act

It was two-thirty in the afternoon and Kevin was so glad to be getting home from work early. This was perfect for the long Labor Day weekend coming up. He couldn't wait to start preparing the surprise dinner he had planned for his wife, Melanie.

Kevin approached his apartment and heard loud music blasting from the stereo. Jay-Z was in full effect in the middle of the afternoon. Melanie must've gotten home early, too. He entered his apartment and saw a trail of clothing leading out the living room. He paused for a second and noticed they were all women's clothes. "What the hell was Melanie doing," he thought to himself.

He followed the trail to the bedroom door, which was halfway open. He heard whimpers and moans under the blasting beat of "Girls, Girls, Girls" and looked inside. His eyeballs nearly jumped out his head when he saw his neighbor, Cindy, the young, stacked girl from across the hall, laying nude across his bed with her legs wide open and Melanie's head buried between them. Cindy was stroking Melanie's head with one hand while holding a large double-headed dildo in her other hand, and she was sucking on it like a real dick. Kevin stepped back and peeked through the crack of the door so he wouldn't be discovered. He watched as Melanie lifted Cindy's legs high off the bed and feasted on her juicy, wet pussy.

"Oh, fuck yeah!" Cindy screamed. "Suck on this pussy, baby!"

Melanie placed both of Cindy's legs over her shoulders and let them rest there, and used both hands to grip Cindy's big, round ass. Cindy still had her hand placed on the back of Melanie's head and threw her own head back and closed her eyes. Cindy's back arched upward, making her perfect thirty-six Cs stick out. Her smooth, light-golden skin was shining and glistening from perspiration. Suddenly, Melanie freed herself and sat up on her knees. "Turn around and get on all fours," she instructed.

Cindy quickly obliged, still holding on to the large dildo. Melanie lowered her head and pressed her face into the crack of Cindy's huge ass.

"MMMMM! OHHH!" Cindy moaned. "Oh, yes! That's it. Ooh, I love when you stick your tongue in my asshole! Yesssss!" Melanie's head started making circular motions, and she was humming as she darted her tongue in and out of Cindy's puckered anus.

Kevin unfastened his pants, took out his thick, eight-inch dick and slowly began to stoke it. He continued to watch as Melanie reached forward and took the dildo from Cindy. Melonie removed her face from Cindy's ass and rose to her knees again. Cindy stayed in the same position and swayed her hips from side to side, anticipating what was about to happen next. Melanie began to slowly insert one end of the large, black, two-headed toy into Cindy's dripping, wet vagina. Then she moved it in and out of her, fucking her with a steady pace.

After a few moments, Melanie turned over on her knees so that she and Cindy were ass to ass. She inserted the other end of the dildo into her own pussy and they started to hump back and forth. Their ass cheeks smacked against each other making a clapping sound as their thrusts became more intense. As loud as Jay-Z was now singing "Give It To Me," the two women's squeals were overpowering him. Cindy's head was turned away from Kevin, so all he could see was her juicy ass. Melanie's beautiful face had a familiar look of passion on it. Her big brown eyes were closed tight. Her long locks draped down the sides of her head. Her beautiful dark skin also glistened with sweat, and her perky thirty-four Bs hung below her, swaying with her as she pounded back to meet Cindy.

Finally, both women collapsed after cumming for what seemed like ten or twelve times each. Kevin was stroking his fully erect dick much faster now. He had suspected that Cindy was lesbian or bisexual, but he never knew his own wife played on both sides of the fence. It turned him on like crazy. He stroked his dick at a rapid pace until a stream of thick, sticky semen spurted out into his free hand. Just that moment, he noticed Melanie getting up off the bed and walking toward the stereo.

"You wanna get in the shower first?" she asked Cindy, who was laying face-down on the bed with the dildo still wedged between her legs.

"No, you go ahead," Cindy grunted.

Melanie turned the stereo down a few notches and started toward the door. Kevin quickly ducked behind the door of the linen closet as Melanie came out the bedroom and went into the bathroom. When he heard the water in the shower come on, he grabbed a towel and wiped the sperm from his hand, then tiptoed into the bedroom. Cindy had removed the dildo from her vagina and was running her tongue up and down its length. She looked back and noticed Kevin coming toward her with his dick in his hand. He quickly put one finger up to his lips and said, "shhhh."

Cindy sat up on the bed with a look of shock on her face. Then, she suddenly started smiling as she focused in on Kevin's semi-erect penis. She threw the dildo across the bed, stretched out both hands and beckoned him to come to her. He dropped his pants down to his ankles and crawled up on the bed to join her. Cindy lunged forward and took his dick into her mouth. She sucked on it furiously until it was fully erect again. She then swung her body around, turned over on her back and spread her legs open wide. Kevin crawled up between her legs, aimed his throbbing, swollen erection at her love hole and shoved it all the way up into her.

"Ooh!" Cindy whimpered, as she felt him penetrate her.

Kevin reached down with both hands and grabbed her breasts tightly, squeezing hard as he pounded his dick into her mercilessly. Cindy threw her legs all the way up and wrapped her ankles around Kevin's neck so that he could get in deeper. She felt his huge balls slapping against her ass as he pumped in and out of her with a mighty force. She held onto his arms as he savagely squeezed the flesh of her breasts. Juices flowed out of her like a waterfall as she came in waves.

Finally, Kevin's body tensed up and he withdrew from her, squirting his jism all over her face and mouth. Cindy licked off as much of his delicious semen as she could with her tongue before grabbing his dick, shoving it back into her mouth and milking the remains. The warm, thick cream oozed down her throat as she continued to suck greedily. Suddenly, they both heard clapping and they turned around to see Melanie standing in the doorway; still wet with a towel wrapped around herself.

"That was great," she said with a big smile on her face. "Encore! Encore!"

Cindy smiled at Melanie and gave her a wink. "Come join us, sweetie," she encouraged. "It's more fun if we all got some."

The three of them spent the rest of the weekend in bed together.

The East Coast Vacation

Valerie's eyes fluttered open as the flight attendant's voice awakened her, instructing the passengers to fasten their seatbelts to prepare for landing. She looked out of the window and got her first look at the lights the New York City skyline. She smiled to herself, thinking about the blind date that she was going on in a couple of hours. She was a bit nervous for traveling all the way from Arizona to meet someone she met on the Internet, but she had been captivated, intrigued and utterly aroused by the many phone conversations she shared with John. The sound of his voice stimulated her. His wit, charm and intellect delighted her. She couldn't wait to finally meet him in person.

John stood in the shower and let the steaming hot water dance off his body. He lathered himself up while thinking about the night he had planned for Valerie. She was due to arrive anytime, and he wanted everything to be right for her. He grinned to himself thinking about how Valerie used pleasant terms of endearment all the time. She was always saying, "yes, dear" or "okay, sweetie" whenever they spoke on the phone or chatted online. Her voice was so mellow and soothing to him that he had to lay back in his lounge chair and turn on the red light whenever he talked to her. The way she giggled at his corny jokes was so innocent. She was silly and playful most of the time, but whenever she talked about something serious, she sounded so knowledgeable and focused. He couldn't wait to finally meet her in person.

Valerie traveled to New York with her best friend, Sophia, who came along to visit Kane, her former booty call from college. They arrived at their hotel room at six o'clock and got a big surprise when they opened the door. On both beds were huge bouquets of roses. On the first bed were yellow and white roses with Sophia's name on it. On the second bed was a larger bouquet of red and pink roses with Valerie's name on it. Both women dropped their bags at the door and hurried to open their respective cards.

"Oh my goodness, Valerie," Sophia excitingly exclaimed. "Who is this man you've come to meet? What does your card say?"

"Shit, girl," Valerie replied, "this was supposed to be a fling, but I might have to relocate if this is what he's all about."

Sophia was still screaming as she leapt from her bed to Valerie's. "Well, what does it say?!"

"Hold on," Valerie said, turning her card away from Sophia's reach. "First tell me what yours say."

Sitting on her knees, Sophia bounced up and down on the bed as she read her card. Valerie's smile widened as she listened. It read:

Thank you for taking the time to accompany Valerie on this trip. I hope your date goes as good as I know ours will. Thanks for being a friend.

Yours truly,
John

Valerie's card read:

My Dear Valerie,

I have been waiting for this moment for many weeks. I'm so glad you made it. I can't wait to finally be able to look into your eyes, touch your lips and feel the caress of your hands. I assure you that this weekend will be time well spent.

Lovingly yours,
John

"Damn, girl. Who is this dude?" Sophia shrieked. "I think you might've struck gold. I can't wait to meet him."

"Slow down, girlfriend," Valerie said, holding up her hand. "Don't be trying to slide in on my date. You have your own."

"Aw c'mon, Valerie. I just want to meet the man, that's all. Don't be like that."

"Well, why don't we just all have dinner together, and then go our separate ways. That way we all can get acquainted."

"That's a good idea. I'll call Kane."

The two women then hurried to unpack and took turns showering. John was due to pick Valerie up at seven-thirty, and Sophia was supposed to meet Kane at eight o'clock. Sophia called Kane to change plans, which he didn't have a problem with.

Kane arrived at the hotel first. Valerie opened the door and her eyes engulfed the man standing before her. Kane stood six-two with a reddish-brown complexion, a shiny baldhead, thin mustache and a long, slender physique. He wore a beige silk mockneck with black slacks and a black leather jacket.

"Hi, there," Valerie said, as she leaned against the door and batted her eyes.

"Hi, I'm Kane. I'm Sophia's date. Is she here?"

"Sophia? Oh, yes, she's here." Valerie opened the door wider and barely moved to the side. "Come in. I'm Sophia's friend, Valerie."

Kane took Valerie's hand and gently kissed the back of it. "The pleasure is all mine, Valerie," he said before proceeding inside.

"Hey, Kane!" Sophia yelled as she came out the bathroom. "Oh, my goodness. You look so good."

"You are looking especially sexy yourself," Kane replied, as he took Sophia's hand and slowly twirled her around. She wore a long, fitted gray wool skirt that showed off her firm, tight ass, with black stiletto-heeled leather boots and a white cashmere sweater.

Valerie was about to close the door when John walked up. "Umm, a woman that fine can only be my date," he said. "Hi, Valerie."

Valerie turned around and saw a six-foot man with neck length locks, a mocha complexion, deep-set eyes and a slick, thin, well-groomed beard. She let her eyes move down across his broad frame and admired his smoky-gray leather blazer draped over a cream-colored, wool-knit sweater and black twilled wool slacks. "Hey, John," she said, holding her arms open wide to greet him.

Valerie only stands five feet tall, so John bent down a bit and hugged her tightly. She felt so comfortable in his arms. Her soft breasts pressed against him, and he smiled devilishly at the thoughts he was having. John was always a breast man, and Valerie had exactly what he liked. He let her go and followed her into the room, watching her big backside bounce. He licked his lips imagining his head up under her short, form fitting Columbia Blue dress. She wore white knee-high leather boots and he admired the smooth, fudge complexion of her thick thighs from behind.

As John entered the room, Sophia looked up and had to cover her mouth to keep from drooling. Her eyes locked with his and her heart began to race. "He looks even better in person," she thought to herself, referring to the photo Valerie showed her online. "Hello, John," she said with a gleaming smile as she marched toward him extending her hand. John took Sophia's hand and kissed the back the same way Kane did to Valerie. The two men exchanged greeting and Kane ordered champagne as the two couples sat around and got acquainted. They laughed and joked through four bottles before Valerie, who was sitting on John's lap, noticed the time. "Oh, wow," she said. "It's after midnight."

"I guess we missed dinner, eh?" Sophia giggled.

"Oh, damn," Kane said. "Well, we can still go out if you want. This is New York City. The parties don't start until midnight anyway."

"I'm gonna start my own party right here," Valerie said, as she threw her arms around John and kissed him passionately.

Sophia walked over to Kane and pushed him back onto her bed. "Mmmm, I like that kind of party," she said, as she climbed on top of him and pulled off her sweater. Kane reached behind her and with one quick snap, undid her bra, revealing her mouthfuls of perky 34Bs. He pulled her close to him and sucked on her hardened nipples.

Valerie was writhing her ass on John's lap against his erection as he zipped her dress down in the back. She jumped up and danced her dress off, then slowly removed her bra and panties and stood before him in just her boots. She looked across the room to see that Sophia was now also naked down to the boots. John didn't take nearly as much time as Valerie did getting undressed. Kane followed his lead and stripped to the buff, as well.

John pulled Valerie close, gripped her ass, buried his face between her breasts and guided her down onto the bed. She wrapped her legs around him as he devoured the flesh of her boobs. Valerie noticed that all the slurping sounds she was hearing weren't only coming from John. She looked over and saw Kane laid back comfortably with his hands behind his head and Sophia curled up in a ball with her head bobbing up and down, sucking on his long, hard dick. She stuck two fingers into her mouth and emulated Sophia's technique. She then felt John open her legs, move down between them and press his lips hard against her clit. "Ohhh!" she cried out with delight. John then slid his tongue into the depths of her heated pussy, and Valerie's back arched as she clutched the bedspreads.

Sophia turned her body around to get into a sixty-nine position with Kane. Kane held onto her waist and buried his face into her vagina. The two of them worked on each other's genitals like they regretted missing dinner. It was obvious that John was also very hungry as he continuously dined on Valerie's cunt. Valerie didn't want just her fingers to suck on and started to ask John to come up on the bed so that they could sixty-nine, also. But before she could say anything or move, she noticed Sophia trying to get her attention. She looked over again and saw Sophia waving her over. Valerie was a little surprised, and showed it with the expression on her face. Sophia returned a "for crying out loud" look and got up off Kane. She grabbed his hand and led him over to John and Valerie.

"Move back on the bed," Sophia instructed Valerie, who immediately complied. John stood to his feet smiling as he realized what was about to go down. Valerie laid spread eagle in the center of her bed and Sophia instructed Kane to feed her. Kane kneeled on the side of the bed, and Valerie opened her mouth wide and took in his dick. Sophia crawled up on the bed between Valerie's legs and picked up where John left off. Sophia's ass was waving in the air as she ate Valerie's pussy. John lowered his head and shoved his tongue into Sophia's wet cunt.

A few moments later, John stood up and patted Sophia on her ass. "Turn around," he said, which she did getting into a sixty-nine position with Valerie. John climbed up on the bed, lifted Valerie's legs and inserted his rock-hard erection into her dripping pussy with one hard thrust.

"UMMMMGGGH!" Valerie moaned, refusing to take her mouth away from Kane's dick. Sophia lowered her mouth to Valerie's clit and flicked her tongue on it as John fucked her. Kane then climbed up on the bed behind Sophia and entered her. His balls hovered over Valerie's face and she lifted her head enough to suck on each one in turn.

"Ohhhh, I'm cumming!" Valerie's muffled scream filled the room. John immediately withdrew his dick from her and stepped back.

"Come here," John ordered Sophia as he walked over to the other bed. Sophia moved away from Valerie and Kane and Kane's dick slipped from her wet pussy. Sophia joined John and mounted him. She rode his dick hard, bouncing up and down on it like a wild woman. Suddenly, she started screaming and her body tensed as she released waves of passion all over John's lap before collapsing on top of him. John continued to thrust upward, but Sophia's body was limp and she didn't move.

At that moment, John heard "UH! UH! UH!" coming from the next bed and looked over to see Kane pounding into Valerie furiously. "ARGGG!" Kane screamed, as he withdrew and spurted thick globs of sperm all over Valerie's back. Valerie began swaying her hips and pushing back to him for more, but he collapsed across the bed and drifted off to sleep. John could feel Sophia's heavy breathing on top of him, as well. He carefully slid her off him and onto the bed. Then, he got up and walked over to Valerie and reached out to her.

"C'mon, baby," John said in a low husky voice. Valerie smiled widely and crawled down the bed to him. She spun around, turned over on her back and spread her legs open wide. John aimed his dick at her love tunnel and drove it inside.

"OHHHHHHH!" Valerie moaned, as she felt the length of John's dick penetrate her. She threw her arms around his neck and they kissed passionately as their hips rotated and grinded together. John reached under Valerie's legs and held them up as he continued to drive his throbbing erection in and out of her. Valerie lifted her hips up off the bed to meet each of his thundering strokes, and her large breasts bounced uncontrollably. Sweat poured from their bodies as they fucked each other like there was no tomorrow.

"Oh, baby," Valerie whined. "I can't stop cumming. Oh! Here it comes again. Ohhhh!"

John quickly withdrew his dick from Valerie's pussy, lifted her legs higher, aimed it at her puckered asshole and slowly slid it in. Valerie's eyes rolled back into her head and she bit her lip. She dug her nails into John's back, causing some skin to tear away. John moved in and out of Valerie's tight ass with a steady motion until he felt his scrotum fill up and shoot streams of hot semen into her rectal cavity. Valerie's body rocked as she felt John's love juices fill up her bowels.

Sophia's eyes fluttered open, and she looked across and witnessed John's drenched dick slide out Valerie's ass. She smiled slightly and drifted back off to sleep. Kane woke up and made his way to the other bed with Sophia, cuddled next to her and fell back asleep, as well. John and Valerie got up and took a shower together. They came back, got under the covers and fucked again before they both fell asleep.

The next day, John and Kane took Valerie and Sophia sightseeing all over New York. After lunch, they went back to John's condo on Central Park North for some afternoon festivities. The four of them spent the remainder of the weekend together, and Valerie and Sophia had the greatest experience of their lives during their East Coast vacation.

A Bonus Story
a collaboration
by Ken Divine & Anna Forrest

Working Together

Ken

Anna was really working my nerves. I wanted to get this project finished so I could get back to New York. I had things to do. I couldn't be spending extra time in Philly messing around with her constantly disappearing into her bedroom. I figured she was probably in there talking on the telephone. I thought this was a bad idea from the start and regretted listening to our editor.

"You and Anna would make a great team," she said. "A collaboration would put the two of you over the top."

Yeah, whatever! This "great team" wasn't clicking. "Over the top" my ass. The whole idea was about to hit rock bottom because I was about to get up and get out of there. I couldn't understand what the hell Anna was doing back there all that time. She got up and went in there every twenty minutes, and she kept the damn music blasting. That same damn R. Kelly song playing over and over again was driving me crazy.

"Anna!" I called out to her. "Anna, can you come out, please, so we can get this done?!"

I didn't think she could hear me over the music, so I got up to go knock on her bedroom door and tell her to bring her ass out. I walked to the back of her apartment, past her kitchen and bathroom to her bedroom. The door was partially open. That pissed me off because I thought she could hear me calling her and was just ignoring me.

"Anna, come on..." I said as I tapped on the door and peeked inside. I wasn't ready for what I saw.

So that's what she kept coming in here for. My frown turned to a smile and my whole attitude changed. Anna was sprawled out across the bed driving herself wild. She was in another world. No wonder she couldn't hear me calling her. Writing those erotic stories must've really been turning her on. She should've told me, I would've been happy to please her fine, mahogany ass.

Anna

I didn't think that Ken would actually walk in on me even though I fantasized that he would. I wanted him to come in and fuck the shit out of me. I know we were supposed to be in there collaborating so we could get this project done, but I couldn't concentrate with all that talk about sex and him looking like a chocolate Adonis. I was picturing his head between my legs and my fingers gripping his dreads as his tongue fucked me like crazy. I came into this room five times since we started and I could see his frustration. He had a funky little attitude, but it wasn't something some good pussy couldn't fix.

I was on the brink of making myself cum. I wanted Ken to walk in. I knew if I played "Imagine That" one more time he was going to snap, but that guitar was doing something to me. Mmmm, I wanted him inside me. The pussy was out, all he had to do was bring his angry ass in and take it. I started working my man in the boat overtime. I swore I'd go to church every Sunday if I could just cum right then. Ohhh, at that moment I knew I'd to have to break out my Sunday gear. It felt so good.

Now, after I finally exploded, I didn't expect to open my eyes and see Ken standing there. He looked like he didn't know whether he was sick at what he saw, or if he wanted to wrap his lips around my pierced clit. My first instinct, after the initial embarrassment, was to cover up and apologize. Then I thought, "Shit, I live here." He shouldn't have had me read all of those freaky ass stories. Just to test him, I opened my legs wider and took one nipple into my mouth, simultaneously stroking my clit. Now what, Mister Book Writer?

Ken

"I...uh...um..." I started stuttering when Anna saw me standing in the doorway. I tried to relax. "Anna, I...uh...was wondering what was taking you so long. I didn't mean to walk in on you. Uh...I..."

I couldn't understand why, while I was searching for something to say, she wasn't saying anything? Then she started up again. She had enormous breasts with nipples that looked like Hershey's Kisses and she was sucking them like crazy. She was also rubbing her clit furiously. My erection made my pants high waters. Saliva built up in my mouth forcing me to swallow hard.

I began to stroke my member through the denim of my jeans as I watched my beautiful co-author lay on her bed batting her eyes, beckoning me, and drawing me to her. I took a step forward and an inviting smile came over Anna's face. Her succulent, pouting lips parted and her tongue slowly glided across the top. I unzipped my pants and started unbuckling my belt when Anna stopped fondling herself, moved toward me and grabbed my belt, pulling me to her. She pushed my hands away, opened my belt and pants and pulled them down to my knees. Then she ran her hands up under my sweatshirt and t-shirt, letting her fingers climb up my back. She pulled both the shirts off together and tossed them to the floor. I took her beautiful face into my hands and kissed her deep. Our tongues chased each other around, back and forth from her mouth to mine.

Anna's hands moved down my back and into my boxers. She grabbed my butt cheeks and squeezed. Her French tip manicure dug into my flesh and that sent a surge through me. I felt an indescribable tingle within my loins and my manhood jerked with anticipation. Anna let go of my backside long enough to pull my boxers down to my knees, as well.

Anna
Ken's tongue tasted like he'd been eating cherry Now and Laters. I thought I had called his bluff, but I was glad to see the man stepped up to the challenge. His body felt warmer than the normal ninety-eight-point-six degrees it should be, and I was glad to see he sported at least ten thick inches. Getting his clothes off was too easy. I hoped he can keep his balance.

I started by kissing the head of his dick, which pulsated involuntarily in my hand. Taking him in a little at a time I continued to stroke him, tasting his pre-cum on my tongue. I leaned back just enough to resume stroking my clit while I worked him over. I looked up at him to see if he was watching. Ken's head was thrown back, eyes closed, and mouth parted slightly with soft moans escaping. I knew he appreciated how my tongue was making him feel.

I wasn't ready for him to cum yet, so I backed away. I lay back on the bed with my legs spread invitingly, softly tugging on my clit ring. He tested the water by inserting two fingers into me, one in my vagina, and the other in my asshole. His tongue was making small circles around my clit. You should have seen me trying to hold it down. I wanted Ken inside me, but I didn't want to mess up his flow. He held me open with his other hand and I kept my hands buried in those wonderful dreads as he devoured me until I came all over those pretty chocolate lips of his.

Ken made sure every drop of my honey was licked up, and he stuck his tongue inside me for good measure. My pussy pulsated in anticipation of him filling my insides and taking me way over the edge.

Ken
The time had come. I had to get up in her. I stood to my feet and watched Anna lying on the bed, rotating her hips, impatiently waiting for my next move. I pulled my jeans and boxers all the way down and stepped out of them, removing my sneakers and socks at the same time. Anna gasped and let out tiny pants as I climbed on the bed and positioned myself between her legs. She raised her legs up high and rested her feet on my shoulders. I kissed and licked her toes and she squirmed from being tickled. She continued rotating her hips as I pushed forward and entered her.

Anna moaned out loud as her labia sucked my organ in and her vaginal walls clamped around it. Her juices began to flow immediately. I thrust into her hard and pulled out slow. She raised herself off the bed, trying to get me to go deeper into her. I thought for a moment that she might've wanted me to push my whole body into her and do a break dance. No matter how hard I thrust, it didn't seem to be enough. She kept wanting more. Now, her ankles crossed behind my neck and just her shoulder blades remained on the bed. I held on to her thighs tightly and pounded into her, trying to keep pace with her. Her moans, groans and squeals drowned out R. Kelly as the song started over for the seventh time. Sweat poured from our bodies, soaking the part of the sheet that still remained on the bed.

Finally, as Anna announced her fourth orgasm, I felt myself about to cum, as well. I drove into her hard one final time and ejaculated into her depths. Anna contracted her vaginal muscles and milked me for more. As our climax subsided, she let her legs down and I rested on top of her. Her gigantic breasts made for nice, soft pillows and her heavy breathing rocked me to sleep.

Needless to say I didn't mind taking my time to complete this project after that. I went down to Philadelphia to spend a few hours and ended up spending a few days. Anna spoiled me the whole time. She even changed the CD for me. I think you can count on seeing more collaborations from us, especially now that we know how to motivate each other.

Menage Quad
By
Anna Forrest

Tongue Tied

The Scenario

I need you to open your mind and use your imagination. I only have one shot at getting this right, and I'd like to do so my first time around. If you have any sexual hang-ups or inhibitions, put the book down slowly, and WALK AWAY! If you're with me, I want you to feel me. Get ready to ride into ecstasy.

The Back Drop

I'm in a large room without windows. Soft yellows, hunter, burgundy... all the colors of fall are surrounding the occupants of this space in the form of plush sofas, cushy lounge chairs, and a few straight back cherry wood dining chairs with padding to match the décor. There is a glass topped cherry wood end table in each corner of the room. On each is a lamp about two feet tall shaped like couples in varying positions of the Karma Sutra topped with butter cream shades. Soft light casts seductive shadows on the walls. A five-foot glass topped coffee table made of the same wood holds center stage on top of a cream and white Persian rug. The rest of the floor is a hard wood so shiny you can almost see your face in it.

On the walls are gold-framed drawings in sets of three. One trio showed a woman lying on her side with her arm extended holding a heart shaped lock on a gold rope. The artist drew her in shades of black and gray with her eyes closed, and lips slightly parted. The second showed her mate standing with his legs apart. Both hands clasped together covering his midsection with the key dangling down in front of him. The third showed the couple embraced. The woman's head is thrown back as her lover caresses her breast and kisses her on the neck. Her leg is wrapped around his waist with a charm bracelet dangling from her ankle, and her right arm is extended over his shoulder holding the lock with the key in it.

The second set of three shows a group of three women in the first picture lying on their back with their legs drawn up to their chest. Three other women held position on their knees with their heads buried between the women's legs. The second showed three of the women sitting in straight back chairs now wearing strap-on vibrators. The other three women are in the riding position, one on the left side, one riding with her back to her mate, and one on the right side. The third picture shows the women coupled in pairs of two holding their mate by the waist with their foreheads touching.

Although they were all equally breath taking, one stood out the most. The first photo is of a man and his woman in the prone position making love. The second showed the woman, now pregnant, perched high on a pedestal with her braids cascading over her right shoulder. Her king is *wearing a crown cocked to the side on shoulder length dreads, and is kneeling at her feet offering her grapes. The final picture shows the couple in a loving embrace gazing down at their son. All the pictures were sketched with pencil on a cream backdrop.*

The Jump Off

    Present are three couples, four women and two men. All of us in varying shades of ebony. Perky breasts, smooth backsides, toned abs, and spirits flow freely. Eyes at half-mast, I am perched on the edge of one of the dining chairs with my knees spread on both sides. In my right hand rests a glass of Moet, my left holds the silky dreads of my chocolate Adonis. Strains of Luther's "So Amazing" can be heard over soft moans and the constant hum of long vibrators. Head thrown back in desire, both sets of my lips spread hungrily just waiting to be fed. I'm performing a slow grind against warm lips. The sensual pulling and tugging on my clit making my body shake involuntarily. His tongue soft against my hardened clit. I rotate a little faster to keep up pace with the two fingers moving in and out of my wet walls.

    Butterflies starting at my toes fan out to my entire body signaling a fast approaching orgasm. My eyes fix steadily on the pictures in front of me. I moan a little louder, my breath coming in short pants. My toes are gripping the floor, and my left hand is now massaging my dark nipples. The feel of my lips cool on hot skin. Taking my nipples into my mouth one at a time, I drowned the shot of Belvedere so I can use both hands. One hand massaging my right nipple while my tongue plays across the other.

    My Adonis picks up the pace by moving his head side to side. My knees are pulled up to my chest, giving him more room to please me. The feel of my explosion rocks my body from the inside out. My cream oozes out warm and sweet on his pink tongue. My Adonis laps at it like a kitten does milk. After shocks pulse through my body as I try to gain composure.

The Coffee Table

 My Adonis motions for me to lie down on the coffee table. I take in the thickness of the glass with strands of gold running through it. A camera, one of many throughout the room, is strategically placed underneath the table on the bottom shelf to capture whatever happens there.
 I straddle the table and ease down slowly, taking my Adonis into my mouth while holding on to the back of his legs. My clit makes a suctioning sound against the glass, its coolness quickly fading. Trailing butterfly kisses along the underside of his sensitive penis before laying my tongue flat on the base and enclosing the head when I reach the top throws off his equilibrium for a millisecond. My Adonis looks down at me through curious eyes, and I gaze up into his, never losing rhythm.
 Moistening my finger with my own love juice, I place it just on the inside of his asshole. My Adonis throws his head back in agonizing pleasure as his seed splatters on my face and drips from my chin. My small hand, barely fitting around the width of his like granite organ, pumps him slowly with just the right amount of pressure until he falls on weak knees in front of me.

The Rules

If a lover screams out you have to switch partners with one of the couples in the room. The person who causes the scream decides who his or her next lover will be. Scanning the room I decide on the ebony Goddess sitting under the picture of a woman holding a heart shaped lock. She has slanted eyes that are just brown enough to match her flawless, chocolate body, but light enough to see the difference. Her jet-black tresses fall in a soft wrap just past her shoulders. Lips lined with dark brown pencil, and accented with clear gloss make her heart shaped mouth look inviting. Perfectly arched eyebrows, a slender nose, and a small butterfly tattoo on the side of her neck complete and complement her features.

Holding a curved dildo and a bottle of mango lube in her well-manicured hands, she smiles wickedly as she makes her way over to me. My Adonis reluctantly joins her partner on the sofa. Before starting my next venture, I go to clean my face. My Goddess sat where I just left a puddle on the table, our juices mixing.

The Gathering

When I come out of the restroom, my Goddess along with The Other Woman is sitting on the edge of the coffee table. The Chocolate Boy Wonder and Sasha make themselves comfortable between their legs. My Adonis is on his knees waiting for me. The two women are leaned back on their elbows with their eyes closed and mouths open in ecstasy. Soft moans could be heard as smooth fingertips manipulate warm flesh, tongues dancing across erect clitorises.

I sit down in front of my Adonis, and his lips find my cave instantly. Automatically, my body language is identical to my counterparts. I gyrate my hips slow then fast, and slow again until my sweetness is dripping off the table's edge. The two fingers inside of me caress my cervix, bringing me one screaming orgasm after another.

I lie back so only my back is on the table, and wrap my arms around my knees, inviting my Adonis into my wetness. Almond eyes smile down at me, although his lips reveal nothing as he enters me an inch at a time. His strokes cause my wetness to spill out on the sides, and run down the back of my thighs while he uses his thumb to stimulate my weak spot.

I close my eyes, and my head falls to the side upon contact when his tongue touches the under side of my breast. His thick tongue makes small circles all the way up to my erect nipples where he moistens them with his wet tongue, and then he blows cool air on them making them stand straight up. Because he is laying on me, and my legs are spread out on either side of me, I can feel his every pulsation. This only makes me even wetter.

Before I can protest, my Adonis pulls out, and moves over to My Goddess, Sasha taking his place. I look to see that everyone on the table remains in the same position, and the person between our legs moves over one. This went in every twenty minutes for two hours.

The Finale

By the end of the night, Sasha, The Chocolate Boy Wonder, and my Adonis are sitting on the couch. Sasha is wearing an eight-inch strap-on dildo with clitoral vibrators attached. I had my knees pressed to the couch, and the lips of my vagina wrapped around my Adonis's soldier. My Goddess and The Other Woman assume the same position right next to me.

By putting my right hand on the wall, I indicate to the other riders that my orgasm is fast approaching. Within seconds we all explode and collapse, trying to still our wildly beating hearts. Not looking at each other, we get up one by one and begin to dress. Once the room was cleaned, we file out, returning to our separate lives until the next time we meet.

Yeah, Just Like That

"Is that how you want it, Boo?"

"Yeah, papi, just like that."

It's like nine in the morning, and as you can see I'm a little occupied. I'm still trying to figure out how the guy I spent getting to know in the video store turned into an overnight guest. I'm sure things like that happen, but not to me. I like to think that I'm selective in the mates I sleep with, and I even surprised myself at the events that took place.

I am in Hollywood Video trying to pick up some smut DVD's on the down low. Not that I should be embarrassed, but I didn't want to have to explain it later. So there I am perusing the aisles trying to find something down right raunchy. Not paying attention I reached for a DVD the same time as the gentleman standing next to me did.

"So, the lady has good taste."

Hesitating at first, I finally looked into the eyes of the most thuggishly handsome guy. I love thugs, and he was definitely it. Standing at 5'11", about 230lbs., dark chocolate, dimples…damn the tape! I found what I was looking for right here.

"You can say that," I openly flirted. While licking my lips, and showing my cleavage I silently wished I had put on some cute underclothes instead of my plain "around the house" ones.

"My Baby Got Back Volume 21? It took that many to get the point across?" He smiled at me seductively, flashing nice white teeth.

"I suppose you can do better?"

"Do you have to ask?"

"So, the gentleman has confidence?"

"Twenty-four seven," was his response as we stood breast to chest.

"We'll see."

"Your place or mine?"

"Yours." I couldn't divulge the location of the Bat Cave.

"Okay, Sporty. I get off in about twenty minutes. Let's make it happen."
"The name is Heaven."
"Heavenly Angel…fits you."
"Seeyouintwenty."

Trying not to run out the store, I practically broke my neck getting home. In ten minutes flat I was showered, and smelling good enough to eat. It wasn't until I got back to the video store that I decided to invite him to my place. Initially I was going to accompany him to his spot, but I knew I would have more control on my own turf.

When I pulled up, he was just pulling the gate down. This man was built like a warrior. Although I've never seen a real live warrior, he would surely be the mold they were made from. I smelled his Curve for Men cologne before he got in the car. It didn't smell like he bathed in it either. Mixed with his natural male scent it was intoxicating, and I was soaking wet.

On the travel back to my home, I found out quite a bit of information. For instance, his name is Patience Robinson. I didn't believe him until he showed me his driver's license. (I learned later on why the name Patience was perfect for him.) Originally from Brooklyn, he's been in Philly for the past three years. At the age of thirty-one he owns his home, holds a bachelor's in early childhood education, and is the owner of the Hollywood Video I frequent.

"So, where's your car?"

"I drive a 2003 Suburban. It's parked in the garage behind the video store. I don't like parking on the street." I was very impressed.

Once inside my apartment, we chatted over shots of Bacardi Limon and fruit. What I thought would be a booty-call with a "would be" thug turned into a very interesting evening. Before I knew it, it was three in the morning.

"Well, I thought I was bringing you here to handle business, but talking was cool too." I was flirting shamelessly, and didn't care. He was there to get inside of me by any means necessary, and that's it. We could talk afterwards.

"We're about to handle business right now."

Patience walked over to my stereo system, and searched through my CD collection. Normally I'd have snapped about someone touching my stuff, but for some odd reason it didn't bother me that he did. Soon after, Dave Hollister's "Chicago '85" began to play. Patience looked me in the eyes, and I was like a deer caught in headlights. I couldn't move.

Slowly he started dancing seductively, and removing his clothes. My man had a six-pack beyond belief, and talk about well hung. If the print in his pants was any indication of what he was working with, then this man had to be part horse or at least a close relative to Mr. Ed. He stood directly in front of me, and his jeans and boxers came down all by themselves. I found myself eye to eye with his soldier, and I resisted the urge to taste it.

When I reached for it, he stepped back, and continued his dance. I was still amazed at the even color of his penis, which sported a big mushroom shaped head. Where most dudes ten inches or longer suffer from what I call the "multi-colored" penis, his was an even chocolate to match the rest of his body. I was anxious to find out if it tasted just as sweet.

As the song changed, Patience stood me up and began to undress me. Patience is a virtue I need to practice because I was ready to get it on. He slowed my fast ass right down and stretched me out in the center of the floor. Thank God for carpet.

Taking his time, he kissed my forehead with the softest lips ever. Not before kissing both eyelids, and outlining my lips with his tongue did he take both nipples into his warm mouth at the same time. I wanted to die right there on the spot. Men normally jump from your neck to your coochi-coo like your breasts don't exist.

Trailing soft kisses down my stomach, I squirmed with delight under his skillful tongue. When he got to the treasure, I was ready. I was completely hairless except for a patch in the shape of an arrow pointing downward. I heard him laugh a little as he raised my knees up to my chest, and teased my clit. It felt a little odd at first until I saw something silver in his mouth. Patience had his tongue pierced, and I was forever grateful.

He took his time circling the little man in the boat before capsizing and drowning him. I was shaking so badly you'd have thought I had epilepsy. He spread my butt cheeks, and proceeded to devour me in the prone position. I couldn't take it anymore as his tongue made contact with my asshole. I begged for him to finally put it in.

Patience leaned up slowly and plunged deep inside of me without warning. He pulled out slowly only feeding me the head at first. Just as I was about to explode, he dove back in, and drove me into an orgasm so electric I could light up all of New York. Flipping me over, he chose the anal entry, and I happily obliged. I loved how he took his time inserting, and didn't try to force it all in. It was on like popcorn. He was talking shit, and smacking me on my ass. I all but told him I loved him.

He then put me in positions I didn't think I was capable of performing. The doozy was when he laid me on my back, and pulled my legs up until only my shoulders touched the floor. He then stood over top of me, and squatted down until he was all the way in. You could never imagine the amount of pleasure I received from that. After what felt like hours, Patience finally came to an orgasm, and exploded all over my stomach. Pure genius. I broke the rules, and let him stay over.

The next morning I woke up to him pleasing me from the side. I was all smiles, and giving it back like it was my job. It was even better, and Patience had me cumming from here to eternity.

"Is that how you like it, Boo?"

"Yeah, papi, just like that."

An Oral Fixation

Call me crazy, but I have a thing for nice straight white teeth. It shows you practice good personal hygiene. How do I look letting a brotha go down on me, and his teeth look like the guy in the Plus White commercial? Now I have to douche with Listerine because you gave me gingivitis. I have a thing for a healthy mouth, and that was my number one reason for becoming an orthodontist.

Speaking of being oral, most women won't admit it, but I absolutely love giving head. It's just something about watching a man's eyes roll into the back of his head right before he explodes in the back of my throat that gives me an instant orgasm. Drives me crazy every time.

As usual I spend my days saving people from yuck mouth. After dealing with gum disease and root canals, it's a rare occurrence to get someone with perfect teeth. Most of my patients come in with chipped teeth from a tongue piercing or rotted teeth from lack of brushing. A few have teeth that look like they haven't brushed since they got their permanent set or they chew on tin cans as a hobby. Sometimes the tarter is so thick it looks like it could be scraped off with a butter knife, and I swear I want to charge them extra.

When Eternal comes in, he is always a constant reminder that I do my job well. This man looked good, you hear me? He wasn't all toned and buffed, but he had his shit together. I noticed that he always brought a book to read at each visit. An intellectual, I like that.

While cleaning his teeth and checking a tooth he said was giving him some trouble, we got on the topic of orally satisfying the opposite sex. What can I say? It happens. We were talking about an article he was reading in an Essence magazine about the lack of oral sex in relationships.

"So, you're telling me that all women give head, they're just in denial?" Eternal asked while I was setting up the tray to clean his pearly whites.

"Correct. When you're young it's considered nasty. When you become a teenager it's not as nasty as you thought, but you vow to never do it. Now that you're all grown up, it's the best thing since sliced bread."

"Interesting analogy, and you believe guys feel the same way?"

"No, I believe guys start kind of early. That's their bragging rights."

He laughed at what I thought about the whole oral sex thing, and I joined in. I have a comfortable relationship with most of my patients. It helps the day go by faster. I maintain what I call a friendly/professional atmosphere in my office. I get most of my patients in and out, but I do have a few that I shoot the breeze with, and am comfortable talking about any and everything under the sun.

I quickly finished up with who is now known as Eternal, and sent him to schedule his next visit. When I came out to greet my next patient, my receptionist gave me an envelope from Eternal. I stuck it in my pocket vowing to read it later as I tended to my next patient.

By the end of the day I was exhausted, but happy. Before leaving, I looked at my schedule for the next day. Afterwards, I shut down everything and prepared to leave the office. Just as I was leaving, I remembered the envelope my secretary gave me, and dashed back in to get it before the alarm went off.

Once inside of my car, I was finally able to gather my thoughts. Further inspection produced an invitation to join Eternal for dinner tonight at eight. Immediately deciding against it, I began to drive home. Soon after, thoughts of my girl friends telling me I don't get out enough started running through my head. I decided as I pulled up to the restaurant to go ahead and live a little.

Tondalayah's is a nice cozy soul food restaurant with a touch of class. The décor was intimate with candlelight and soft music. The food tasted like your grandmother was in the kitchen putting it down, and it was reasonably priced too. When I walked in, I spotted Eternal sitting at the bar. He looked up as I was walking towards him, and gave me a smile so pretty it made me proud of my work.

"Glad you could make it," he said.

"Hey, I never disappoint my patients." We were seated in the far corner of the restaurant away from the conversation of the other patrons. After getting settled, the waiter took our drink orders.

"I'll have a diet coke, no lemon, and give the lady whatever she wants."

I really wanted a glass of wine, but I went with the flow and ordered a Sprite. After giving our meal orders, we wasted no time picking up our conversation from earlier.

"I've been thinking about what you said all afternoon," Eternal began.

"Okay, and what conclusion did you come to?"

"After careful deliberation, and being true to myself," he said with a sly grin, "I decided you're right."

"Good. I'm glad somebody else in the world see things the same as I do."

"I hope this doesn't sound offensive, but…"

"But what?"

"I was hoping you were open to getting to know each other orally."

"Excuse me?" I had to wonder if for a second I was indeed getting too close to my patients. I'm sure the look on my face spoke volumes.

"I'm not trying to offend you, and I truly apologize if I have. It's just that I've been wondering what you taste like since we've met."

"I don't know what to say."

"Don't say anything, just think about it."

The food came right on time, and we began to eat. I made sure to take small bites, and chew my food twenty one times just like I learned in dental school. Before I knew what hit me, Eternal was sitting extremely close to me, and was pulling my panties to the side. Good thing I wore a short skirt.

"What are you doing?"

"You know exactly what I'm doing, Ms. Cook. You want me to stop?"

Instead of answering, I sat back and enjoyed what Eternal was doing to me. Just as I was about to have an orgasm, he stuck two fingers inside of me, and I had to kiss him to keep from screaming out in ecstasy. When it finally passed, he pulled his fingers out and proceeded to lick all my juices off. Afterwards, he stuck his tongue in my mouth so I could taste my own honey.

"Lets finish this somewhere more private," Eternal whispered in my ear as he simultaneously took my earlobe between his perfect teeth.

"Come on."

After the waiter wrapped our food to go, Eternal paid for dinner leaving him a generous tip. I decided to leave my car in the parking garage, and we took his car back to his place. He only lived about two blocks down, so walking back to my car was an option.

His home was beautiful. He gave me a tour of his humble abode ending with the pool. It reminded me of something out of Better Homes & Gardens. Eternal offered me something to drink. I thought it might be soda, but to my surprise he bought back a glass of White Zinfandel.

I sat back on the lounge chair, and Eternal began to strip. I almost choked when I saw how buffed he actually was. He has a chiseled physic, but not one that looks like he spends his every waking moment in the gym. His looks like he exercises on a daily without over doing it.

"Care to join me?" he stood in the water at the pools edge offering me his hand. He didn't look like he would let me drown, but for some reason I still hesitated.

"I…I can't swim." I must have looked like a scared little girl standing there even though I tried to put on a brave face.

"Come on. I won't let anything happen to you." He dipped his body down into the water up to his chin. When he stood back up the water droplets on his skin looked like he was a chocolate bar melting a little bit. I wanted to remove every drop with my tongue, but my legs wouldn't move.

"I don't know. Maybe I should be heading home." Eternal looked at me like I had to be kidding, but because he is a gentleman he stayed calm in his approach. He flashed his pretty white teeth at me before dipping his body back down into the water. The more his eyes caressed my skin the more I wanted my body pressed up against his.

"Serena Cook. I know you're not scared."

"Of whom?" I tried to be cocky, but this playing hard to get act was wearing me down. I know I wanted to be in the pool and all over him, but I didn't want to seem easy.

"No, not of whom. Of drowning."

Eternal got out of the water, and strolled over to me. I watched the water glisten all over his body. My mouth was dry as a desert.

"Serena, I swear on everything that is good I will not let anything happen to you. The pool ranges from six to eight feet. We'll stay at the low end. I promise."

"I don't have a bathing suit."

"Neither do I."

"Besides, it's getting late."

"I won't hurt you, I promise."

Before I could make any further protest, Eternal began kissing me and fondling my breasts. I was out my clothes, and in the water before I could blink. The coolness of the water gave me goose bumps all over.

"Now, rest your head on my chest, and just feel the waves."

Eternal floated me around the pool, and soon I was comfortable with floating. Deciding to sit on the edge of the pool was not a good idea. As soon as I sat down, Eternal swam up between my legs and began tasting me. Reflexes made me lean back and put my feet up on his shoulders.

As good as it felt I wanted to satisfy my own curiosity and taste him. Somehow, I maneuvered myself back into the pool, and gave him the blowjob of his life under water. As he eased up the steps, I moved with him. I was determined not to let him go until he exploded, and he gave me what I was looking for.

We got into the sixty-nine position on the side of the pool, and drove each other crazy. After both of us experienced multiple orgasms I got up on wobbly legs and started to get dressed.

"Why are you leaving?" he asked with a worried look on his face.

"I have to work in the morning, sweetie."

"Will you come back tomorrow? Stay here tonight."

"Eternal, I enjoyed the evening, but I really have to get going."

"We will get together soon, right."

"Call me," and with that I was gone.

I walked back to my car, and my smile never left my face. When I got home, I enjoyed a nice warm bath, and smiled myself to sleep.

A couple of months went by before I saw Eternal again. As usual I was in the clinic willing the day to end. I had my last client scheduled early so I could get out into the sunshine. After taking a quick caffeine break, I went to service my last patient of the day. When I walked into the exam room, Eternal was sitting in the examination chair smiling brightly.

"What can I do for you today?"

"The usual."

As I got my tray ready to clean his teeth, Eternal got up and locked the door.

"What are you doing?"

"Enjoying you."

"But I'm at work."

"That means you won't be loud, huh?"

Eternal kissed me, and it was on and popping. We made love right in room number six. Four months into the future found me pregnant, and Mrs. Eternal Gooding. I couldn't help but smile when I treated patients in that room. I almost felt bad about what I did, but hey, that's what Lysol is for, right?

Old Flames

Running into an old girlfriend can go one of two ways. Depending on how things ended, it could actually lead to new beginnings. That's how I felt when I ran into Anai.

It was kind of awkward at first. I was standing at the bus stop on my way to pick up my car from the shop when I was side tracked by this woman in red. She looked good, and oddly familiar. Just as the bus pulled up, memories of our lovemaking flashed temporarily. Before I could control my thoughts, I was calling out her name.

"Anai? Hey girl, wassup?"

"Eugene?"

"You know it."

"Long time no see. How's life been treating you?"

We got to talking, and pretty soon I forgot all about the bus. While reminiscing about old times, I set up a date to meet with her later on in the day. We exchanged numbers, and she gave me her address in case I wanted to stop by after I picked up my car.

Oddly enough, I found myself thinking about Anai the entire day. She pretty much looked the same. I noticed she gained a few pounds, but it was cool. She was thick in all the right places, and if there were places that weren't right it would be worked off from the pounding I would be giving her. I was looking forward to this evening.

Later that evening I made my way over to Anai's place. She has a cute little apartment over in West Philly. I found myself wondering if she had changed much or was she still the same easy going person she was back in the day. After stopping to get a bottle of sparkling apple cider, I got my heart together, and knocked on the door.

"Who is it?"

"Eugene."

"Hey, you made it."

Anai looked good. She had her hair in that wrap style the ladies are wearing now days, and a nice one-piece negligee covering her frame. She was barefoot, and I noticed her toes had French tips. I sort of have a foot fetish. She definitely had curves that she didn't have before, and I wasn't mad at her. Thinking about how her head game was back in the day had me stiff as a joint, and I was hoping it got better over the years.

We sat, and talked for hours. Catching up on old times made the day get away from you like that. When I looked at my watch, it was almost four in the morning. Anai was looking damn good to me, and I figured I should leave before I said something stupid.

"You can stay if you want."

"I think I should be going. I have an early start in the morning."

"If you insist."

Anai then stood up, and stepped out of her nightgown. She was a little thicker than I remember, but I could look past that. It took everything in me not to jump on her when she walked away toward her bedroom.

I stood in the living room stuck on stupid. My mind was telling me to behave, and go home. Justice (my johnson) was telling me to get in there, and handle my business. Curiosity took over, and I made my way to the back.

Upon entry, I found Anai spread out on her back in the middle of the bed. Her knees were pulled up to her breasts, and she was teasing her clitoris with a silver bullet. Wasting no time undressing, I quickly joined in the festivities.

I started at her toes, taking each one in my mouth. She tasted like chocolate. Like she had some kind of flavored syrup spread all over her body. I took my time caressing her thighs, and tasting behind her knees. When I got to her clitoris, she tasted like peaches.

I spread her lips apart, and her clit popped right out. I stuck my tongue inside of her to get a taste of her warm walls, and she grabbed my head putting my whole face in it. I wasn't going to stop until she came. Anai started moaning louder than before, and her whole body began to shake. I made sure to be right there to swallow every drop.

I then moved up to the top of the bed so I could taste those nice breasts of hers. Anai immediately sat up, and began kissing my neck. I closed my eyes, and enjoyed the attention as I felt her tongue flick across both my nipples. She trailed kisses down my stomach, and deep throated Justice until I couldn't stand it.

Just when I thought I was about to cum, she pulled Justice out of her mouth and began rolling my balls around on her warm tongue. I felt her lift my balls up, and her tongue began to play around my asshole. Damn, this girl is a freak!

Gaining control of my penis, I gestured for her to get on top. She easily put the condom on me, and positioned herself over Justice. Anai started by riding the head, and that was driving me crazy. Slowly she began to lower herself on me, and I felt her walls squeezing me when she rose up. I sat up on my elbows, and she fed me her nipples both at the same time.

I flipped her over and began to long stroke her, and play with her clit simultaneously. That had her calling my name, and squirming under me.

"You ready to cum, papi?"

"Whenever you ready, ma."

Next thing I know she did something with her hips, and my heart stopped beating for about five seconds. I've never had an orgasm like that. I was ready to pull out a ring. We finished up in the shower, and pretty soon it was morning.

"I hope we can get together again soon," I said

"I hope so, too."

"Okay, ma, I'll call you."

I found myself thinking about Anai all day. I was almost becoming extra whipped, and started to call her a couple of times. Better judgment changed my mind. A few days had gone by, and I finally got a call from her.

"Hey, girl, wassup?"

"Just wondering if you could come over. I got an itch that needs to be scratched."

"I'm on my way."

When I got there, Anai had candles burning all around the apartment. I noticed her room now had a swing hanging from the ceiling, and a table set up on the side with a variety of dildos, body creams, and gels. Anai offered me a glass of Alize, and immediately began to undress me.

"Do you mind handcuffs?" Anai asked while twirling a pair of fuzzy pink cuffs around her index finger.

"Not at all."

I stretched out on the bed, and Anai handcuffed my hands and feet to the four corners of the bed. She began to rub me down with warm scented oil, and I closed my eyes to enjoy the treatment. I thought it was just my imagination. It felt like more than one pair of hands was on me, and when I opened my eyes two other women had joined the party.

"Anai, what's this all about?"

"Shhh...just sit back, and enjoy the ride."

The women stood around me in their birthday suits, and the game of ménage quad began. I made sure I was properly protected with a cherry flavored condom. Anai and Sheila, the woman I later called Ms. Nasty, gave me head at the same time. Sheila straddled me in the sixty-nine position, and joined the other women in their heart-stopping act of fellatio.

Anai was using a vibrator on Ms. Nasty from the back. The smell of sex hung so heavy in the air it felt like a blanket on our skin. Flipping the script, Anai rode the head of my nightstick while Candy sat on my face, and they stroked each other into screaming orgasms. Anai was riding me like a pro while Sheila simultaneously tongue kissed their nipples.

In the midst of our play, I noticed all three women had the same exact butterfly tattooed on their right shoulder like they were a part of some kind of secret sorority. The girls took turns pleasing me and each other for hours.

Roughly around five hours later, Anai took me out the handcuffs, and we took it up again in her custom made shower. While I was dicking Sheila from the back, Anai and Candy were in their own little world on the shower floor in a sixty-nine position that would put Heather Hunter to shame. It wasn't until we were showered and dress that I found out our fiasco was videotaped. What a night.

Although I hoped for something on a more personal level with Anai, we decided it was best to just remain friends. We still get together with Candy and Sheila every so often, but our friendship blossomed into something wonderful.

Happy Birthday To Me...

Today is my 25th birthday. You would think I'd have reason to celebrate, right? All of my family and friends were bugging me about going out, but I just wanted to be home alone with a nice stiff dick. Not just any o' dick, either. I'm talking about some booty-bustin', don't need no KY-Jelly, fuck me till I pass out then get up and smack my momma for not telling me it was so good dick. The kind that'll make you leave work early.

So I'm sitting in my cubicle flipping through my mental Rolodex. Like most women I was picturing all of the men that I've slept with, and pointing out their flaws. I was looking for perfection, and just as I was about to let it go, Malachi popped into my mind. Just thinking about him made my mouth water. I called him Snickers. He was just that chocolate!

I called him on his cell phone, and left him a sweet little message informing him on what I had in mind. He must have been listening in on the call because no soon as I put the receiver back on the cradle, my phone rang.

"Hello. Thanks for calling Howard, Kenny & Greg, Inc. This is Storm. How can I help you?"

"You can start by sitting on my face, and letting me taste you."

"Is that so?"

"Yeah..."

"Tonight at nine. Don't be late."

"Cool. Got a surprise for you."

"Later."

Simple as that. Set up the rendezvous, and try not to pass out from all the excitement. I was a tad upset that he didn't remember my birthday, but the pounding I was going to get later would make up for that. By 3:45pm, I was in my car and zooming out of the parking garage. I had five hours to get ready for the freak of my life, and I wanted everything to be perfect.

It took no time getting the love nest together. Handcuffs? Check. Feathers? Check. Hector and John (my vibrators)? Check. Passion fruit and whipped cream? Double check. Everything was ready, and so was I.

By nine o' clock I was dressed to kill in a red backless chemise, and my red strap to the knee sandals. My hair lay perfectly, and I applied a light lip-gloss to perfectly heart shape lips. Just as I finished misting my body with Clinique Happy my doorbell rang. I took my time answering because I knew Malachi would wait.

When I opened the door, I was truly impressed. Malachi was the bomb in chocolate slacks and a cream button down shirt that made his muscular frame look even more delicious. The surprise was the equally attractive woman he had on his side. Naturally I started to question the couple, but I'm always game for something new, and decided to let them in. Malachi presented me with a butter cream cake. The two and the five were curved penises with chocolate heads. I was even more surprised that he remembered my birthday since he hadn't mentioned it when I talked to him earlier.

Normally I wouldn't admit it, but the woman he called Amber was actually easy going. She had a sense of humor that was contagious, and she was very attractive. It shocked me even more when I started thinking about ways to turn her out. Now, don't get me wrong, I'm strictly dickly. I love me a nice stiff one, but I'd be lying if I said I never thought about what a woman could do to me. We held conversation for a while longer before I invited them to my bedroom.

Determined not to be nervous, I allowed Amber to undress me. She took her time running her soft as silk hands over my exposed flesh. All I had on was a thong under my chemise so it wasn't much to take off. I saw Malachi lounging on the love seat strategically placed by my bed. He was completely nude, stroking his massive penis slowly and deliberately. He never took his eyes off us.

The warmth on my nipples turned my attention back to Amber. She now had me completely naked, and was simultaneously sucking my nipples and fingering my clit. My mind kept reminding me how crazy this was, but my body was screaming yes, yes, yes!

I don't even remember lying on the bed, but I found my head buried in my pillows while Amber drove me crazy with her tongue. Further inspection showed Malachi pleasing Amber with his tongue from behind.

Amber was definitely a pro at this. I stretched my legs wider, and she parted my lips and drowned my clit causing all kinds of electricity. Call me Spider Woman because I was definitely climbing walls. She licked me from my asshole to my belly button, and not specifically in that order. I was loving the work that Amber was giving me, but I was ready to be fucked into oblivion. I wanted all 11_ inches of Malachi, and I wanted it now.

"Malachi, I want you, Boo."

"Now…"

"Right now."

"Open up, ma."

After properly protecting himself, he teased me with the tip of his nightstick. Amber levitated just above my lips, and I wasted no time hooking her up. She held my legs up while Malachi fondled her breasts.

We went from one extreme to the next as we switched from one position to another. We ended up in a three-way doggy style position that was off the chain. Amber brought along a strap on that she diligently stepped into. She took me from the back, and Malachi had her. On the same rhythm we rocked ourselves into the greatest orgasm of all times.

Five minutes before the next day, we finally settled down to some gentle stroking and petting. I made myself comfortable in Amber's arms. Just as I was dozing off, Malachi came back into the room carrying the cake we abandoned earlier. Amber sang happy birthday in the most beautiful voice I've ever heard. We shared a bottle of Moet, and devoured the cake and each other well into the next day.

tongueandcheek.com

    I found myself in this chat room one night, tongueandcheek.com, a very popular site among the 25 to 35-age range. The site offered everything from shopping for sex toys to playing erotic board games. The chat rooms ranged from "dating only" to "something extra", everything you could want, and more from a website. It didn't hurt that it was free.
    One lonely night when I couldn't find anyone to go out with me I decided to check it out. I remembered receiving a flyer advertising the free membership when I was out with a few people from the office at a happy hour spot close to the job. While my slower than molasses modem connected me to AOL, I got myself a glass of juice, and settled in for the night. After checking my mail, I immediately logged on.
    The site opened with prompts for the basic membership information. I wanted my screen name to stand out, and after careful contemplation I came up with the perfect name. Just plain old Tasha wouldn't due. For now on I would be known as *nyce&wet247*. Describes me perfectly. After adding a few pictures and telling the world a little bit about myself, I was ready to browse the chats. For an hour or so, men and women alike quizzed me on how I came up with my screen name. I was up to my ears in instant messages, and was honestly having a good time.
    I never entertained the thought of actually meeting anyone face to face. I was content with the images flashing across my screen until I received an IM from T.Y.A.N.
    "What does T.Y.A.N. mean?" I typed back as quickly as possible.
    "Do you really want to know?" the stranger responded.
    "Yeah…"
    "Tasting You All Night."
    I was very impressed. We went back and forth for a while exchanging pictures in the midst of our conversation. His screen name did nothing for his looks. I tend to go for men of a darker complexion. T.Y.A.N. was a light skinned guy, a little on the thin side, about 5'8", and had freckles. Nothing to scream about, but friends are always good to have. He comple-

mented me on my looks several times, and before I logged off for the night I added him to my buddy list. For a little over a month we IM'd each other. Late one night T.Y.A.N., now known as Talib, invited me to a masked ball.

"You mean like a 'Phantom of the Opera' type thing?" I typed back excitedly. I was becoming a pro at this.

"Yeah, everyone is in lingerie, but you have to keep your mask on at all times," he responded anxiously.

"Sure, why not."

"I must warn you though. It starts getting a little wild as the night goes on."

"I'm the epitome of wild," was my response. On the inside I'm really laid back, but I could be spontaneous sometimes.

"Okay, here's the address…"

Talib proceeded to give me the address and date of the party. It turned out to be popping off this coming weekend, and he also gave me his home telephone number just in case I got lost. The very next day I ran out to Lane Bryant, and got me a sexy one-piece man catcher.

I picked out a lilac slip dress that fell to my ankles with a split on the right side up to my waist. The back was out all the way down to just above my ass crack, and was held up by a thin strap that tied around the neck. I'm every bit of a size fourteen, but at 5'8" my weight is well proportioned to my height. Most people would say I'm pear shaped. I have a healthy amount of booty (thanks to my ancestors), and nice perky breast with dark nipples that sit up all by themselves.

The dress fit perfectly. I know this because when I stepped out the dressing room to look in the full-length mirror the guys in the dressing area waiting on their girlfriends confirmed. I finished the outfit off with a diamond and lilac choker, diamond-studded earrings, and perfectly manicured nails to match. I willed the remainder of the week to go by fast.

It was a day before the party, and I was truly excited. I had my hair appointment set for the next morning. I wanted my wrap to be freshly done for the event. I spent all evening after work getting my legs waxed. I can't have any hair on me. The party was in Elizabeth, New Jersey, and I didn't want to drive old Betsy that far. Quick thinking led me to a Budget Rent-A-Car, and into a 2003 Benz Jeep.

Once I got home, I waxed my bikini line, and trimmed the remaining hair into a triangle. Before applying my avocado facemask, I e-mailed Talib to let him know I would see him the next evening. He told me what he would be wearing, and I called it a night.

I woke up bright and early the next day to get my hair done. Shyce hooked me up as usual, and I gave him a nice tip when he was done. By then it was early afternoon. A Touch of Class Hair Designs is always packed on Saturday mornings so I was happy I made my appointment early. I contemplated taking one of my girl friends with me if for nothing but safety reasons. For some odd reason, I knew I had nothing to worry about, and the idea left my mind as quickly as it came.

By eight o' clock, I was adding the finishing touches. I found a great mask with vibrant feathers at a costume store. It had an elastic band that snapped at the neck, so I didn't have to worry about holding it up all night. I purchased some jasmine scented body glitter from Bath and Body Works that went perfectly with my outfit. I made my face up in neutral colors that made my almond shaped eyes shine. Last, but not least, I slipped into my lilac sandals.

I arrived at the party by 10:30 that night. The band was in full swing, and everyone seemed to be enjoying themselves. Mask in place, I entered the party and prepared to mingle. Lets just say I turned heads all the way to the punch bowl. Just as I was testing the bright red concoction a deep masculine voice was close to my ear.

"Nice and wet is right."

I turned around to a sexy vanilla brother with the whitest teeth I've ever seen on a man. If it weren't for the light dusting of freckles peeking out from under his mask I would have never known who he was.

"Talib?"

"In the flesh."

He looked good. Talib was dressed in silk p.j.'s the color of the sky just before a down pour. His mask was silver with ice blue jewels adorned by navy blue, black, deep purple, and white feathers. He was amazing.

"Hi. Thanks for inviting me."

"Sure, no problem, enjoying yourself?"

"Yes. I just got here, but yes. Thanks."

"Good...care for a tour?"

I linked on to his arm, and he showed me around what appeared to be a mini mansion. Fourteen rooms, six baths, a gorgeous garden, and a stunning wrap around porch were spread out in front of me. Come to find out the place was his. Just as we entered the ballroom *This Woman's Work* by Maxwell began to play. Everyone coupled up so we did the same.

Talib kissed me on my neck, and caressed my exposed back. I felt so right in his arms. Slowly I noticed the partygoers gathered in groups of four and five began to strip down to their birthday suits leaving only their mask. The smell of sex was heavy in the air, and it made me extremely horny.

My better judgment took over, and I tried to pull away. Talib held me tighter, and I felt him teasing my clitoris through my gown. I wanted to leave, but my feet were planted. I saw him get down on his knees and lift my dress up to my hips. I opted to go bare bottom, and was very happy I did.

Talib stroked me into ecstasy. Next thing I know four men circled us, and joined in. I found myself perched on Talib's lips with one of the guys giving me a rim shot. I had one on each nipple, and a nice long dick down my throat. Isn't life grand?

I never thought I would be able to handle five men at once, but I held it down. If only I had a video camera. None of my friends would ever believe me. I didn't get home until eight the next morning. Before I left, Talib informed me that tongueandcheek.com was, in fact, his website. That's how he was able to live so lavishly. I also found out he threw those parties four times a year. One for each season. At a twenty-dollar cover charge and at least three hundred people there, lets just say I was very impressed.

Monday morning came, and I fell back into my normal routine. I stayed away from the website for fear of what I might get sucked into. Months went by, and that party was now a memory tucked into the back of my mind.

I was chilling in my loft apartment watching *Media's Family Reunion* when the bell rang. I started to ignore it because I wasn't expecting any visitors. Who ever it was became persistent. I took precautions and looked through the peephole. A Federal Express truck was parked out front, and a scrawny delivery boy held a package. I signed for it, and closed the door.

The box was from *Fetishes*. I didn't remember ordering anything from there, but I opened the box anyway. Inside was an invitation from Talib, and a navy blue slip dress similar to the one I wore to his party. A pair of sandals, matching accessories from Tiffany's, and a single white rose completed the assemble.

It disturbed me that he knew my address, but then I remembered he owned the website, and I volunteered that information when I signed up. Curiosity took over, and I went.

A limo arrived to pick me up at nine that evening. I gave my best friend Talib's address just in case I popped up missing. When I got there, I was escorted straight to the master bedroom. I should have been offended, but it never crossed my mind.

The room was decorated in deep burgundy and black. The California king size bed was made of a heavy cherry wood. The view offered a well-manicured lawn with a duck pond in the middle. At least three swans floated amidst them.

Just as I made myself comfortable on the bed, Talib came in. I'm not into vanilla, but I could surely get into him. He was a little taller than I remembered, and his body was toned.

"You know I waited for you for months. Why'd you stay away?" Talib quizzed in his deep sexy voice.

"I honestly couldn't answer that."

"I want you here with me."

"But we don't know each other."

"You'll love me. Believe it."

Before I had the chance to answer, Talib was inside me, wrapped around me, and in my pores. I couldn't take it. When would I wake up from this dream? The deeper question was, did I want to? Just as I was getting my head together, he slipped a three-karat diamond ring onto my finger. What could I say? I'm a sucker for diamonds.

Two months later I was Mrs. Talib Saheem, and I was extremely happy. Most would say it's because he's paid. The truth is I opened my heart, and allowed Talib to love me. In return I loved him more. We continued throwing parties, but this time the only woman he was sexing was me.

Comfort Zone

I'm in search of poetry in motion. Liquid love on the tip of my tongue that wraps around my body, and frees my spirit. Intense friction on the crest of my being that is mind blowing beyond belief. A love so pure it can only be touched by angels descending from heaven, and landing on my soul. I'm in search of poetry in motion.

Take me to the moon. Led only by your beating heart and natural attraction, I will follow you to the end of the earth. My body is wrapped in your essence, tears of joy moistening my flesh. I'm in search of soul shattering love that leaves me floating amongst the clouds. My high is an all-natural feeling of being in love with you.

Take my hand. From here on out, your fear of flying is nonexistent. I'm prepared to climb walls. Moaning in your ear as you caress my chocolate body is part of my every day fantasy. Imagine being so into it we don't even realize we're levitating above the bed in a forbidden dance made for lovers.

We have no limitations. The sky is made for us to float upon the clouds and become one in any position your heart desires. Take my hand. Your fear of flying is nonexistent. You'd be surprised at the things you actually like.

Our hearts will become one as we take the path to bliss and ecstasy ever lasting. Take the lead. Your fear of living is nonexistent. Plunge into my cavern, and drink from the fountain I call Life. We will nurture each other and become warriors. The invincible less intimidating. We have no boundaries. Only you, me, and our lives before us. Your fear of the inevitable is nonexistent.

We will walk proud, hand in hand through the gate of our souls until we are surrounded by butterflies in the Garden of Peace. Keep in mind we have no limitations. Your fantasy starts now.

Let go. Let me take you there so you can see, and feel your fantasies come to life one at a time. Up close and personal. Follow your hearts vision, and I'll take you back to the day you became mine. Take my soul. Your fear of loving me is nonexistent. I'm here to take you to levels beyond your wildest dreams. We'll walk the earth as king and queen, and you'll reign supreme as I watch you from my pedestal. Forever is the limit, so ask yourself how high you want to fly.

Come in and relax yourself. Only those with an open mind and content heart are welcome. Steady your heart, and prepare your soul for tantalizing ecstasy. Go on… it's okay to relax in the comfort zone.

Rest your weary shoulders, and enjoy the feel of my body wrapped around you. Ease your mind as I take your toes into my mouth one at a time. Your senses come alive as you enjoy the scent of body butter being massaged into your skin. Leave all of your burdens at the door. I'm not done yet.

You are in a realm of divine peace. Your every desire and most lewd fantasies can happen if only you would let go of your troubles. Allow me to slip into your mind, and make you a very happy man.

We'll start with a warm coconut bath, and a double shot of Hennessey. Me and my partner will be your servants for the evening. You will not have to lift a finger except to please either of us in any fashion you choose. Let's start by seeing what my tongue ring does for you.

I'll begin by circling the head of your rod with the tip of my tongue. The moans easing from your slightly parted lips tell me you're enjoying it. My partner is messaging your neck while the bubbles tickle your rib cage.

I decide to be daring and insert a well-oiled finger into your anus while I give you the best head of your life. I whisper in your ear that nobody will find out. Trying new things are okay in the comfort zone.

Now stretched out on a bed so soft it feels like clouds is our playground. My partner eases down on your love stick while I play with her pierced clit with my tongue. You insert one finger into her anus while you watch us play through the ceiling mirror. Colored lights reflecting off the all white back drop cast provocative shapes on our bodies, making the game that much more interesting as we work ourselves into heaven beyond belief.

Things are about to get sticky, but I believe that's exactly how you like it. Warm caramel is drizzled all over your body. I'll start at your nose, my partner will start at your toes, and we will meet in the middle. You squirm as my tongue flicks over your nipples, and she nips at your heels. Trailing kisses down to your belly button, we both work diligently to remove all traces of the syrup from your body. Our prize is in close view and you're definitely ready.

Switching positions, my partner sits down on your face and swallows your erection whole as I remove caramel from your testicles. I then join her in removing the last bit from your penis before I get up to straddle you. Being kinky is okay in the comfort zone.

While I'm riding you, enjoy the feel of my warm walls gripping you as you devour my partner while smacking her on the ass. My partner then moves to the side of the bed, and masturbates while we do our thing. She then gets up, and pulls out a leather whip for your approval. You take it happily, and demand us to get in position.

The night is almost over, so we have to work fast. You begin by sexing me from the back, and satisfying my partner with the handle of the whip. It looks like we are playing twister as we switch from one position to the next. Upon orgasm, we fade away until next we meet in the comfort zone.

The More, The Merrier

I'm into the group thing. I want nothing less than five men who's been drinking Hennessey all night. I mean I keep a bottle on reserve just in case. If you've ever been fucked with a Henney dick, you know exactly what I'm talking about.

I don't discriminate either. No man is off limits. My motto is "return the favor." If you don't get it, I'll be glad to break it down for you. Men have been scagging women for years. Treating us like it ain't nothing for them to bone, and leave. Which is cool if that's what you're into. In return I treat men like the smuts they are, and at the end of the night their asses gots to leave.

My favorites are the "attached" males. The ones that like to step out on their wives and girlfriends. They can come bone, but I tell them from the gate "I ain't got but one wash cloth, and I'm using it." They better go to the 7-11 and get some wet naps. My thing is if you don't care about your girl enough to go out and cheat, then you shouldn't mind going home smelling like my pussy.

Now, I don't know how most women get down, but I love sex. I have three holes, and I want them all worked thoroughly. Shit, you can put it in my ear if you want to. I'll hear you cumming. You don't have to come by yourself either. Feel free to bring two or five of your friends with you. I like it like that. I want nothing less than a bunch of well-hung niggas running a train on me. If you can't find a friend don't fret. I have a box full of dildos at your disposal. Do what you have to do to make me cum.

I'm not one of those prissy girls either. I don't run from the dick. I look that shit right in the eye, and take it to the head with no problem. I have no problem with giving out brains. That's what I do, giving head is my specialty. Don't worry about having to clean up anything. I'm swallowing all of that. Either get with it or lose my number.

So, I'm in the house one night looking through my phone book. I'm in the mood for some butt fucking that'll have me regular for a couple of days. I know me, and one dude ain't going to be enough. It's like I have a fetish for orgies, and I don't plan on going to get help any time soon.

Jamal and his cousin Scott instantly popped into my mind. They like playing with whips, and I'm in the mood for something wild. I love the way leather feels on my skin. It reminds me of a lover's caress, and it puts me in the mood to do some things. Red leather especially. It's my power color. Whether it's a jacket or a pair of sandals, I step into diva mode whenever I'm in it.

It's a typical New York night. I'm sitting on my balcony in the nude taking in the view from the forty-second floor. It's times like this when my body starts to itch for the feel of warm hands that don't belong to me. My mind starts to wander back a few months when I was living care free with Jamal. He was the one that turned me on to the group thing. He made my body tingle just thinking about him. One night in particular stands out, and it made me want to explode just thinking about it.

We were getting it on so intense, I broke out into a cold sweat, and all he was doing was giving me a rim shot. I found myself gazing up at the stars as I demanded him to "fuck me harder." The feel of cold concrete on my back mixed with his warm body on top of me is a sensation every woman needs to experience.

The feel of bodies causing friction as a cool breeze slips between us took me over the edge. I scratched Jamal's back drawing blood as I tried to gain control of my senses. He didn't even flinch, and kept a steady pace as I begged for him to slow down, and let me breathe.

Relaxing was not an option. Jamal pushed my knees up to my chest, and put all of his thickness in me, leaving me exhausted and extremely happy. Deciding that he wasn't playing fair, I took his Hershey Kisses flavored nipples into my mouth one at a time making him lose his cool if only for a second. That gave me time to get a grip on the situation.

Coming back to the present, I decide that mere memories won't suffice. Jamal only lived ten minutes away, and I could always count on him to fuck me like I wanted it. He has a baby mom, but who cares? I'm here to do what she won't, and if that means sucking his dick and getting back shots then so be it.

He answers his Nextel on the first ring. Jamal has that Barry White/Jaheim thing going on with his voice that gets me wet instantly. It's like I can feel his lips on my clit when he talks to me.

"What chu doin'?" I asked him in my sexiest voice.

"You, if you're down."

"Depends…"

"On what?"

"If you're fucking me with that Henney dick." He giggled a little at my boldness.

"Girl, you are too much."

"How fast can you get here?"

"Five minutes. Why?"

"You know why."
"Yeah, but Cindy be whilin'."
"I'll make it worth while…"
"You better. Just have the door open."

I hang up the phone without responding. I have five minutes to rid myself of pubic hair and light candles. Jamal likes his pussy clean-shaven, and I have no problem accommodating him. I had the na-na smelling like candy in no time and was butt naked, playing with my clit and waiting for his arrival.

I heard my door open up two minutes later, and it sounded like more than one pair of footsteps. When I looked up Jamal and Scott were standing at the foot of my bed. At the time, I had not entertained the thought of having more than one man at a time, and I'd be lying if I said I wasn't shook by the idea.

"You didn't tell me you were bringing a guest." I say as if I had a problem with him doing so. Scott is cool, but I don't know him like that. I've seen him around the way every so often, but that was about it.

"Chill, he won't hurt you."
"I don't think I can handle both of you."
"Ma, you're in good hands. Just relax, and enjoy the ride."

Now Jamal is a chocolate Adonis. Standing at six feet two inches, weighing in at two hundred and forty pounds, and working with about nine and a half inches, Jamal was not to be fucked with. Scott wasn't to be questioned, either. Caramel complexion, six feet even, two hundred and thirty pounds, and eleven and a half inches? I was happier than a dyke in clit town. I knew I was in for some shit, and I was hoping my ass could take it.

Both men wasted no time stripping, and joining me on my sleigh bed. Scott took post between my legs, sopping me up like he was the biscuit, and I was the gravy. Jamal got on his knees next to my head, and his dick instantly disappeared into my warm mouth. Yes I do swallow, and wasn't letting him go until my thirst was quenched.

Scott was doing the thing to me. He took the liberty of inserting anal beads into my saliva lubricated ass hole, and tongue fucked me with no mercy. That made it hard to concentrate on the task at hand, and Jamal ended up slipping out of my mouth, and squirting all over my breast. That was cool, too. I just rubbed it in like lotion, and kept moving.

Switching places and positions, I found myself riding Scott while Jamal was tearing my ass up. Literally! It seemed like the faster I rode Scott, the harder Jamal stroked me from the back. Holding my breath only increased my orgasm, and I was soon exploding all over the place.

We were like tag team wrestlers up in this piece. Jamal and Scott fucked me six ways from Sunday, and a sistah needed a break. Putting all I had into it, I finally got those fools to explode.

They rained on me from both sides, their cum hot on my skin. It was cool, I just rubbed it in with one hand and jerked them with the other. Before they left I made sure to get Scott's number… just in case. Maybe next time they'll bring someone new.

Snakes and Caves

It wasn't until recently that I realized that I, too, had fetishes. Being in a lesbian relationship for the past three years helped me see things in a whole new light. I love the entire "snakes and caves" thing, but I realized that the snake didn't have to belong to a man, if you know what I mean. I much prefer the hands of a woman.

At one point in my life, I wanted nothing less than nine inches all up in my insides making me explode into oblivion. Men tend to be a little on the rough side, and the gentle ones are few and far between. My good friend Tasha, who had been trying to bring me to the other side for months, invited me to a swing party.

"Girl, I'm strictly dickly! You know I don't get down like that. Tasha, your ass stay trying to recruit."

"That's what all lesbians in training say."

"Yeah? Well I'm dead serious. It ain't nothing a woman can do for me that I can't do for myself."

"You can't go down on yourself."

"That's what I got your dad for."

"Honey, hush. All I'm saying is you don't have to do anything you don't want to do. Just go and see what it's about. No one will force anything on you."

Tasha went on for about ten minutes before I decided to at least go and observe. I figured it wouldn't be harmful to watch, and I might luck up on a nice looking guy while I was there.

When we walked in, it was nothing like I expected. I was bracing myself for a room full of women in compromising positions using dildos in all shapes and sizes. There turned out to be a mixed crowd watching a sex toys demonstration.

The partygoers differed in age and ethnicity. There were both hetero and homosexual couples present, and a few flying solo. There were bowls of condoms in different colors and textures placed strategically around the room, and whips and handcuffs at your disposal.

This one chick was steady checking me out, but wasn't shit poppin'. The look on my face said everything, and she averted her eyes to the situation at hand. The hostess instructed us to fill out a nametag to place on our shirts, and to grab either a penis or vagina taste tester out of the bowl by the door. They are small flexible toys that are used to sample the different creams and jellies presented during the demonstration so that you won't end up buying something you don't like. I immediately went for the penises as Tasha reached for the vagina at the same time.

"I'm sure you'll be reaching for one of these before we leave."

"I'd rather get a back shot with no lubrication instead." Tasha laughed at me, and found us seats as I checked out the buffet and dessert tables.

Everything was in the shape of penises and vaginas. The buffet included penis pasta salad, clitoris chip dip, and other dishes in that category. I giggled out loud at the "Swallowing Babies" punch. It was cream in color, and had sperm shaped fruit mixed in. I got a cup before I took my seat.

The hostess finished up her show, and invited everyone to browse and purchase. I noticed there were five doors in the room numbered accordingly. The oddest thing was the five was in the middle. I was trying to ask Tasha what was up, but she was too busy feeling up the girl next to her.

"I guess I'm on my own now," I said to no one in particular.

"You don't have to be."

I looked up into the prettiest eyes I'd ever seen on a woman. She stood at about five feet six inches, and her wrap laid like she had a fresh perm. She had a serious hourglass figure going on, and close inspection revealed a silver belly ring with a diamond butterfly dangling from the end. In short, she was beautiful.

"I'm here with a friend," I said to Pretty Eyes as she noticeably checked me out. I didn't think to ask her what her name is because I wasn't interested.

"So am I, but he went into room three with Chad," she pointed to a handsome man built like a football player standing at door three with five equally attractive men. I just glanced over at them and silently hoped I never slept with any of them.

"He's gay?" I asked just to have something to say hoping to take the spotlight off me. Him liking men was so obvious, and I didn't realize how stupid the question was until it was already out.

"Bisexual, but tonight he felt like packing a little fudge," she answered nonchalantly never taking her eyes off my face.

"Okay? So, what's with the numbers on the doors?" since Tasha abandoned me I got the scoop from Pretty Eyes since she was all in my face. I at least wanted to know what to expect if someone invited me into one of the rooms.

She went on to explain that the numbers indicated how many occupants were allowed in a room at a time. The one meant that only one couple at a time was allowed, and so on.

"So it's like multiplication," I said.

"Yeah, but the only exception is room number five. The number of people in the room has to always be divisible by five. She only invited fifty people to the party, and there is enough room for all of us to be in there at one time."

"What if someone wants to leave?"

"Then he or she has to take four people with him."

"How does she keep track of all that?"

"You should have received tickets upon entry to the party. Those allow you to visit the rooms. Or at least the first four. The hostess does scramblers, and other games to win special passes to room five. She has men on post at each door to stamp your hand for each room."

"Damn, how long have you been coming?"

"Active member since 1995," she offered with a slight grin. I didn't see myself getting that comfortable with my sexuality, and I definitely didn't want a lifetime membership!

"So, which way do you swing?"

""Excuse me?" I was still on the whole membership thing.

"Which way do you swing?" she asked again doing a pendulum motion with her arm.

"Oh, I like men."

"Snakes and caves, huh?"

"Yeah, I guess."

"Let me show you something."

Sis walked away from me, and went to purchase vibrators from the hostess. I busied myself with the buffet as I spotted Tasha going into room number four with seven other girls. I just shook my head, and continued to put food on my plate. As soon as I was done eating from the buffet she came back with a bag of goodies, and tickets to room number two.

"Come on, I have something to show you."

"I don't get down like that."

"Oh c'mon. What ever happens at the party stays here."

I noticed a guy and another girl waiting for us. I was cool as long as there was some testosterone in the room. I figured I would just kick it with him, but I soon found out it wasn't going to be that simple.

Once we all settled in the room, I found out the woman's name was Candy, and she introduced me to John and Trish. John is a stockbroker on Wall Street, Trish is a pediatrician at the Michigan Children's Hospital, and Candy practiced law in Center City, Philadelphia.

"So everyone comes from all over?"

"Yeah, we have everyone from doctors and lawyers to electricians and hair stylists."

"I see..."

"Okay, gather around everyone. We're about to play a game."

Candy went on to explain that the game we were about to play was called "Snakes and

Caves." The rules were as follows:

1. The maximum number of players is four. One being a male, and the rest female.

2. Each player gets a flavored condom, and two taffies that are all to be used before the game has ended. To use the taffy, place one or both on any part of your body that you want someone to taste.

3. The object of the game is for everyone to have pleased each other by any means necessary.

"So, you're saying that if the game calls for me to go down on a female I have to do it?" I asked with a frown on my face.

"Yes, John has provided one of the snakes, and I have three more in this bag. We'll start off by spinning the wheel to decide who goes first."

"Okay, y'all go ahead. I'm out." I jumped up to leave, but Candy stopped me in my tracks.

"Come on, I won't tell a soul."

John came over to assure me everything was cool. Pretty soon I found myself in the nude with everyone else, and the festivities began. I turned the wheel first, and it landed on giving head to one of the players. I chose to hook John up, as Candy spun the wheel. I sat down on the chair as John stood in front of me, and fed me his dick. Next thing I knew Trish had stuck her head between John's parted legs, and started lapping at my clitoris.

I lost myself in the feel of Trish's warm tongue on my clit while I swallowed John whole, and watched Candy give Trish a rim shot. Trish parted my lips with her petite fingers to easier devour my clit. I didn't know a timer was set until I heard it go off.

"Time to switch." Candy said as she got up to reset the timer.

The rest of us walked over to the bed. Trish lay down, and John slipped on the first of the condoms and slid into home base. Trish placed both her taffies on each nipple indicating she wanted us to suck on them. I hesitated at first, but soon found the feel of her nipples in my mouth inviting. Women definitely taste better. Candy took the other one, and I felt myself wanting so bad to taste her. I let go of Trish's nipple, and walked around to the other side of the bed to taste Candy.

She was lying on her back, so I took the liberty of placing my head between her legs. She smelled fresh like she just showered, and I hesitated before parting her lips. She was clean-shaven, and I wasn't sure if I preferred that or not since this was my first time taking the plunge.

With her lips now spread open, I closed my eyes, and sucked on her clit softly. She tasted as good as she smelled. Holding her open with my thumb and index finger, I took the index finger of my other hand and probed her soft folds gently. Doing to her what I would want done to me, I continued to lick, suck, and finger her until she exploded into my hand.

"Are you sure this is your first time?" Candy asked like she didn't believe me.

Instead of answering, I placed both of my taffies into my cave and laid down for her to fish them out. Using only her teeth, she pulled them out one by one, and fed them to me. The sweet and tangy taste only heightened my senses. John took over, and plunged his snake deep into my cave, but I wanted Candy to continue tasting me.

We went on like this for another hour, and finished up in the shower connected to the room. Upon exiting the room, Candy slipped me her number, and I made sure to grab a plate before I left.

That was three years ago, and Candy is now my girlfriend. We don't go to the parties as much as we used to, but I never pass up the chance to explore her cave. This time, the snake runs on two D batteries.

Photo Opportunity

I've always wanted to be a photographer for as long as I can remember breathing. I got my very first camera for my seventh birthday. Capturing the smiles of people has always brightened my day, even when it didn't start out so great. I specialize in children's photos and family portraits, but this one woman changed all of that.

Saturdays are my busiest days. As usual, before I sit down for breakfast I check to see what my schedule looks like for the day. I noticed a Ms. Jones requested my services for three hours at the end of the day. It doesn't even take twenty minutes to do a family photo, so I assumed my assistant made a mistake.

"Kia, who is Ms. Jones, and why does she need three hours?"

"She called five times yesterday, and insisted that she see you at the end of the day."

"At four o'clock? Normally I'm packing up to leave by then."

"I know, but then she offered to pay three grand for your services because you came highly recommended."

"Is it a family photo, child, what?"

"She wouldn't say."

"Aren't you leaving early today?"

"Yeah, but if you need me to stay..."

"No, it's cool. You requested for the day off last month. Let's just try to get through the morning."

As curious as I was to solve the Ms. Jones mystery, the front of my studio was filling up with the day's appointments. I put on my best smile, and neglected breakfast. Kia was a Godsend, and a lot of days I didn't think I would make it without her.

With all the energy it takes to make babies smile and line up disgruntle adults for a family portrait, I still seemed to have a lot of energy by the end of the day. I don't know if it was from anticipation or what, but when I finally got a chance to breathe, it was ten of four, and I had yet to eat lunch. Kia had already been gone for three hours, so I had to do everything myself.

Popping my food in the microwave, I took time to straighten up the shop, and put things in order. The bells on the door and the microwave sounded at the same time. When I looked up, a woman dressed in sexy red sandals was standing in the doorway. She stood before me in a tan trench coat with a bucket hat that she flipped up on the right side and dipped over her left eye. She held a Fendi overnight bag on her shoulder, and I could only guess what was inside.

"Can I help you?"

"Hi, I have an appointment for four o' clock."

Forgetting all about the microwave meal, I walked up to her. This woman was gorgeous. At five feet seven inches, she had legs that went on forever. I wanted to see what she had on under the coat, and quickly showed her to the studio.

After breaking down the cost of the packages and putting a new roll of film in, I was ready. I showed her what backgrounds we had to offer, the entire time trying not to stare at her cherry red lips. Her bottom lip slightly bigger than her top made me want to tongue her down on the spot. Flashes of her pink tongue as she licked the corners of her lips had me about to burst on sight. I could almost feel her lips wrapped around me.

Ms. Jones took the liberty of placing all of my oversized pillows on the floor in front of the plastic fireplace background. I just stood there trying to get my penis to stay down. This girl was getting me so hard.

"Will all of the pictures be in front of the fireplace or will we be changing the background?"

"No, this is fine, but I will be changing outfits. Better yet, lets just go along with the flow."

"Okay, lets get started."

The first pose was of her straddling a chair in the trench coat, and matching hat just covering her right eye. Her hair lay down on her shoulders in soft wispy curls, and I tucked the auburn strands behind her left ear before taking the picture.

Ms. Jones toyed with the camera, and I made sure to get every pose from all angles. She stood up posing with one foot resting on the chair giving me a peek at her red garter. I was ready to put the camera down and take her standing up just like that. It took everything in me to compose myself as I told my man to chill. Pulling her hair back off her face revealed a better view of perfectly arched eyebrows, and a button nose that only added to her character. Her lips covered the whitest teeth, and her eyes danced for the camera. She reminded me of Janet Jackson on the cover of her Design of a Decade CD. Just sexy all over.

"What's your name?" I asked never missing a beat.

"Carmen…"

She took off her trench coat causing my mouth to drop wide open. All that was left was her hat, a diamond studded Baby Phat belly ring, a red garter with matching lace thong underwear, and sexy red sandals. Her toes were suckable, and painted the same crimson red as her perfectly manicured finger nails. Carmen posed on the pillows lying on her back. Looking at her pretty nipples pointing skyward had me damn near about to cum on myself.

Carmen took one nipple into her mouth, and pulled her thong to the side for easier access to her swollen clitoris. If any juice dripped off of it, I got it on film. Watching her masturbate was killing me, and I found myself wishing I had a camcorder.

I couldn't help moaning right along with her as I placed the camera on automatic run, and took a seat so I could get a better view. Carmen pulled out a dildo from under the pillow, and began doing herself. That shocked me because I don't remember seeing her put it there. Before inserting it, she wrapped cherry lips around the head, leaving behind a wetness I was sure was as warm as the inside of her nether lips. Using her first two fingers, she spread her caramel lips invitingly, exposing her sweet pinkness. She inserted only the head, pulling it out slowly. Her juices dripped off the edge of the chair and formed a puddle on the floor. She used her thumb to play across her clitoris in a constant back and forth motion never losing rhythm with her other hand. Stroking myself through my sweat pants, I finally pulled out my partner, and enjoyed the show.

Carmen never took her eyes off me as she got on her knees, and pleased herself from the side. The build up of her orgasm was like watching a thunderstorm through her eyes. By then I was exploding all over the place, and had to find a towel to clean up the mess.

"I think I'll change into another outfit. I want these photos in black and white." Carmen gathered the items off the floor, and went back to change.

I didn't even answer. I couldn't. While Carmen was changing outfits, I changed the film in my camera, and the background. Instead of pillows, I put down a bearskin rug with an actual bear head on it. I placed eight large feathers on the rug, and decided to let her be creative. I started to put out some whipped cream and cherries, but I decided that would be too cheesy. I keep all kinds of props such as rose petals and sequins because I shoot a lot of models and strippers that want to take sexy pictures.

Carmen came out dressed in a crotch less leopard skin two-piece bikini, and I was so glad I put the feathers out. She opted to go bare foot, and her toes were painted a delicious shade of raspberry that made me want to eat her ass up! It amazed me how fast she changed her polish, and I knew that Carmen wasn't leaving until I tasted her.

After stretching out and making herself comfortable, Carmen wasted no time giving it up to the camera. She started out lying on her back. I took the liberty of pouring honey on her body from head to toe, and then I stood behind the camera to take pictures. We were getting into it, and I had to giggle a little when she positioned the head of the bearskin rug to look as though the bear itself was eating her out. This girl was very creative. By the time I was ready to change the film again, she was completely nude.

Carmen asked me to join her, and I wasted no time. Stripping down to my birthday suit. I was glad I worked out on a daily basis. My six-pack looked nice on film, and I made sure Carmen felt it. I positioned her over one of the props shaped like a log, I took her from the back with her legs wrapped around my waist. Never in my life had I felt like I was going to explode as soon as I put it in.

Carmen wasn't a slouch either. She got down on her knees and took everything in, including my testicles. I've never had a girl do that before, and she didn't choke not one time. Her steady rhythm had me creaming all over the place, and she swallowed everything. I laid down on the rug, and Carmen squatted on top of me, and rode me like that until I came again. Life doesn't get any better than that.

Finishing up, I took a few pictures of Carmen stretched out on a cream chaise lounge dressed in a feathered two piece, and cream and gold sandals. Her hair framed her perfectly made up face, and she looked well rested as I took pictures with her eyes closed.

While Carmen changed, I got dressed and cleaned up the mess we made. She came out of the dressing room in the trench coat and sandals she came in with, and an envelope in her hand. While she gathered her belongings, I counted out the three thousand dollars she gave me for the session. I was willing to do it for free after all of that, and told her the same.

"Carmen, you don't have to pay me this kind of money. If you insist, just pay me for a basic package."

"No, it's fine. You *cum* highly recommended."

"By who?" I asked. I was curious to know what friends we had in common.

"A mutual friend."

Before I had a chance to say anything, she left out of the door as silently as she came in. I find myself looking for Carmen through my window everyday since she never came back for her pictures. Now, every time I see a woman in a trench coat, I smile at the memory of having her.

Dream Girl

I've been coming to the *Pink Panties* strip club for as long as I can remember. It's an average club with average chicks, but something about it keeps me coming back. I decided to get a drink after work, and figured I might as well see some ass-naked women in the process. Upon entry, I noticed an advertisement for a new dancer they called Dream.

This girl looked like the others that worked there, but her eyes did something to me. Mesmerized by the almond shape of her hazels, I could have sworn she spoke to me. Stepping back from the poster, I took one last look before I found my usual seat close to the stage.

I ordered my usual, Butt Naked Back Stage, then got comfy and waited for the show to begin. The first couple of girls that came out did okay. It was the same tired show from last week, and I wanted to see what this "Dream" girl could do. An hour and three drinks went by before the M.C. announced Dream's presence to the club.

Snake by R. Kelly and Big Tigga started playing. R. Kelly said he wanted to see her body move like a snake, and she did just that. Dream wiggled and gyrated around the stage so good I damn near creamed on myself. She squatted down in front of me on the stage, and started pulling toys out of her vagina like she was a magician. In no time a nice pile of assorted colored condoms, silk scarves, and a few toys sat in front of me. I was waiting for the Verizon guy to step out, and ask could we hear him now. This girl had talent.

I pulled out a New Port, and Dream danced over to me and asked for a puff. I lit the cigartte, and went to put it to her lips. She took the cigarette from me, and put it to her kitty-cat, and puffed the cigarette like it had lungs to accept the smoke. If that wasn't enough, her coochie-coo started blowing out rings of smoke that floated into the air before disappearing. I had to give her a tip after that. She ended the dance with one of the partygoers giving her head. Now that's what I call a show!

I didn't want to see anyone after that, and gathered my things to leave as Dream collected her hundreds of dollars from the stage floor. I couldn't wait to get home. I had a vibrator with my name on it, and I was dying to use it. If I weren't such a chicken I would have taken her to the back in one of the private rooms, and had my way with her. As if being in the strip club wasn't enough.

Following my daily ritual, I ran bath water while I brushed my teeth. My tongue felt thick in my mouth, and I was so damn horny it wasn't even funny. After adding pear scented bath beads to the water, I stepped in and sank down until the water was up to my shoulders. Closing my eyes, I began massaging both nipples, and imagining Dream's lips all over me. My right hand found its way to my triangle, and kept up a steady rhythm until I exploded.

When I opened my eyes, Dream sat in front of me on the side of the tub. I had to blink twice to make sure I saw what I was seeing. She looked just as radiant as she did in the club. Even better from this viewpoint. Her slanted eyes had a hint of Asian ancestry behind their hazel gaze. Her breasts sat high and perky with dark chocolate nipples looking back at me. Her stomach was flat, and rounded out to nice curvaceous hips. Her triangle sported a perfectly trimmed crescent moon, and her little man in the boat winked at me.

I soon noticed my surroundings had changed, and I found myself at the shallow end of a pool. Dream stepped into the water, and swam her way to me until she was between my legs. They parted automatically, and she drowned the man, and capsized the vessel. I felt myself pushing her head away from me, but I knew I didn't want her to stop. Dream was fingering me, and I felt my head going under water. I couldn't breathe, yet I didn't want her to stop.

I closed my eyes to enjoy what she was doing to me, and I realized I really couldn't breathe. Gasping for air, I jumped up and was suddenly back in my own bathroom with a now drenched floor. Dream was gone, and I was tired. I got out the tub and crawled in the bed, leaving the mess for the morning.

For most of the night, I kept dreaming about Dream and all the positions I wanted to try with her. An active imagination is a bitch because I had yet to have sex let alone have something to go on. Okay, the one time with Brian Randall on prom night, but it was over so fast I didn't even count that. My fingers and my vibrator kept me company for the past six years and that was cool until I saw Dream.

Waking up late for work the next day, I ran into the office with my head still wrapped in a scarf. Ignoring the stares from my co-workers, I ran into the ladies room to make myself presentable. When I looked into the mirror, I saw my face, but Dreams eyes stared back at me. It wasn't until my co-worker Megan tapped me on my shoulder that I realized I had been standing there for ten minutes just staring at the mirror.

"Girl, you look like shit. Long night?" Megan commented as she fixed her always gorgeous weave in the mirror next to me.

"You wouldn't believe me if I told you."

She looked at me willing me to share what happened the previous evening, and instead of responding I combed my hair out in silence until I was satisfied with my look. Ignoring eye contact, I gathered my things and went to my desk. I had a lot of work to do, and no time in which to finish.

My computer took forever to reboot, and as much as I complained to my manager I was still stuck with this out-dated contraption. Checking my e-mail, I noticed I had mail from the Pink Panties strip club. I was almost scared to click on it, but curiosity took ever, and I was double clicking on the icon before I could stop myself.

As the web paged opened, I busied myself by putting the millions of papers on my desk in some kind of order. I just hated clutter, and looking at it was giving me an instant headache. Hell Yeah by Ginuwine and Baby started playing, and a miniature sized Dream danced around the screen, coaxing people into coming to see her show Friday night. I looked at my calendar. It was only Wednesday, but I knew I would be there.

I somehow made it through the day and got home in one piece. I knew the girls at the office thought me to be a prude, but who gave a damn. I wasn't there to make friends; I was there to get work done. That's what they paid me for. I ate lunch by myself, and barely conversed with any of them if it wasn't work related. I don't have time for a bunch of cackling hens that have nothing better to do than spread everyone's business. Megan included.

When I got home, my cat Mr. Whiskers met me at the door. I fed him and made my way to the bedroom. Climbing onto my cherry wood queen sized bed, I picked up the phone, and called my best friend in the whole wide world. Destiny and me had been friends since the sixth grade. I transferred to Philly from North Carolina, and couldn't fight all that well.

One day this big bitch of a bully named Gertrude decided I would be the one she fucked with that day. During lunch she decided that my Twinkies were more appealing than her spam sandwich, and snatched them out my hand. I was the shortest person in my class, and she looked to be at least six feet. I was scared so I just gathered my things and left the schoolyard.

This went on for about two weeks until Destiny saw what went down one day, and stepped to her. They got into a heated argument, and Destiny laid her down in front of everyone. I haven't had any problems from anyone since then. It wasn't until we were juniors in college that she told me she was a lesbian. Shocked the hell out of me.

She didn't look like a lesbian to me. She wasn't all butch like the ones I saw in the pizza place on campus. She was feminine just like me, and even prettier. All the guys were on her, and lord knows she was getting it in on the regular, so her coming out of the closet was something for the books. She was the one that introduced me to the Pink Panties nightclub, so I didn't hesitate to call her.

We quickly decided we would go to the show, and before I knew it, Friday was here. I called out from work, and spent the day pampering myself. It was long over due, and felt like heaven. After purchasing a new outfit, I made my way over to Destiny's apartment. Wasting no time, we got dressed and headed to the club.

Late as usual, when we walked in Dream was just starting her show. My girl worked it out as she sat half way down on a forty-ounce bottle. That damn near floored me, and Destiny had to pat me on my back to help me breathe. Toni Braxton was singing about speaking in tongues, and I wanted to feel Dream's tongue all over me. Dream slowly peeled off her feather costume as she twirled around the stage, allowing patrons to stuff money into her garter. I sat back and watched her do a head stand with her legs spread apart in a perfect V. she moved like a snake until her body was lying flat on the stage in front of the pole. She was winding her hips and pulling herself up the pole. My dream girl gyrated her hips slowly and sensually as the song came to an end, and Etcetera by R. Kelly began to play.

I was so wet I was sure there would be a wet spot on the back of my skirt when I stood up. Dream turned me on in ways I didn't think a woman should be able to, and what scared me the most was that I liked it. After her show she walked around to the patrons that wanted lap dances, making more money.

"You want a dance?" Destiny asked me almost teasing.

"I don't know if I should. I don't get down like that."

"Girl, who's going to know besides me and you?" Before I had the chance to object, she was in the chair, beckoning Dream to come over. My cheeks were so red I looked like a charms blow pop.

"My friend would like a dance," Destiny said.

Dream took the money, and started her private show for the two of us. My mind kept flashing back to the tub scene at my house, and I felt my thong becoming drenched with my juices. She took her time gyrating on my lap while she caressed my nipples through my sheer dress. I wanted to scream out in ecstasy, but my voice was stuck in my throat.

For some reason, we made eye contact, and I damn near passed out. I kept wondering why Dream's eyes were haunting me, and it jumped out clear as day. Dream worked on the third floor in my office building. She was the secretary for the CEO of the corporation. She looked at me, and smiled like she knew my thoughts and moved on to the next patron.

When I saw her in the elevator the next morning, we smiled at each other through our greetings, and I went on about my day. I never went back to the club, but I still have the pink carnation I took out of her hair that night. It's a small world after all.

The Life of a Spider

    Love is much like that of a spider's web. I know that might have confused you, and I'll be glad to explain. The spider, this being a female spider, takes her time to build a web. She works diligently creating her well-proportioned masterpiece then lays low and waits for her victim to get caught in its silkiness.
    The victim, this being a male insect of any species, struggles to get loose because the spider is now approaching. At the last seconds of breathing the spider spins her prey into a cocoon, and sucks the victim dry of all of it's blood leaving it for dead. The most deadly, I believe, is the black widow. With her long legs, and flashy red marking, any male insect in it's right mind would fall for her. That's how I felt when I met Sinai.
    This girl was it, you hear me? She was thick in all the right places, and had legs that went on forever. Sinai was the color of warm caramel with a voice equally as sweet, and could out sing a humming bird on her worst day. The woman I should have married.
    We went to school together from the sixth to the twelfth grade. She moved to Philly from Miami because her dad's job relocated to open a branch office in Center City. I remember teasing her when I was around my boys because she talked funny. Secretly I loved her accent. So we played the games children play until we graduated from high school, and went our separate ways.
    It had been nine years since I've laid eyes on Sinai, and it caught me off guard to see her looking back at me from the cover of the April edition of *Essence* magazine. Everyone hopes to be a success, and it looked like the girl from Miami was now doing it up in the Big Apple. I don't normally read *Essence* magazine, but this issue was a must buy. Rushing to meet my publisher, I tucked the magazine safely into my briefcase, and made my way through crowded Center City barely missing the El train.
    I'm not doing too bad myself. I have a nice crib in the Malvern section of Pennsylvania, and a 2003 Lincoln Navigator parked in the garage. I'm currently working on my third novel. I write mystery with a twist of romance, and the ladies love it.

As of yet, I'm single with no children, and in no rush to turn in my playa's card. Not that I'm picky, but my wife would be nothing like the women I meet in the clubs. I meet women in every shade of ebony, but none of them have any will power. The fact that I'm able to bone two hours after we've met does nothing but add another notch to the list of women I've already laid. My woman won't be that easy. What makes it even more comical is I write about the kind of woman I'm looking for in my novels. I watch women flock to the book signings and seminars, yet none of them seem to get it. My number one reason for being a player.

Finally getting to my meeting, I notice the sign stating the parking garage is full, and I'm suddenly glad I opted to take the train. Once in the office I notice a wonderful pair of legs resting in the far corner of the conference room. The woman's face is hidden behind the same *Essence* magazine I just purchased from the newsstand. She didn't look up when I came in. Then I noticed the head set from a disc player peeking out of the purse at her side.

Always the gentleman, and on the hunt for new game I sat down my belongings, and walked over to introduce myself. As I got closer I could hear her softly humming whatever she was listening to. I didn't want to startle her, so I tapped her on the knee. I was prepared to make myself "irresistible" when she dropped the magazine to her lap, and I looked into the prettiest eyes I've ever seen on a woman.

"Sinai?"

"Quincy? Nice to see you!"

Sinai jumped up out the chair, and into my arms knocking the contents of her lap onto the floor. Her embrace was soft and warm. She smelled deliciously feminine, and felt just as good. Exactly how the woman in my life would.

"Hey, sweetie. What are you doing here?"

"I'm here to see Simon, you?"

"Here to see Simon."

We fell into an awkward silence, and found ourselves staring at each other. It was so much I wanted to say, but my lips wouldn't form the words. Some how I felt like Sinai was the woman I wanted to be with. I don't necessarily believe in love at first sight but the childhood crush I had on her came back instantly. Sinai always had the perfect smile, soft hair that I used to tease her about because I didn't want my boys to know I liked her, and she always smelled like she had just finished bathing. Even after gym class. I knew if I ever got a hold of her I would always love her, and the beautiful children we would have.

She never made it easy to get close to her. Every woman I met made it entirely too easy to get the panties. I guess because I'm a well known author they probably think they can get me for some money, but little did they know it's not sweet like that. Not that I'm a stingy person, but how could a woman expect me to take her seriously when it took all of ten minutes getting to know her before I'm ripping her back out the frame? Give me something to look forward to. If I know I can hit on the first night, I'll just wreck shop and leave you wondering if I'll call you. Just as I was about to ask for her number, Simon, our publicist, walked into the room. Saved by the bell.

"I see you've met," Simon said in his deep baritone voice.

Simon is a big man whose voice demands your attention. He always has a smile on his face, and puts you in mind of the Santa Claus at the mall. His marketing skills made him number two in the publishing business, and he goes out of his way to keep his clients happy.

"Yes, we went to high school together," Sinai answered in her honey-coated voice that I've always loved. I noticed she hadn't lost her accent.

Always business conscious, Simon got right to the purpose of our meeting. Paramount Pictures wanted to turn my first novel, A Thieves Reprise, into a motion picture and Sinai would be writing and singing for the movie soundtrack. She's here to work with me so she could get a feel for my book, and that in its self is a blessing. Sinai, along with Baby Face, Method Man, Kelly Price, L.L. Cool J., and various other artists would aid in making my novel a successful movie, and a slamming soundtrack.

"So we're looking to create a schedule that works for both of you. One that doesn't prevent you from finishing your novel, and you can get back to working on your next hit CD."

"That sounds good to me. Sinai, what do you think?"

"Sounds perfect. Let's get started."

Sinai and I decided on a four-day workweek with days starting at nine in the morning and ending at three in the afternoon. That way I could still work on my novel until early evening, and Sinai could work on her CD in the studio.

Preparing to leave for the day I learned that Sinai would be staying at the Marriott until she found an apartment to lease. Being the playa/gentleman that I am I offered her a room in my home.

"Quincy, I couldn't invade your privacy like that."

"It's okay. I live alone so there's plenty of room. I have four bedrooms and three baths. I have plenty of space, and it will cost you nothing."

"I don't think that's a good idea."

"Sinai, I know we weren't the coolest in school, but I'm not that little boy anymore. Please, let me do this favor for you. It's not a problem, I swear."

I ended up helping Sinai move her things from the hotel to my house where she set up shop in the back room, the second largest bedroom in the house. I know I messed up any chance I had of us being together as a teenager because I was too stupid to realize what my friends said didn't matter. I was to blind to see that they wanted her, too. Now is as good a chance as any to make amends, and stir her in the path of wanting me. She only got sexier with age and I want her to be mine so I could smother myself in her softness. I gave her the back room so that she could feel at home. That way she would have her own bathroom, and more privacy. Now I could work on making her mine.

... ...

Sinai turned out to be a wonderful houseguest. It made my house feel more like home with a female within its walls. Every female I've ever met only made it as far as the nearest Motel 6, and if she was good I gave her my pager number. I've never bought anyone home, so having Sinai here was a welcome change.

After Sinai settled in, I gave her a tour of the city in case she needed any feminine hygiene products or had any late night cravings. As a courtesy, I set up an in-house phone so she could make personal calls, and conduct business. I showed her where the clean linen was located, and left her to relax. We had an early start tomorrow.

The way my house was built, the master bedroom had an adjoining bathroom, as did the back room. Both bathrooms connect to save water. A wall was built in place of the door for added privacy. Mine was slightly larger, and housed a Jacuzzi and custom-made shower. Decorated in silver, black and white, one wall was mirrored, and a double sink made of black opal completed the décor. The other bathroom was similar, minus the Jacuzzi, and was decorated in cream and gold.

Sinai and I must have been thinking the same thing as our showers were turned on simultaneously. Following my daily ritual, I tried not to think about Sinai naked on the other side of the wall. Stepping into the steamy water only heightened my senses, and my soldier stood at attention.

I tried washing as quickly as possible, but as soon as my soapy hands made contact with my manhood I immediately began to stroke all nine and a half inches of myself with thoughts of Sinai nude in my mind.

My fantasy had both of us in my shower. I had one nipple in my mouth while the other hand was busy teasing Sinai's panic button. Leaned against the wall I inserted my middle finger into her warm walls until she exploded into my hand. I slowly pulled my finger out, and inserted myself deep into her wetness, causing Sinai to hold on to me tighter as we rocked ourselves into a wonderful explosion.

I finally opened my eyes after releasing all over the shower wall. Quickly cleaning up the mess, and my body, I made myself comfortable in my king size bed to get some much needed sleep.

At three a.m., I found myself wide-awake, and horny as hell. I could smell the nectarine shower gel Sinai bathed with, and it was driving me crazy. Different scenarios played over and over in my head. I wanted Sinai in so many positions they haven't made numbers for them yet. Curiosity got the best of me, and I decided to peek in on her.

When I got to the end of the hallway I found her bedroom door cracked open. Jaheim's *Ghetto Love* CD was playing n the background, and I could hear her humming quietly to track number eleven, "Redy, Willing & Able." After tapping on the door I waited for the lamp light to come on before I walked in.

Sinai had the sheet wrapped around her body, clearly indicating she was completely nude underneath. I was forever thankful that my t-shirt covered my partial erection. Her shoulder length hair was kind of tousled, and made her look very sexy. It's not like all I wanted her for was sex. I want Sinai to have my last name, but sex appeal just surrounds her like a bee does honey. You can't help but want to taste her.

"Couldn't sleep?"

"Jet lag probably. You know how it can be sometimes."

"Yeah…"

"Thanks for letting me stay."

"No problem. Just making sure you're comfortable."

"Very much, thanks."

"Okay, see you in the morning. Try to get some sleep."

"See you then," was her response as I walked away. "Oh, Quincy, I really appreciate this."

"No problem. Breakfast at 8:30 sharp."

Instead of going back to my room I went to the den to try and work on my novel. That proved to be fruitless since all I could think about was Sinai, and what our children would look like. Hey, I may have player tendencies, but I do have a soft side.

As promised, breakfast was ready by eight thirty on the dot. Sinai was looking extra fine in a cream and peach cotton skirt set that accentuated all of her curves, and showed the world her lovely legs. I was the perfect gentleman. As soon as the table was cleared we set up shop in the den, and got down to business.

Sinai admitted to having read both of my books, and was anxiously awaiting the third. We talked about all the excitement of my book making it to the big screen. Although I never gave the music soundtrack much thought, I was glad an old friend was apart of the process. Surprisingly, I still entertained the thought of settling down, and doing the family thing.

"So, I have three songs written for the soundtrack so far. One will be done by Toni Braxton, and two by Mary J. Blige. As part of the contract, I'm required to sing two songs on the soundtrack also."

"Sounds to me like somebody's on the ball."

"Hey, you have to rise early to stay on top."

I told her what direction I was taking in my newest book, and what hopes I had for the movie. Sinai sang a couple of bars for me, and by noon one song was half done.

"I think it's time for a little break. It takes a lot more to write a song than I thought."

Sinai stood up, and stretched like a cat to get the kinks out. Her top rose up a bit, and I saw that she had a navel ring. I think that is so sexy. My mind instantly wandered to the two of us on the floor. Her legs were wrapped around my head in a warm embrace as I satisfied her orally. She exploded without much effort, and I made sure to get every drop.

We changed positions, and Sinai wasted no time handling business. I like to watch, and Sinai's soft tongue circling the head of my man was doing the thing to me. She took the thickness of my soldier with ease. Sinai couldn't deep throat the entire nine and a half, but what she could get had me about to burst.

It was feeling so good that I swear I heard myself moan. The cream was rising to the top, and fast. Just as I was about to cum I heard someone call my name.

"Q...Quincy, you okay?"

"Oh, umm, yeah. I'm sorry, I didn't sleep all that well last night."

"I know. I couldn't seem to close my eyes for even five minutes."

"Yeah..."

We fell into our usual silence that found me staring at her lips. I'm a lips and teeth man. I stay clear of yuck mouth at all cost, especially on the ladies. If you don't take the time to brush your teeth, I'm sure the rest of you can't be too clean.

"How's about we go have lunch. My treat," Sinai suggested breaking the silence.

"Only if it's my treat. I know this nice little Mexican restaurant down on Route 30. Best fajitas in Pennsylvania."

"Okay, let me grab my purse."

... ...

"It doesn't surprise me that you became a singer. You've always had a beautiful voice."

"Really? When we were younger, you said I sounded like I was choking on chimney smoke."

"You know I didn't mean anything by that. Kids tease each other all the time. It's a part of growing up."

"How 'bout that."

"I truly apologize. No harm intended."

"No sweat."

"So, I read in the *Essence* magazine that you're living in the Big Apple. How's that going?"

"Well, Long Island isn't exactly the city, so it's pretty quiet."

"Yeah. My neighborhood is the same way."

Sinai went on to explain that after graduating from college she, and her parents had a falling out about what direction she was taking in her career. She wanted to sing. They wanted a doctor. Naturally she went on and did her thing, and now she's about to blow up.

After downing our Mexican feast, we made our way back home to finish the song we were writing earlier. During the car ride we talked about the music industry, and publishing. The entire time we were talking I kept picturing Sinai on top of the hood of my car. Her hair fanned out around her, and her legs were spread invitingly. It would have been impossible for me to not drink from her fountain, and I placed my tongue on her clitoris anticipating her reaction.

"Q...Q!"

"Oh...uh, sorry. What did you say?"

"You've been day dreaming for the past five minutes. Keep your eyes on the road."

"I'm sorry. I have a lot on my mind." Like getting to taste her sweet body.

"Well, you can think about your millions of women when we get home."

I chuckled lightly at her accusations, and got us home safely. If only she knew that she was the woman I was fantasizing about. I found it hard to concentrate with Sinai being so close, and opted to sit by the window in an attempt to control my erection. This girl is hot!

We got through the song just shy of three in the afternoon. Sinai ended with singing the entire song, and that damn near brought me to tears. She had one of those voices where if she were in a church choir she would definitely tear the house down. I let her hold my jeep, and went into my office to work on my novel. By eight I had three chapters done, and I noticed the woman in my story was a description of Sinai to the fullest. I found it much easier to write with her in mind.

I'm at the point in my story where the main character, a smooth 'James Bond' type detective, is falling for the woman he is trying to help. Her ex-husband is stalking her, and with her being an up-and-coming singer, it's hard to keep her out of the limelight. The detective never mixes business with pleasure, and he's having a hard time controlling his Love Jones for the doe eyed Sasharey.

Sinai came in at around ten that night. I was in the den watching "In Too Deep", and eating broccoli pizza from Pizza Hut. Sinai looked tired, and it took everything in me not to strip her down, and give her a full body massage.

"Hard day at the studio?"

"Kind of. It's hard dealing with so many different personalities. The positive is the songs are almost done. Between myself, and Baby Face the soundtrack will have fourteen songs. As a bonus track we're including the interview you did on Oprah for the new book."

"That's wonderful! Do you anticipate getting done ahead of schedule?"

"Well, I'm hoping to finish right on time."

"Good. Congratulations on another success."

"Thanks."

"Would you like some pizza? It just got here about ten minutes ago."

"Sure, but let me get in the tub first."

"Look, you go ahead and eat. I'll get a bath ready for you."

"Q, you don't have to do that."

"No, I insist. I don't want the food to get cold."

I took her bags out of her hand, and put them on the love seat. After she sat down I took her sandals off, and pushed the play button on the DVD player before I did something to offend her. I figured if I didn't get a chance to wash her she'd at least let me give her a hot oil massage.

When I came back down Sinai was curled up on the sofa fast asleep. She looked so cute, and innocent. I was going to let her sleep for a while, but I figured she'd be more comfortable in my bed. What shocked me more was that I didn't want to just bone, and let it be. I truly wanted her as my wife.

"Sinai…c'mon sweetie. Your bath is ready."

"Oh…I'm sorry. I didn't realize I was that tired."

"No problem. Being beautiful…I mean the studio can be tiring."

"Yeah…"

Instead of letting her walk up the stairs, I opted to carry her. She didn't seem to mind, because she laid her head on my shoulder and wrapped her arm around my neck. She smelled like peaches, and I almost lost it.

When we got to the top of the stairs she tried to get down, but I took her to my bedroom. After carefully placing her on the side of the bed I let her know that the Jacuzzi was ready for her, and left the room to give her privacy. I was on my way downstairs when Sinai called me back to get a towel out for her.

I looked through the linen closet for my softest towel, and walked into the bathroom to sit it by the Jacuzzi. Sinai had added jasmine scented bath beads to the water, and it turned the water a soft lilac in color. I could see her clearly, and rose to the occasion. She didn't try to hide herself either.

I instantly soaped the washrag that I bought in with me, utilizing the Caress shower gel hanging on the bar. I know my eyes resembled the look a deer has when it's caught in headlights, and I breathed deeply in an effort to calm my racing heart. I've been waiting for this moment since I first laid eyes on her back at the office, and I swear I almost exploded at the thought of finally being able to touch her.

Starting with her neck, I allowed my right hand to slide down to her chocolate nipples. Sinai closed her eyes, and leaned her head back into the neck rest built into the Jacuzzi. I leaned forward to taste them feeling like I was about to wake up from a dream. The water rippled under me as Sinai pleased herself, and that only proved to make my soldier grow into an almost painful erection.

Stepping away from the tub, I disrobed with lightening speed, and joined her in the warm water. Lifting Sinai up to straddle me, she slid down on me, knees bent, feeling oh so good. She hugged her body tightly to mine, kissing me with strawberry flavored lips. The up and down motion was causing water to run over the sides of the tub, her walls gripping me the entire time.

I felt my orgasm fast approaching, and started thinking about baseball as not to end my stay in heaven so soon. Sinai started quickening her pace, and I made sure to look directly at her so I could see her orgasm play out.

"Mmm…mmm…" she moaned while keeping her eyes closed. "Q, can I come, baby?"

"Slow down, and let it ease out." I replied while rubbing her back. Sinai was now biting her bottom lip, and grinding her clitoris against my pelvis.

Never in my life have I seen an orgasm so beautiful. In that instant I was surer than ever that I wanted Sinai in my life. I reached up to move the hair that escaped from her bun off her forehead. She opened her eyes, and looked at me. Before I had the chance to respond, she stood up on wobbly legs trying to get out of the Jacuzzi.

"Sinai, why are you leaving…where are you going?" my voice was bordering on panic as I watched my dream girl leave the bathroom in haste.

"That wasn't supposed to happen, Q."

By the time I got into the hallway Sinai had already closed her bedroom door, and placed the lock on it. Still in the nude, I slipped and slid my way down the hall toward her door. I raised my fist to knock on her door when the sound of her radio blaring suddenly found its way to the other side. Defeated, I made my way back into my room not knowing what to do to mend our broken friendship.

… … … …

Barely getting any sleep, thoughts of Sinai invaded my mind. All these years I was afraid of getting caught in the web, and here I am so tangled up in my emotions I can't even function. For days we avoided each other like anthrax on U.S. mail, saying no more than what was necessary. Our sessions were so tense a few times she just walked out leaving me to deal with my heart by myself.

I tried to bring up the subject to clear the air between us, but Sinai was strictly business. We worked until the afternoons like usual, and in the evenings she went to the studio. Sometimes she didn't get home until late, and I found myself on more than a few occasions peaking through the blinds until I saw her car pull up into the driveway.

I was truly miserable. I wanted Sinai to know the love I had for her. I wanted her to know that she wasn't just some fling, a booty call, or some smut that I boned on the regular. This woman held my heart in the palm of her hand, and she didn't even know it. For the first time in my life I understood the pain a woman endures when she gives her heart to a man and he stomps all over it.

On her last day I volunteered to help her to the airport. She was on her way to Chicago to do a video with Mr. Cheeks from the movie soundtrack. The song, Mend My Wings, played over and over in my head. Sinai gave me an advanced copy of the CD, and that's all I had been playing ever since. It talks about a man and a woman who are in love, and don't exactly know how to say it. The song ends with the woman leaving, and never getting the chance to talk about her feelings. That was Sinai and I all the way.

Upon arrival to the airport I took Sinai's luggage out of the car while she checked in for her flight. I wrote her a letter, but was scared to give it to her so I stuck it in her carry-on before taking the rest of her belongings to baggage check. Honestly, I was trying not to cry as I felt Sinai slip through my hands like sand. I wanted to beg her to stay and become my wife, but my mouth wouldn't form the words.

"So, this is it, huh?" I asked.

"Yeah, I guess it is." Sinai refused to make eye contact. If I could just get her to look at me maybe she could see the love I had for her.

"Thanks for all of your hospitality. It was really nice of you to let me stay at your place."

"My pleasure. I'm glad you agreed to come by."

Before I had a chance to say another word, Sinai's flight was announced over the intercom system. At first we hesitated, but then we leaned in at the same time to embrace. I held her close to my body and she didn't pull back as I inhaled her scent for the last time. I memorized the feel of her body, because I knew I would need it to keep me company from here on out.

Without so much as a "see ya later", Sinai stepped away from our embrace finally making eye contact. As I watched her walk away from me I had the urge to scream to the rooftops how much I was in love with her. Pride wouldn't let me do it. It wasn't until her plane had taken off, and I could no longer see it from my spot by the window that I went home.

… … … …

ONE YEAR LATER

Sinai never called. I know she got the letter because I made sure to tuck it into her day planner in the side of her carry-on bag. I waited by the phone for days; a few times picking up the receiver to make sure it was working. Although I finished my novel, my mind and heart didn't belong to me.

I had girls throwing sex at me left and right, but none of that was appealing to me. I not only turned in my playa's card, I cut it up in little pieces and scattered it amongst the ocean. I finally came to grips with not having Sinai, and decided to clear my heart for my next love. I went on with my life doing promotional tours for my previous novels, and going through the tedious editing process for A Thieves Reprise so that it could be released on time the following year. I threw myself into my work as a means of getting Sinai out of my system, and coming to the decision that I wanted a steady relationship. I had my movie premier to get ready for and I vowed the next one I go to I'd have the love of my life on my arm. Whoever she may be.

I sat on the side of my bed in a tuxedo that Giorgio Armani made for me personally. It was the premier of my movie, and I was extra excited. My mother was accompanying me to tonight's festivities, and it felt good to have her by my side.

"Mom, can we leave today? The limo is waiting." I never could understand why women took so long to get ready.

"You can't rush good looks, baby. Didn't I teach you anything?" My mother stepped out the bathroom looking sharp as ever. At the age of sixty-two she didn't look a day over forty. In a slinky one-piece number that exposed her back, and hugged her size eight frame, the old bird looked damn good.

On the ride over I was giddy and nervous at the same time. Every writer dreams of their book becoming a best seller, and the few that make it to the big screen have a lot to be proud of. My mom had been smiling with pride since day one.

"Quincy, I want you to know I am proud of you. It warms my heart to see your dreams come true. I'm happy for you, baby."

"Thanks, Mom. That means a lot to me."

"Now, I want you to know I see the sadness in your eyes. Things will work out, I promise."

"I'm not sad, Mom. I just have a lot on my mind."

"Listen, baby. Your momma is ol' school, and I know love when I see it. She cared about you, she was just scared. Just know if it was meant to be she'll come back."

Words of wisdom are just what I needed at a time like this. I was finally at the point where I was able to watch Sinai on television. She looked good in her videos, and sounded even better. I had every last one on tape. My love for her was still alive and thriving, but I could better cope with it now.

Minutes later we pulled up to the hall. Upon stepping out of the limo all I saw were cameras flashing, and we smiled for the public. Almost a half hour went by before we made it inside. Rubbing elbows with Denzel Washington and Will Smith, I made my way to the middle where our seats were located. My mother decided she just had to go and talk to Aretha Franklin so I went to take my seat. As happy as I was to be there I wanted the night to be over.

While taking my seat I accidentally bumped into the woman in the seat in front of me. My apology was stuck in my throat when she turned around to look at me. I hadn't seen Sinai for almost a year, and here she was staring me in the face.

"Q…I…uh…" before she got a chance to finish, I was kissing her in the aisle. I wanted her to know just how much I missed her, and needed her in my life.

"Sinai, I missed you so much. You have to know that I can't let you leave again."

"Q, I'm so sorry I ran out like that. I was scared. I didn't know what to do…"

"Shhh… baby we'll talk later. Lets just enjoy right now."

Sinai stepped into my open arms, and when I looked up both of our parents were smiling at us. We joined in on a group hug, and that turned out to be the best night of my life. I now have the woman I've been writing about all of these years only I didn't know it. Sometimes you can't see the forest for the trees. A good thing could be looking you dead in the face and you don't even notice it. I never thought that I would end up with Sinai but if it's supposed to be things have a way of working itself out.

All these years I've been afraid of getting trapped in a web of deception and money hungry women that I'm sure I've passed my wife by plenty of times. Sinai made me see things clearly. I've been building a web around myself and didn't even realize I was the spider all this time. It only takes one woman to open your eyes and make you see what's in front of you. Life can't get any better than this.

-the end

BIO's

KEN DIVINE

Ken Divine was born and raised in Brooklyn, NY where he still lives and grew upon an aspiring artist. He loved to draw and won scholarships to programs at the Brooklyn Museum, Pratt Institute and Parson's School of Design. He also dabbled in other various fields over the years, including the music industry as a rapper, song writer and producer. Mr. Divine found his niche as a writer in junior high school when he was asked to write articles for the school newspaper. Upon entering high school, he continued to do journalism work as the sports editor, which earned him the journalism award upon graduation. Mr. Divine has also written two plays, "To Rise and Never Fall" in 1986, and "Rise of the Phoenix" in 1993, which he will be producing in 2004. An accomplished high school and college basketball coach, Mr. Divine also publishes a monthly scouting report and newsletter on girls' basketball in the New York City area.

ANNA FORREST

Anna Forrest started writing at a young age. Starting with children's stories at the age of ten and moving on to poetry and short stories as a teenager, it wasn't until Anna picked up her first romance novel and decided that she could write the same kind of stories with a lot more spice. This started her to write erotica, and her first collection of short stories entitled Ménage Quad. Anna resides in Philadelphia, and is now working on her next book.

Erotic Anthology: Bedtime Stories
By Simone Harlowe & Caroline Stone

Jillian Walters scanned the revisions of her latest novel, a collection of erotic short stories, her editor had just overnight mailed to her office. Clutching the thick folder to her chest, she could smell the heady perfume of the paper. Her throat went dry the scent got to her every time. A dream realized, she thought. For a second she let the pride bubble inside of her. This was the best work she'd done so far.

Opening the top flap and scanned the letter from her editor. She had less than a week to get them in tip-top shape and ready for publication. Nervousness roiled inside her. This was the book, the one that would make her name and enable her to complete the restorations on her house in downtown Charleston, South Carolina. The manuscript had to be flawless.

The buzz of her intercom could her attention. Reality interrupts again. Placing the file on her desk, she sighed. She hit the receive button. "Yes sir?"

"Walters, I need you," the upper-crust, English accented voice of her employer barked loud enough not to need an intercom.

She hit the intercom answer button again. "What do you need sir?" Hopefully he didn't need her to run to his rescue and she could get out of here early.

"Now!"

Jillian groaned. Her master calls. Dropping the manuscript on her black laquer desk, she stretched her sore neck muscles hearing her tired bones creak. Before standing, she put on her tortoise-shell eyeglass and smoothed a strand of hair behind ear. Checking the tight bun and the base of her neck, she slipped her feet into her black low heeled pumps. One had always to maintain the charade.

Walking into the office she found her boss, Gavin Alexander rummaging through the stacks of files on his desk. Five minutes alone in his office and he managed to wreak her neat files. Naked from the waist up, his smooth mahogany skin glowed from his afternoon session in the employee gym. The powerful chest muscles flexed as his movements became more agitated. Gavin was smoking. He had the most delectable nipples for a man. Pert and brown they always reminded her of milk chocolate *Hershey's Kisses*, ready to be devoured. How she wanted to snack on him. Jillian bit the inside of her bottom lip until the pain radiated throughout her mouth.

She'd imagined a number of salacious scenarios a countless number of times. The fantasy of tangled limbs and sweaty sheets fill her mind until the twinge in her lip brought her back to careening back to reality. Seducing her boss would be against her rules and would be counterproductive to her plans for the future. She had to keep this job for few more years. Until she was financially solvent again, she couldn't quit her job. When that goal was accomplished, then she could leave behind her role of Gavin Alexander's prim, repressed executive assistant. Only then could she be emancipated of his forbidden temptation forever.

He straightened as she closed the double doors to his office. His fulls lips were twisted in a grimace. His dark eyes stormy.

Oh he was in a fine mood. He must have lost something again. She stopped herself from laughing at him. "You need something?"

A thick file waved in front of his face. "Damn it where is it?"

Jillian let her hungry gaze travel down the taut muscles of his stomach to the waistband of his snug black nylon shorts. Her heart pounded. Her nostrils flared as she caught his subtle scent of musk. He always smelled like sex in the afternoon. Her toes curled inside her heels, she had to fight the strongest urge to walk over to him and lick the perspiration from his glistening body. Drop by glorious drop. Squeezing her hands into fists behind her back, she reigned in her ever present lust filled thoughts. "Where is what, sir?"

He ran both his hands over his damp hair. "The file on the Telnaco merger?"

The muscles in his biceps rippled. She stopped herself from smiling. This man could pick a stock that would hit the roof without a second thought. He could negociate a deal that God couldn't wiggle out of. He held the undying loyalty and trust of his employees from executive to janitors. But let him try to locate a file and he was clueless. Gavin's knack for misplacing things always forced her to wonder how he managed to head a major international corporation. He couldn't find his butt with a GPS system and bloodhound.

"In your briefcase. Where you had me put it this morning." And to add a bit of insult to injury. "After your meeting."

Gavin pushed aside another file with his hand and raised his head. "Are you sure?"

His dark eyes burned into to her. Jillian met his gaze squarely. *He never believed her the first time.* Enjoying their game of hide and go seek the important file, Jillian pulled herself up to her full height. "Aren't I always." She gave him a wide eyed look of innocence.

Narrowing his hazel eyes at her, he bent over and grabbed his briefcase. Gavin didn't answer; she didn't expect him to.

Subscribe to Blackboard times today and enter a chance to win a Caribbean vacation for two

Blackboard
African-American Bestsellers, Inc.

The African-American Entertainment Magazine
Get the latest in book reviews, author interviews, book ranking, hottest and latest tv shows, theater listing and more...

Coming in January 2004
Call for more information
1-800-303-9442 or go to
www.blackboardtimes.com

Valentines Sweepstakes

Win An Expense Paid Trip to Barbados*

NAME _____
ADDRESS _____
CITY _____ STATE _____ ZIP _____
DAYTIME PHONE (____) _____
E-MAIL _____ @ _____

RULES & REGULATIONS

1. **ELIGIBILITY:** *Sweepstakes open only to legal U.S. residents, who are 21 years of age or older and have Internet access as of 12/17/04.* Void in CA and where prohibited by law. Employees of Genesis Press Inc. USA, and its agencies, parents, subsidiaries, affiliates, vendors, wholesalers or retailers, or members of their immediate families or households are not eligible to participate. Federal, state and local laws and regulations apply. Grand Prize Winner is required to complete and return an Affidavit of Eligibility/Publicity Release and a Travel Release. Travel companion must be 21 years of age or older and must sign a Travel Release/Publicity Release. Affidavit of Eligibility/Publicity Release and Travel Releases must be returned within 2 days of notification or the Grand Prize will be forfeited and an alternate winner will be randomly selected. Must be 18 years old or older.
2. **DRAWINGS:** *Prize Winner* will be selected in a random drawing on or about 1/10/05 from among all valid entries received. Grand Prize winner will be contacted by telephone on or about 1/10/05 at the daytime number listed. If, after two (2) attempts, contact has not been made, prize will be forfeited and an alternate winner randomly selected. Winner will be randomly selected before a panel witnesses and judge.
3. **NO PURCHASE NECESSARY. YOU MUST BE 21 YEARS OF AGE OR OLDER, A LEGAL RESIDENT OF THE CONTINENTAL UNITED STATES, AND HAVE INTERNET ACCESS AS OF 12/17/04, TO ENTER. VOID IN CALIFORNIA AND WHERE PROHIBITED.**
To enter the Tempting Memories Sweepstakes, send above information to by postmark date 12/17/04 to P.O. Box 782, Columbus, MS 39701-0782 beginning at 12:01:01 am ET on 12/10/05 log on to www.genesis-press.com and complete an Official Entry Form. Entries must be received by 11:59:59 pm ET on 12/17/04. Proof of entry submission does not equate to proof of receipt. Limit one entry per person, per IP address per 24-hour period. All other mailed entries will be matched by name and address. If multiple entries are received, only the first entry will be entered into the Sweepstakes and all other entries will be disregarded. In case of a dispute over winner's identity, entry will be deemed to have been submitted by the IP address owner (who must meet eligibility requirements). Sponsor not responsible for entry submissions received after deadline, incomplete information, incomplete transmission defaults, computer server failure and/or delayed, garbled or corrupted data. All entries become the exclusive property of the Sponsor and will not be returned or acknowledged. Any attempts by an individual to access the site via a bot script or other brute-force attack will result in that IP address becoming ineligible. Sponsor reserves the right to suspend or terminate this Sweepstakes without notice if, in Sponsor's sole discretion, the Sweepstakes becomes infected or otherwise corrupted. By entering this Sweepstakes, entrants agree to be bound by these Official Rules and the decisions of the judges which shall be final, binding and conclusive on all matters relating to this Sweepstakes. Sweepstakes starts at 12:01:01 am ET on 1/10/05 and ends at 11:59:59 pm ET on 1/10/05.
4. Winner will be notified by certified mail.
5. Prize is non-transferable, nor redeemable for cash.
6. Once travel dates are selected by winner, they can not be modified. Any changes will forfeit the prize.
7. If winner does not respond within 30 days, prize will be forfeited.
8. One (1) Winner will receive a trip for two (2) adults to the. Trip includes round-trip coach airfare for Winner and Guest to Barbados from the major airport nearest the Winner's residence 4-days/3-night hotel stay (standard room, double occupancy accommodations/hotel to be selected by Sponsor. Prizes provided by Barbados Tourism Authority.
9. **RELEASE OF LIABILITY & PUBLICITY:** Prizewinner consents to the use of his/her name, photograph or likeness for publicity or advertising purposes without further compensation where permitted by law. All entrants release Genesis Press USA, and each of its parents, affiliates, subsidiaries, officers, directors, shareholders, agents, employees and all others associated with the development and execution of this Sweepstakes from any and all liability with respect to, or in any way arising from, this Sweepstakes and/or acceptance or use of the prize, including liability for property damage or personal injury, damages, death or monetary loss.
10. **Genesis Press Inc.**, nor any of its subsidiaries or partners are will be held liable from any and all damages, accidents injuries, negligent actions, breach etc., that might incurred by WINNER during the acceptance of the prize pursuant to the services performed and agreed to herein.

ESCAPE WITH INDIGO !!!!

Join Indigo Book Club©
It's simple, easy and secure.

Sign up and receive the new releases every month + Free shipping and 20% off the cover price.

Go online to www.genesis-press.com and click on Bookclub or
call 1-888-INDIGO-1

Order Form
Mail to: **Genesis Press,** Inc.
P.O. Box 101
Columbus, MS 39703

Name _____
Address _____
City/State_____ Zip _____
Telephone _____

Ship to (if different from above)
Name _____
Address _____
City/State_____ Zip _____
Telephone _____

Credit Card Information
Credit Card # _____ ❏ Visa ❏ Mastercard
Expiration Date (mm/yy) _____ ❏ AmEx ❏ Discover

Qty.	Author	Title	Price	Total

Use this order form, or call 1-888-INDIGO-1

Total for books _____
Shipping and handling: _____
    $3 per book* $3 x_____ = _____
Mississippi residents add 7% sales tax _____
Total amount enclosed _____
FREE shipping and handling for 6 or more books

Visit www.genesis-press.com for latest releases and excerpts.